FAR *Grander* THAN *Paradise*

Endorsements

A missing father, orphaned twins, a dashing ship's captain, adventure on the high seas, a heroine with a mind of her own, a swoony happily ever after ... *Far Grander Than Paradise* has it all!
—**Elizabeth C. Hull**, as Izzy James, award-winning author of Christian Historical Romance

Far Grander than Paradise is an intriguing work of fiction with an engaging, fast-moving plot to hold reader interest. The storyline has a hint of suspense with desirable twists and turns to keep the reader curious to learn how the conflicts resolve. The characters are well-developed, causing you to care about what drives their actions. I am thankful this gifted author has returned to her craft and will look forward to her future work.
—**Joan C. Benson**, author, speaker, educator, BS, MSE, University of Kansas

Full of sparkling prose and vibrant characters, *Far Grander than Paradise* is a unique historical romance that will fill your imagination. From the shores of Norfolk,

Virginia, the author takes the reader on a delightful sea voyage with romance and adventure at every turn.
—**Dina Sleiman**, Award-winning author of the Valiant Hearts Series.

Barbara Blythe is a talented and engaging storyteller who has crafted a novel packed with rich historical details, exotic destinations, and vibrant characters. The romantic tension between Blythe's roguish sea captain and her strong, independent heroine is palpable. I have no doubt *Far Grander than Paradise* will captivate readers from the first page to the last.
—**Kelly J. Goshorn**, bestselling author of *The Undercover Heiress of Brockton*

A swoon-worthy romance, a taste of adventure, and family lost and found will transport you back in time from the first page in *Far Grander than Paradise.*
—**Roseanna M. White**, bestselling, Christy Award-winning author

FAR *Grander* THAN *Paradise*

BARBARA BLYTHE

A Christian Company
ElkLakePublishingInc.com

Copyright Notice

Cover and Interior Design: Kelly Artieri, Deb Haggerty
Editor(s): Carol McClain, Cristel Phelps, Deb Haggerty

PUBLISHED BY: Elk Lake Publishing, Inc., 35 Dogwood Drive, Plymouth, MA 02360, 2025

Library Cataloging Data

Names: Blythe, Barbara, Barbara Blythe
Far Grander Than Paradise
392 p. 23cm × 15cm (9in × 6 in.)
ISBN—13: 9798891344655 (paperback) | 9798891344662 (trade paperback) | 9798891344679 (e—book)
Key Words: Christian historical romance high seas adventure; Christian romance 1800s ship captain bold lady; Faith-based romance clipper ship enemies to lovers; Historic romance South Pacific grump captain Jesus; Christian love story captain lovely woman danger; Christian historical fiction love story sailing; Spiritual romance enemies to lovers south seas
Library of Congress Control Number: 2025946920 Fiction

Dedication

In memory of my parents—Barbara Mae Rice Brown and Timothy Joshua Brown—my inspiration for Zorinda and Carris.

My mother loved all places exotic and tropical. She was a gifted artist and unwavering supporter of all my endeavors. As an example of faith and service to the Lord, she instilled in me a desire to honor the Lord with the talents he's given me.

My father's tales of his service in World War II aboard the *USS Aquarius* fascinated me. Seeing action in and around the Pacific Islands, the *Aquarius* stopped briefly at Bora Bora, an American military supply base in French Polynesia. His descriptions of the people and the island made a lasting impression

> Thus saith the Lord, which giveth the sun for a light by day, and the ordinances of the moon and of the stars for a light by night, which divideth the sea when the waves thereof roar; the Lord of hosts is his name. (Jeremiah 31:35 KJV)

Acknowledgments

I want to thank Deena Adams, ACFW Virginia President and Chesapeake, Virginia Cluster leader for reaching out to me in 2023 with an invitation to join the group. Though I was previously published, I had stopped writing after losing my husband, my father, and my brother within a seven-month period. After attending several meetings, I finally sat down at my computer and started writing again.

I especially want to thank three great individuals at Elk Lake Publishing, Inc.

Deb Haggerty, author, publisher & editor-in-chief; Cristel Phelps, managing editor fiction; and Carol McClain, editor and author. Less than a month after I was offered a contract, I received a serious medical diagnosis. They were understanding and encouraging while I tried to make sense of my situation. Carol was very patient with me as I blocked out my previous publishing experiences (from ten years earlier) and embraced the changes and expectations so essential in today's publishing world. I'm so glad to be working with Elk Lake and these dedicated women.

Most importantly, I thank God for using these individuals to prod me along my writing journey and for giving me a second chance with my writing. All praise, honor, and glory to him.

Chapter 1

Norfolk, Virginia
Waterfront harbor
Early May 1850

Zorinda Wemblish decided no man would ever again tell her what to do. More importantly, what she couldn't do. A decision she'd made one week ago.

Her thoughts churned as rapidly as her walk to Norfolk's harbor, urging her to either scream, cry, or laugh hysterically. The incredulous visage of Banker Sharp, the first to be subjected to her resolution seven days earlier, had been exhilarating. Yet, memory of his threats still summoned the burn of unwanted tears.

Sadly, Wil Goodwell's effrontery later the same day had delivered her shame and torment. How she wished she had the strength to knock him witless and silence his offending tongue.

Then, yesterday—learning of the heartless, mercenary sea captain.

Righteous anger seethed violently within Zorinda, wishing a confrontation with the piratical captain who was a disgrace to humanity. He was a villain to require payment to deliver the Norfolk Mission Society's supplies to San Francisco. He must know the place was bursting at the seams with lost souls vainly seeking the golden touch of Midas. The cataclysmic need among the miners and their families was no secret, and the Norfolk churches had combined their collecting efforts filling at least fifty large crates with non-perishable staples and clothing destined for the town. This loathsome, uncharitable captain made Ebenezer Scrooge seem a saint. If she'd thought to ask his name, she'd find him and skewer him.

Which left her father. Her amazing father who'd return home from his voyages sharing his adventures, bearing gifts, and earning her adoration with a childish naiveté. How dare he disappear? How could he leave her here, where people politely avoided her, painfully tolerated her, and directed unsubtle whispers her way?

Zorinda paused in the shade provided by the newly leafed branches of a towering oak, momentarily overwhelmed. Shoppers, approaching the bustling market across from her, hurried by, unaware of her life-altering metamorphosis brought on by Banker Sharp. If only her mother had experienced the same before Zorinda's father broke her heart. But even if given the chance, Zorinda knew her mother wouldn't have wanted anything different. Because she had loved Thaddeous Wemblish with everything within her.

"I will never love a man as she did," Zorinda whispered fiercely, allowing a solitary tear to slip free. She impatiently brushed the moisture with her lace-gloved finger then cringed at the hand accessory. The ridiculous, mandatory glove. Useless for a woman who would never achieve society's definition of perfection.

Aggravated over her momentary despondency, Zorinda opened her beaded reticule and withdrew the paper she'd brought along. "Uncle" Teig had eliminated those ships with questionable crews and given her the name of a ship and the captain, reputedly of sterling character. This clipper, having arrived the day before, was scheduled to be in port for a brief time before sailing to San Francisco.

She should have thought of this solution sooner. The opportunity stared her in the face each time she passed the ship-berthed waterfront. Since receiving the news her father, his ship, the *Scheherazade,* and crew had been lost at sea, Zorinda refused to believe the report. As time passed, her hope dwindled. Then her uncle—actually her father's oldest friend and a second father to her—had delivered a small measure of hope. Uncle Teig had discovered her father had reached San Francisco, then mysteriously sailed to the Pacific islands.

Hence, her destination. All she had to do was obtain passage to San Francisco. She would search for her father no matter where she had to travel and for however long doing so required. And once she found him, she'd be free of the constraints now choking the life from her. If only God would help her shake these shackles. Was her wish sinful?

As calming as the shade provided by the nonjudgmental oak was, she resumed her walk, nearing the wharves aligned along the waterfront. She knew she sought a clipper at Newton Wharf and Captain ... what was his name?

Footsteps—light, child-like thuds on the planks—sounded behind her, and she turned. The approaching boy and girl, identical in height and possessed of fiery red curls, raced toward her. Openly sobbing and gasping, they hurtled forward at breakneck speed. As the distance closed, they cried out to her. In French.

"Aidez nous—il va nous tuer! Aidez nous!"

"Help us. He is going to kill us."

Baffled by who *he* was, Zorinda had no time to ask because the breathless children slammed into her. The impact shifted her balance, and she instinctively wrapped her arms around them. When she looked down, their terrified eyes and trembling bodies unnerved her. Whoever had so frightened them deserved the thrashing she'd dreamed of giving Wil. Or the skewering she'd planned for the captain.

"Madam, release those children. Immediately!"

The menacing voice flayed every nerve in Zorinda's body as though Poseidon's trident had summoned a scourging maelstrom. Childhood fantasies inspired by sailor's yarns flashed before her eyes, a shocking plunge into the ocean's impenetrable depths suddenly real. Efforts to surface were restricted by a tall, broad-shouldered shape. Words rumbled in her ears, drowning her sensory perception. She'd never shied from confrontation, but uncontrollable quaking commenced as this incomprehensible demand stilled her tongue and rattled her mind. Logic and reason fled in the face of the man's imperious command. Zorinda, warring with fear and panic, was certain if she looked up at him, her eternal imprisonment at the bottom of the sea was inevitable. *Papa, you never told me there was some truth to your far-fetched, seafaring tales.* Lower lip quivering, she braced herself intending to raise her eyes.

"He is going to kill us."

The repeated French plea broke through Zorinda's debilitating haze, and she focused once more on the two who tugged on her skirt. Two pairs of watery green eyes begged her. The children were well fed, clean of face and clothing, and bore no visible signs of physical abuse but were clearly terrified. All the years conversing in French with her mother, Cappy, had suddenly become crucial to understanding this bizarre moment.

"Must I repeat myself?"

His voice was less Poseidon-like but still domineering. English. Authoritative. Arrogant. His voice exuded power, but the children's whimpers strengthened her resolve. She would accept his challenge—she would upbraid this man—a stranger to the concept of decorum. Zorinda raised her head, looked up and up, regret snaring her as she nearly choked on a shriek.

The darkly bronzed man towered over her. The wind ruffled straight hair the color of deepest mahogany, and his eyes were a penetrating blue green. A scar marred the sculpted plane of his right jaw, evincing a sense of danger. He held a hat, and his attire, elegantly delineating his muscular build, indicated he was in a position of authority on a ship. But not an officer of the American Navy or of Great Britain. Zorinda knew those uniforms, and she suspected, this man was not a member of any sanctioned naval force on the face of the earth.

Intimidation was his weapon. The children scooted closer, whimpering as they clutched her arms. They peered up at him as though he were a fire-breathing dragon. Their reaction and his beastly glare banished her dismay and unfurled her tongue. Her father had cautioned her on more than one occasion to have a care lest her unruly temper lead to her downfall. This wasn't the day to heed her father's warning. Zorinda mirrored his glare while the children buried their faces in her skirts. She ignored his harsh question, certain no one had dared such before. But she still feared his reaction. Crouching, she pulled the children closer.

"Pourquoi pensez-vous que?" Zorinda asked. "Why do you think that?"

The little girl—judging by the shared green eyes and red curls, unmistakably the twin of the boy—looked up at the man, her lips trembling when she looked back at Zorinda.

"Vous nous comprenez?" "You understand us?"

At Zorinda's nod, the girl gave her brother a triumphant, although weepy look as she continued in French. "We must escape him." She gestured at the man, whose expression had gone from angry to livid. "He is cruel. He will flog us." The words poured from the child's lips in rapid French.

"*Avec un chat à neuf queues,*" the brother added.

The girl nodded vigorously in agreement, her curls bouncing from the effort.

They feared a beating with a cat-o'-nine-tails? Though the children were clearly frightened, the words held a touch of drama. A tiny twinge of doubt niggled Zorinda.

"Take us away from here," the boy begged.

Zorinda grasped a hand of each child and turned, walking away as swiftly as her hindering skirt and petticoats would allow. The boy and girl trotted to keep up with her as she hoped to elude the enraged madman following. Surely, with so many people about, he wouldn't try to harm them. Even so, Zorinda increased her pace. So did the captain. And he walked much faster than she, causing her to detest her heeled shoes.

Grasping her arm, he forced her to stop.

The children sobbed harder. For the second time, Zorinda would test her new creed.

"Step aside. I will deal with this matter." His voice was cold, forceful, yet the fire in his eyes nearly threw her off course.

No more being told what to do by a man. She found her voice. "Unhand me."

An inexplicable giddiness filled her when he obeyed. An untapped confidence surfaced.

"What right have you to demand anything when you've terrified these children? They sought my help. They told me you wanted to kill them." She raised her chin defiantly, and his aqua eyes reflected ... amusement?

"You believe their nonsense? This boy and girl," he waved a large, callused hand at the children, "are my nephew and niece. I'm to deliver them to their maternal grandfather."

"Here? In Norfolk?" Zorinda asked sharply, not ready to accept this man's plausible explanation after frightening children who looked to be hardly more than seven or eight years of age.

"No. My ship is only in port to make repairs and take on cargo."

I was right. He is a captain. Just like Papa. Always leaving—always breaking hearts.

Where had such a thought come from? She forced herself to concentrate on his words.

"Their grandfather owns a plantation in the South Pacific on the island of Bora Bora in the Society chain—not far from Tahiti."

"Which doesn't explain why they're afraid of you."

The captain sighed and ran a hand over his face, drawing her eyes back to his chiseled jaw.

As though with a mind of their own, her eyes traced his well-formed lips, then studied his unyielding chin. When he ran his fingers through his hair, she found herself wanting to smooth the untidy strands. His motion hinted at defeat, tugging at something unexpected within her.

"Might we speak privately?"

Zorinda started at his words. Looking around, she noticed they had captured the attention of several market vendors and patrons who openly gawked. The last thing she needed was to make a spectacle of herself. Glancing across the brick-paved street opposite the market, she spied an old, weathered bench.

"The bench there." Her tone was curt, unwilling to display any softening.

The man followed her gaze with his own. "Yes." His reply was brusque, while his cleanly shaven jaw twitched. Accepting a dictate from her clearly rubbed against his grain.

Nodding stiffly, Zorinda guided the children, who still grasped a side of her lacey overskirt. They passed the stalls of the fish seller, the butcher, and the poulterer, all of which contributed unpleasant odors to the crowded, noisy market. Even the refreshing spring breeze couldn't erase the stench. Upon reaching the bench with its wonderful view of the waterfront, and less pungent air, she sat while the twins scooted close on each side, clutching her for dear life. Still ignoring the captain, she addressed the children in French.

"Now tell me who you are." Zorinda gave them her attention while their uncle braced his right shoulder against the unyielding column of a streetlamp. "Are you twins?"

"We are. I am Valeraine, and my brother is Valeron. Our *maman* called me Raine and my brother, Ronnie."

"And where is your maman?"

The man huffed, assuring her he was greatly displeased. Good.

She refused to look at him as she awaited an answer.

"She is in heaven with our *papa*," Valeron answered, his voice tearful. "Sister Lyonetta told us so before we were taken away." Tears glistened in the boy's eyes.

Outrage at this overbearing captain threatened to strip Zorinda of all civility. These children were orphans.

Zorinda looked up at the captain, tightening her lips in disapproval. His brows lowered and his storm-churned eyes met hers, restricting her breath. She silently reminded herself God was in charge of this situation. She sincerely wished he would make this man go away.

"I thought to have a private word with *you*," he growled.

Zorinda restrained a wild desire to laugh. She imagined this captain was not one to tolerate defiance.

"My time is precious."

"As are these children," she retorted, coming to her feet. She was more than ready to defend the twins. Was God prodding her to do battle?

The man sighed again, this time in resignation. "I've no experience with children as I'm without family. Their antics are," he paused as though searching for the right word, "exasperating. They were responsible for a shipboard mishap at breakfast, and I confined them to their cabin. Apparently, they weren't happy with my punishment, and they ran away."

"You were going to flog us," Raine cried in French. "Ronnie and I overheard you tell *Monsieur* Cavenley such a crime deserved a whipping with the cat-o'-nine-tails."

"Speak English—I know you can," the captain said.

The children's expression hinted at guilt, and they dropped their heads.

"I suspect you've told this woman I've treated you poorly." His tone was harsh, and Zorinda sent him a warning flash of her eyes. His next words to the twins were softer. "You know my French is lacking, but I believe you overheard a conversation between myself and Mr. Cavenley concerning a crewmember on another ship. Have you seen anyone flogged these two months past?"

Zorinda looked down at the twins.

Slowly, they shook their heads in the negative.

"You know eavesdropping is impolite?" Zorinda asked in English. "Doing so often lands one in trouble."

Those identical, sorrowful, sea-green eyes looked up at her.

She wanted to laugh and cry and hug them all at the same time. When she looked at their uncle, a touch of humor quirked his lips and lightened his eyes. He suddenly didn't seem so monstrous. Somewhat attractive. *Oh bother—he's the handsomest man I've ever seen.*

Self-conscious, she managed a smile. "Apparently, we're entangled in a misunderstanding perpetrated by two very charming and imaginative children. I am Zorinda Wemblish." Zorinda extended her hand, which the captain firmly clasped. A shocking warmth breached her glove and sent tingles up her arm. She was once again rendered breathless by this pseudo-Poseidon. Had she forgotten her initial animosity?

"Carris Trewellyn of Cornwall, England." He still gripped her. When she lowered her eyes to their joined hands, he immediately released her and put his arms behind his back.

"Could I help by keeping an eye on Raine and Ronnie while you see to matters of your ship? My father was a captain, and I know a captain's focus is on his ship and men."

Ship captain ... Wemblish ... Wemblish ...

The pieces slipped into place as Carris Trewellyn looked down at the dark eyed, ebon-haired beauty. Thad

Wemblish's daughter—the sea captain lost somewhere in the South Pacific two years ago. He'd heard the rumors swirling along the Boston waterfront. Recalling his manners, he offered sympathy. "I knew of your father, Miss Wemblish, though we never met. My condolences."

Her eyes flared. "There's been no confirmation of his death."

"I meant no offense. I had heard of his ... disappearance."

"I apologize for my rudeness. You'd have no way of knowing how deeply troubled I am. Everyone urges me to accept his death and move on, but I can't. Something tells me he's out there." She failed to mask the pain and determination evidenced in her voice and eyes. "My mother died from the grippe five years ago, and not a day goes by I don't miss her. Now, to believe I've also lost my father ..." She turned her face aside as though fearful of displaying emotion.

"Again, please forgive me. You shouldn't give up hope."

Zorinda Wemblish looked at him again. Though her eyes glistened with unshed tears, they conveyed gratitude. There was a slight tilt of those eyes, fathomless and exotic. A natural, golden glow tinted her face, arms, and neck. He'd heard talk Wemblish had taken an island woman as his wife. The woman standing before him served as verification, the union producing a beautiful daughter.

"As to Valeraine and Valeron, I would never presume upon you. They are a handful."

She now looked at a slip of paper she'd been clutching in her left hand. Lifting her head, her expression noticeably altered. "Actually, Captain," Miss Wemblish settled once again between the children, folding her hands before her while fiddling with her purse. "I was on my way to see you. Before—"

Her words abruptly ended. Something akin to alarm twisted within Carris as he waited for her to continue. Uncomfortable seconds passed before she resumed.

"I've been told you are sailing to San Francisco."

"San Francisco is our first stop, and the *Bird of Paradise* is to sail with the tide Monday."

Why the interest in his destination? Miss Wemblish seemed hesitant to elaborate. With a decisive motion, she lifted her chin, meeting his eyes.

"I wish to seek passage on your ship."

Chapter 2

"Absolutely not!" burst from Carris's lips. Had this woman lost her mind? Sail to San Francisco—around the Horn? No genteel woman would willingly undertake such a voyage. And a woman who defined exquisite ... no, no. No.

"Excuse me?" she asked, a trace of iron lacing her words.

Carris struggled against his inclination to tell her she was mad. "I'm not taking passengers on this voyage. Other than the children."

"My source tells me you have available cabins."

"Your source is wrong."

"He's not. He's my godfather as well as a ship's captain—Teig Witherspoon. He knows of what he speaks."

So certain, so insistent. Who was this creature who believed she could demand and receive? Beautiful, yes, but clearly unaware with whom she was dealing.

"I am not accepting passengers." Silence enveloped them, causing Carris no end of discomfort.

"So, you say." Her eyes hurled spears at him.

Something inside him tightened uncomfortably as she held silent.

After an eternity, she finally spoke. "I believe the three of us can manage very well. Return to whatever you were doing prior to this incident. I have a meeting at the local orphanage, and my new *amis* can come along. You can join us for the evening meal, and afterward, escort the twins back to the ship."

Carris started to tell her he would do no such thing. Nor would she watch the children. Even though his pulse annoyingly heightened, and Miss Wemblish's classical features reminded him of the carved woman gracing the prow of the *Paradise*, he had no need to further their acquaintance. Zorinda Wemblish belonged somewhere else—not surrounded by the sights, noises, and smells of a seafaring town somewhat rough around the edges. Her attire bespoke moderate wealth—the pale green gown swathed in lace appeared fashionable. The bodice displayed her elegant neck, a hint of shoulder, and intriguing curves. But the woman within the gown was as out of place as a swan among honking geese. And for all her bravado, there was sadness in her eyes.

"Are you certain, Miss Wemblish?"

What was he thinking? He wasn't thinking. His mind was spiraling out of control. "I consider this an imposition." He had to reverse course and even the keel.

"Nonsense," Miss Wemblish said. "I will give you my address." Opening her small, beaded bag, she removed a slip of paper and pencil, writing quickly then handed him the note. "I live on Bank Street." She gestured northward. "The only home with brick columns. Bank is about four blocks from here. Li Ling serves the evening meal precisely at seven o'clock."

She actually smiled, and his heart hammered. Carris managed to return a half smile, a feat given his discomfort.

"I'll be there at seven o'clock. Are you sure ..." There was still time to make this go away.

"I am." She glanced down at the children who looked at her with something akin to adoration.

A knot of guilt twisted in his gut—he'd been a terrible guardian of his half-brother's children. Though Carris held Lance a grudge, there was no reason to subject the twins to his rancor.

"We'll have a wonderful time," Miss Wemblish promised as she stood with the twins, taking a hand of each child. "Are you ready?" Far too eagerly, they nodded. "Good day, Captain Trewellyn. We'll be expecting you."

Her clipped tone brooked no argument.

Lovely, aggravating despot. Carris watched them walk away, insanely wishing seven o'clock were at hand.

Zorinda learned two things about the captain's niece and nephew—they were extremely intelligent, and the little scamps had an adequate command of English. As Zorinda headed toward the orphanage, she held tightly to a hand of each child. One of the places she'd planned to visit before all the excitement, the establishment was located on Brigg's Point in a section of the town in the easternmost part of the city beyond Barry's Row. Here, run-down, poorly kept tenements clustered at the south end of Church Street. Constructed more than thirty years ago when Captain John Maxwell left $2500 to the Norfolk Female Orphan Society in his will, the orphanage still depended on donations from the community to stay afloat. Zorinda had voluntarily visited and wrote the area churches requesting cast-off garments, serviceable enough to be washed and repaired for the girls who lived there. Through the grace of God, many of the churches had responded to the need even though she'd been the one asking for help. They'd managed to overlook her societal deficiencies for a greater good.

The children's French-English chatter diverted her troubling thoughts as they skipped along beside her. Pedestrians, carriages, and a varied assortment of wagons shared the street, invoking numerous questions from a fascinated Raine and Ronnie. Unfortunately, there was no ignoring the odor of horse droppings and human sweat, a reminder the sweltering summer would soon be upon the region. At least the twins were much happier than they'd been when they'd clung to her in abject terror.

"How do you know our language?" Raine was the most vocal and curious of the two.

"My maman spoke French, and she taught me. Her stepfather was a French sailor."

"*Oui*. Yes. Our papa was a sailor too. "You are as beautiful as a *princesse*."

Zorinda laughed. "What an imagination. Believe me, I am anything but a princess. Well, here we are. I'm visiting the girls' orphanage, but I won't be long."

Both children ceased skipping, staring up at the place as though they expected a monster to peek out a window.

"What's wrong?" Zorinda asked.

"We were in an orphanage," Raine whispered. "Until Oncle Carris came for us. The sisters were very strict except for Sister Lyonetta. We cried a lot after we went to the orphanage."

"And we've cried a lot since we left," Ronnie said. "Oncle Carris doesn't want us. I know he would like to throw us to the sharks. Did he ask you to leave us here?"

"Of course not." Zorinda knelt, still holding their hands. "I was coming here before I met you. As for your uncle—he's, ah, distressed by children."

"But you're not." Raine smiled as Zorinda stood.

"Because I'm often around children. I volunteer here several times a month and sometimes teach the children at my church. I love children." By now they had mounted the steps and paused at the front door, badly scarred and in need of a fresh coat of paint. As was the rest of the building.

"Why don't you have children?" Ronnie asked.

"Because I'm not married."

"Why not?" Raine was also the most prying twin.

Zorinda chewed her lower lip as she struggled for an answer. *Because when a man looks at me, he can tell my lineage isn't as pure as his. I'm acceptable as a mistress, nothing more. But God has given me many children to love and nurture. I'm content.*

Fortunately, the door swung open, preventing her from stumbling through an explanation. Matron Catharine Redman stood there, smiling a welcome.

Zorinda had never known a more energetic and compassionate soul than Catherine Redman. The amazing woman loved the girls living at the orphanage and had a knack for getting more out of a penny than anyone Zorinda had ever known. So when she'd received the matron's distressing note a few days ago, she knew matters were serious. Numerous windows in the building needed replacement before winter, and there was no money to pay for them. Zorinda would have gladly financed the repairs had she access to her father's Exchange Bank accounts. But Banker Sharp had frozen her father's funds, refusing to release them unless she had her father declared dead. Her only income—adequate but not excessive—came monthly in the form of an allowance her father established before his last, ill-fated voyage. But she had one source of income only three dear friends, Sarah Simmons, Joseph Arnell, and Catherine Redman, knew about.

Zorinda and Matron Redman retired to a small sitting room, sharing tea while discussing the facility's lack of funds. Afterward, they walked to the library where one of the younger teachers settled Raine and Ronnie earlier.

"I visited Taylor Darrow. The mission society's funds have been pocketed by a weasel of a ship's captain who hasn't the decency to take the supplies without recompense."

Catherine Redman sighed. "Most unfortunate. But the captain seeks an honest profit. Not unlike what the Darrows do as ship chandlers. Was Mr. Darrow upset?"

"No." Zorinda now sighed. "He believed the request fair. Surely this captain knew the crates contained items sorely needed by so many in San Francisco. He was more worried about the cotton or tobacco he could cram into the hold."

The woman chuckled. "A necessity for those in shipping, Miss Wemblish. But at least the items will reach their destination."

"You're right, but still ..." Her voice trailed off as she pondered the matron's words. "However, I do have some encouraging news. I visited Mr. Arnell and delivered one of my newer paintings to him to display in his shop. When sold, I've asked him to give you the money."

"Are you sure?" Matron Redman's brow creased. "You've done so much for us."

"Let me at least leave you some hope." Zorinda smiled sadly. "As I told you, I may be away for some time. Those windows must be replaced soon." Sales of her paintings had allowed her to donate to the orphanage and the School for Indigent Boys during her father's absence. She'd recently completed a painting she called "Promise of Paradise." When she'd delivered her artwork, Mr. Arnell, giddy with excitement, had predicted a quick sale.

"You've already donated enough to purchase shoes and socks. How can we expect you to do more?"

"My joy comes from helping."

Having reached the library, Zorinda noticed a dozen or so girls seated at reading tables while the librarian sat behind her desk. Raine and Ronnie sat close at a corner table, their heads bent over the same book. *Twins—they are naturally close no matter what they're doing.* Zorinda smiled to herself. "I'll have Fergus deliver more of the donated garments in a few days. Mrs. Simmons and I are nearly finished with the repairs and the laundering. I want you to have those as soon as possible."

"You've been such a blessing, Miss Wemblish, seeking donations and teaching the art classes here expecting nothing in return. I wish there were more like you. And now you're sailing to California. We're going to miss you."

Zorinda shook her head. "My father's disappearance is of great concern. This may be my only opportunity to search for him. But I have loved working with the children."

"Thanks to you, our halls are filled with their drawings."

Zorinda laughed. "What a unique way to paper the walls."

Matron Redman joined in her laughter, nodding her head. "Time for me to gather the children for afternoon prayer." Smiling a goodbye, the eternally positive woman walked toward the occupied tables.

Zorinda joined Raine and Ronnie. "What are you reading?"

Raine answered. "We think the story is about a ship. There are drawings on some of the pages—a ship, palm trees, a beach, and a hut. Will you read to us?" Two eager faces looked at her.

Zorinda picked up the book entitled, *A Voyage to Paradise*. She laughed.

"What's so funny?" Ronnie asked in French, wrinkling his nose.

"Nothing, really. I'm sure Matron Redman will lend us the book. But I warn you, you may be bored." She idly flipped through the pages, scanning the print haphazardly. "Apparently, a man who sailed to the South Pacific wrote this."

"That's where we're going," Raine said. "To our *grandpère*. Please read to us."

Zorinda nodded and clasped the book to her chest. How coincidental she had named her latest painting *Promise of Paradise*, Captain Trewellyn's ship was the *Bird of Paradise*, and these children picked a book with paradise in the title. Zorinda shook her head at her foolishness, then beckoned the children to follow as she paused at Catherine Redman's side to ask if she could borrow the book.

Chapter 3

Though Carris's day was full, his thoughts never strayed far from the raven-haired female with the irritating demeanor and the mesmerizing eyes. At the oddest times, he'd take the paper bearing her address from his inner breast pocket to look at her artistic script. Her handwriting flowed, decoratively executed with tiny curlicues and flourishes. He couldn't help but smile.

"Somethin' funny, Cap'n?"

Pete Surrell's question prompted him to refold the paper. His second mate eyed him strangely—because he was distracted or because he was smiling? Carris knew he'd done none of the latter since learning his half-brother's children were residing in an orphanage in Marseille. Lance, the spoiled and pampered only child of his father's second marriage, had lived unwisely and selfishly, murdered a year earlier in a tavern in Madagascar. No one knew of his marriage to the French courtesan until four months ago when Carris received the letter from the Sisters of Supreme Mercy informing him of the passing of Amalie Montagne Trewellyn. He still wasn't certain Lance had wed the woman. But Valeraine and Valeron were indisputably his brother's offspring—possessed of his green eyes, stubborn chin, and penchant for mayhem.

"No. I'm hoping Miss Wemblish isn't sorry she kept the children." When Carris had returned to the ship without the twins, the crew was so alarmed he'd no choice but to share the peculiar happenings on the wharf. He felt gut-punched knowing his men had warmed to the children when he hadn't even tried. He carefully omitted his combative conversation with Miss Wemblish who was sadly mistaken to think she'd sail anywhere on the *Paradise*.

"If Miss Wemblish is anythin' like her father, she'll keep them in line. Firm, but fair. I spent the better part o' five years sailin' with him on the *Scheherazade*. Said his little girl suggested the name."

Turning away from the activity on deck, Carris's eyes scanned the bales of cotton littering the wharf's planks awaiting storage in the hull. His men would then use the jack screw to compress them for optimum storage, not an easy job even under the best of conditions. Carris walked to the port side with Surrell and looked out over the Elizabeth River, noting the smaller town of Portsmouth and its shipyard on the opposite bank. After slipping the note within his pocket, he leaned his arms on the rail. Muddled thoughts returned, annoying when he prided himself on clarity. All he could think about was the woman who'd somehow managed to win the affection of his wayward charges in mere minutes. He drew a deep breath while clasping his hands.

Surrell continued. "Mr. Tenney says there are more repairs needed on the spars and sails than he originally thought."

A nasty late spring squall had caught them off the eastern shore of Maryland and played havoc with the clipper's vast and complicated rigging. "What of our scheduled departure?" Carris asked, dreading Surrell's answer.

"We should be fit to sail no later than Monday. Mr. Tenney's had the men at work since before sunup." Surrell shifted his hands behind his back, awaiting his response.

Looking up and to his left, Carris spotted the rigging monkeys high in the masts, most stripped to the waist as they labored while the bosun shouted orders. Carris nodded. "Tell Tenney to keep the work going and spare no expense—no short cuts. We've a long voyage ahead and expensive cargo to get to San Francisco. We'll stay longer if we have to."

"Aye, sir. I'll let Mr. Tenney know."

Surrell hurried off, leaving Carris to wrestle with his mercurial thoughts. His sparring with Miss Wemblish had summoned long suppressed memories—all painful. Why couldn't she accept the fact her father was likely consigned to Davy Jones's locker?

"Captain Trewellyn."

The voice of Denford Cavenley, first mate and quartermaster upon occasion of the *Paradise*, brought Carris to attention as he turned, assuming his official captain's mien. The man mustn't catch him in maudlin musings.

"Mr. Cavenley. Have matters been finalized with the Darrow brothers?"

"Indeed, sir." Den Cavenley smiled. No wonder young ladies found him so charming. Fortunately, the man never took advantage of his popularity. Otherwise, Carris wouldn't have made him first mate. He'd learned his lesson with Lance. "I have a check for half the sum agreed upon. The remainder to be paid upon our return."

"Excellent." Carris's fingers warred with his senses, those calloused digits tempted to pull the paper in his pocket free once more. Why was he so maddeningly intrigued by Miss Wemblish's lovely script?

"Taylor Darrow seemed most relieved when I confirmed the agreement," Cavenley said.

"As well he should. Those crates will take up space begging to be filled with profitable cargo. And we well know the value of cotton."

"I'm sure, sir, you're doing a good thing."

"Not from a businessman's point of view." No sooner had he spoken than an unwelcome vision of dark eyes, blue-black hair, and perfect lips crowded Carris's mind, leaving him oddly unconcerned with cotton, the Darrows, or anything else.

Cavenley cleared his throat forcing his attention back on his first mate. "All is well with the twins?"

Carris struggled with his momentary distraction before delivering a proper answer. "Not exactly, but they are presently in the company of a young woman, the daughter of the late Thaddeous Wemblish."

Cavenley remained silent though his brows raised.

"I'm fed up with their mischief. The incident this morning assures me I must wield a firmer hand. We've endured soup tainted with soap shavings. We've hoisted painted sails on painted masts, forcing us to lock up our ship paint. We'd be the laughingstock of the seven seas with our sails bearing pictures of birds and flowers."

Cavenley coughed suspiciously. Carris knew the man was covering a laugh.

"I'd like for us to join Mr. Tenney and Mr. Surrell to review the list of repairs."

"Aye, sir," Cavenley said.

Carris pushed away from the rail and proceeded toward the hammering and sawing, welcome sounds assuring him his ship would soon be sailing.

"You did what?"

Sarah Simmons's outrage confirmed Zorinda's fear she shouldn't have invited Captain Trewellyn. She loved Sarah dearly and was accustomed to the housekeeper's matter-of-fact manner. But now the woman seemed apoplectic.

"I invited him to supper. He needs to understand I'm sailing on his ship. Is Uncle Teig dining with us tonight?"

"No changing the subject, Miss Zorinda. Why invite a man to dine here after he insulted you and terrified two children?"

"I didn't assess matters accurately," Zorinda hedged. "The children had engaged in mischief putting them at odds with their uncle. Hence the attempt to run away."

"Sit yourself down, Zorinda Wemblish," Sarah commanded while Li Ling, stirring something which smelled wonderful on the stove, paused long enough to look at her and Sarah, her dark brows raised.

Zorinda glanced out the kitchen window to see Raine and Ronnie watching Fergus hoeing a trench in the vegetable garden. Her introduction of the children to the Wemblish cook, Li Ling, Sarah, and the Negro gardener-handyman, Fergus Tucker, had gone well. Until she'd shared her lack of success in securing passage on the *Bird of Paradise* and the captain's blunt, ungentlemanly refusal. Thunder clouds gathered in Sarah's sharp eyes, forcing Zorinda to send the twins to Fergus outside.

"I've a mind to take a rolling pin to Witherspoon's noggin for telling you to see that Trewellyn captain." Sarah's glare was worse than Captain Trewellyn's.

"He was helping me. And his is the only ship in port Uncle Teig says I could safely sail on. I will convince Captain Trewellyn he must accept me as a passenger."

"Why?" Sarah demanded, taking the seat she'd ordered Zorinda to fill.

Zorinda remained near the window, fidgeting with her hands. "I'm not taking no for an answer."

Sarah shook her head.

"Miss Zorinda, this is a bad idea. I know the banker and his nephew and some of the women have made things hard for you since Captain Wemblish was reported lost. But to sail halfway around the world, leaving your home—and us—behind? I fear for you."

Zorinda took the chair opposite Sarah's and reached out to take the woman's hand.

"I'm prepared, Sarah. I'm already packed." She waved a hand at two mid-sized trunks nestled in a corner of the kitchen. "I've spoken to Papa's attorney, and Mr. Arnell has the documented authority to handle all matters in my absence. Banker Sharp will have to comply. But he still has the power to restrict access to Papa's bank assets. I've familiarized Mr. Arnell with the household needs—he can access the monies Papa put aside for me before he last sailed. As for Wil, he's made his choice and selected a bride approved by his family. I succumbed to his charm, but I won't endure his insults. I'm tired of the whispers and stares of forced politeness and raised brows, reminding me I'm tolerated because of my father. And I will never forget how miserable local women made Maman. Most importantly, I need to find Papa."

Sarah drew a deep breath, her eyes now sharpened daggers. "Witherspoon is sending you on a wild goose chase. And no, he's not eating here tonight. He received a letter from his sister today. She's not doing well, so he may head north soon."

"The sun was rising when the wind caught the sails." Zorinda paused to look at Raine and Ronnie, the three of them sitting in the garden of her home, the space filled with lilac bushes, hyacinths, and bright yellow marigolds. She'd promised to read to them before dinner, and as soon as she and Sarah had shuffled aside their squabble—to be further discussed—she'd gathered the twins. Now on page one of chapter four of the borrowed book, there were no signs of boredom from her rapt audience, though she'd been reading for the better part of an hour. Seven o'clock neared, and dusk slowly slipped around them.

Zorinda resumed. "I'll never forget the majesty of the early morning rays, the canvas tinted mauve and pale blue and cool lemon—the colors crisscrossing intricately to form a myriad of patterns. The breeze fanned my face, and I was reminded of a loving caress—gentle and unforgettable. Not much given to romance, my thoughts unpredictably created an image of me sharing a quiet moment with my beloved."

"What's a beloved?" Raine whispered as though afraid to speak too loudly.

"Well, for us ladies, it would be a gentleman who has stolen our hearts. For you, Monsieur Ronnie, a fair and winsome girl who has set your heart aflutter."

Ronnie giggled. "Aflutter?"

"More like poleaxed."

The deep-timbred, masculine voice brought them to their feet, the captain nearly upon them. How had he appeared so silently? Carris Trewellyn's cryptic expression was unnerving and his disparagement of affection deplorable. She couldn't control her frown but tightened her lips to withhold a comment.

"Please continue reading," he urged. As he removed his hat, a wayward hank of rich dark brown fell over his brow. "After your housekeeper—Mrs. Simmons, I believe she said—greeted me at the door with a censorious look, she told me you were out here. She suggested I walk directly to the garden to join you, as the meal is still several minutes from serving. She didn't seem to want me in your home."

Not surprising, Zorinda thought, lowering her eyes lest she reveal her understanding of Sarah's displeasure and her own irritation at his cynicism. After settling again on the stone bench, as did Raine and Ronnie, she schooled her expression then raised her eyes, clamping down on her annoyance with his bit of loosened hair. Captain Trewellyn seated himself on a stool then smoothed his wayward strands before resting his arms on his bent knees.

Swallowing hard, Zorinda resumed.

"By midday, we were out to sea—ah, the sea. Turquoise and jade"—*like his eyes*—"with depths so clear, I could see the vividly hued fish darting beneath the surface when I leaned over the ship's rail. In the distance rose another island—one we'd not be exploring. Exotic trees soared heavenward, the fronds of palms swaying to and fro as though beckoning me nearer. Had I been captain of the ship, I'd have taken her in—"

"And ended up dead."

Lowering the book, Zorinda glared at the captain, wiping away his smile. If he thought his comment humorous, Raine and Ronnie's gasps assured her his words had frightened. She'd had enough. "Was that necessary?" Her tone was sharper than she'd intended. This man brought out the worst in her.

Instantly, his eyes darkened to the color of a vicious, gray-green sea. "I made an honest comment. Having spent most of my life at sea, I'd never put ashore on an uncharted island."

"Nor fall in love for fear of being poleaxed? Your honesty is unfit for a child's ears. No wonder they ran away from you."

His eyes narrowed.

"You misunderstand, Miss Wemblish. I'm only pointing out the fallacies in this man's rendering of his voyage—romanticized tripe."

"I assume you could write a better novel?" She lifted her chin challengingly.

"Had I the time or inclination, I could. But I have better things to do." He came to his feet, forcing her to look up at him. "Obviously, I'm not as welcome as I'd been led to believe, so I shall bid you good evening. Children, we're leaving."

A clamor and wailing arose, the likes of which Zorinda had never heard. The twins grasped her as though for dear life, and tears ran profusely over pink cheeks. Gathering them close, she glared at Carris Trewellyn.

"I can't decide if you're simply an unfeeling cad or a monster. You promised to dine with us, and now because I've taken you to task, you want to punish the ones who are innocent. Lash at me if you need an outlet for your ill humor, not these children."

Zorinda had heard the expression, "took the wind out of his sails," but had never witnessed the happening.

Captain Trewellyn's shoulders loosened, and he dropped his head, a man who seemed, oddly, lost. When he raised his head, his eyes locked with hers. "You've made your point. I will keep my thoughts of danger to myself if your invitation still stands."

Zorinda fought the urge to accept his apology. Though his eyes were fascinating, and his face was possessed of a sculpted, bronzed visage, she would not overlook his poor behavior.

"Mademoiselle, would you let Oncle Carris stay?"

Zorinda looked down at Raine, surprised by the girl's request on behalf of the captain. "If you make him leave, he won't get dessert."

The fight whooshed from her.

"You're right." When Zorinda looked at the captain, she was surprised to see his expression somber when she'd expected smugness. "There's no need to leave, Captain."

"Thank you." She accepted his hand as he drew her to her feet.

His roughened flesh encircled her fingers, his grip firm and oddly welcome. Unexpected warmth wrapped around her, and heat rose to her cheeks. Sarah mercifully appeared at the rear door, announcing supper was about to be served. Even after he released her hand, Zorinda could still feel the strength of his touch.

Miss Wemblish led Carris into the interior of the home. The twins followed, whispering to each other. There was no mistake Wemblish had provided well for his family though the furnishings and décor were quite different than what he'd encountered in other American homes. From the unique Chinese porcelain objects d'art to the bamboo accents and the bold, flowered wall hangings, he was reminded of another world—one far removed from the two-hundred-year-old port of Norfolk, established when Virginia had been a British colony. Zorinda Wemblish fit perfectly within the walls—the appropriate background for her unusual beauty. As he passed what appeared to be a sitting room, he noticed a portrait centered over the fireplace, painted with skillful realism. The older woman, whose image filled the canvas, possessed an uncanny resemblance to his hostess. He hadn't realized he'd stopped until Miss Wemblish spoke.

"My mother, Cappouitti. Papa called her Cappy, and she called him Teddy. They loved each other very much. But life here was hard because of her differences, having come from a world so unlike this one."

Carris glanced over at her. Miss Wemblish, though her skin was fairer than her mother's, faced the same obstacles. He wasn't sure what to say because society in England might regard her in the same manner as in America. He had no tolerance for narrow minds, but sadly, he was one of the few who saw things differently.

Continuing, Carris peered into a smaller room, possibly a study or library, filled with charts and nautical instruments. How he would love an opportunity to look at the volumes lining the shelves and twirl the globe suspended on an ivory and teak pedestal.

A print depicting a Chinese village and garden papered the dining salon, and on a far wall, the harvest of the tea leaves. The furniture was more formal, dark and heavy, lightened by the brightness of a lacquered coromandel standing screen and the alabaster finish on several decorative pieces. The mantle was elaborately trimmed with pillars and a large starburst medallion in the center, smaller stars positioned at the corners.

"Your father had exceptional taste."

Zorinda Wemblish laughed. "My mother furnished our home. Had she left things to Papa, everything would have been gray, beige, and dark blue. I'm afraid I've inherited her love of color."

"How fortunate." Carris was truly impressed. With the woman and her preference for color.

The disapproving—of him or his profession?—housekeeper bustled about settling the children in their seats, and the Chinese cook emerged from the kitchen with the first course. A riot of impressions invaded his senses as he absorbed his surroundings and studied the woman who so effortlessly presided at the table.

Chapter 4

Droopy-eyed, yawning twins told Carris the time had come to take Raine and Ronnie back to the ship, yet leaving the Wemblish home held no appeal. Generously sampling each dish prepared by the diminutive Chinese cook—not to mention two slices of strawberry pie—he could think of nothing better than relaxing in one of the overstuffed chairs in the sitting room. But duty came first, which meant returning to the *Paradise*. Zorinda—at some point during the meal he'd decided she was Zorinda—sat on the green brocade settle, a child on either side. Their heads rested on each shoulder while she read from a worn edition of *Arabian Nights Entertainments*. Though listening to her melodic reading voice was bliss, this companionable moment had to end.

"Miss Wemblish," he said as he stood, "we've overstayed our welcome. We should depart and give you some peace."

"Would you consider allowing them to spend the night? They needn't return to the ship when they're clearly exhausted. And if they stay, you'll have a few extra hours of uninterrupted ease."

Carris restrained a grin. What a tactful way of saying she would keep them out of his hair.

"Meaning more work for you and your staff. Though my day is full tomorrow, I'll have someone on the ship keep an eye on them. Admittedly, we're in the midst of repairs, as the ship suffered minor damage when we encountered a storm off Maryland's eastern shore."

"Don't take a crewman from his duties. The twins can stay the night and spend the day with me tomorrow. Join us again for our evening meal at seven o'clock. Then you can decide if the children may remain another night."

Carris knew refusing was his only choice until the children, now alert, looked up at him with silent pleas. A tender thread wound about his heart, and shame assailed him. He'd been abrupt and impatient with two abandoned children whose welcome from a grandfather who lived thousands of miles away was uncertain. Their father had been a conscienceless womanizer, and their mother supported herself by selling her favors. Raine and Ronnie had never truly known peace and contentment until today when they'd crossed paths with Zorinda Wemblish. He'd never seen them happier or more appreciative of a meal, giggling and teasing one another, a side to them he'd never witnessed.

"I hesitate ..."

Miss Wemblish stood. Her beautiful smile set her face aglow.

"Don't. I have a busy day tomorrow, as well, so the children will have plenty to see and do." She paused, drawing a breath. "Might we speak outside?"

Carris had sailed through unpredictable storms frequently enough to sense one approaching. She'd been the perfect hostess, smiling and laughing. Now her determined side resurfaced—the side which waged verbal war with him earlier. She was not sailing on the *Paradise*. He would make certain she understood.

Before he could plot his course, four small arms wrapped around him somewhere between his kneecaps and hips. He hadn't noticed Raine and Ronnie stand, so fixed was he upon Zorinda.

"Thank you, Oncle Carris," Raine and Ronnie chimed as one.

Looking down upon their curly heads, he ruffled their hair, silky and springy to his touch—the curls must have come from their mother. Their unexpected gratitude created a new emotion. Affection?

"Remember—best behavior."

Looking up at him, they nodded solemnly, released him, and then scampered off to the rear of the house.

"Li Ling promised them a tart and warm milk before bed," Zorinda said.

"You'd already decided you'd keep them tonight." His words were a confirmation rather than a question. Carris couldn't keep the grin at bay any longer. Miss Wemblish had a sweet, but manipulative side. Something to remember when she resumed her war to gain passage on his ship.

"I hoped you'd be agreeable. They are both incredibly bright and endearing."

"Something you've brought out in them."

Mrs. Simmons appeared, handed him his hat, and turned away without a word. There was no mistaking the sharp look the housekeeper gave him before heading off in the same direction as the twins. A slight frown dimmed Miss Wemblish's eyes while watching the woman depart.

He cleared his throat reclaiming her attention. "Your servants are very different from those we have in England. Not in a bad way, mind you."

She greeted his words with a tiny, upward tilt of her lips, no longer frowning. "How tactful of you, Captain." After looking once more down the hallway to make certain no one lingered, she lowered her voice and continued, her tone soft with sadness. "My father came upon Li Ling in a Hong Kong alley, badly beaten by a brothel client and half-starved."

Carris knew well the brutal life women—known as sing-song girls—suffered in such places. He often wondered if abuse had contributed to Amalie's untimely death.

"On the voyage home, my father asked her to help the ship's cook who taught her his American recipes. I was but a child when she became our cook. Mrs. Simmons," she began, then hesitated before resuming. "I know she lost her husband in a tavern brawl here in Norfolk and had no place to go. Maman found her wandering the market. They talked and took to one another immediately. She became our housekeeper." Miss Wemblish smiled at the memory.

"Fergus Tucker who maintains the house and yard and tends the horses was a slave on a South Carolina plantation. After his daughter and her husband died, he took their child and escaped to the Great Dismal, an endless maze of swamp and towering cypress not very far from here. I don't know all the details, but when Papa and he met, Papa offered him a job and gave him a new name. Fergus and Violet, his granddaughter, live over the stable. Our servants are a varied lot, each with stories to tell. But then, so am I. All one has to do is look at me."

I could do so for the rest of my life. Pulling his thoughts together, he managed to speak. "I choose to focus on what lies within a person. Outward appearances mislead. I hope my curiosity hasn't offended."

"There is nothing wrong with an inquiring mind. I indulge in curiosity from time to time." She gifted him with one of her incredible smiles.

They faced each other in the large foyer with its flooring of gold-veined marble and walls painted a warm ivory. Miss Wemblish stood beneath a painting of a ship centered over an ornate, oriental commode. Unable to resist a better look, he stepped closer, admiring the sure, forceful strokes replicating a ship caught in a storm. The subdued shading of the sky and menacing clouds reflected in the gray green waves pulled Carris into the drama as though he were aboard. Proportion and detail of the sails and rigging told him the artist was well acquainted with ships. The composition was beyond magnificent. The initials *R.I.N.* had been signed in the lower corner, along with the date, January of '47.

"Where did your father find this amazing scene?" he asked, unable to look away from the painting.

"This isn't something he found."

Miss Wemblish's vague response caused him to turn toward her. She was fumbling with a lace-edged handkerchief, her eyes lowered.

"The painting was a gift, given to him by a ... friend."

She looked up and smiled, but the smile was forced. Mention of the painting had doused her spirit. But why?

"And presented to him for his birthday before his last voyage. The ship is his, the *Scheherazade*."

Reason enough for her odd reaction. He'd inadvertently recalled sad memories. "What a treasure," he said and smiled.

Zorinda noticeably relaxed. Placing his hat upon his head, he strode toward the front door where Mrs. Simmons had silently positioned herself. Her sudden appearance startled, but he gave no outward sign. The woman bid him a crisp good evening, then opened the door, her lips thin with disapproval. There was no mistaking her dislike. Carris turned to Miss Wemblish.

"I believe you wished to speak to me before I depart."

"Yes, thank you."

He allowed her to proceed him, received another suspicious look from Mrs. Simmons, followed Miss Wemblish out onto the wrap-around porch, and closed the door. How was this woman even more beautiful when bathed in the glow of a streetlamp?

"I will be direct, Captain. I wish to continue our earlier conversation."

"Ah, of course. And here I thought you'd revised your opinion of me and wished to be friends." Would his attempt at humor unfurl her sails?

"You, sir, would be the last person I'd wish as a friend."

Apparently not.

Instead, her cold tone invoked his reefing-the-sails mindset. She'd soon learn he could remain steady no matter what storm she tossed him. He was no stranger to feminine ploys and the resulting humiliation, his broken engagement to Ivy akin to scraping barnacles off a ship's hull. Yet, Zorinda Wemblish might be equipped with enough spine to make an effective combatant.

"I'm wounded, Miss Wemblish. But please—continue."

"I need to travel to San Francisco. Then possibly to Tahiti."

"This is connected to your father?"

"Not your concern. I wish to purchase passage. I was told you have availability."

"I told you I wasn't accepting passengers."

"Have you an issue with my heritage?"

Her words exposed her vulnerability. He'd never meant to make her think anything of the kind. Carris's anger evaporated, and without thinking of his actions, he laid his hand on her arm. "The voyage is dangerous. I have to keep a ship afloat, keep my crew as safe as possible, and on this voyage, keep watch over two impetuous children. I'm refusing you because I don't want you in harm's way. My answer is still no."

Miss Wemblish stared up at him, her lips tightly clamped. She finally lifted her regal chin. "Would you answer differently if I were a man?"

Rather than reply, he removed his hand from her arm and descended the steps, stopping when he reached the flagged path leading to the street. After turning, he looked up at her—a shimmering apparition in the low light—her hands tightly clasped. He should at least depart with polite words.

"Thank you for the meal. And thank you for looking after the children. I've never seen them this happy. I've not been a good caregiver."

"You need practice," she said without the scathing tone he'd anticipated. "Perhaps I can share a few tips before you sail."

"A kind offer. Until tomorrow, Miss Wemblish." He made a small bow then straightened, "Should you need me—"

"We'll be fine."

"I'd expect no less. Good night." His feet refused to move as he continued to look up at her. Though her facial features were wreathed in darkness, he easily recalled her lips. Unnerving thoughts raced through his mind, taunting him mercilessly. This would never do. He'd watched his mother suffer through his father's absences much like the late Mrs. Wemblish and Amalie. No woman deserved such agony.

Firming his resolve, he moved back and pivoted but took only two steps when Miss Wemblish spoke.

"I am sailing to San Francisco. I've spent the past week packing and putting my affairs in order. You may have told me no, but I'll find someone who will tell me yes."

Something in her words rattled his resolve, shaking his certainty. An irrational longing welled up within him, urging him to do something disastrous. He took several deep breaths, regained control and managed to reply. "May your search prove successful."

Freshly scrubbed and smelling of scented soap, wearing borrowed night clothes destined for the Female Orphanage, Raine and Ronnie eagerly climbed under the covers of the trundle bed. Once Zorinda's bed as a child, the piece now presided over the guest room. Ronnie took the lower section, and Raine hopped upon the upper bed.

Though seething from Captain Trewellyn's second refusal to take her to California, Zorinda buried her anger. She seated herself in a rocker by the lamp, opened the borrowed book, and resumed reading. The children soon lost their battle to remain awake. Placing the book on the small table and turning down the lamp, Zorinda quietly slipped out. As soon as she shut the door with a soft click, she noticed Sarah in the hall heading her way.

"I've turned back your covers and left warm milk and toast. You've had quite a day."

Zorinda sighed. "I am relieved the children aren't in an abusive situation."

"Only frightened half to death."

"The captain is struggling. Perhaps his manner will gentle before they sail."

"Humph!" Sarah resumed walking, headed toward the stairs. Zorinda fell into step with her. "Him gentle in a few days? I doubt a year would bring him up to snuff."

"You've identified his faults in one meeting?" Zorinda had a wild urge to giggle. But Sarah's disapproving scowl stilled the impulse.

"He's a hard one. Handsome, but no feelings. He's all about sailing and business."

"And you know this how?"

"I've seen his look on the face of many a sailor. Mostly acquaintances of my late husband and your father. Have a care, Miss Zorinda."

"Don't fret, Sarah. The captain and his wards will soon be sailing. And according to the captain, without me."

"Which may be fortunate. So why invite him to dine here tomorrow evening? You've never invited any man to share a meal in this house. Not even that no account Goodwell."

"I'm only doing so because of the children."

By now they'd descended to the lower level. Sarah paused as she met Zorinda's eyes. "I saw the way he looked at you. Like a shark about to have a meal."

"He's been nothing but a gentleman." Even though she'd bordered on inexcusable rudeness on the porch.

"Outwardly, yes. But I saw his eyes. Don't lose your heart to him. The sea will always come first. Though your father was one of the finest men I ever knew, he too was snared by the sea."

"You've never spoken to me like this." There was a hint of bitterness, perhaps regret, in Sarah's voice. Zorinda couldn't help but wonder about her housekeeper's late husband.

"With Captain Wemblish gone, I'm responsible for you. You've already had your heart broken."

Heat flushed Zorinda's cheeks, the reminder of the Wil debacle singeing the raw wound with burning shame. "Don't fret, Sarah. Thank you for your help this evening. I'm sorry for the extra work falling to you and Li Ling."

"Not a problem. You haven't laughed this much in months. The children are good for you. The captain isn't."

Sarah walked on, leaving Zorinda standing in the hall. Turning, she looked at her painting, the one Carris Trewellyn had admired earlier. Why hadn't she told him she was the artist? She'd kept her painting a secret because Mr. Arnell would have difficulty selling her work locally. As no man wanted to marry a woman stained with the blood of an islander, no connoisseur of art would purchase a painting by an unknown woman.

Shaking her head, she walked to her father's library hoping to find a book to read and encourage sleep. She had a feeling warm milk and toast would not suffice given her disturbing thoughts. How would she ever reach her destination?

Chapter 5

Breakfast was lively, Raine and Ronnie eagerly devouring the bounty Li-Ling placed before them. As they ate, Zorinda mapped out a list of activities she believed the twins would enjoy—a tour of Market Square, a picnic along the banks of the river, and a visit to Mr. Arnell's shop. She shared her plans with Sarah who suggested she ask Violet to assist. When invited, Fergus's granddaughter happily accepted, volunteering to pack a basket for lunch. Fergus readied the buggy, and the excited group set off on what Zorinda hoped would prove special for all.

As Zorinda neared the market, she recognized Taylor Darrow approaching, his purposeful strides eating up the distance. She called out a greeting as she slowed the buggy.

The silver haired, portly man stopped and smiled. "Hello, Miss Wemblish. Seems you've a merry lot on board today."

"Indeed, Mr. Darrow. You remember Violet?"

The man nodded at the girl.

"And these two are my temporary guests. Their uncle is in port."

"Heading to California, I'll bet." He gave the twins a smile before returning his attention to Zorinda. "I'm glad

I've run into you. I wanted to tell you again how sorry I am about the orphanage windows. But the supplies," he lifted his hands in a helpless gesture, "needed to be delivered. The miners gamble, spend recklessly, and die needlessly leaving their families in great want. Their attraction to certain improper places harkens back to the time of Sodom and Gomorrah." Mr. Darrow paused and cleared his throat, embarrassment reddening his face.

Zorinda sought to relieve his discomfort. "I understand, but I'm aggravated with the captain's payment demands. He should have welcomed an opportunity to bring Christ's compassion to those hopeless and in need." Loathing for the captain flared while she silently condemned his greedy soul.

"He's a fair man of business. Those crates will take up space better used for more profitable cargo. I dare say we were lucky he agreed at all. I'm content with the arrangement but touched by your concern." Mr. Darrow smiled. "I well know you are a champion of the needy."

Zorinda managed a smile. "Thank you. Whatever I may have done to help is a blessing to me. I pray donations will continue to support the Mission Society while I'm away."

"I will greatly miss you. But I wish you well."

Zorinda nodded, afraid she might cry. Once Mr. Darrow walked on, Zorinda found a spot to secure the buggy near the market.

All alighted. Raine and Ronnie eager to see everything. Zorinda led the twins and Violet to the strawberry vendor but gave a wide berth to the butcher's and fishmonger's stall. After completing her purchases, Zorinda and her helpers carried several baskets back to the buggy. The most important item, however, was the bag containing the licorice.

Zorinda guided them to a shaded spot on the bank of the Elizabeth River. After spreading a blanket, Zorinda and Violet unpacked the weighted basket bearing Li Ling's enticing dishes. All ate their fill while enjoying the waterfront activity. An hour later, Raine and Ronnie were yawning and soon settled on the blanket for a nap.

"Should I go to Mr. Arnell's alone?" Zorinda whispered to Violet.

"Why not? I'll be here, and the children can rest. You go ahead and make your visit."

Knowing Violet had matters in hand, Zorinda returned to the buggy, arriving at Mr. Arnell's shop in minutes.

The dear man was dusting his collection of bric-a-brac when she entered his gallery. Paintings hung on the wall in no order or pattern. Landscapes hung beside unidentified portraits, and still lifes nestled between depictions of an assortment of animals, both wild and domestic.

One of her paintings—*Wind's Song*—was no longer on an easel in the bow window. The ship, with its billowing sails turned golden red by the setting sun, had been replaced by her most recent delivery, *Promise of Paradise*.

The owner, bald and bewhiskered, gave her a wide smile. "Zorinda, dear, how fortunate you've dropped in." Mr. Arnell tossed his duster aside. "I sold your other painting yesterday. The buyer was disbelieving of the modest sum. I told you all along you should set a higher price."

"How wonderful." A tiny thrill raced through Zorinda. She was always excited when one of her paintings sold knowing someone would enjoy what she loved to create. How grateful she was to God for his gift. And what a balm to her loneliness.

"The buyer was Mrs. Sharp."

Zorinda felt ill, her smile turning to a grimace. "Really?" The word came out as a squeak.

Mr. Arnell chuckled.

"She convinced herself the painting was by a famous French artist and was, somehow, stolen from the Louvre."

"I hope you didn't intentionally mislead her." If Mrs. Sharp thought she'd been duped, she'd sue Mr. Arnell. Zorinda would have no choice but to come forward and admit she'd painted the picture.

"Mrs. Sharp convinced herself. She has a penchant for the dramatic. Don't worry your pretty head. I can hardly wait to see what this new one fetches. Should Mrs. Sharp drop in, I'm certain she'd pay three times what she paid for the other one."

"Remember, when sold, the money goes to the Female Orphanage."

"Absolutely." His smile dimmed a bit. "Zorinda, have you booked passage yet to San Francisco?"

"No." She had to tamp down her threatening despair.

"Don't think I'm meddling, but shouldn't you let your father rest in peace so you can move on with your life? You're a beautiful, young woman. Find yourself a good man and marry. Thad would be joyous to look down from Heaven and see you surrounded by children—your children. Not the ones from the orphanage or our church."

As she twisted her hands, Zorinda lowered her eyes, willing away potential tears and swallowing embarrassment. Mr. Arnell's words recalled memory of Wil's announced engagement to the bank director's daughter. And Wil's suggestion she become his mistress. She raised her eyes welcoming Mr. Arnell's kind regard.

"I will await the Lord's will. Until then, I'm content. Thank you for everything."

"You don't have to thank me. Before I forget, let me give you the money from yesterday's sale." Mr. Arnell walked toward his office at the back of the shop.

While Zorinda waited, two women entered, setting off the welcoming bell attached to the door. Recognizing them as attendees at a recent church meeting, she gave them a smile. The women delivered a cursory nod then put their heads together as though whispering. They walked to an opposite wall displaying an assortment of paintings while keeping their backs to her. The dreaded prick of tears burned.

Mr. Arnell's return eased the sensation, and after greeting the new arrivals, he handed Zorinda a generous sum. She hoped he'd deducted his commission. Slowly, she closed her gloved fingers about the bills. The women, having turned, openly stared, making Zorinda uncomfortable.

Mr. Arnell leaned close to whisper. "I'm going to give those old hens something to cackle about." Then he kissed her cheek.

Zorinda nearly giggled. What would she do without dear Mr. Arnell?

After leaving the gallery, Zorinda returned to the picnic site, Raine and Ronnie awake and ready for another adventure.

"Where are we going next?" Raine clasped her hands together expectantly while Ronnie tried to hide his half-eaten licorice stick.

"Why don't I surprise you?"

Both heads bobbed, and after Violet loaded the empty basket and the children in the buggy, Zorinda had an idea. A daring one. After the snubbing at the gallery, she was ready to be bold.

Zorinda guided the buggy toward the commercial waterfront, heading opposite from the avenue leading to

Bank Street. Her secret hope was to see Carris Trewellyn's ship at Newton Wharf. Her spontaneous change of course took her past at least a dozen ships where longshoremen were storing either cotton or tobacco in the holds. A lesser number took on crates of supplies, most likely bound for the gold fields of California. Upon sighting the clipper, as indomitable as her captain, Zorinda noticed the intricate figurehead of a winged woman positioned on the ship's bow. Emblazoned in gold, the lettering above her declared the vessel, *Bird of Paradise*. Compelled to enjoy more than a cursory glance, she halted the buggy.

Even with the sails furled, the ship was magnificent, luring Zorinda's imagination to far away countries and unimaginable adventure. How often had she dreamt of sailing with her father and seeing something of the world? All she'd ever known was Norfolk, having ventured but once to the Atlantic Ocean on an outing with her parents more than ten years ago. She could still feel the waves tugging at her bare feet and the wind snatching the ribbons from her hair. The tangy taste of the salt spray and the jewel-like shells scattered across the sand. If only—

"Miss Wemblish?"

Zorinda reddened, embarrassed. Captain Trewellyn had caught her. Would he be arrogant enough to think she'd hoped to see him? As he hurried down the gang plank, Zorinda glanced behind her. The children had dozed off again.

"Have you decided to return them?"

When the captain reached the buggy, Zorinda quickly put her finger to her lips to indicate he lower his voice.

"You've put them to sleep?"

"More likely the fresh air," she replied softly. "A hearty lunch. And licorice."

"This isn't the way to your home."

Zorinda groaned inwardly. Honesty was her only option. No matter the poke to her pride. "I was hoping to have a look at your ship. She's a marvel."

"Have you ever been on a clipper?"

"No. My father's ship was a barque."

"I'll give you a tour."

"I'm expected at home."

"Where are we?" A sleepy Ronnie sat up and looked around. "Is that Oncle Carris's ship?"

"What? Are you bringing us back?" Raine popped up, rubbing the sleep from her eyes, her voice quivering with unshed tears. *What a mistake I've made.*

"Not at all. Your uncle has offered to give me a tour. The two of you could help him." Zorinda gave their uncle a pointed look, and he grinned. He was a charmer when he grinned. Sarah had warned her.

"Oui," Raine agreed eagerly. "I could show you my dolls. My papa bought them for me and left them with my maman for when I was older and would better care for them. They are *très belles*—I mean very beautiful." Raine cut her eyes quickly to her uncle who was trying not to smile.

"And I have a ship one of Oncle's sailors carved for me," Ronnie said.

"I'd love to see your things. May Violet come along for a look?" Zorinda held her breath as she looked at the captain, awaiting his reply.

Violet lowered her eyes and fussed with the cuff on her sleeve.

"She's more than welcome."

Zorinda couldn't contain her smile. She stood and accepted his hands about her waist as he lowered her to the ground. They faced each other longer than necessary.

Then the captain, as though remembering his manners, helped Violet alight, then swung each child down, producing happy squeals.

The children seemed to have overcome their fear of him. Could this be the softer side she'd hoped to bring out in the captain before he sailed out of her life?

Carris could hardly believe his good fortune. Surely luck had led Zorinda Wemblish past his ship while he took a turn on deck with Cavenley. Luck or something of a divine nature? Shaking off the ridiculous notion, he offered his arm to the stunning woman, garbed in a gown the color of the flamingos he'd once seen in Brazil. Valeraine and Valeron each took one of Violet's hands, pulling her toward the gangplank.

"I trust the children have behaved?"

"Absolutely." Yet a slight sigh escaped her perfect lips.

"But?" Carris prodded.

"Truly, the children have been no trouble. I'm upset over another matter. The Female Orphanage needs several windows replaced before winter. Unfortunately, I don't have the funds to donate. Nor anyone else, I've been told. Yet, I know there is someone who can help."

"Someone?"

"Our heavenly Father. Surely, he will work out matters."

Zorinda's easy reference to God, as though he were her best friend, unnerved him. Carris's mother had also thought of God as a personal friend. Uncomfortable with his thoughts, he quickly changed the conversation. "After I completed my business this morning with the local banker, I was extended an invitation."

"To what?"

"An affair hosted by your mayor, a Mr. Delaney, tomorrow night at his home."

"Oh." A shadow passed over her eyes, and Carris pondered the cause. "Do you know the mayor?" she asked.

"Not personally. But the banker whose cotton I'm transporting to San Francisco requested an invitation on my behalf."

"Which banker?"

Her arm stiffened beneath the fabric of her gown. "The president of the Exchange Bank, Mr. Sharp."

"I see."

Her tone was frostier than the South Pole. Which happened frequently when he was around. He stopped and covered her hand with his. "Would you consider accompanying me? The invitation also included a guest."

"You refuse to allow me passage on your ship, but you ask me to attend a social event?"

The pleasant moment disintegrated more rapidly than a snow squall could form around the Horn.

"Why not?"

Her expression darkened. "You know very well why not. I appreciate your efforts to be tactful, but I'm not highly regarded by Norfolk society."

"I'd like to be the one to change their minds."

"You have no idea what you're saying." Zorinda shook her head, her eyes taking on a glassy sheen. "Mr. Sharp is also my father's banker, and because I refuse to have my father declared dead, he won't grant me access to my father's deposited funds. I receive a comfortable monthly allowance Papa arranged before his last voyage. But there are charities and causes I'd like to support and can't because of Mr. Sharp's unreasonable demand. Instead, I'm forced to ..." She clamped her lips tightly, pulling free of his hold. Lowering her eyes, she fidgeted with the chain of her embroidered reticule.

Carris failed to stop his frown. "Perhaps I could assist—"

"Certainly not. Forgive my rambling." She drew herself up stiffly, elevating her adorable chin. "But I must decline your invitation."

"Because I won't take you to San Francisco?" Anger tightened his neck cloth.

"I really must be going. If you would be so kind as to summon the children?"

"They've already disappeared with your maid. They could be anywhere."

"Please find them." Her agitation was palpable, and she looked close to bolting as though an exotic bird poised for flight.

"If you must leave, I could bring the children and Miss Violet back at seven."

"They should accompany me now." There was no softening in her tone or look.

"So, you would interrupt their enjoyment because you're angry with me?" He intentionally flung an accusation similar to the one she'd used on him the previous evening.

Her eyes widened.

"Are you being fair?" he asked.

"Then I will see you—later." Her tone sharp, she turned and rushed down the pier, reaching the buggy and dozing horse in record time. There was no missing her desperation to be away from him.

There were secrets inside Zorinda Wemblish Carris had an insatiable desire to uncover. And little time to do so. Unless he changed his mind ...

Carris arrived as the tall case clock chimed seven, neatly garbed twins and the maid, Violet, with him. Zorinda appeared recovered from earlier and was now the charming beauty who irritatingly invaded his thoughts when least expected. He soon discovered the cause of her pleasant demeanor. There was another guest for the meal, introduced as Captain Teig Witherspoon—the man who'd directed Zorinda to him and his ship. Carris suspected the meal would be rife with tension.

"Captain Witherspoon is my father's oldest and dearest friend," Zorinda explained after introductions were made. "They both grew up on Virginia's eastern shore and were inseparable until they each acquired their own ship."

Carris acknowledged the man with a dip of his chin while extending his hand.

Witherspoon hesitated for a moment, obviously sizing him up, his brow furrowed. The captain was a bit shorter than Carris, leathery skin, all-seeing eyes sharp with inspection as though probing Carris's soul for secrets. Silver liberally streaked Witherspoon's hair and beard, though a few blond strands were still in evidence.

"Captain Trewellyn." Witherspoon's grizzled voice rumbled around him.

Carris glanced at Zorinda who was watching him. Closely.

"We meet at last."

As Carris pondered any unspoken meaning to Witherspoon's words, the twins made their presence known to the grizzled captain. And Mrs. Simmons summoned all to the dining salon. But Carris knew the reprieve was temporary.

Chapter 6

After the meal, Carris intended to follow Zorinda and the twins to the sitting room. She held the book she'd been reading to Raine and Ronnie in one hand while they reminded her she'd promised to continue the story.

Witherspoon, behind Carris, cleared his throat.

Time to be taken to task. Again. When Carris turned and met the man's glare, he knew what was coming.

"Captain, a word with you outside." His tone brooked no refusal.

"Of course. I'm prepared for my next verbal flaying."

Witherspoon frowned then exited the front entrance. Carris dutifully followed. The man veered to the right of the spacious veranda where several wicker chairs provided seating. Settling in one, Witherspoon lit his pipe.

Carris leaned against a brick column, folding his arms. He hoped the anticipated hostile exchange would be quick.

Witherspoon didn't disappoint, coming right to the point. "I know you're busy, and I'm due to sail within the next day or so north to New York. My sister is doin' poorly, and I've spent precious little time with her these years past. She's a good woman. Right with the Lord. Her voyage is plotted. But your eyes tell me you're not sure o' your direction."

Carris shifted uncomfortably, but remained silent, waiting for the man to continue.

"Zorinda is my goddaughter. I've tried to be a father to her since learnin' Thad was nowhere to be found. When she took a notion to search for him, I wanted to discourage her. Then I realized she needed to do this to find peace." Witherspoon fell silent as he drew in on his pipe, then slowly released a smoky plume. "Mrs. Simmons tells me Zorinda met those children before she reached your ship."

"She befriended my niece and nephew the day after we arrived. They were ..." Carris paused and cleared his throat. "... lost, and she encountered them on the wharf." He couldn't very well tell the man they'd run away from him.

"I was told you'd scared them."

So much for salvaging his reputation. "They were disruptive and hindering the crew's work—"

"They were bein' children," Witherspoon snapped, leaning forward, pointing the end of his pipe at Carris. "Zorinda helped you. Anyone can see the lass and lad admire her. Do they admire you?"

Guilt gripped Carris. He held silent.

"Zorinda needs your help. I sent her to you because you have a reputation o' runnin' a tight ship. Your crew is orderly, and you are a fair man of business. I made the mistake o' sharin' a tale I was told when the *Hailstrom*—my ship—had a layover in Tahiti. I cautioned her some o' what I told her was likely scuttlebutt. But I believed she had a right to know. I'm not so sure now." Witherspoon shook his head then continued.

"While in Papeete, I encountered the captain o' a French ship. We ended up eatin' together, and in the course of the conversation, I mentioned my concern over Thad's strange disappearance. This captain knew o' him. Some o' what I'll be tellin' you, I haven't told Zorinda—things I didn't want her to know.

"This captain—Goudreau—recalled meetin' Thad in San Francisco. Some o' Thad's crew were shanghaied by what was believed to be a ship o' French registry but captained by an Englishman."

A privateer, perhaps, with a letter of marque from Louis-Napoleon Bonaparte?

"Captain Goudreau helped Thad make contact with French authorities in the town, but they were little help. However, one o' the men workin' with the French sought Thad later and told him what he knew about the incident. What it came down to was the ship bearin' Thad's missin' sailors was involved in the illegal opium trade—how some wealthy Frenchman livin' in the Pacific was smugglin' opium into China for huge profit."

Unlikely a privateer.

"Thad swore to find this man and expose him. The *Scheherazade* sailed the next day, bound for the Pacific islands."

"Did he know which island?" Carris instantly regretted asking. Could the island be Bora Bora? What if Montagne was the Frenchman involved in the opium trade? What if Lance ...? Now wasn't the time to let his imagination run wild.

Imagination? I've never had an imagination.

"He didn't.

"When did you speak to Goudreau?"

"Six months ago. He last saw Thad in September of '48."

"What do you think?"

"I know he would have made every attempt to rescue his men. What he met up with along the way, only the good Lord knows."

"After a stop in San Francisco, my destination is Bora Bora."

"Actually Pora," Witherspoon corrected. "Part of the Windward Societies—recognized by the French and English as an independent kingdom. Not very large and about one hundred forty miles from Tahiti. Ask about Thad when you reach Papeete." Witherspoon paused. "I've taken enough o' your time. Thanks for hearin' me out."

Witherspoon got to his feet while Carris straightened from his position.

"Oh, one thing more, Captain. I know you're refusin' to take Zorinda to San Francisco. I've learned o' another ship put into port today in Hampton headin' to the west coast. I've checked out the captain and crew. They're a solid lot and accepting passengers. I'm goin' to let her know, and possibly they'll take her. Why don't you want her on the *Paradise*?"

Because she's stubborn and opinionated—enchanting and good-hearted. Far too determined. And for the first time in years, I've been reminded I do have a heart, which is terrifying.

The silence deafened.

Witherspoon's sigh conveyed disapproval. "I only hope one day she finds a man deservin' o' her, one who will treasure her. Not rob her o' her spirit. I saw what happened to Thad's wife, a good woman, Cappy. But a little bit o' her died each time Thad sailed away. Zorinda has a beautiful soul and zest for life. I should be thankin' you for turnin' her down."

Seated in the sitting room, Zorinda's voice was as tired as her spirit while she struggled to remain alert. She continued reading, unwilling to disappoint the children.

"The oarsmen got us swiftly to shore, and we disembarked, wading some as we approached the beach. It appeared deserted until we neared a line of palms and prickly vegetation. Then a woman emerged, a beauty like no other—part of the island yet somehow part of me."

A soft snore forced Zorinda's eyes off the page and onto two red-haired moppets. Both children were fast asleep. As she pondered how best to get them upstairs, she heard booted feet moving through the front entrance and down the hall.

"Uncle Teig," she beckoned softly. Rather than her godfather, Captain Trewellyn entered and recognized her dilemma. Moving to the settle, he lifted Raine in his arms then headed toward the stairs while Zorinda guided a groggy Ronnie.

When they reached the guestroom, Violet was already within the space, having laid out the twins' night shifts and pulled back the counterpanes. When she offered to ready them for bed, Zorinda eagerly accepted her help. Witnessing the captain's gentler manner was disconcerting. As was the hint of sandalwood, citrus, and clean linen clinging to his person. She lost no time in leading the way from the room and down the stairs, Captain Trewellyn following too closely. Drawing a steadying breath, she moved into the long hall then turned. Zorinda found him mere inches from where she stood. What had Uncle Teig said to him?

"Thank you for your help. They've had a busy day. I'm surprised they remained awake as long as they did."

"I'm amazed at how you've turned them into different children. I fear we'll not fare as well once we sail." The captain seemed to move closer.

"You'll manage. I've explained the enormity of your responsibilities and reminded them to do everything they can to help, not hinder, your efforts. I often felt neglected by my father, although he loved me dearly. A captain's burden is balancing a personal life with the sea."

"You are overly generous to justify my negligence of the children."

His humility was unnerving, so she averted her face. "Is Uncle Teig—"

"Smoking his pipe in your garden. We had an interesting discussion."

Now Zorinda warmed, certain the captain knew curiosity was about to get the best of her. "I hope things went well."

"Well enough. But no, I haven't changed my mind."

"I didn't expect you to," she retorted, aware of her icy tone. "Shall I watch the children tomorrow so you can prepare for your special evening?" *Sarcasm doesn't become you, Zorinda.*

"Will you reconsider attending? I would be truly honored to escort you."

"Absolutely n—"

"You should go, Miss Zorinda." Sarah slipped from the shadows. "I can't remember the last time you went somewhere special."

Had the housekeeper gone mad? She'd warned Zorinda not to trust Carris Trewellyn, and here she was encouraging her to go to a social event, knowing Wil would be there.

"Violet and I will watch the children."

Panic flooded her. "I–I really don't have anything appropriate to wear," she offered half-heartedly. Did she want to attend? If so, she was the one who'd gone mad.

"You've yet to wear the lovely turquoise and gold silk Captain Wemblish sent to you from Paris. The one fashioned by the new dressmaker with Gagelin—Worth, I think is his name."

"I don't know—the gown was Papa's last gift to me before—"

"Nonsense. What good is a gown if not worn? I'll go up now and have a look. What a waste for something so lovely. After you've seen the captain out, come up, and we'll decide if alterations are needed." Sarah didn't tarry long enough for Zorinda to protest, for she quickly started up the stairs. Zorinda watched her go, aware her life raft had been snatched, and she was sure to drown. Slowly, she turned to face her tormentor.

"I ... accept?"

His grin took years off his face, and he seemed rather boyish.

"As close to a yes as I need, so I will take my leave so you may join your housekeeper. I don't want anything to prevent you from accompanying me. I shall call for you tomorrow. Precisely at seven."

Shock spread through Zorinda, his jest both stunning and amusing. She'd assumed he was a stranger to humor.

"I don't expect your staff to watch the children," Captain Trewellyn said. "I could pick them up in the afternoon, or you could bring them to the ship and take the tour?"

"Raine and Ronnie will be no trouble. They can remain here with Mrs. Simmons and Violet. I'll be awaiting you. At seven." There was no need to see his ship. There was no hope to be found there.

To her amazement, he took her bare hand, leaning forward slightly. She was stunned by the feather-light kiss upon the back. How dare he? She could barely tolerate him. Or had her intolerance moderated? Heavens, no. No. No.

"Until tomorrow." Releasing her, he went to the door and let himself out.

Zorinda remained motionless, breathless, and bereft of something she couldn't name. The shutting of the door roused her from her stupor. As though caught in a pleasant nightmare she walked out into the hall while drawing a painful, sharp breath. When the man had pressed his warm lips to her bare hand, a thousand lights exploded in her head. She dare not think of her reaction had he kissed her lips.

"No!" Her fierce whisper echoed around her, followed by a series of more silent nos. Pacing the length of the hall, she turned, paced to the front door, turned again and repeated the process. Whatever she felt didn't matter. He was the man who stood between her and her search for her father.

I will not waste one thought on Carris Trewellyn. He's opinionated and inflexible and infuriating—too regimented and arrogant. He is going to sail away, and I'll never see him, Raine, or Ronnie again.

When Zorinda neared the staircase, she dropped down on a low tread, covering her face with her hands. What disaster awaited her tomorrow night at the mayor's soiree?

I kissed her hand. What was I thinking?

A sleepless night awaited Carris as he paced his cabin. He'd nearly barked at his steward earlier, abruptly dismissing the puzzled but unruffled John Rollins. Even

Cavenley's carefully penned note informing him repairs would be completed sooner than expected, failed to soothe him. Nor the news the Darrow's crates had been stored and the last of the cotton had been loaded. Everything was out of kilter—his mind, his direction, his heart. All because of Zorinda Wemblish. The news the *Paradise* could sail earlier was less than welcome. And the half payment received from Darrow seemed a lot less satisfying now than when the contract had been finalized. He had no regrets for taking money from Banker Sharp considering the difficulties he'd created for Zorinda. But Darrow was sending supplies to San Francisco for those who'd fallen on hard times.

He reasoned through his actions as he paced. He was a captain and a businessman. The welfare of his crew and Trewellyn Shipping rested entirely in his hands. Thanks to the irresponsibility of Lance, who'd never done anything unless of benefit to himself. Carris Trewellyn, the senior, had been a skilled captain, shrewd, and an unmatched negotiator in financial matters. Carris had developed his father's acumen but not through his father's tutelage. He and his father had become strangers after the birth of Lance. Carris resented the man's devotion to his second family as though his mother, Madeline Trewellyn, had never existed. To this day, Carris couldn't forgive his father.

As a child, Carris believed in a loving God who freely dispensed miracles and forgiveness. But in the years following his mother's death, Carris had struggled with his faith. After his fiancée ended their engagement by marrying his best friend, Hubert Mayes, he'd forgotten how to hope. Though many years had passed, her rejection still tarnished Carris's opinion of females. Until now.

In two short days, he'd discovered a woman who was more concerned about others than herself, who would spend what money she had on those less fortunate. Her good heart had welcomed those who were society's castoffs—a Chinese prostitute, a former slave and his granddaughter, and a woman widowed and destitute. All part of the Wemblish family. Zorinda loved them, and they loved her. Her honesty and pureness of spirit threatened to topple his barriers. Distance and an emotionless existence served him well where women were concerned. There would be no broken hearts—no dalliances in ports of call. No children left without a home or family. No broken-hearted lad of six mourning a dead mother or longing to see a father thousands of miles away. *"No tears, Carris. Be stout of spirit ... there's no time for tears ..."*

A knock sounded on his door, banishing his father's harsh words. He took a seat behind his desk bidding whoever knocked to enter. Den Cavenley opened the door, holding what appeared to be a packet with sides bulging in an odd way.

"Sorry to disturb you, sir, but this arrived right after you left with the twins." Cavenley moved inside the cabin and handed him the sealed item. Carris recognized the impression in the blue wax as the seal of his London solicitor, Malcolm Truesdale. A knot tightened in his throat.

"Thank you. So, we may be ready to sail on Sunday?"

"Aye, sir. Have you need of anything?"

"No. Miss Wemblish has agreed to accompany me tomorrow evening to the mayor's affair."

"Shall I make arrangements to have the children watched?"

"They will remain at Miss Wemblish's home while we're out."

"I'm sure the twins won't mind," Cavenley said then displayed a mischievous grin. "She is quite lovely. A rare flower, most certainly."

Carris lowered his brows, annoyed by the man's comment. Was he so idiotic as to think no other man would have noticed her breathtaking beauty? Not many of his men had missed her short visit earlier in the day. He made no response to his first mate's observation.

"Is there anything else, Cavenley?"

"No, sir. Good night."

Cavenley nodded, then turned sharply in a display of his naval training.

After the door closed behind him, Carris sighed. He looked about his private space—the large bunk, the scarred desk, and the nautical paintings covering the walls. The trappings and tools of a sea captain, many once belonging to his father, were scattered about. Opening a drawer to remove a small knife, his fingers brushed the worn leather of a book. Taking hold, he pulled the book free, clearing a space on his desk. His mother's Bible, much read and much treasured, tugged uncomfortably at something inside him. Had the time come to seek wisdom from the worn pages, still bearing a trace of his mother's scent?

He sliced the envelope's flap with his knife, the object creating the bulge tumbled out, striking the desktop. Carris stared at the small nondescript box. Removing the top, a thick band of gold, centered by an aquamarine stone nested in a bed of white satin. With a shaking hand, he removed the ring. The scrolled etching on the band emulated waves.

His father's ring. The one Carris senior had given Lance on his sixteenth birthday. The ring Carris had one day expected to receive as the eldest son. Foreboding filled him as he unfolded the accompanying missive. The letter had been written four months ago. Though he'd given the attorney his itinerary and planned ports of call, how amazing the package had caught up to him. Dread threatened to steal his soul as he read the page.

Chapter 7

Unfolding the letter, Carris braced himself, knowing he had no choice but to read. Anger flared within him when his right hand began to shake.

> Carris, I've startling news. As you know, I asked the captain of the HMS Treasure, Harless Peerley, to investigate your brother's death while in Madagascar four months ago. He discovered Lance was not killed. A man bearing a striking resemblance to him acquired your father's ring while gambling with Lance. This man was wearing the ring when he lost his life. Naturally, those who saw the ring assumed the deceased was your brother. The tavern owner knew otherwise and in a most unexpected but honorable manner, took possession of the ring for safe keeping. This means Lance could very well be alive.

The pages slipped through Carris's fingers as he pondered the revelation. Lance—alive? Good news—or disaster? This guaranteed he'd have no sleep.

Carris spent Friday alternating between rage and disbelief. If Lance was alive, why hadn't he sent word? Why hadn't he searched for his children? Cavenley and Surrell knew something was wrong but had the sense to give him a wide berth, limiting their verbal exchanges to brief updates on the ship's repairs. When he wasn't mentally flaying Lance, he was wondering how kissing Zorinda Wemblish would feel. At moments, he even missed Raine's and Ronnie's antics. His world had lost its predictable precision, but fortunately he had errands to complete—and quickly so he could prepare for the evening's event.

Carris's first visit was to the apothecary to resupply the ship's medicinal chest. In possession of Rollins's list, he purchased spirits of camphor, alum, and blue vitriol. Rollins had previously served as a surgeon's assistant in the Royal Navy and now provided care for the *Paradise's* injured or ill in addition to keeping Carris organized.

Carris located the postal office and sent off a letter to Truesdale, then ventured into a mercantile to purchase cooler clothing for the twins. A pleasant, older woman greeted him, and after explaining his need, she gathered items she assured him were appropriate for warmer climes. Had he sought Zorinda's help, she would have known exactly what to purchase. And proved a distraction.

Errands completed, he planned a hasty return to the ship. But his pace slowed when he neared the Darrows' place of business. Zorinda's charitable spirit filled him with guilt. How much would refunding the Darrow's payment cost him in the long run? Not enough to ruin Trewellyn Shipping. Yet, a successful business only remained thus if managed responsibly, and he couldn't very well provide free transport to all who sent goods and supplies to the poor. There would be a sizeable loss of revenue over time.

Carris's brisk walk brought him to a side street, its cobbled surface worn smooth. The town market was ahead, and he lengthened his strides, until a painting displayed in the window of an art gallery halted him. A ship rested peacefully at anchor in a cove of a tropical island. The style and technique reminded him of the painting in the Wemblish home. Peering closer, initials of the artist—*R.I.N.* and the date painted in the lower right corner—confirmed his assessment. A bell tinkled merrily when he impulsively opened the door proclaiming Arnell's Gallery.

A balding man of middle age with a fringe of whiskers looked up, spectacles perched on his nose. "Good day. I'm Joseph Arnell. Might I be of help?"

"The painting in the window—how much are you asking?"

"I must apologize. I sold it about an hour ago and neglected to remove it from the window. The buyer purchased the art as a companion piece to another painting."

"I'll double whatever they agreed to pay." Desperation consumed Carris, dampening his brow and tightening his collar. He had to possess the painting.

The man arched his brows.

"The buyer has committed to a generous sum. To double—"

"How much?" A tic commenced in Carris's jaw. What was wrong with him? *I kissed her hand. I've lost my mind.*

"I know the artist—perhaps you could commission—"

"My ship sails Sunday. I won't return to Norfolk until January. Has the buyer paid you?"

"Not yet. She insisted on speaking with her husband first."

"There's a possibility she won't complete the purchase?"

"Possibly, but unlikely. Her husband is most indulgent." The man smiled.

Carris could only frown. "Did you promise to await her decision?"

"No, I didn't expect anyone else to be interested."

"Why? Who could ignore this amazing scene?" Carris asked. Clearly the man had no idea this was a treasure. Rather like Zorinda Wemblish—those blinded by her mother's island blood were imbeciles.

The owner pressed his lips together as though pondering his words. "You're right. Mrs. Sharp—the wife of a local banker—has things her way far too often. Besides, I'm certain she'll return to haggle over the price. I'll sell this to you for twice what I agreed to sell to her. One hundred fifty dollars."

Carris blinked. Only once as he digested the amount. But worth every penny. And he'd already earned some extra because of the supply crates bound for San Francisco.

Withdrawing American currency from an inside breast pocket, he counted out the bills and handed them to the man.

"You've made an excellent purchase. And you've helped a fine individual in ways you can't imagine. May I ask your name?"

"Of no consequence," he assured the man. "But the next time you see the artist, please tell him his work is without equal."

"I certainly will." The man smiled though there was a slight quirk of his left brow.

Carris wondered what he'd said to produce his facial reaction. "Thank you."

Carris and Mr. Arnell went to the window, and the two of them removed the painting. Carris estimated the size to be about eighteen by twenty-two imperial inches, perfect for the space between the window gallery and the top of his bunk on the ship. The precise place for so restful a scene.

Arnell wrapped the painting protectively, then offered to have a lad make a delivery to the ship as soon as possible.

Carris declined the offer, afraid the spoiled banker's wife would find a way to reclaim the painting before the delivery. After shaking the man's hand, Carris left, humming as he walked—of all things—*Amazing Grace*.

Zorinda's eyes reflected her troubled thoughts in her vanity mirror as Violet artfully braided and curled her hair, draping several locks over one shoulder. Shaking free of her preoccupation, Zorinda found her voice. "You've outdone yourself, Violet. However do you manage such an elaborate coiffure?"

"I enjoy arranging your hair." Violet smiled. "I suspect the captain will take notice."

"I doubt he'll care."

"He'll care," Violet murmured as she fastened a jeweled feather to a section of ringlets. "There. Now, your gown."

Violet's help made the ordeal of dressing tolerable, and soon Zorinda stood before her Cheval mirror while Violet clapped her hands in glee.

"My word, Miss Rinda. You're quite a picture."

Zorinda turned a little to the left, then the right, amazed at what the shade of the gown did for her coloring. Vibrant and somehow soothing at the same time. Her father had selected well. She wore her mother's gold necklace with the lapis lazuli stones, matching earrings, and bracelet, a reminder her mother was with her in spirit. Zorinda reached out and hugged the girl.

A light knock sounded on the door, followed by Sarah's entrance.

"The captain has arrived and is in the parlor. But the children have asked to see you."

"Sarah." Zorinda hurried over to her housekeeper before she could dash off. "Why did you encourage me to accept Captain Trewellyn's invitation?"

"I had no right to speak as I did because my sailor husband broke my heart. You've a good head on your shoulders. You're brave and strong."

Zorinda shook her head. "I'm not."

"You are, and you'll make the right choices. Listen to the Lord. Let him lead you. Now go see the children." Sarah made a few tiny adjustments to Zorinda's bodice and smoothed the necklace which encircled her neck.

Lifting her chin, Zorinda fought back the urge to run and hide. She had to face her fears. And Wil. This night could be a new beginning. Violet held out her light, gauzy wrap, and after taking it, Zorinda hugged Sarah. Leaving her room, she hurried toward the children's bedchamber to tell them goodnight. *Please don't let me be sorry, Lord.*

Carris couldn't help staring at the vision entering the Wemblish parlor. Shades of blue, green, and gold blended in the skirt and bodice of Zorinda's gown. He was reminded of waves bathing the white-gold sand of a Mediterranean beach. The rustling silk of her skirt mirrored the sound of the wind riffling palm fronds. When he dared to look at her, something long buried flared to life. His brittle, battered soul struggled with his loss of control, shredding his mastery of order. Desire for what he didn't have, and would never have while clinging to a ship and the sea, nearly brought him to his knees. *I've been in port too long. I need to feel the sway of the deck beneath my feet, breathe the salt air, cool my brow with the sea's mist. I don't want or need this complication.*

“Good evening, Captain. I didn’t mean to keep you waiting.”

Carris struggled to speak. Zorinda stood before him, and he knew he would never again look upon such beauty. Without thinking, he raised her gloved hand to his lips, vibrantly aware of her blue-black curls, her exposed shoulders of palest gold, her gardenia scent a heady elixir. He nearly groaned when he released her. “Rest assured, the minute I waited was worthwhile.”

Zorinda blushed and uttered a silvery laugh.

“I spent more than a minute with the children.”

“Which was a treat for them. Shall we?” He offered his arm, and she laid her hand upon his sleeve, giving him a smile.

“I’ll wait up, Miss Zorinda.” Sarah hovered nearby, her eyes flicking back and forth between them.

“There’s no need.”

“Indulge me. The mother in me wants to be sure you’re home safe.” After giving Carris a warning flash of her eyes, Sarah headed toward the rear of the home.

Carris restrained a chuckle.

Within a few minutes, Carris settled in the seat across from Zorinda in the rented carriage. After the driver put the conveyance in motion, conversation lagged while Carris pretended to ignore the press of his legs against Zorinda’s skirt and petticoats. Thoughts of Lance churned through his mind. Zorinda stared out the window. He doubted she saw anything. “We both seem to have gears and cogs rattling in our heads.” His comment broke the silence, and she looked at him.

“My mind is wandering. Uncle—Captain Witherspoon—has shared information of a ship now in Hampton leaving for California within the week." She fell silent, and Carris sensed her inner tension.

"And?" Carris prompted, leaning forward, closing the distance between them.

Her eyes lifted to his. "As Uncle Teig has spoken to you, you're aware my intention is to search for my father."

Don't say or do something you'll regret. Yet, this other ship—will they accord her the respect due her?

"Though hopeless, I fear."

The light of a streetlamp revealed a telling dampness on her cheeks Carris ached to brush away. "I can't imagine you as a woman prone to hopelessness. As a matter of fact, I've received some news."

"Do you wish to share?"

"I'm told the *Paradise* will be ready to sail Sunday."

Zorinda's eyes widened, but she remained silent.

Carris sighed. "And Lance—my half-brother and the children's father—may not be dead." At his words, a bitter taste swirled in his mouth.

"How wonderful for Raine and Ronnie."

"Not really. Lance has always been unpredictable. And selfish."

"But he loves his children."

"He hardly knows them. He hasn't been involved in their lives."

"How sad. And hard for their mother when she took ill."

"Lance prefers pursuing pleasure and avoiding complications. If he's alive, his silence is intentional."

"Perhaps he's not in a position to get word to you or the children."

"What are you suggesting?" Carris's tone conveyed his vexation. Was Zorinda attempting to excuse his brother's blatant indifference?

"Well, he could be injured or ill—"

"Or drunk in a brothel." His words were harsh, bitter.

Zorinda gasped. "Surely not."

"How do you think he met the children's mother?"

"I have no idea."

"The sisters at the orphanage said Amalie Montagne ran away with a sailor when sixteen years of age. He deserted her in Marseille leaving her destitute and desperate. My brother met her in a brothel. And soon after found himself a father."

"The children," Zorinda's voice faltered. "Do they know?"

"Some things don't need to be shared. At least, not until they are much older." The carriage slowed before a three-story home ablaze with light. The stone façade was imposing and bespoke of wealth. Other conveyances were in line, the occupants systematically alighting. The driver of Carris's rented carriage maneuvered behind those ahead. Several minutes would pass before they reached the front entrance. "You understand my aggravation."

"If he's alive, there's always a chance the Lord is working on his heart."

Carris's inclination was to scoff, but Zorinda spoke with such sincerity, he remained silent. The carriage suddenly lurched forward, ending any need for comment. All too soon the door opened, and Carris stepped out, turning to assist Zorinda.

Chapter 8

This wasn't Zorinda's first time at Mayor Delaney's home. She'd been there with her father and had taken tea with the mayor's wife and several other women while working together on a mission project. Zorinda had been treated courteously, but never the recipient of an enthusiastic welcome. Tonight would be no different.

As expected, the mayor's wife was the consummate hostess, graciously welcoming her and the captain—especially the captain, complimenting him on his regal bearing while batting her lashes. Banker Sharp made his way over to them, minimally acknowledging Zorinda, but smothering the captain with a bombastic greeting. When she realized the man planned to monopolize him, she drifted off, mingling with several of the ladies affiliated with the local mission society.

Their conversation centered on the current need of the Female Orphanage. The women were sympathetic but not in a position to help. They too were saddened by the information the Darrow brothers had to use the Society's funds to ship the supplies and Bibles to San Francisco. Conversation turned to the recent engagement of Wilson

Goodwell and Frances Southgate, the bank director's daughter. Relief filled Zorinda when Mrs. McIntosh, the directress of the Female Orphanage, joined them—for attention centered on her, leaving Zorinda unnoticed. Half listening to the discussion, she dared to take note of Norfolk's elite. Then her perusal brought her to Wil, laughing loudly at something the mayor said, followed by a hearty sip from his cut-glass tumbler. His eyes shifted, meeting hers. Ice pricked her veins. Panic and anger stiffened her spine. Wil murmured something to the mayor and walked her way. Looking around, Zorinda debated her choices, quickly realizing her only recourse was to rejoin the cluster of women surrounding Mrs. McIntosh. Until a hand gripped her elbow.

"I hoped to find you." Captain Trewellyn paused as he looked at her. Far too closely. "Is something amiss?"

"I ..." She couldn't tell him about Wil. The humiliation was unbearable. "I was admiring this portrait."

His brows furrowed while studying her, ignoring the stilted representation of the Delaney ancestor she'd waved her hand toward. Her evasive skills were sadly lacking.

"So, all is well?"

"Of course."

Snapping open her fan, she vigorously waved, hoping to cool her temper and her skin. From the corner of her eye, she saw Wil turn aside, directing his steps to a group of unattached females, which did not include the inestimable Miss Southgate.

"I believe the call to the table was delivered," Captain Trewellyn said, offering his arm.

Zorinda accepted, allowing him to lead her toward the ornate dining room. Unfortunately, they would not be sitting together, for Mrs. Delaney had names at each place. Zorinda found herself between Mrs. Sharp and Mrs. McIntosh. Wil sat across from her, eyeing her speculatively. Thankfully, Mrs. McIntosh was eager to chat.

The meal blurred. She vaguely noticed a course consisting of she-crab soup, a leafy salad garnished with radishes and corn relish, and a main course of lobster and scallops. The subject of clippers dominated the dessert course, with many of the men present questioning the captain about the *Bird of Paradise*. The mayor admitted a fascination for the Greyhounds of the Sea, as did several others.

Then Wil joined the conversation, his tone setting off warning bells in her head. "I've heard, Captain Trewellyn, clipper masts, spars, and rigging have been known to topple with very little cause."

Captain Trewellyn regarded the man evenly, a tiny tic in his jaw indicating his displeasure.

Zorinda quickly averted her eyes, not wanting to appear overly interested.

"Usually the result of inaccurate estimates of the amount of sail needed."

"Don't clipper captains agree the more sail the better?"

As if Wil knows the difference between a clipper and a dinghy.

"Conditions must be favorable when setting all possible sail. Maximizing speed in order to achieve what amounts to notoriety is a sure way to lose a worthy lady and her crew."

Zorinda inwardly shivered from the ice in the captain's voice.

"Isn't fame and fortune the very essence of these *ladies*?"

Wil is provoking the wrong man.

"Mr.—?" Captain Trewellyn seemed about to pounce.

She held her breath.

"Wilson Goodwell." Wil's tone resonated with self-importance.

"Mr. Goodwell, a captain's concern should be for his crew first. A legion of hard-working men, bound by love of the sea and the ships they sail honor a profession as old as time. For one to infer anything less is insulting. As for the *ladies*, we would do well to treat them with the respect they're due."

Heavens—is he speaking of a ship? Or women, perhaps a woman? Another shiver.

"Here, here," erupted from several of the male guests while Zorinda held her breath.

Mayor Delaney stood, putting an end to Wil's baiting. "I believe we should make our way to the ballroom for dancing."

The captain exchanged a glance with Wil, then rose to his feet, making his way to where she sat. As he leaned forward to assist her from her seat, he whispered. "Egotistical landlubber."

Zorinda nearly giggled, but when Wil shot her an angry glare, her amusement evaporated. He was not done with her.

As they entered the grand salon, all furnishings were against the walls. The musicians played the opening strains of a Strauss waltz, Carris easily sweeping Zorinda out upon the floor. They joined the mayor and his wife, Banker and Mrs. Sharp and several prominent members of the Norfolk community, earlier introductions and names having blurred into sameness. His only concern was the woman in his arms. And the fact she'd seemed anxious before they'd taken their seats at the table. Had one of the women insulted her?

"You should have warned me you're an accomplished dancer."

Zorinda commanded his full attention, an amused light lurking in the mysterious depths of her eyes. She was incredibly graceful, and Carris floated on a cloud. Her curved lips beckoned mercilessly. Summoning Herculean restraint and exerting the labor required to steady a gale-tossed ship, he fought the urge to kiss her. He chuckled hoarsely. "You've encouraged me to display my refined side."

"How so?"

Was she smiling? And teasing?

"When I was very young—still in leading strings—my mother decided I would be a gentleman in all ways. I wanted to impress her. I suppose I'm attempting the same with you."

"You needn't do so. Save your efforts for your mother." Her eyes sparkled in the light cast by the ceiling's crystal chandelier.

Carris shook his head. He so wished his mother was alive for him to do so. "My mother died when I was a young boy."

Zorinda gasped. "I'm sorry. How thoughtless of me."

"Don't apologize." He knew a ghost of a smile touched his lips. Had his mother lived, would he be different—a man of deep convictions and unshakable faith in God? Sadly, he would never know. "She lavished me with love but died not long after I turned six. Nearly a score and nine years ago."

"I was blessed to have my mother for twenty years. Even so, I think of her daily." She fell silent, a deep sadness reflected in her eyes. "What of your father?"

Carris felt the familiar pain slice his soul, but he would answer her.

"My father was a hard man, made more so after my mother's death. But he remarried, and his world revolved around his lovely young wife and, eventually, Lance. Rather than try to please my father, I forged a path separate from his."

How neatly he'd summed up the most unsettled years of his life—his mother's replacement, Esmé Glisson, a China doll come to life, delicate and unfit for the rigors of childbirth.

"Which you've navigated successfully." She gave him a half smile.

"I've done well enough. How fortunate you had two loving parents."

"They always encouraged my dreams. My mother gave me the gift of color. And Papa—he gave me a love of adventure. He made the sea come alive for me, and I could see the water, calm and serene, then raging and merciless. The pictures are painted in here." She removed her hand from his long enough to tap the side of her head, all without losing time to the music.

"I was always a disappointment to my father."

"Your mother believed in you. Others believe in you."

"I once thought if I could find a woman who had the faith in me my mother did, I'd never let her go."

"Do you think you'll find her?"

"Possibly." Carris watched her intently, and her hand trembled. He tightened his grasp, and Zorinda looked to her side. Was she afraid to look at him?

"Surely there must be someone in England."

Carris pondered her comment. Did she harbor more than a passing interest in him? Why was his pulse racing? *She's not sailing on the* Paradise. *She's not sailing.*

"There isn't." Her eyes met his, her lips parting. His breath hitched. The cravat tightened. *What is wrong with me?* Zorinda Wemblish would be nothing but a memory in two days. And even if not the case, she was out of reach. Kind, generous, compassionate. And on good terms with the Lord. Something he would never be.

Carris banished the somber moment. "But I am dancing with the loveliest woman here, and I'm enjoying myself immensely. I'll remember this night when I'm halfway around the world sailing through the snow and freezing rain." The intensity between them eased.

She smiled. "You might think me without sense, but I've often wondered what a sail around the Horn would be like. Papa's descriptions—the majesty and ferocity." Zorinda's eyes glowed.

She pulled Carris into her dream, seeing the scene as she did. With the eyes of innocence. But innocence could prove deadly.

"Imagination isn't reality."

Her eyes clouded, and he hated himself for smothering her joy. But Zorinda deserved the truth and not idealized versions of exotic, wondrous places. Nothing like the book she'd been reading to the twins.

The waltz ended, and Zorinda pulled away, turning her face aside. She hurried across the room and disappeared into the hall.

Carris followed.

He caught up to her in the dimly lit corridor and clasped her arm, halting her flight. She used her other hand to brush at one cheek.

"I didn't mean to upset you. Sailing isn't a lark. Or an adventure. Anything can and does happen. Men lose their lives. Ships sink."

"I know." Zorinda pressed a hand to her lips until she recovered. "I'm being foolish. I miss my father, and I'm certain he's out there, lost and alone. He needs me."

"Don't let Captain Witherspoon's tale influence you—"

"He would never pass on idle gossip. If he believed what he heard, so do I." She shook her head and pulled her arm from his grasp. "I … I believe I'll go into the garden for some air."

"I'll come with you."

"No." Zorinda was emphatic. "Perhaps you could dance with one of the ladies who've been smiling at you so frequently. Excuse me."

Shouldn't he go with her even if she didn't want him? Or should he give her time—time to realize she was unlikely to find her father? He only hoped the captain of the ship in Hampton had the sense to turn her down.

Zorinda settled on a stone bench in the Delaney rose garden.

"Hello, Zorinda."

The voice filled her with dread. *Lord, help me.*

The string of Japanese lanterns clearly illumined the clean shaven, patrician visage of Wilson Goodwell. "May I take a seat?"

Panic threatened, but Zorinda managed to speak. "Where is Miss Southgate?"

"She's suffering from a meddlesome headache. You look well."

Zorinda refused to comment.

"Still crusading for the orphanage?"

"Yes, I still am." Zorinda allowed herself to look at him, unavoidably comparing him to Carris Trewellyn. Wil wasn't nearly as tall or as broad through the shoulders. Evening attire looked natural on the captain. Wil lacked innate elegance. He also lacked the captain's commanding presence. And arrogance cloaked Wil as did his cologne. To her dismay, he took the seat she'd never granted.

"Why won't you meet me? You know I would marry you if not for my uncle."

"You needn't explain. If you'll excuse me." She rose until he gripped her arm, forcing her back down beside him.

"I know your father's funds are tied up by Uncle Sharp. And they will continue to be unless you have your father declared dead."

"He's not dead," she snapped, snatching her arm free. "You've no reason to look into my affairs."

"You liked me well enough when I first came to Norfolk. Remember our picnic by the river?" Wil reached up and trailed his index finger along the side of her face. She jerked back, and he laughed. "I know you arrived with Captain Trewellyn. I passed his clipper earlier today at Newton Wharf. Nothing exceptional."

Rage boiled within her.

"Uncle said five years ago when the *Houqua* caused such a stir in the New York to Canton run clippers were the future. I don't agree."

This time, Zorinda stood and glared at Wil.

"I don't care what you think of clippers or why you can't marry me. You're engaged. Leave me alone." She clenched her fists, breathing as though she'd been running.

Wil's eyes drifted to her décolletage. He too came to his feet. "I would hate to make you regret your words. You prize your reputation but think what would happen should I mention we shared a private picnic."

"As nothing occurred, do whatever you please." She turned away, but Wil grabbed her roughly, hauling her against him.

Zorinda bent her arms and wedged her elbows between her and Wil. She could smell the inebriating spirits emanating from his harsh breaths.

"Zorinda, I want you."

"I. Don't. Want. You." Anger burned deep in her soul, and she made no effort to hide the fiery emotion. "Release me. You've chosen to marry a woman who meets your family's requirements. If your new wife falls short of your expectations, I suggest you lower them."

He tightened his embrace. "By sunset tomorrow, no decent man or woman in this city will so much as speak to you. I suspect the charities you so nobly support will sever all connection with you."

Tears burned Zorinda's eyes, threatening to spill. *Don't let me break down in front of this insufferable being. Make me strong. Help me.*

As though an avenging angel from heaven had appeared—one without wings—she was miraculously freed.

Wil was shoved so forcefully he stumbled and landed on his bottom amidst the thorny rose bushes. Carris Trewellyn edged her aside striding toward the fallen man like a tiger stalking its prey. Leaning over Wil, he took hold of the lapels of his coat and pulled him to his feet. "Don't ever lay a hand on Miss Wemblish again. The next time I'll do more than knock you on your backside. I'll make sure you don't get up."

"The next time?" Wil snarled. "You're leaving. You won't be here to protect your mistress."

The captain's blow sent Wil reeling. He careened into the trunk of an elm, face first. Blood trickled from his nose and stained the pristine white of his silk shirt. As he looked up, he wiped his coat sleeve across his face, leaving a red trail on the cloth. "You're going to be sorry."

"How so?" Carris Trewellyn's jaw twitched, and his scar pulsed.

Zorinda swallowed. Hard.

"I'll tell my uncle to find another ship for his cotton."

"I don't think so. Get out of here."

Wil looked as though he was about to say something, clamped his lips, then turned away. He staggered the first few steps then righted himself as though to convince them he was in no way damaged. Zorinda looked at the captain. "How did you find me?"

"Your someone led me here." The warm huskiness in his voice as he grasped her hands was certain to be her undoing.

Chapter 9

"Would you take me home?"

Zorinda's request wasn't unexpected, heightening Carris's protective instinct. Without hesitation, he pulled Zorinda into his arms, her head resting perfectly against his shoulder.

A shudder rippled through her when a tiny sob escaped her perfect lips.

When her trembling eased, Carris raised her chin. How he hated the distress Goodwell had caused. When he'd located her in the garden with the bullying jackanapes, he'd been sorely tempted to do more than knock the man off his feet. "We'll leave immediately."

Zorinda nodded, her eyes filled with gratitude.

The need to kiss her returned tenfold, so Carris quickly dropped his arms. "I'll retrieve your wrap and make our goodbyes."

Once they were in the carriage, Zorinda fell silent, her eyes fixed on her clasped hands.

Carris warred with himself. No matter how fiercely he fought, there was a tension between them. A bond. An attraction he could never acknowledge. And one Zorinda would never encourage. Could there be a future for them?

Carris looked out his window struggling with an unknown emotion. Had this woman entered his life to remind him of what he would never have?

Zorinda roused herself when she realized they were on Bank Street. "I've been terrible company, and you've been nothing but considerate. I'm sorry you left early."

"I'm not. I've had the pleasure of a beautiful woman's company. A grand meal, if somewhat overdone. And engaged in fisticuffs with a bilge rat. I couldn't imagine a finer evening." He gave her a lopsided smirk.

Zorinda couldn't help but smile at Carris Trewellyn.

"What is or was this Goodwell to you?'

There was a hint of command in the captain's voice, angering and encouraging her. What a blessed relief if she could share the truth without fear of repercussions. To tell someone who might shed a different light on the matter. And the captain would be gone by Sunday.

Zorinda sighed. "We courted for several months until I realized he had no serious interest in me. His uncle, Banker Sharp, had decided the daughter of a bank director would be a suitable match for Wil." Zorinda drew a deep breath. "Though engaged, he has proposed we continue ... an acquaintance."

His sculpted jaw tightened, anger turning his eyes a now familiar shade of a raging sea. "Has he forced—?"

Zorinda shook her head while quaking inwardly.

"Thank God." He lifted his eyes to the carriage roof as though sending his words heavenward. When he looked down at her again, he leaned forward and clasped her hands in his rough, callused ones. "Flogging wouldn't be punishment enough for him. But I fear I've added to your trouble."

"Had you not come upon me when you did, Wil would have done more than ruin my reputation."

The carriage slowed, but he made no attempt to open the door. He still held her hands, and for the life of her, she had no wish to be released. When the horses' impatient movements jerked the carriage, Captain Trewellyn released her, exited and turned to assist her. When she leaned out, he clamped his hands about her waist and swung her down.

Zorinda softly gasped as she met his piercing eyes now a deep aqua in the glow of the streetlamp. An unfamiliar warmth warred with common sense, Zorinda keenly aware of his hands gently stroking her sides. Instinctively, she tilted her head as he lowered his—warm breaths whispering across her heated face, sending her into a spiral. *What am I doing?* She backed away, and he made no attempt to stop her. "I must bid you goodnight." Zorinda turned, hoisting her skirt and petticoats as she ran up the steps to the house. Breathless, she grasped the brass doorknob.

"Goodwell isn't worth jeopardizing your well-being."

Releasing the knob, she walked back to the edge of the steps.

"What do you mean?" She knew anger cooled her tone. He was about to tell her once more she shouldn't seek her father.

"Don't let him force you into running away."

Restraint snapped. She'd suffered Wil's insults. She would not endure a lecture from this man.

"Though you've no wish to find your brother doesn't mean I'm wrong to search for my father."

"I've little belief Lance is alive. Given his preferences and peccadillos, I still believe he was murdered—if not in Madagascar, somewhere else."

Shock quivered through Zorinda. *Murdered?*

"Though I respect my solicitor, he may be wrong."

"But if my father—or your brother—is alive, they are most likely in terrible trouble. I would never allow doubts and misgivings keep me from helping my loved one."

"There's no love lost between my half-brother and me."

"But what of the children? Raine and Ronnie have never known security. They are being delivered to some faraway island to a man they've never met. I know the sadness when one has lost both mother and father."

"As do I. Sometimes children might be better off if an irresponsible parent isn't part of their lives. Knowing Lance, Raine and Ronnie will fare better without him. Their grandfather will provide for them far more adequately than Lance ever could. They are but eight years of age. At some point, he will be little more than a fuzzy memory."

"They may remember more than you realize. Don't allow pettiness blind you to what might be best for the children."

"Really?" Harshness tainted Carris's response, and the telltale tic spasmed along his jaw. "After meeting them but three days ago, you know what's best for them?"

"They could only benefit by knowing their father."

"If their father is alive, and he wanted to find them, he would have already done so."

"We're of two different minds. I thank you for your intervention this evening. Tomorrow, I'll arrange for passage on the ship in Hampton harbor." Zorinda turned back to the door, her breathing unsteady as she grasped the knob once again. Carris Trewellyn would not alter her course.

After parting from Zorinda, Carris had wasted hours before falling asleep. When a knock sounded on his cabin door, he turned over in his bed with a groan, wondering if he could ignore the summons. Was it time to rise already? No light filtered through the gallery, so dawn still hid. He needed to gather his wits, but Zorinda Wemblish would give him no peace. He shouldn't have warned her not to seek her father. He shouldn't have disparaged Lance. Saving her from Wil would probably cause her more harm than good.

"Captain Trewellyn?"

Rollins. Carris was in no mood to face the efficient, unflappable man. Yet, there was work to be done and even though he'd managed to destroy any kind feelings Zorinda may have harbored for him, he wouldn't neglect his men or his ship. The *Paradise* would sail on the morrow.

"Come in," he bellowed as he threw the coverlet aside and managed to sit. He wore his shirt and trousers from last night. When Rollins entered, the man's shocked look grated on Carris's nerves.

"Sir, are you well?"

Coming to his feet, Carris fell to pacing. Running a hand through his hair, he knew the wiry, untamable strands took on a life of their own whenever he bypassed proper grooming.

"I've made a mess of things."

"I don't understand, sir." Rollins's brows drew together.

"Miss Wemblish will never speak to me again."

Why was he baring his soul to Rollins?

Why not? The man is level-headed and understanding.

"I'm sorry, sir. Was the soiree not to her liking?"

"I'm not to her liking." Carris slammed his hands on his desk, scattering papers. Drawing a deep breath, he raised his eyes, meeting his steward's widened ones. "I'm sorry.

I shouldn't bother you with a personal matter. Please tell Mr. Cavenley I'll meet him on deck for inspection in fifteen minutes."

"But Captain, you're in last evening's clothes—"

"I'm capable of dressing myself," Carris snapped then was immediately contrite. "Forgive my ill temper. I mean no offense."

"Of course, Captain. Pardon my saying so, sir, but I've never seen you like this. If you've formed an attachment to Miss Wemblish, shouldn't you let her know before you leave?"

"Things will improve for Miss Wemblish when I do leave."

"Captain, you're exaggerating."

"I'm not." Carris drew a deep, fortifying breath as he straightened to his full height. "Please take my message to Mr. Cavenley."

"Shall I have Amos prepare a plate for you?"

"Thank you, but no. And Rollins, I haven't taken leave of my senses."

"Of course not, sir."

Rollins's face remained impassive, his prior military training serving him well. "I believe the term for your malady is besotted."

The man quickly vacated the cabin, but he left Carris in worse condition than when he'd first risen. Of one thing he was certain—he would never allow himself to fall in love. Never.

Then why did Zorinda Wemblish wrap silken bands around his heart? Why couldn't he be glad she would secure passage to San Francisco on the ship in Hampton? How could his life ever return to what he'd known before he met her?

It couldn't.

There was but one solution.

Ready a stateroom.

For one enchanting, irrepressible, vexatious woman.

Once decided, Carris hurriedly dressed. Assured he was shipshape and Bristol fashion, he sought Cavenley and Surrell. His announcement—Zorinda Wemblish would be accompanying them on the voyage—widened their eyes and raised their brows while each held silent. Rather than field pointless, irritating questions, Carris instructed the two men to conduct inspection without him then left the ship, walking rapidly to the Wemblish home. There was more to Zorinda than what she'd shared. Undoubtedly, she wanted to find her father. But he sensed she unduly suffered the dictates of society. Would he ever know what truly lay beneath her controlled, restricted manner? Was there more fire than ice in her veins?

Deep in disturbing thought, he'd made a wrong turn somewhere along the way, now noticing he was about to pass a building whose door bore an identifying plaque. *Female Orphanage*. He looked up, mentally counting the numerous windows. Replacing all of them would be expensive, and easily covered by a small portion of what he'd collected from recent shipping contracts.

Guilt stabbed. Yet ...

This was a matter of business—his business. And he shouldn't feel guilty at having spent hard-earned quid on a painting. He was about to risk his life, his crew, and the *Paradise* for Banker Sharp's cotton and the ship chandlers' supplies.

Which brought him to another thought. Didn't the Darrows realize whatever they'd packed in those crates wouldn't matter much to gold miners—men who'd be lucky to find so much as a cap of yellow dust? And what kind of men dragged their families to an uncivilized, dangerous place where death hovered on every corner and life was cheap?

Carris made an abrupt turn soon arriving at Zorinda's home. Childish voices floated on the air, and he suspected the twins were in the garden. Was Zorinda right about Raine and Ronnie? If Lance was alive, was he ready to be a real father? How hypocritical to judge his brother when he was no saint himself?

Witherspoon's mention of a Pacific island rumored to be a base for opium smuggling weaseled into his consciousness. *What if ...*

Carris shook his head in dismissal. His priority was Zorinda.

He hurried up the steps and forcefully rapped the knocker. Light footsteps approached from the other side, and the door cracked open a few inches. Li Ling peered through the crevice, not the expected Mrs. Simmons. The petite woman looked up at him with wide eyes.

"Good morning, Miss Ling."

She bowed in deference as did Carris while removing his hat.

"Is Miss Wemblish at home?"

Li Ling pondered his words, then brightened, giving him a smile.

"She no here."

Worry gnawed at Carris, but he reminded himself to be patient and not surrender to whatever madness had gripped him.

"Is Mrs. Simmons available?"

Li Ling shook her head.

"She no here. At market."

Disquiet seeped through Carris, perspiration beading his brow.

"What of Mr. Tucker?"

"He with Miss Zo. They leave early morning. Ship in Hampton town."

"Is Captain Witherspoon still in port?"

"He leave. Go to sister—veery sick."

Carris wracked his brain wondering how to better communicate.

"*Nĭxiăng yòngnĭ de yŭyán shuōhuàma*?"

At Carris's question spoken in Cantonese, a huge smile spread over Li Ling's face.

"*Shide*," was her reply. She would be happy to speak with him in her native tongue.

Carris might not know French, but he'd been able to converse with Trewellyn Shipping's Cantonese contacts since the age of twenty. He would try anything to keep Zorinda from making a terrible mistake.

Chapter 10

The morning had been busy, and Zorinda was glad Fergus had accompanied her in the wagon. After obtaining more details about the *Game Cock*, a clipper built in Boston and on her first voyage, Zorinda had sent a telegram to the captain requesting passage on the ship.

Her next visit was to Mr. Arnell to tell him she'd requested a cabin on the ship in Hampton harbor and might be leaving soon. She was beyond amazed when he described how a finely dressed gentleman purchased the painting she'd delivered two days ago for an exorbitant amount. Mr. Arnell, after giving her an impish grin, confessed to some enjoyment when he told Mrs. Sharp, who'd also made an offer, she'd been outbid. Only after leaving the shop, funds in hand, did Zorinda realize she hadn't asked Mr. Arnell the purchaser's name.

With Fergus's help, she delivered the clothing to the Female Orphanage and presented the proceeds from the sale of her two paintings. After sharing hugs and tears, Zorinda remembered to ask Matron Redman if she could purchase the book the twins had borrowed, hoping they would continue reading in English on their long voyage.

The grateful woman had told her they could have the book, then hugged Zorinda again.

Reality descended with such gravity, Zorinda didn't think she could take much more. Fergus cast her a worried glance when she asked him to take her to the cemetery located behind the church the Wemblishes had attended since Zorinda's childhood. Heavily shaded, the serene expanse allowed for unobserved reflection. After alighting, she made her way to her mother's grave, overwhelming sorrow threatening to suffocate. Kneeling, she brushed aside a few leaves and twigs, wondering what her mother would have thought of her search for her father. What would her mother have thought of Carris Trewellyn? Zorinda would miss Raine and Ronnie but would pray their grandfather was a kind and loving soul. She would pray for a safe voyage for the men on the *Paradise*. She would pray for the captain who'd challenged her, infuriated her, yet, somehow, comforted her.

"Miss Wemblish?"

The voice drew her like no other, possessed by the man who had refused to grant her most desperate wish. Zorinda raised her head and met his eyes. *I will not change my mind.*

The captain held out his hand.

She hesitated, then reached out, his fingers tightening about hers. The calluses were still there, as was the unwelcome warmth of his touch.

He drew her to her feet.

"Why are you here?" Puzzled was too mild a word for her current state.

"Li Ling told me you were going to the orphanage and several other places—she couldn't recall them all. But she shared you spend time at your mother's grave when you're troubled."

Li Ling knew her far too well. How amazing the woman, who understood English, but hadn't mastered conversational proficiency, had conversed so easily with the captain.

"Are you troubled?"

Zorinda refused to answer.

"Are you here to tell me goodbye?" Anger and despair sharpened her tone.

Captain Trewellyn shook his head.

"I've come to tell you there's a cabin waiting for you. If you're set on a voyage, I can provide one you may never forget."

She was certain the earth shook at his announcement.

Zorinda and Sarah watched the captain pace the sitting room, deep in thought, weighing his options, choosing his words. Zorinda could almost see his thoughts spinning as he worked through this anomaly in his plans. That lock of dark hair hanging over his brow called to her, but rather than obey her wayward thoughts, she clasped her hands. How could she worry about his hair when her life had drastically altered?

"I have one request." Carris Trewellyn halted looking directly at her.

Now what? Had he changed his mind? Was he concerned about receiving payment for her passage? "I have the funds to pay," she said.

"Not payment. Raine and Ronnie require structured supervision. Something I can't provide, and I haven't a crew member to spare. Instead of running amok for the next three months, they could be at lessons or engaged in more appropriate pursuits administered by a firm hand."

Zorinda's heart beat so painfully she couldn't steady her breathing. What was he suggesting?

"In exchange for passage on the *Paradise*, will you accept a position as their governess?"

Carris knew the man who asked Zorinda to be governess to his wards was not he. The fact he'd told her he would grant her passage on the *Paradise* still made no sense, undoubtedly proving to be the worst decision he'd ever made. No matter how Zorinda's dark eyes and tempting lips reminded him of his own desires, hidden years ago in a heart he'd believed numb. Why now had they flared to life? She stared, too stunned to speak. Goodwell was certain to hurt her with his threats, and Zorinda didn't deserve the resulting condemnation. Society would blindly accept the word of a so-called gentleman over the claims of a woman of unconventional parentage. No matter how wrong.

Mrs. Simmons rested her hands atop Zorinda's, drew a breath, and spoke to her.

"I've always known you wanted to see something of the world—this yearning's in your blood—whether a gift or curse from your father. You're ready for this voyage. Maybe you'll find Captain Wemblish. Maybe you won't. But you will have tried. And by the time you return, Wil Goodwell will be a balding, fat, married man with a shrewish wife and a dozen children."

Zorinda uttered a weepy laugh, and Carris's heart lightened.

"How long will I be gone?" She gave him a questioning look.

Was she agreeing to be a governess to the twins? How could he exist so close to her and not want ... *Oh, God, I've made a terrible mistake. How do I get out of this?* The offer had been made, and there'd be no rescinding. The children did need her. They admired her. And he—well, he wouldn't be able to live with himself if he allowed her to sail on another ship. The *why* he refused to consider.

"A year at the most," Carris said. "Hopefully less. If all goes well, three months to San Francisco. A short layover there to deliver the cotton and sundry crates. Then to Bora Bora where Raine and Ronnie's grandfather, François Montagne, lives. We should sail home no later than mid-October." *So I can collect the remaining payments.* Rather than instill satisfaction, he was disappointed. Now was not the time to dissect his contradictory emotions.

"Then, I leave in the morning."

Carris released a sigh—of relief—or distress? "Shall we speak to the children?" he asked.

Zorinda nodded and stood.

"I believe they will be pleasantly surprised," Carris said clasping her hand. Then immediately released her. *Mrs. Simmons may carve my heart from my chest.*

Zorinda smiled, her eyes fixed on him. Why did he have this maddening urge to kiss her? What would stop him once she became a passenger? What would keep him from wanting more than impersonal interaction? There was no room in his life for marriage—a disastrous engagement, the loss of a beloved mother, a disapproving father, and an irresponsible brother had replaced dreams with stark reality.

But Zorinda, possessed of a beauty of spirit and an unshakable faith he envied, might be good for him. He could only pray for as much in the weeks and months ahead.

"What have I done?"

No one was present to answer Zorinda as she looked around her room. Moving slowly across the floor, she fingered one beloved item after another. Most were gifts Thaddeous Wemblish had given her over the years whenever he returned from a voyage. There was the porcelain princess doll her father brought from Prussia, embroidered Turkish slippers, a Japanese fan, a shawl from India. She was about to leave them and the only life she'd ever known. At her spinsterish age of a score and five, she should have more sense. She should have sought God's will.

But she hadn't. She'd decided no man would control her life. She'd decided to search for her father. She'd decided to accept Captain Trewellyn's offer. Her selfish desire to break free had driven her decisions the last ten days.

"Mind if I come in?"

Recognizing Sarah's voice, Zorinda turned to her partially opened door. "Not at all."

The woman entered, bearing a mug, and joined Zorinda by her dresser. "I knew you'd be awake. Here's some warm milk to help you sleep."

Zorinda accepted the mug Sarah offered and sat on the stool before her vanity. "I'll never sleep. My mind is awhirl."

"Why?" Sarah took a seat on an upholstered chair. "You're ready. And the children are thrilled."

"Sarah, suppose I'm wrong?" Zorinda paused and tucked her lower lip between her teeth. "I've never done anything so impulsive. Have I been over hasty in declaring my independence?"

"I think you'll find some of the answers you seek. You possess your mother's kindness and good heart, but you also have her eyes and her golden skin. You're a lovely woman, yet different, and people readily blame things on those who are different. Why should you suffer when you have an opportunity to see how your life could change?"

"You think more kindly of Captain Trewellyn?"

"I can't discourage you because I bear scars from the past. The captain might be what you need. I believe he needs you. He's searching, Miss Zorinda, even though he would never admit as much. I sense the Lord isn't captain of his life. Until he turns to the Lord, he'll never find what he seeks."

"What does he seek?" Zorinda sipped from her mug. The taste of the warm milk flavored with honey brought back childhood memories of her and her mother snuggled together in bed on a cold night reading together, her father thousands of miles away.

"What we all seek. A place to belong—someone to belong to. A heart filled with love and a strong faith."

"Carris Trewellyn doesn't believe he needs those things. In case you haven't noticed, he's the quintessential, self-sufficient man."

Sarah chuckled softly as she stood.

"Those are the ones who most need love and faith. I will miss you, Miss Zorinda."

Zorinda sat her mug aside and accepted Sarah's hug.

The woman's eyes clouded with unshed tears.

Zorinda's eyes immediately filled.

When they separated, Sarah straightened, adjusted her pinafore and folded her hands before her. "We'll be here waiting. You'll be back in no time at all, sailing on so fast a ship."

"In no time at all." Zorinda whispered while fear and excitement warred within her.

Now in his cabin, Carris sat at his desk, his eyes resting on his mother's Bible. He'd never prayed before a voyage, but something urged him to drop to his knees and petition the Almighty. He'd never been responsible for anyone other than his crew, his ship, and male or married passengers. This time, he was sailing with two children and a woman. He had no power over life and death. Only God could truly protect them.

A single lantern cast its flickering light over the space while he clasped his hands. When a child, his mother had taught him his first simple prayer. Right now, though, his thoughts were disorganized. But God, who made the sea and the sky, who created and calmed storms, could make sense of his tumultuous thoughts.

"I'm not sure what to ask. Anger and resentment have been my constant companions for years, but on this voyage, Lord, I carry my brother's children. They are innocent and undeserving of pain. I ask you to allow me to deliver them safely into the arms of one who will love them and give them the security they've never known. I ask you to watch over and protect Zorinda. If her father is out there, please reunite them. And grant Zorinda the desires of her heart—she's everything I'm not but wish I could be. Lord, please hear my prayer."

Carris stood on the deck of the *Paradise*, restless and consumed with second thoughts as the ship slowly came to life with sunrise a good two hours away. He watched his crewmen as he stood at the helm, their movements across the pine planks efficient while orders were issued and seamlessly obeyed. The ship rocked gently at her berth, belying the power and speed she possessed. Clipper sailings in New York and Baltimore always generated public excitement, but Carris had no need of such.

The *Bird of Paradise*, named for his mother's favorite flower, had been built by two brothers. One trained with John Griffiths, the man credited with the creation of the clipper. The other brother was once employed by the Boston boat builder, Donald McKay. The ship's design was a mix of the extreme sharpness of the clippers and the rigging of New York packets. With enlarged capacity, floor length, and buoyancy, the *Paradise* possessed rounded lines and finely formed ends. A vessel to depend on in heavy seas. And worth every bit of the $70,000 American dollars he'd spent. This run to San Francisco would substantially whittle away at the initial cost and allow him to recover the purchase price in less than two years.

The bow, bold and graceful, supported the figurehead of a Grecian clad woman embellished with wings. Carris wondered if his selection of the winged woman had been prophetic, for he now thought of Zorinda as a mythical creature in need of wings. The ship's name, in gilt lettering, decorated the head and quarter boards while gilded, carved scrollwork adorned the stern's window gallery. With the exterior painted black, the interior a pale shade of sand, and the waterway's blue, the ship struck a chord of pride within Carris. Yet, he couldn't shake his mother's long-ago admonition of pride going before a fall.

Though the ship could equal—perhaps surpass—any of the statistics set by other clippers, Carris had no need to break speed or time records. As his eyes swept the towering masts, his only wish was to take her to San Francisco with a minimum of problems, even if doing so took a little longer. He would never jeopardize the children, Zorinda, or his crew for the sake of a record.

Carris groaned as he checked his pocket watch. Zorinda and the children weren't due for another hour. For the thousandth time, he wondered why he'd put himself in this position. There was no denying he was attracted to Zorinda Wemblish. Yet, he was wrong for her and had nothing to offer but endless, empty days waiting for him, never knowing if he'd return. She deserved a man with sound prospects who was compassionate and loving. Carris's bucket of compassion and love had sprung a leak years earlier.

Cavenley called up to him, mercifully ending his agonizing uncertainty. He hurried down the steps to join his first mate, ready to lose himself in the work, that until now, was all he'd ever needed.

An hour before dawn, two sailors from the *Paradise* arrived with a wagon. As they loaded Zorinda's bags, hat boxes, and two trunks—one packed with a collapsible easel, palette, canvases, paints, cleaning and sketching supplies—the other with her clothing, Raine and Ronnie flitted about. They were unmistakably eager.

Zorinda couldn't concentrate, thankful the children were happy, but distracted by their ceaseless chatter. Art classes with the girls at the orphanage had in no way prepared her to be a governess. The twins' welfare would be her responsibility, their education in her hands. And in a way, their future. *Oh, Lord, help me be your instrument.*

Allow me to show them your grace and mercy so whatever storms beset them in life, they will be prepared.

Zorinda and the twins were lavished with hugs, tears, and pledges of prayer for safe travels. Mr. Arnell surprised Zorinda when he joined the small group, crediting Sarah for getting word to him through Fergus. He assured her everything would be fine in her absence and looked forward to a rousing clash with Banker Sharp should the man prove difficult.

When Sarah hugged her a final time, Zorinda feared she wouldn't survive the heartbreak of parting.

"Be careful, Miss Zorinda." Sarah sniffed. "I love you like the child I never had. Promise me you'll take care."

She managed a nod.

An intentional throat clearing drew Zorinda's eyes up to one of the *Paradise's* sailors seated on the wagon's bench. She believed he'd introduced himself as Doherty.

"Miss, time to be leavin."

"Of course." She lifted her gloved hand to the young man's extended one. He leaned over, gripped her and helped her up.

As soon as Raine and Ronnie joined the other sailor seated in the loaded wagon's bed, Doherty clicked to the horses and the wagon rolled away. A chorus of goodbyes followed them, while Zorinda felt the dampness on her cheeks. *Dear Lord, let this be the right decision.*

Chapter 11

Dawn closed in with merciless swiftness, the activity aboard ship frenzied. Carris was bombarded with the familiar yells and bellows. Discordant discussions rose and fell in volume according to the severity or success of the task performed. Men scurried up and through the rigging like their namesake—monkeys—shinnying up banana trees. Others labored over the endless yards of canvas sail, soon to be hoisted into place. Carris's anticipation—feverish and exhilarating—was a familiar emotion when about to set sail. This time, he was heading into the unknown and this unknown transcended geography, wind, and currents. This unknown had something to do with his heart, which he'd carefully guarded.

Above the dull roar came the unmistakable sound of wagon wheels. Now on the starboard side of the quarterdeck, Carris strode to the gangway to meet the arrivals. Seaman Sanders helped the children out of the wagon while Doherty assisted Zorinda.

For a moment, his gut clenched as he watched the man's competent hands clasp her waist. Then she was firmly on the ground and moving toward him.

Raine and Ronnie raced up the gangplank and darted past him with a breathless. "*Bonjour*, Oncle."

But he could only see their new governess. The brightening bands surrounding the rising sun illuminated her perfectly, her traveling costume of deep blue complimenting her dark hair and glowing eyes. The sleeves of her embroidered jacket were slashed to expose billowing folds of ivory silk while her black curls were tucked beneath a shallow bonnet.

As though she sensed his stare, Zorinda looked up and leveled one of her own. She lifted her chin as though a soldier marching into battle.

Carris sincerely hoped nothing resembling battle came to be. He intended to make sure she felt welcomed. And safe. "I promise you will not regret your decision."

"Did you say something, sir?" Cavenley paused in mid-run, having nearly rushed past.

Carris shook his head, unaware he'd spoken aloud.

"The cabin next to the children is in readiness?"

"As you requested, sir. Doherty and Sanders will see to the trunks as soon as Miss Wemblish arrives."

"She's here."

Carris's attention remained riveted upon the vision moving closer. He was suddenly impatient for her to be on board.

Cavenley sighed and Carris frowned at his first mate. The man reddened and coughed to cover his embarrassment.

"I believe you're needed at the capstan," Carris said. "Time to winch the canvas up to the yards."

"Aye, sir." Cavenley saluted and dashed off.

By then, Zorinda was nearly at the top.

He held out his hand to help her through the brow in the bulwark. Ballooning skirts and heeled shoes might prove hazardous on a ship, but he'd never seen a woman more beautifully arrayed. Zorinda placed her gloved hand within his and raised her eyes. He felt as though someone had knocked the breath from him. Somehow, he found his voice.

"Welcome aboard the *Paradise*. I've had the cabin beside the twins' cabin prepared for you—hopefully satisfactory and comfortable."

"I've no doubt my accommodations are fine. I would like you to review the lesson plans I've created, but I need to know what level the children are at in their studies. Their spoken English is adequate, but reading and writing in English should be reinforced. I'll also need to assess their grasp of mathematic fundamentals." She stopped. "Am I making sense?"

Carris knew his expression reflected amused confusion. There was no doubt Zorinda intended to take her new duties seriously. He had no idea what grasp Raine and Ronnie had of mathematics. He could only surmise the nuns had provided some sort of education.

"Of course. But I suggest you and the children settle in first, then we'll discuss lessons."

As though they knew they were the topic of conversation, the twins hopped into sight and surrounded Zorinda, speaking simultaneously, their excited English-French chatter contagious. Taking hold of Zorinda, they pulled her toward the companionway stairs.

Before disappearing, Zorinda turned and gave him an apologetic smile.

He smiled in return until Doherty spoke.

"We've got Miss Wemblish's trunks, sir. Shall we take them to her cabin?"

Carris turned, certain his mouth widened in shock as he viewed Zorinda's baggage—two trunks, two smaller bags and several hat boxes. Apparently, she was determined to be the best dressed governess on a ship or anywhere else. Carris suppressed a chuckle.

"By all means, Doherty. But will Miss Wemblish have any room to move about?"

Doherty produced a crooked smile.

"Hard to say, sir."

The man hurried off, calling to other sailors for help.

Carris glanced at the eastern horizon, the sun now reflecting a slight reddish hue. Possibly a storm later? Regardless, the anchor would soon be raised. Closing his eyes, he silently repeated the same words he'd prayed in his dark cabin, covering the possibility God had missed his original petition.

When his name was called, he opened his eyes, glanced once more at the east, then hurried to join Cavenley and Pete Surrell.

"Are you an artist?" Raine ran her hand lightly over several brushes Zorinda removed from her valise.

Ronnie examined the capped tin tubes containing her paints.

"I like to think so. Would you care to paint?"

Both red, curly heads nodded. "When?" they asked simultaneously. Since stepping foot on the ship they'd exhibited a contagious excitement.

Zorinda laughed. "Hopefully soon. I'll need to unpack today and, later, speak with your uncle. We must arrange our daily schedule around his. We mustn't keep him from his work."

"We were always doing so before." Ronnie punctuated his words with drooping lips. "I think we were—what did Oncle call us?"

"Annoying," Raine said. "We made Oncle *tres misérable*."

"This time, we won't start out on the wrong foot."

Raine and Ronnie looked at each other in confusion then lowered their heads to examine their feet. When Zorinda realized they'd taken her literally, she shook her head. "On the wrong foot means we don't want to upset your uncle."

There was a chorus of "oh" and "*Je vois*."

"I think," Zorinda surveyed her cabin filled with her trunks and bags, "this is going to take some time. Would you like to help?"

Raine and Ronnie bobbed an agreement.

After removing her bonnet and jacket and placing them on the bunk, there was a knock. Ronnie raced over to open the door, revealing their uncle.

An unsettling tension raced through Zorinda yet produced an inexplicable warmth. His smile only heightened the feeling, and she nervously clasped her hands.

"Would you be upset if you observed our departure?" Captain Trewellyn asked.

Zorinda shook her head. "I might be sad, but I wouldn't miss this for the world."

Raine and Ronnie dashed around the captain each of them promising to beat the other to the weather deck. Shaking his head at their antics, he offered his arm, which she took without hesitation.

Once on deck, morning sunlight cast its welcome glow over the *Paradise*. Zorinda could now see all those things she'd missed on her abbreviated tour of the ship. The vessel was an intricate composition—like a work of art formed by masts, rigging, and sails. The grinding creak of the capstan kept tempo with the sailors' sea shanty, "The Saucy Arethusa," while the mechanism ploddingly raised the massive anchor. The great sails hoisted into place, the wind catching and filling them, one by one. Now unfurled canvas sheets, painted pale gold by the morning sun, billowed aloft, and the ship took on a life of her own.

Childlike excitement gripped Zorinda, her laughter escaping as the wind tugged loose the curls Violet had so carefully created.

The captain grasped her hand, his touch jolting to life an unfamiliar awareness. He led her forward, the twins now on each side of them. Light mist peppered Zorinda's face, her gleeful shrieks mingling with Raine's and Ronnie's.

All around them shouts and orders lifted skyward. The wild cry of the wind in the lofty rigging pounded in Zorinda's ears, and the sails stretched taut like the covering of a drum. Behind her, an older man at the helm guided the *Paradise* farther into the ever-widening river. For a moment, her heart cried at leaving her family. When Captain Trewellyn smiled down at her, she fought the threatening sadness as a tentative excitement demanded release.

The *Paradise* skimmed the water's surface, a veritable bird in flight as the water churned by the cutting prow parted in a delicate froth. Men hung in the rigging above them as though suspended in air. Raine and Ronnie cried out then laughed when the sailors completed their tasks safely and swung down. For one heart-stopping moment, the ship careened crazily. Directives were shouted aloft, adjustments made, then the *Paradise* settled. Zorinda had never felt more alive, more wonderful, more hopeful.

"What do you think, Zorinda?"

She looked up when Captain Trewellyn uttered her Christian name. His eyes searched her face as though seeking her approval. This was going to be a long voyage.

Rules of propriety seemed ridiculous given this most unusual situation. With a most unusual man.

“This is more than I ever dreamed, Carris.”

With his free hand, he tucked back several stray curls and allowed his thumb to slide along her cheek to her chin.

Raine and Ronnie interrupted the moment by throwing their arms around her. “I think we’re on the right foot,” Raine said.

“I believe so.” Zorinda then turned back to look once more at her vanishing home.

By midday, the *Paradise* had passed through Chesapeake Bay and entered the Atlantic Ocean. The sun glowed in a perfectly blue sky, and the men had slipped into the routine altering little until the weather unleashed a tantrum. At the helm, Carris scanned the gray-green waters, intermittently marred by a few choppy swells, and his thoughts strayed to Zorinda. As usual, he struggled with the emotions playing havoc with his reason. When she’d guided the children back to their cabin, she’d taken his joy with her. Watching her, feeling her excitement when they’d sailed from Norfolk, brought back memories of his childhood and the first time his father had taken him aboard a Trewellyn ship. The sheer wonder of the masts and sails and—

“Cap’n, Miss Wemblish has requested a meeting with you.” Surrell spoke from his left, the man having moved beside him with unnerving silence. “She says she’s ready to review the children’s study plans.”

When Zorinda set her mind on something there was no ignoring her. Carris swallowed what could have easily escaped as an audible oath.

“And she wants to look through their lesson books.”

Carris looked at him—blankly. Lesson books?

Surrell must have noted his confusion. "Remember, the nuns gave you several books for the children?"

Carris nodded.

"They're in a chest in my stateroom. I'll find them and deliver them to Zor–Miss Wemblish. Would you mind—?"

"I'll take your watch, Cap'n. No need to keep Miss Wemblish waiting."

Surrell grinned as though privy to a secret, but Carris didn't have time to correct the man's erroneous assumption. He needed Zorinda to watch the children. And she needed him to facilitate her search for her father. Nothing more to their relationship.

Fifteen minutes later, after locating the requested books, he presented himself at her door. His one solid knock earned his immediate admittance. Raine stood there smiling up at him. A real smile—not a grimace.

"I'm in search of Miss Wemblish."

"Do come in, Captain," an unseen Zorinda summoned.

Raine opened the door wider, and Carris entered.

Zorinda sat on her bunk, Ronnie next to her on his knees gazing out the porthole.

"I see you found their books." She gave him a brilliant smile.

"I admit I have been remiss in my instructional duties. I'm afraid the children will need to tell you how far along they are. These books," he handed them to her, "are in French."

Zorinda examined each tome, and when she looked up, no condemnation shone in her eyes.

"You can safely remove teaching responsibilities from your list. Between the three of us, we'll determine where to start. Thank you for bringing them."

Carris turned, planning to leave though nonplussed by Zorinda's professional manner, inexplicably preferring the woman who'd laughed with such abandon on deck. Even so, he loathed vacating the crowded cabin. Looking back at her, he fumbled about in his mind for some excuse to remain. "Would you care for a brief look about my cabin?"

Her eyes widened, and her lips parted.

Carris quickly rephrased his question. "My steward, sometimes medic and purser, John Rollins, is there making sense of the mess I make on sailing day. Unintentionally, of course."

A laugh escaped Zorinda's lovely lips. "I can't imagine you making a mess. Yes, I'd like a tour. Raine, Ronnie please look at the mathematics book first. We'll begin with a review of even and odd numbers on the morrow."

Both heads bobbed as they took a seat on the bunk and shuffled through the books. Carris held out his hand. When Zorinda placed her hand in his, he tightened his hold, bringing forth her soft gasp. And a beautiful blush. Was this a good sign?

Zorinda discovered Carris's steward doing exactly what Carris had promised, though little seemed out of place. Perhaps the man had already made order of the captain's *mess*. After Carris introduced him, Zorinda considered the middle-aged man, his pate covered with sparse red strands, his demeanor serious, but approachable. John Rollins soon excused himself but assured them he would be on the other side of the paneled door Zorinda had noticed upon entering the cabin.

After Rollins exited, the door was left ajar revealing a narrow passage likely leading to officer's quarters and dining space. As Zorinda moved farther into Carris's comfortable—but far from lavish—cabin, she assessed the area as functional, yet inviting—upholstered seating, wooden armrests and sturdy legs highly polished, a carved sea chest bolted to the floor, and a hip bath tucked in a corner. The large bed was centered beneath the stern's window gallery, and an enormous desk dominated the remaining space, sides and top marred with the scars of time and use. Charts, nautical instruments, and books—tide tables, a nautical almanac, and an edition of Maury's *Wind and Current Charts and Sailing Directions*—resided on the surface in no particular order. Rolled charts rested by Carris's glass and barometer. Beside them his captain's log lay open. Nautical paintings hung on the walls, and the front of a painting rested against the legs of the desk. She was tempted to have a look but restrained the impulse.

"I can almost imagine my father sitting at his desk. When I was a child, he'd place me on his lap, and I would play with these." Zorinda ran her fingertips over the items displayed before her.

"Pretending to be a captain?" Carris smiled.

"Not pretending. I was the captain." She gave him a challenging grin.

His fascinating aqua eyes lightened as his brows lifted. "I would expect no less," he said, still smiling.

His smile accelerated her pulse, and she turned away, lowering her eyes.

He moved closer. But not in an alarming way. "May I invite you to dine with me this evening—with the other officers, of course?"

"Thank you, yes. What time shall I be ready?"

"Six bells—seven o'clock. I'll have one of the men escort you. I hope you and the children enjoyed your time on deck."

“We did. Forgive my exuberance.”

“Your enjoyment reminded me of my first time on a ship—I was about two years younger than the twins. What do you think?”

Zorinda moved to face him, her pulse skittering from the intensity of his eyes. Then she noticed his mouth. *Oh my—*

“My bailiwick?” he prompted.

“Functionally arranged. And comfortable,” she managed breathlessly.

There was no further reason to tarry, so Zorinda murmured a need to return to the twins, slipped away and took the companionway stairs leading below deck at a steady clip. She hadn’t been on the ship a full day, had nearly swooned when Carris took her hand, and lost her ability to breathe when she’d fixated on his mouth. Carris’s appeal had intensified. Staggeringly so.

Chapter 12

Carris wasn't honest with himself as he dressed for the evening meal. He'd always prided himself for looking at matters directly—no circumventing reality by painting a situation in an unrealistic light. Buttoning his embroidered waistcoat, he could only attribute his unnatural attention to his attire to the presence of Zorinda. He'd hoped to look sharper than Den Cavenley whose appearance was always reproachless. Rollins had offered to assist him, and now he wished he'd accepted the help.

Carris worked on his cravat, adjusting the length of navy silk about his neck. All the while, he marveled Zorinda hadn't chastised him for his failure to see to the twins' studies. She had every right to say something, but she'd excused his negligence. A knock on the door broke into his disturbing thoughts.

"Mr. Surrell has gone for Miss Wemblish."

Carris recognized his first mate's voice.

"Cook says the food is ready for serving."

Carris picked up his coat, strode to the door and upon admitting the man, was subjected to Cavenley's look of shock. The man obviously hadn't expected him to take such care dressing. The knot anchoring his cravat tightened.

"Close your mouth, Mr. Cavenley, less some pesky insect find its way inside."

Cavenley's brows lifted.

"Sorry, sir. Our unexpected passenger has inspired us all to look our best."

"Mr. Cavenley," Carris began, torn between raging at the man and laughing at his own foolishness, "I want Miss Wemblish to see we can dine as civilized men." Carris slipped on his coat, his eyes never leaving Cavenley's. "I hope such meets with your approval."

"Yes, sir." Cavenley barely suppressed a grin. The man had the good sense to turn and walk away.

Zorinda hoped she'd hadn't overdressed for a simple meal with Carris and his officers. She'd never dined with her father on his ship. Her mother had, of course, but what she wore on those occasions was lost to time. Taking advantage of the mirror fastened to the wall of the twins' cabin, she critically eyed her gown of copper silk. Ecru lace edged the silk bodice and her puffed, elbow length sleeves.

"You are magnifique," Raine whispered from her place on the lower bunk, Ronnie sprawled on the one above hers. Each child lay on their stomachs, already attired for sleep. Supper had been delivered to them earlier by a cabin boy who looked to be but a few years older than the twins. Resting their chins on the back of their hands, they watched her closely. "I wish I had a gown like yours."

"There's no reason you can't. We'll find some fabric in one of the ports we visit, and we'll work on a design."

"But I can't sew."

"I'm adequate with a needle, but perhaps we can find a seamstress in San Francisco who will make you a gown."

"Really?" Raine's eyes shone with anticipation.

"Why not? Now, both of you settle. I'll tuck you in."

"Will you come kiss us after the meal?" Ronnie asked.

"I will give you a good night kiss now because the two of you had better be asleep before the captain's supper is over."

"May we read our book?" Zorinda knew Raine referred to *A Voyage to Paradise*.

"Of course, but not tonight. Remember—lessons tomorrow."

The twins frowned until Ronnie's eyes lit up. "And painting?" he asked. "You promised to teach us."

"We'll work on a schedule, so we can fit in our studies, our art lessons, our Bible stories, and our special book. We'll be busy until we reach San Francisco."

Zorinda kissed the top of their heads with another warning to go to sleep. But ruined the warning by laughing when they poked out their lips in displeasure. As she opened their door, one of Carris's officers approached. He looked ill at ease in a neat jacket and trousers. Obviously, the man was more comfortable in his sea-faring garb.

"Evenin', Miss Wemblish. I'm Pete Surrell, the cap'n's second mate. My, but you're something to see. Mr. Cavenley asked me to bring you to the saloon—that's where we eat, not drink or anything."

Zorinda hadn't the heart to interrupt the man's serious explanation, although she knew about designated dining sections on a ship.

"The captain doesn't tolerate drinking at sea." The man's Adam's apple bobbed comically. "Are you ready?" His gravelly voice pitched like a rogue wave. Time to end this man's misery.

"A pleasure to meet you, Mr. Surrell. And I am most ready."

He awkwardly offered his arm, and Zorinda placed her gloved fingers on his sleeve, determined to ease the man's discomfort and help him survive this traumatic experience. She closed the cabin door behind her.

Carris was hard-pressed to keep his distance from Zorinda when she entered the saloon on Surrell's arm. With his hands clasped behind his back, he greeted her with a stiff bow while Cavenley and the other officers openly stared. The color of her gown brought out the golden tone of her skin, and her upswept curls framed her face beguilingly. Heart thumping loudly, he was certain all present heard.

"Welcome, Miss Wemblish. We're honored by your presence."

"Thank you, Captain. I'm honored by the invitation." There was a hint of mischief in her dark eyes as she glanced about. "Good evening, gentlemen."

Multiple introductions ensued. Carris saved Cavenley for last.

"A pleasure to meet you, Miss Wemblish." As expected, Cavenley was the consummate gentleman. He gave her a smile and a bow.

"Mr. Cavenley." Zorinda curtsied.

The man's rapturous expression forced Carris to look everywhere but at him for fear he would say something he'd regret. He struggled to regain his composure. "Denford Cavenley is my first mate. This will be our third voyage together."

"The first two times we sailed from Liverpool to Hong Kong," Cavenley elaborated. "This will be my first voyage to San Francisco. And my first sail around the Horn."

“How momentous,” Zorinda said. “Hopefully, the voyage will be a successful one.”

“Only if wind and wave cooperate.” Cavenley grinned.

Carris moved between them, determined to be the one to seat her at the long table. As he drew out her chair, her gardenia scent transported him to an enchanted garden. Once he had her safely positioned to his right, Zorinda proved far too charming and complimentary, most of her praise lavished on Cavenley seated across from her. Had she even noticed him? He was certain he looked as presentable as the first mate.

The initial course arrived—lobster stew. Amos Lester, the ship’s cook, prepared this for what he apparently considered an auspicious occasion. Lester could do more with ship’s rations than Carris had ever imagined possible in the years he had employed the man.

Cavenley offered grace.

Carris secretly peered at Zorinda during the prayer and afterward while she spooned the stew’s broth through enticing lips. Two cabin boys, wearing white jackets, their hair slicked back, faces shiny, and nails as clean as the bosun’s whistle, served the salad course. Carris almost didn’t recognize Bo and Tate.

The conversation danced through several topics, all involving Zorinda who shared stories of her father’s seafaring adventures and his descriptions of her mother’s native Pacific islands. Each of his officers hung on Zorinda’s every word and laughed at her every anecdote. By the time the main course of broiled chicken and seasoned stuffing appeared, his mood bordered on irascible. Why should he care Zorinda hadn’t addressed one comment directly to him? Or how she fascinated Cavenley and captivated the other men? She was a passenger, but first and foremost, governess to his wards. Their relationship was convenient and professional. So why did the flash of her eyes and her brilliant smile for his first mate and the others rankle?

When a sudden silence filled the space, Carris looked up from his plate and the pile of peas he'd been pushing around the china. Everyone looked at him. Hot coals of embarrassment moved up his neck, realizing he'd been asked something, and those present awaited an answer.

"Miss Wemblish asked you a question, sir." Cavenley ended the awkward moment. "She was wondering how long before we reach Brazil."

"You have the answer, Cavenley," Carris grumbled, dissecting the food before him.

"But I asked you." Zorinda's statement snapped his eyes to hers.

"My apologies. My mind has rudely wandered. About a month."

"Will we be there any length of time?" she asked.

"Two days to take on fresh water and supplies."

"I've heard so much about Rio de Janeiro. I can't wait to arrive."

"Don't expect to see much. Ship matters will be my concern and the crew's. There won't be leisure time to give you a tour." His cold tone earned him her frown. *Something is wrong with me.*

"I would never think of taking you from your duties, Captain, nor any of your men. I'm sure a local resident could be persuaded to show the children and me around."

"Far too dangerous. You'll remain on board."

"But, Captain," Cavenley said, "Sanders or Doherty could be spared. They're both familiar with Rio."

"Not familiar enough to take a woman and two children about a city filled with countless dangers. Have you forgotten Elbert's fate?" The men fell silent.

"Who is Elbert and what happened to him?" Zorinda Wemblish was too persistent for her own good.

"Jacob Elbert was our master carpenter." Carris lifted his water goblet and sipped before continuing. "He went out with a group of men but didn't return with them. He attempted to make his way back to the ship alone. He was robbed and killed."

Zorinda visibly started, her face paling. "How terrible. But the children and I wouldn't attempt anything dangerous. Raine and Ronnie will benefit from exploring the city and contribute to their geographical knowledge.

"Geographical knowledge won't keep the three of you safe." Carris resumed eating, convinced the matter was settled. As soon as he forked a manageable chunk of the succulent chicken into his mouth, Zorinda spoke.

"Your edict is unfair and senseless. The children have a unique opportunity to see places in the world other children will never have. Surely, you're not so culturally indifferent you can't see the merit in my suggestion."

"Miss Wemblish." Carris's fork clattered to his plate as the chicken slid uncomfortably down his throat, working its way past his too tight collar. "As you well know, I'm captain of this ship and the children's guardian. You are here in a professional capacity at my request. There are rules for a reason."

Zorinda's perfect brows drew together, and her captivating lips tightened. To his surprise and displeasure, she gracefully stood, carefully placing her napkin by her plate.

"I am also a passenger, and your manner is unpleasant. Your *rules* are in no way acceptable. If you will excuse me." Turning away, she headed toward the door.

Cavenley and the officers stood quickly while two of their number managed to reach the door, swinging it open for her departure. As soon as she'd left, all eyes turned on Carris.

"Let me assure you, gentlemen, I won't change my mind. Do not aid or abet Miss Wemblish in taking the children ashore. Understood?"

"Aye, sir," rang through the saloon. But when the men retook their seats, the earlier banter and jesting was but a memory. Zorinda had taken the enjoyment of the meal with her. And Carris could only blame himself.

As Zorinda entered the twins' cabin, she struggled with embarrassment. Why would Carris humiliate her so publicly? An hour or two spent in Rio—or any port—would open new worlds for Raine and Ronnie. She would make sure they stayed by her side. Were they to be prisoners for the entire voyage?

She knelt by a sleeping Raine, brushing back a red curl. In a few years, the child would blossom into a beautiful young woman. And Ronnie would be quite the handsome charmer. What about their father? Lance Trewellyn must have looked something like Carris, which would have made him popular with females. She supposed the younger brother had a more engaging personality and didn't hide emotions behind stoicism. What would Carris be like if he ever threw off his suffocating reserve?

Zorinda sighed as she rose on her tiptoes to check on the softly snoring Ronnie. He too was gripped in the throes of peaceful repose, his worries far away at the moment. Carris's behavior should have come as no surprise even though he'd inexplicably allowed her passage on his ship. Not really inexplicable, she admitted. His change of heart had everything to do with the two children in this cabin, now her responsibility.

But children needed adventure—granted, supervised adventure. Words in a book weren't the same as life experience. Rio de Janeiro was but one of several places they would visit. And to think of sailing around the tip of South America—Antarctica less than five hundred miles away. Amazing! Yet Carris wanted to keep her and the twins sequestered on the ship.

She would tell Carris his decision was unacceptable, and if he sent her back to Norfolk, she'd find another ship sailing to San Francisco. Even if she had to travel north to New York or Boston to find one. Carris Trewellyn would not have the final say.

Chapter 13

Even on the familiar planks of the gently rolling deck, Carris continued his self-chastisement for his behavior during the meal. He displayed an overbearing, intractable side of himself. There really wasn't a reason Zorinda and the children couldn't go ashore when in port. Thieves and miscreants abounded everywhere in the world, but seasoned sailors knew what to look for and what to expect. He could escort them himself and eliminate his worry.

What had been the real source of his bad humor? Zorinda's unmatched beauty, her winsome ways, the manner in which she delighted the men without artifice. She was nothing like Ivy, a woman obsessed with status, position, and wealth. And though she had endured ignorance and prejudice, Zorinda exuded poise and consideration for others. Her compassionate spirit had filled two lonely children with joy, a miracle given Carris's obvious failure with the twins.

As he looked up into the star-studded sky, words from the Bible tickled his memory. "If I take the wings of the morning, and dwell in the uttermost parts of the sea; even there shall thy hand lead me, and thy right hand shall hold me."

The words from Psalms settled in his battered soul. He'd ignored God's words and admonitions for years, struggling with betrayal by those he'd loved. How could he dismiss his father's disapproval or Ivy's unfaithfulness? Lance's desertion of his lover and their children had filled Carris with loathing. Each disappointment added to a seething, violent sea trapping him.

Lost in troubling thoughts, Carris mounted the stairs to the bridge, the wheel currently under the control of Helmsman MacCurdy. Carris leaned against the pedestal supporting the binnacle.

"She's holding steady, sir."

"I'll relieve you."

"My watch isn't over, Captain."

Carris shook his head. "No need to wait."

"Then I'll be going below for a few winks. Goodnight, sir." MacCurdy departed, leaving Carris alone to reexamine what he feared was his misspent life. The wind tugged at his hat and whipped across his face. The sensation was like the caress of a woman's fingers—Zorinda's?

I've got to stop thinking of her. I have to focus on my responsibilities. Get the ship to San Francisco, deliver the cargo, deliver the twins to their grandfather, avoid ...

The rustle of silk, the swish of petticoats, and the accompanying scent of gardenia enveloped him. Zorinda, a shawl about her shoulders, mounted the steps. So much for his plans.

"I've something to say to you."

He held his tongue, looking up at the billowing sails to avoid looking at her. "I'm not surprised." Carris uttered a rough laugh. "Condemnation of my overzealous affirmation to keep you and the children safe?"

Her silence answered his question.

"If we're in port for a day or two, you and the children may go ashore. I could possibly escort you." Carris dared to look at her. She was smiling.

"Most acceptable." Silence fell between them for several seconds until she tilted her head back exposing her graceful neck. Carris swallowed. Hard.

"The stars seem so different when viewed from sea."

"When I look at the night sky, I instinctively search for the North Star," Carris said.

Zorinda laughed softly as she lowered her head to look at him.

"With or without the North Star, I'm sure you know exactly where you are and where you're headed."

"Are you saying I'm methodically predictable?"

"Could a sea captain be otherwise?"

He heard teasing in her voice. "Perhaps not. But he can be misdirected a time or two."

"I doubt you deviate from a plan once you've set a course."

"Plans have a way of surprising us, Zorinda." Her name was sweeter than honey on his tongue.

Zorinda turned around and crossed her arms, leaning against the traverse board filled with the most recent readings. "One night, when I was about twelve, Papa took me with him to the wharf when he was summoned to the ship. While on deck, he had me look through his glass while he pointed out the North Star. He told me if ever a sailor was unsure where the North Star was he—or she—need only visually trace a line between Ursa Major's two outer stars."

"Dubhe and Merak. Your father taught you well." Carris hesitated a moment then continued. "I apologize for my earlier behavior." He had to fight the urge to tuck a loose curl behind her delicate ear.

"And I regret sharing my opinions when you hadn't asked for them. You are the children's temporary guardian."

Both slipped into silence. Carris wrestled with strange but insistent emotions. He'd never experienced such madness. With a strength taxing his limits, he turned away. His mind and efforts had to be directed to his ship and whatever the darkness hid. But the need to share a part of himself beat uncomfortably beneath his breast. He wanted her to know why he harbored such animosity for Lance.

"You had every right to say what you did about my brother the night of the soiree. I can't let go of the anger, and I'm ..." Carris fell silent unable to utter the word.

"Jealous?" Zorinda whispered.

Carris sighed. Her insight pierced his control, but he wouldn't salvage his pride by lying. "Yes."

"Your stepmother—does she live in England?"

Something hard and sharp crushed his chest. Another time when his father was needed and the man half way around the world. Esmé's screams filling the halls for hours. Followed by sickening silence ... another babe dead, and this time, Esmé, as well. But Lancelot Arthur Trewellyn played in the nursery, kept away from all unpleasantness, cossetted, pampered.

"She," Carris began, then hesitated, gathering his thoughts. "She suffered the loss of several infants in childbirth, Lance the only one to survive. Eventually, childbirth claimed her, as well."

"I'm—I'm so sorry. You cared for her?"

"She was kind to me, but more like a sister than a mother. She was but ten years my senior."

If Zorinda was shocked, she said nothing. After what seemed an unbearable silence, Zorinda joined him, though looked ahead. The rush of wind and wave broke the charged air. She tugged her shawl closer.

"Are you chilled?"

"I'm fine. Where are we now?"

"Nearing Hatteras Island, off the North Carolina coast.

"So, you don't snug down at night?"

"Depends on the situation." Carris paused. "I've heard sailing at night is the best time to test your nerve. You've only yourself to judge the carrying of canvas and how long the sails and spars will tolerate the stress."

"Is this a self-imposed test?"

Her words struck another chord of truth. Zorinda was right—another of his futile attempts to prove himself of more worth than Lance.

"More akin to a rite of passage. The waves along this stretch are rough and currents unpredictable. For centuries, wreckers used lanterns to lure ships onto the sandbars. I'd rather be at the wheel when so much uncertainty abounds. And barring no unforeseen hazards, we should arrive in Charleston the day after tomorrow." Carris intentionally redirected the conversation, unnerved by Zorinda's perception.

"How fast are we traveling?"

"Last reading, eighteen knots."

"When you delivered the children's books, you accidentally included a volume of navigational basics. I'll return the book immediately—"

"Keep the book for research. In case you want to captain a ship someday."

"There's a thought." Zorinda tapped the box atop the stand near the wheel. "I already know a few things. This is the binnacle which holds the compass. And the sextant determines the angle between the stars and the horizon. The chronometer determines longitude by observing the stars. Stars are very important."

He loved this playful side of her. *Loved?*

"How am I doing?"

"Exceptionally, Miss Wemblish. I'd say you're well on your way to captaining your own ship. Would I be correct in assuming you've knowledge of dead reckoning?"

She laughed, the sound sending heat through his veins. "I'm not seeking your job. But my father says no sailor is worth his—or her—salt if unable to master dead reckoning. What say you?"

Her fathomless eyes sparked something else within him—admiration. A ship relied on dead reckoning—a series of measurements and readings taken throughout the day at watch changes—to stay on course. In inclement weather, lacking celestial visibility, the compass's reliability depended on accurate assessments of the current, wind, and ship's speed to pinpoint the vessel's position. He had no doubt Zorinda was fully capable of determining direction, using the lead line to measure fathoms, and reeling out the chip log to calculate knots. This woman defied every preconceived notion he'd embraced regarding the fairer sex. Ivy would have fainted if asked to hold a compass, much less make sense of one. Carris cleared his throat.

"I'd say you're well-versed, and I'll not hesitate to make use of your skills should the need arise." He hoped conditions wouldn't deteriorate to where he'd need to ask Zorinda to assume any duty.

Zorinda nodded, her eyes taking on a faraway look as though reliving old memories. "As a child, I'd cry whenever Papa left on a voyage. Sarah would tell me I was better off at home with my mother where things were safe. But I still wanted to sail with him." Zorinda looked up at Carris and offered a sad smile. "Though Papa generously shared his knowledge, I always wondered how I'd feel if allowed to use what he taught me."

"Don't despair." Carris tightened his hold on the mahogany wheel. "This voyage should give you a real taste of life at sea and, hopefully, will be everything you've dreamed of."

"All I dream of is finding my father alive."

The poignancy of her words pained him. Taking a hand from the wheel, he captured her chin, her warmth and beauty igniting a thousand fires inside him. Longing and anguish mounted so powerfully, breathing was difficult. He'd told himself repeatedly marriage and—yes, love—were not for him. He detested uncertainty and the accompanying loss of control.

As soon as the thought took root, Carris saw the question in Zorinda's eyes. He couldn't mistake her vulnerability—much like his own. He released her.

"I'm sorry." His voice grated on his ears, raspy and unnatural. He should never have yielded to his impulse to touch her. Even so, he wanted nothing more than to take her in his arms and feel her heart against his.

"The hour is late. I should return to my cabin." She moved a few steps away, her back to him then stopped. "You should know you've no reason to be jealous."

Her words cracked the ice encasing his heart. Then she was gone, like a wraith, dissolving into the light mist now surrounding the ship. The *Paradise* was entering the dangerous Carolina capes, and Carris, recalling the red of the morning's sun, could sense an approaching storm in the very marrow of his bones. One certain to test his nerve. As well as the sails and spars.

Though Zorinda had donned her nightdress and slipped beneath the coverings of her berth, there was no sleep. She couldn't forget the way Carris had clasped her chin as though leaning in for a kiss. Then he'd changed his mind leaving her teetering on the edge of a terrifying chasm.

Zorinda didn't know why she'd shared old memories with him. She wasn't seeking sympathy. Carris had as much said the chances of finding her father were nonexistent. Still, she wanted to prove him wrong.

She'd left a lamp burning, illuminating the interior of her small, but comfortable cabin. Her space was larger than the twins' and exhibited the fine craftsmanship standard for the ship's public and private rooms. Two portholes—one above her bunk and the other over a small desk—allowed light to filter in even on dismal days. Furnishings were custom made to accommodate the cabin's size, and the linens had a feel of luxury. As in Carris's stateroom, a hip bath nestled in a corner, currently surrounded by her trunks and other baggage. What an unexpected luxury and one she and the twins, whether or not to their liking, were going to use to full advantage.

A sudden lurch in the ship's motion brought her upright, and a sudden dive forced her from bed. She staggered to the porthole above the desk and attempted to peer out, but the wind and rain pounded with such intensity she couldn't see anything. Thunder rumbled, rising above the roar, and lightning penetrated the murky vortex. A storm had materialized in the short time since her presence on deck. Would this prove to be one of Carris's personal tests?

Knowing the children would be frightened, Zorinda left her cabin and traveled the short distance to theirs. When she entered, she found Raine and Ronnie huddled together on the lower bunk, softly whimpering. Rushing over, she threw her arms around them and gathered them close.

"We're afraid," Raine said in French, the language she spoke most naturally. "Will the ship sink?"

"No, dear ones." Zorinda pressed a kiss to each curly head. "Your uncle knows what he's doing, as do the other men. We must pray for them. Raine, you begin." A pitch and roll silenced her as the three of them fell against a chest. Shards of lightning momentarily brightened the cabin as Raine shrieked and Ronnie wailed. Zorinda wanted to join them, but she had to remain calm. Even when she was falling apart inside. *Lord, help me be strong for the children. Please be with Carris and his men.*

A frantic hammering commenced on the outer door, sending her heart into her throat.

"Zorinda! Zorinda! Are you there?"

Grasping the edge of the chest, Zorinda pulled herself up, tottering precariously as she made her way to the door. As she reached for the latch, the door swung in so forcefully, she stumbled back. She dropped onto the lower bunk as Carris, water cascading the length of him, towered over her.

At the moment, he could have been Poseidon summoned from his ocean kingdom glaring as he was. "I heard a scream. Are you hurt?"

"No ... the children and I fell against their trunk. We're somewhat shaken." An understatement if ever there was one.

"You weren't in your cabin." His tone was accusatory—angry.

Why was beyond her reasoning. And why was he looking at her so oddly? She needed to explain. "I came to the children as quickly as possible."

The ire drained from Carris, and his voice softened.

"Stay here. No wandering." Turning abruptly, he left, slamming the door behind him. If Carris thought his irate display conveyed concern, she could do without his overtures. He was fiercer than the storm. What was wrong with the man?

Looking down at herself she gasped aloud. Stars above, Carris had seen her in her nightdress. Unexpectedly, a cry escaped her lips. Raine and Ronnie pressed their quaking bodies close to hers while she wrapped her arms around them. *Oh, Lord, calm the sea and the winds. And remove the painful shadows within Carris.*

The storm aged Carris twenty years. Not because the event was overly serious given the time of year and the weather patterns along the Carolina coast. But for several interminable minutes, Carris had feared Zorinda had gone on deck for a closer look at nature's fury. When there'd been no answer to his knocks on her door, he'd assumed the worst. He should have known she'd be with the children. Once he'd discovered her, he'd felt like an idiot. And having seen her in her soft, shape-defining nightdress, her hair draped about her shoulders, he knew the sight would haunt him. Which would never do.

With the forenoon watch, Carris was relieved of his duties at the helm and made his way to his stateroom. Stripping off his sodden clothing, he donned dry trousers and a shirt. Not bothering with the buttons, he sprawled across his bunk and immediately fell asleep. Yet, his dreams were filled with a vision in white leaning over the rail of the *Paradise.*

After breakfast, Zorinda and the children ventured on deck to see what damage had been done to the ship. Mr. Cavenley explained the night's storm had been little more than a squall and there would certainly be worse before reaching San Francisco. Zorinda allowed the children to watch—at a safe distance—several sailors accessing the masts and rigging. Several crewmen explained what was damaged, how badly damaged, and the repairs required. The sailor Zorinda knew to be Jep Sanders, and one of the two who'd brought her and the children to the ship, allowed Raine and Ronnie to hit some nails into a wooden plank, replacing a splintered one.

She was about to take the children below to begin their studies when Carris emerged. Dressed simply in trousers, boots, and a loose-sleeved shirt gaping at the neck, he looked rather like a pirate captain. His recalcitrant lock of hair partially obscured one eye. Dark whorls spanned an exposed expanse of his upper chest, and there was no ignoring his muscled arms and shoulders.

Noticing her and the children, Carris joined them, a wry smile shaping his lips. "I must apologize for my irrational conduct during the storm. I should have known you were with the children."

"Two apologies within a few hours? This must be a record for you."

"Unusual, I admit."

Is a tiny grin softening his lips?

"I'm afraid I frightened you more than the storm."

"Both frights were mercifully brief. I'll be better prepared next time."

"No one is ever really prepared for a storm—too many variables. We do what we can and hope for the best."

"Praying could be useful."

Carris's eyes reflected skepticism. "I shall allow you to intercede on my behalf. I suspect God would respond to your petitions far more favorably than mine."

"I suggest you offer your own prayer."

Carris's brows lifted.

"Come, Raine, Ronnie. Lessons won't wait." Not daring to look back, she directed the children toward the steps leading to their cabins, sensing Carris's eyes following her until she moved out of his sight.

Chapter 14

The twins' progress during their first official class was better than Zorinda anticipated. After two hours of writing basic words in English and reviewing simple equations, she was satisfied the nuns had done an excellent job. When she showed them Carris's navigation book, they were eager to learn about the different instruments and their uses. Now, sitting alone in her cabin, she mentally considered activities for the children, wondering if Carris would allow the twins a look through his glass. Maybe he'd even explain the rigging and sails and the yards.

Someone knocked on the door. "Zorinda?"

She was becoming more comfortable with his use of her name. Even so, her heartbeat escalated as she left the small desk and crossed to the door. Carris, still dressed as he'd been earlier, smiled.

"Captain?"

"I thought we'd decided no formality." His eyes strayed to her lips.

"A wise decision?"

He chuckled.

"I'm not sure wise could apply to recent decisions. But here we are. I say we make the best of things."

His comment nettled. "Are you inferring this is a bad situation?"

"You misunderstand."

"Do you regret my presence?"

"Not in the least." His tone brooked no argument.

Her temper heightened.

"We may be addressing one another familiarly, but there will be no easing of other formalities." She wanted him to understand a repeat of last night could not happen again when she was improperly attired.

He obviously caught her meaning, for he scowled. "Such would be unthinkable." Carris's sarcastic words brought heat to her cheeks. "In the future, don something more concealing should you venture from your cabin at night."

"Did you want something?" Tension flared within her, and there were darts of flame in Carris's eyes. This man pushed her to fits of pique, totally anathema to her manner.

"I wanted to see how lessons went today. But knowing you, and your adherence to formalities, things went swimmingly. Good day." He walked away, rigid and angry.

Upon shutting the door, Zorinda dropped her head in her hands, wishing she'd held her tongue. *Soft words turneth away wrath.*

Carris avoided Zorinda and the children for the next day and a half. There was no missing her on deck with Raine and Ronnie as she encouraged members of his crew to share their shipboard responsibilities and explain the rigging and sails while she consulted the navigational book he'd told her to keep. Disappointment filled him, for he'd hoped to have the pleasure. Now his men—lucky blokes—entertained the children and Zorinda.

The layover in Charleston was to be brief, but there would be time for Zorinda and the children to go ashore. Summoning Cavenley to his cabin, Carris asked him to have Sanders prepared to escort them after they arrived. In truth, he'd hoped to take them about the city. But Zorinda had clearly expressed her preference for an impersonal acquaintance. Surely the wisest option. Then why his disappointment?

Yet, several hours after the *Paradise* arrived in Charleston harbor and the ship now anchored, Carris, from his position at the bow, watched Seaman Sanders row Zorinda and the twins to the pier. Carris already missed them—their laughter and chatter, their excitement over things he considered mundane. Looking at his crew efficiently carrying out their duties, he realized there was nothing crucial demanding his immediate attention. His log was updated, and he'd reviewed last evening's recordings on the traverse board. Though the last person Zorinda would want to see, he reasoned the children might enjoy learning about the area's fortifications and their history. He was knowledgeable enough on some subjects to contribute to their education.

Carris returned to his cabin, made some adjustments to his appearance, and tucked his cap under his arm. He assured himself he was only venturing into the city for the sake of the twins.

Charleston's quaint charm fascinated Zorinda, reflected in its uniquely romantic architecture. The front facing, narrow porticos of most residences disguised the length of the homes and the beckoning galleries hidden by the street-side entryways. Mr. Sanders, their appointed guide, led them to a row of shops clustered together surrounded by palmettos, primrose, and trumpet vines. After the seaman suggested another activity for Ronnie, leading him off in the opposite direction, Zorinda led Raine to several shops, hoping the child would find the fabric she sought. Though they combed the area, nothing appealed to the girl who insisted her new gown had to be the same color as the one Zorinda had worn the day they'd first met in Norfolk. Zorinda didn't have the heart to tell the child her father had purchased the silk for the gown in Morocco. Hopefully, there'd be other places to search.

When Zorinda and Raine returned to where they were to meet Sanders and Ronnie, Carris was there showing Ronnie his compass. The boy, clearly engrossed with the object, listened intently while Carris explained its importance. They looked up hearing their approach, and Carris smiled, making the sun seem brighter. Zorinda hoped her pleasure wasn't obvious. She would not suffer another man's edicts, even though her traitorous heart now beat faster.

"Where is Mr. Sanders?" Zorinda hoped her cool tone would slow her racing pulse.

"I hope nearing the ship."

"He returned to the ship?" Zorinda frowned. "Why?"

"I relieved him of his duties. I hoped you and the children would join me for a picnic." He held up a hamper.

"I thought you were otherwise occupied."

Carris grinned. Not helping her heart rate.

"Do you prefer I lea—"

"Oh no," Raine interrupted. "We'd love a picnic. Wouldn't we, Ronnie?"

Her twin nodded enthusiastically.

Zorinda wanted to refuse, but the children were so eager she hadn't the heart to deny them. "We accept, Captain." Zorinda assured herself she'd only agreed because of the children. But after entering the park bordered by the Ashley and Cooper Rivers, she inwardly confessed a picnic was an excellent idea. Carris drew her eyes far too frequently, and his unexpected conversational efforts ruined her plans to remain aloof.

Towering live oaks dripping Spanish moss canopied the spot they selected for their picnic. Carris asked Raine and Ronnie to spread a large cloth while Zorinda helped him unpack the overflowing basket. Everyone helped themselves, selecting from the cook's ample provisions, and the children's laughter eased Zorinda's earlier apprehension.

Having eaten their fill, the twins chose to explore, particularly fascinated by several cannons overlooking the Cooper River and in direct line with the fort Carris said was Sumter.

Zorinda was repacking when Carris caught her busy hands, removing the plates she held to place them in the hamper. She didn't want to look at him. She didn't want to misinterpret this moment or wish for something more.

"Zorinda, we've a long journey ahead. I don't want us to be at cross-purposes. You're a marvel with Raine and Ronnie. Something I'm not."

"You must be patient."

Carris sighed. "Patience doesn't come easily for me." He smiled ruefully, looking down at her hands. He slowly rubbed his thumb over the back of one. "I apologize for making you uncomfortable when I sought you the night of the storm. Never think I would take advantage of our arrangement."

Zorinda's cheeks flamed, and she prayed the tightening in her throat didn't choke her. After freeing her hands, she clasped them tightly. "I only wished to clarify my position on our, uh, affiliation."

"I see." Carris nodded stiffly before turning, his long strides taking him toward the children who had climbed one of the cannons. Zorinda shook her head in frustration while resuming her task. Sarah had a saying that one was "jumping from the frying pan into the fire." She feared this voyage might drop her into both. At the same time.

Though two days had passed since the picnic on the Charleston Battery, the twins had done little but talk about the fun they'd had. Zorinda could see the change in their relationship with Carris. They'd been discussing the forts Carris had identified as part of the day's history lesson while sitting on deck.

"Oncle Carris knew all about the battles fought between England and the colonies and how France helped win their freedom." Ronnie was clearly still excited.

Not to be outdone, Raine piped up. "And how the people here didn't like the king. Or taxes."

"As you grow older, you'll discover no one likes taxes," Zorinda said.

Looking up from the sketch pad she'd brought on deck for drawing and giving the children a brief lesson, her eyes sought Carris. She'd already begun an outline of Carris's figure as he stood at the helm with Mr. Surrell.

Suddenly, he looked up. And stared.

Flustered, she lowered her head, angered by her shaking right hand marring the lines she'd diligently perfected over the past half of an hour.

"May we see?"

Raine's question forced her to lay aside her pencil. "Of course." She held out the tablet, and the twins crowded close.

"You've drawn Oncle and Monsieur Pete," Ronnie said.

"They look real." Raine lightly traced her uncle's face.

"Amazingly so."

Zorinda's head snapped up at the sound of Carris's voice. "You didn't mention you're a gifted artist."

"Thank you, and if I am gifted, the gift is bestowed by God."

"May I?" Carris held out his hand.

Flushed with embarrassment, Zorinda handed him the tablet.

Carris was silent as he examined the partially completed sketch. "You so perfectly define our expressions and body language. I can almost hear myself conversing with Mr. Surrell. You've even captured his twinkling eyes. This is marvelous."

"You are most kind." Zorinda's secret now belonged to someone she wasn't sure she trusted. Wariness had kept her silent when Carris had asked her about the painting of the *Scheherazade*. Logically there wasn't any way he would connect her with the paintings Mr. Arnell sold in his gallery.

Carris returned the sketchbook. "Would you consider drawing the twins? I'd very much like to have a portrait of them before ..." Carris halted when he noticed Raine and Ronnie looking up at him with sorrowful eyes. The children weren't eager to meet their grandfather.

Zorinda quickly nodded.

"I would love to. Though what a challenge to keep these two still long enough to do so." She chucked each child beneath their chin bringing forth giggles. "Raine, Ronnie, why don't the two of you pick something on the ship to draw. This will be your first art lesson."

Nodding eagerly, they each took a smaller pad she handed them, along with a charcoal stick then scampered away to find their subject. Carris remained, crossing his arms as he looked up, his eyes fixing on the clouds scudding high overhead. Zorinda realized the wind had strengthened. "Where are we now?"

"Not far from the Florida Keys. We should be in Havana tomorrow. Unless ..." His words ceased as his eyes shifted to the sails.

"Unless there's another storm," she finished for him.

Carris looked at her. "Mr. Surrell reported the pressure is dropping. There'll probably be a pesky skirmish a little after sunset. Not as sudden as the one we encountered the other night."

"I'll prepare the children." Zorinda folded her pad, hoping the twins hadn't made their way to an upper deck.

"Remember what I told you about storms?"

Zorinda looked up at Carris. "We can only do so much and hope for the best."

His lips quirked in a wry smile.

Why did she think of kisses? Zorinda pressed a hand to her heating cheek.

"So you were listening."

"I've listened to everything you've said—the good and the bad. But when a storm is involved, I still prefer prayer."

Carris's eyes darkened to a stormy shade of teal. She'd obviously struck a nerve.

"If you'll excuse me." He nodded and walked away.

Oddly bereft at his abrupt departure, Zorinda felt as though he'd taken away the brilliance of the day. Looking up through the billowing sails, she realized the thickening clouds had shuttered the sun.

The storm hit swiftly and moved on, leaving only a small amount of disarray in its wake. Carris moved among his men, inspecting the areas of concern with Mr. Tenney, making a few suggestions while praising the diligence of his crew. Childish voices and one very soft feminine one reached his ears, and he excused himself to seek the sources.

As expected, Zorinda, Raine, and Ronnie were on deck raptly attentive as Cavenley pointed at the masts explaining something to his enthralled listeners. Carris noticed how eager Ronnie was to learn, and if he'd but taken the time to recognize as much, he and the boy would have gotten off to a better start.

The same with Raine. She was quick and intelligent and though very much a little girl who loved ribbons and lace, was interested in everything around her. And Zorinda effortlessly tapped their potential with encouragement. Seeing Cavenley and the three of them together, Carris experienced an emotion so crippling his breath hitched. For the first time in his life, he feared he would succumb to raw, ugly jealousy over a woman. Reason told him to turn away. Emotion propelled him toward the group.

He made no effort to disguise his approach, and he was secretly gratified when Zorinda and Cavenley put distance between them, like guilty children caught with their hands in the biscuit tin.

"We're in the midst of making repairs." Carris inwardly cringed at his harsh tone.

Cavenley stepped back.

"We have no intention of interrupting anyone's work." Zorinda lifted her chin in silent challenge.

Rather than meet her challenge, Carris glanced up at the sailors navigating the rat lines, as did Cavenley. When one of them called for a fid to repair the damaged sail, the first mate immediately responded to the request and slipped away. Carris turned his attention to Zorinda, inwardly chastising her for destroying his well-ordered world.

"The three of you seem to have come through unscathed." Carris managed a civil timbre.

"We did." Zorinda's voice held a touch of asperity. "Did you require something?"

"I only wished to give you a caution. This deck isn't the safest place for you and the children at present."

Without awaiting an answer, Carris turned sharply then strode off in the opposite direction. How unreasonable of him to be annoyed with Den Cavenley. Repair assignments had been made, and the men were hard at work. Cavenley's few minutes spent with Zorinda and the children hadn't interfered with or interrupted anything. Carris owed the man an apology. Cavenley was a natural gentleman, the sort of man who made a woman feel appreciated and valued. But Carris could too. If he could show Zorinda—

"Captain?"

Carris halted at the sound of Zorinda's voice. Looking around, he watched her approach, aggravatingly stirred by her graceful walk across a moving deck. And achingly reminded of her appearance the night of the first storm.

"Your behavior is unacceptable," Zorinda said.

"My officers and crew must stay on task." There was the bite back in his voice.

"Mr. Cavenley wasn't neglecting his duties. I could see you were displeased to see us speaking. Why?"

Carris watched Zorinda gather her shawl closer, drawing his eyes momentarily to the slim column of her throat and the modest exposure of a creamy gold shoulder. He quickly looked away, hating the painful beat of his heart. He hated knowing his control was tenuous at best. Curling his hands into fists, harsh breaths labored beneath his breast. "Perhaps I want to make sure you don't lose your heart to the wrong man."

"What? The wrong man? Mr. Cavenley?" Zorinda's eyes narrowed, her glacial question freezing his veins. "Utterly ridiculous. Mr. Cavenley is first and foremost a gentleman."

"Which I'm not." Carris growled the words as he met her furious glare. Her anger sparked something deep inside him, something no other woman ever had. He was torn between shaking her and crushing her in his arms.

"Obviously you know the answer." Zorinda stood before him, hands now on her hips as she glared.

Why should he care if she considered him less than a gentleman? Yet, he did. *God, help me.*

"Cap'n, might I have a word with you?" Surrell strode toward him.

Carris turned to the man allowing Zorinda to use the interruption to leave, her stride purposeful and her posture stiff. Even if she'd remained, he couldn't tell her the sight of her laughing with another man ripped him apart. Though he well knew a determined woman was not for him.

Chapter 15

After the unsettling encounter with Carris, Zorinda herded the children back to their cabin to begin lessons. Fury with Carris built to a fever pitch, and she had difficulty concentrating. Somehow, she completed the day's selected subjects with extra time for them to return to the drawings they'd begun the day before. While the twins worked diligently on their tablets—Raine finished a lopsided basket, and Ronnie attempted to complete his sketch of the *Paradise's* wheel complete with a very thin captain—Zorinda began a rough drawing of the twins. Why she would even consider fulfilling Carris's request was beyond her. He was insulting, overbearing, officious, controlling, and sadly, inordinately handsome.

She gave up her efforts, putting her sketchbook aside, and offered to help the twins. After showing Ronnie how to flesh out his captain, she made suggestions to Raine on how to convey depth and straighten the basket's tilt. Instructing them eased her anger, and the afternoon passed pleasantly.

Zorinda dined with Raine and Ronnie, and after they settled for the night, she ventured up to the main deck, much quieter now than earlier. One minute, the ship could be caught in a tempest of wind, waves, and rain, and within a few hours, one would never suspect there'd been a storm.

Coming upon Mr. Surrell, she paused to listen as he played his horn pipe.

He stopped when he saw her.

"Please continue," she said.

"I'd rather talk. Not often a pretty miss comes my way."

Zorinda laughed. She'd quickly learned Carris's second officer was full of what the Irish called blarney. She'd overheard some of the amazing tales he'd shared with the twins, thankful they'd found the stories more amusing than terrifying.

"One would hardly suspect we had a storm last night."

Surrell lowered his pipe. "We've patched up the topgallants. We'll do more once we reach Rio. Last night's storm wasn't much, and the cap'n brought us through like he always does." Mr. Surrell, oblivious of her inner turmoil, looked toward the rising moon. "He has a rule to never lose a man. Unless a soul is foolish enough to place himself in danger."

"Please continue with your playing, Mr. Surrell." She smiled. "I've always loved the sea shanties."

Mr. Surrell grinned then complied. Zorinda leaned against the rail, the soft, warm breeze loosening her hair of its bonds as she wondered what an affectionate Carris Trewellyn would be like. Something she would never know.

Carris sat at his desk, his concentration nonexistent. Each time he picked up his pen to record in his log, all thought evaporated. At least he'd managed to apologize to Cavenley for his unnecessary rudeness earlier, providing him some measure of peace. But not enough on this evening as the *Paradise* narrowed the distance to Havana.

He dropped his fountain pen in frustration, left his chair and paced, running his hands through his hair. Thoughts of Zorinda raced through his mind—sitting on deck with the children as they sketched, enchanting Cavenley and Mr. Surrell. Laughing with the children over a silly yarn spun by one of the crew. Making excuses for the father the twins barely knew. Reminding him with a look that God should be his compass, and he should forgive his brother.

Lance is incapable of being a father. Carris snorted at his unspoken assessment. Then stubbed his booted toe.

"Blasted ..."

Biting an oath in half, Carris looked down, discovering he'd made contact with a corner of the painting he'd purchased in Norfolk. Preoccupied with storms and damaged masts—and Zorinda—he'd neglected to display the breathtaking scene.

Crouching, he turned the painting around, enticed by the passion and emotion evoked by the sure strokes and realistic colors. Noting the open space between the headboard of his bunk and the window gallery, he grasped both sides of the painting, hoisting while gaining his feet. There was a knock on the door, and he lowered the painting face first on the coverlet. Rollins had been dismissed for the evening. Perhaps Cavenley? "Come in."

"Captain ... Carris, it's me."

Knowing Zorinda was on the other side of the door accelerated his heartbeat. Shutting his eyes, he prayed for patience and the ability to say the right thing. For a change. The door opened and she stood there, clad in sprigged muslin and lace. Without the shawl, he had an unobstructed view of her shoulders.

"I know the hour is late. But I was wondering if Mr. Cavenley—"

Cavenley. Always Cavenley.

"Or Mr. Surrell might take Raine and Ronnie to see the Morro Castle tomorrow. We've been studying American colonization, specifically the time of Columbus and the Spanish explorers. They are very excited about seeing a Spanish fort. Ronnie is keeping a journal listing the forts he and Raine see on the voyage."

"I'm not sure." *Carris, you idiot.*

A frown marred Zorinda's lovely brow.

"Really? Then you will take them?"

"I will," he snapped before thinking. "The three of you will be ready at four bells—that's—"

"Ten o'clock in the morning. I've mastered the bells and watches." There was no mistaking her sarcasm. He nearly chuckled until she added. "But I'm not going. As you've volunteered, this outing will give you time with the children and opportunity to improve your guardianship skills."

Now Carris frowned.

"I will engage in other pursuits."

"You've not asked permission."

One perfectly arched brow lifted.

"All governesses are given a day off at least once a week. I'm taking mine tomorrow."

"Because you don't want to spend time in my company?" Could this woman be any more infuriating?

"There are some matters I've neglected. If you watch Raine and Ronnie tomorrow, I'll have time to complete them."

"What matters could you have neglected?"

"Not your concern."

Carris felt his facial muscles tighten. "You are not to go off on your own." His eyes locked on hers, but she appeared unperturbed, tilting her adorably stubborn chin. "If you're upset—"

"I've no reason to be upset." She smiled with her lips but not her eyes. "I'll take my leave now and allow you to get some much-needed sleep."

"After this conversation, do you think I'll sleep?"

"If you're seeking sympathy, don't look to me." With her words ringing in his ears, Zorinda left.

Carris slammed the door.

The following morning Zorinda watched the twins and Carris depart, secretly wishing she were going. Carris had informed her he would take Raine and Ronnie to the Morro Castle first, reviving memories of her father's description of the fortress protecting Havana Bay. She'd never considered she'd be excluded from the outing, certain Mr. Cavenley, Mr. Surrell, or another crew member would be their escort. She could only blame herself for provoking Carris into taking the twins alone. At least now, she had time to paint.

Motivated by her objective, she asked Mr. Surrell if he could spare one of the sailors to assist her with her easel, painting supplies, and canvas. After leaving the ship with Jep Sanders, Zorinda found the perfect place for setting up not far from the *Paradise* on a section of pier with a marvelous view of the Morro Castle. Within a few minutes and with Sanders's help, she settled on a stool, her easel before her. How wonderful to hold her brushes as she planned the portrait of the twins. Their black and white faces stared back at her. Now was the time to bring them to life. The day was perfect for painting. The fresh air and light breeze minimized the scent of her paints, gesso, linseed oil, and turpentine.

As the sun moved higher, Zorinda tied on her wide brimmed straw hat, providing some shade on what was turning out to be a sweltering day. Sanders returned with a small basket, explaining Cook had made her lunch. Leaving her pier-side studio, Zorinda found a shady tree where she sat and ate, watching the activity around her. When finished, she returned to her painting, losing track of time. With the faces of the twins now fleshed out, she removed and covered the portrait, placing a prepared blank cotton canvas on the easel. Looking toward the fortress guarding the harbor, she roughed in the fort, capturing the effect of the afternoon sun on the stone walls. A ship rested at anchor beyond the Morro Castle, its sails alight from the sun's golden rays.

Zorinda worked steadily until the westering sun threw portions of the fort into shadow. Deciding to pack up and return to the ship, she paused when she heard childish squeals. Turning, she saw Raine and Ronnie racing toward her, each carrying a sack. Carris followed behind, covering the distance with his long, powerful strides. As the children neared, their squabbling reached her ears.

"I'm showing her mine first," Ronnie declared.

"No, I am," Raine insisted.

"You're not."

"Wait and see. I can run faster than you."

Zorinda had no idea what each child wanted her to see, but so engrossed were they in their rivalry, they increased their speed, unaware of their proximity to her. They commenced tugging, both trying to slow one another.

"Valeraine! Valeron!" Carris's bellow carried clearly to her ears. "Stop. You're going to topple—"

No sooner had he uttered the words than the twins stumbled and pitched toward Zorinda. Knocked from her stool, she fell against her easel, and the canvas plunged into the water, followed by the easel, her tin paint tubes, her palette, and several brushes.

Zorinda shrieked.

Covering her face with her hands, Zorinda's heart shattered. Her parents had given her the easel, and she'd purchased the paint set only six months ago. Tears streamed down her face as she lowered her hands, looking up at Raine and Ronnie, both children crying.

"We're so sorry. We wanted to show you our seashells." Ronnie paused to wipe his face with his sleeve. "We are so very sorry."

"Mademoiselle, this is très terrible." Raine said with a sob. "We never meant to do this."

Carris arrived, having run the remaining distance. After assessing the disaster on the pier and the items floating away on the water's surface, Carris dropped his hat, removed his coat and boots, and dove into the water. Her paint box and brushes had already disappeared as had the easel. And the canvas, though floating, might be unsalvageable.

"Carris!" Zorinda screamed. The twins clutched her, their sobs louder. "Carris!"

Amazingly, he resurfaced with the easel. He kicked forward while shaking the water from his eyes and reached out to grasp the canvas and bobbing palette. After turning on his back, he floated to the pier as he propelled himself with his free arm.

Still on her knees from her tumble, Zorinda held out her hands and retrieved the items he held, laying them aside. She reached out to Carris, grasped his extended hands then pulled him closer to the wooden planks. By the time he clutched the edge, four crew members of the *Paradise* had arrived to haul him out.

Once on the pier, he loomed over the quaking twins while he caught his breath, water pooling around his feet.

Although Zorinda was distraught over her loss and the children's disobedience, she prayed Carris wouldn't publicly berate them.

"Do you realize what you've done?" Carris's voice roughened with anger.

Zorinda cringed, wanting so badly to gather the children close but unwilling to jeopardize Carris's authority.

Raine and Ronnie nodded, remorse etched in their teary green eyes.

"How do you plan to replace Miss Wemblish's paints?"

Zorinda held her breath while brother and sister looked at each other.

"We could buy her some," Raine offered. "But we haven't any money."

"What if we help on the ship?" Ronnie asked. "And earn money?"

"Oui," Raine agreed eagerly.

Zorinda released her breath when she saw a glimmer of approval in Carris's eyes.

"An excellent plan. In the future, you'll listen to me when I tell you to do something. Another incident may resort in more serious punishment."

The children's eyes widened, and Zorinda feared they imagined a flogging. When she chanced a look at Carris, there was no missing the tic in his jaw. Could he be angry with her, as well?

Still dripping, his shirt clinging to his firm, muscled torso, Carris moved past her and hoisted the rescued painting while Sanders took up her easel.

Forcing herself to move, she collected what remained of her supplies, dropping them in the basket in which Cook had packed her lunch. She took up the covered painting of the twins, thankful their portrait hadn't taken a dip in the water. Zorinda hoped she'd be able to finish the one Carris had saved.

A somber group returned to the *Paradise*. Carris retired immediately to his cabin, undoubtedly to bathe and change.

Zorinda took the twins to theirs. As soon as the door closed, Raine and Ronnie launched themselves at her, both still sniffling. Zorinda wrapped her arms around them.

"We wanted to show you our shells." Ronnie tearfully spoke in French.

Zorinda didn't have the heart to tell him to use English.

"I wanted to prove I could run faster than Ronnie," Raine said. "Then my toe stubbed on a board, and I lost my balance."

"And caused me to trip," Ronnie added.

"Raine, Ronnie, I still have my charcoal. I can sketch. The paints can be replaced."

"We're going to be like Monsieur Fergus. One day in the garden, he told us when he does chores, he earns money. Maybe Mr. Cavenley will let me help him?" Ronnie's face brightened at the thought.

"And maybe I could help Cook," Raine suggested.

"I know someone on this ship needs the help of two smart and hardworking children. Enough of the tears. Tell me about your outing before the, ah, incident."

Tears evaporated as the children told her about the fort filled with soldiers, the meal of tapas they shared at a small outdoor eatery, and how Carris laughed and joked with them. All was très merveilleux until the pier disaster.

Zorinda assured them all would be well, then seated herself on the floor. Locating their geography book, she found the lesson on Cuba. Raine and Ronnie joined her. The twins' despondency lessened as they read the description of the island and Havana, comparing the book's details to their sightings. Time passed quickly, the three unaware of the hour until a knock sounded on the door and one of the cabin boys, Bo, announced he'd brought their meal. Zorinda left them to eat and went in search of Carris.

Hoping no one noticed her taking the companionway up to Carris's quarters, she'd nearly reached his door when the man she sought emerged. Dressed in his usual captain's garb and likely on his way to dine with his men, he snapped to attention, his eyes reflecting surprise.

Suddenly nervous, Zorinda fidgeted with her hands. There was no mistaking the scents of sandalwood, citrus, and soap. "I'm sorry."

"You've no need to be sorry. Raine and Ronnie caused the mishap."

"I'd chosen a precarious place to paint."

"This is not your fault. I'll be sure your paints are replaced."

"Don't be too hard on them. They were simply excited."

Carris chuckled wryly. "Certainly an understatement. As soon as they spotted you, they were determined to show you the shells they'd collected along the beach. They adore you. You have a powerful effect on people."

"Unlikely." Zorinda arched one brow. "But I thank you for saving my easel and the painting."

"Will you finish it?"

"After drying, I hope to."

"Your strokes and technique remind me of the artist who painted your father's ship—vivid and intense."

"You're most generous with your praise," she said though her heart drummed with uncertainty.

"And assuredly the truth. Have you eaten?"

"I'm about to join the children. But I wanted to make sure all was well with you."

"I'm none the worse. Thank you for goading me into today's outing—enjoyable and eye-opening. They're like sponges, soaking up everything they see, asking questions, fascinated by discovery."

"Much as you were once, I imagine." Carris's eyes darkened as though her words had reminded him of something unpleasant.

"Perhaps, I was. I was wondering," He cleared his throat and hesitated, uncharacteristic for him. "Would you consider dining with me?"

Zorinda's eyes widened.

"At a local *posada*?" he added,

Her tension eased. "I would."

Carris gave her an arresting smile. "Could you be ready in an hour?"

"Certainly. I'll let the children know I've had a change of plans."

"I'll come for you at two bells."

Zorinda nodded, turned toward the stairs but suddenly halted. Looking back at him, she laid her hand on his arm. His eyes locked upon her fingers, and self-conscious, she removed her hand. "Your handling of the mishap is to be commended. The children sincerely want to earn the money to replace my paints."

"If I've earned your approval, I don't regret all the grinding of my teeth. Should you look closely, you'll find them much reduced."

Zorinda laughed. "I hope you'll still enjoy the meal."

"Rest assured, I will." His eyes flared, and he moved closer.

Distrusting her emotions, Zorinda stepped back. Perhaps dining with him wasn't such a good idea. But she'd committed.

"I should change." She departed quickly, her heart thumping and her hands oddly clammy, unable to breathe until entering her cabin. After donning a silk gown of periwinkle, she went to the twins' cabin to let them know of her plans. But when she entered, she found them sitting together on the lower bunk, both crying, their meal untouched.

"What's wrong Raine, Ronnie? You haven't eaten." Zorinda knelt and clasped their hands.

"We are *très désolé*," Raine said. "Because we know Oncle is terribly angry." Ronnie nodded, his unruly curls bobbing as he silently agreed. Raine reached out to touch the embroidery on her bodice. "Why are you wearing such a beautiful gown?"

"Um—no reason." Sadly, Zorinda would not be sharing dinner with Carris. But her smile hid her disappointment. "Why don't the two of you try to eat something? And afterward, I'll read to you from our book."

Both children smiled through their tears. They were one of the reasons she was here. She would do everything in her power to keep them safe and happy. While she searched for her father.

Chapter 16

From his position on the poop deck, Carris could see Zorinda and the children seated below on the main deck, heads together as they worked on their lessons. Yesterday, Carris had informed Ronnie he would work with Mr. Rollins and learn the responsibilities of cabin boy. Raine would help Amos in the galley. Lessons would come first, then the afternoons would be spent performing their duties. He had already decided he would purchase new paints and a box for Zorinda in Rio. However, the children wouldn't be relieved of their duties until arriving in San Francisco.

"Captain?"

Carris turned to see Cavenley had joined him, all good humor and cheer. Though he wanted to snap a curt "What?" Carris refused to succumb to his mood, wavering between resignation and frustration. Cavenley had no part in Zorinda's change of heart last evening. Nor could he blame the children for her decision. Zorinda's note—delivered via Bo—had explained how Raine and Ronnie were so distraught they hadn't touched their supper, certain he was furious with them. Zorinda's words, penned in her flowing script, had hit hard. As had her request to allow *her* to address the children's concerns alone—a subtle suggestion he shouldn't interfere.

"Mr. Cavenley. You seem most jolly."

"No more so than any other day. I wanted to inform you, Mr. Surrell expects we'll run close to 250 knots today."

"The wind is cooperating. I believe she can pass 250. Raise all royals and studding sails. Let's see what she can do."

"Aye, sir. As soon as the sails are in place, I'll order the chip log released at the stern." Cavenley grinned.

"Let Surrell monitor the hourglass. Not a second more than thirty. Be sure there's no twisting in the knotted rope."

"I'll have Sanders feed the line. She may reach 300." His first mate paused. "Captain, might I speak forthrightly?" The man's serious tone wiped away all thoughts of speed.

"I've never known you to do otherwise." Carris met Cavenley's earnest expression.

"I don't want there to be any misunderstanding between us. I am not seeking Miss Wemblish's favor. She's a beautiful woman and I, as well as the other men, only want to see to her comfort. My overtures to Miss Wemblish are friendly. I've enough sense to know where her affections lie. I've never mentioned this, but there is a young woman in my shire whom I have admired for some time."

"Miss Wemblish harbors no affection for me." Carris spoke honestly, though the truth hurt.

"Sir, I can see how she watches you when she's on deck—how her eyes light up when you're near. You're most fortunate."

"You are mistaken, Mr. Cavenley. She can barely tolerate me."

"She said as much?"

Carris didn't care for the mischievous twinkle in the younger man's eyes. Glaring, he ignored Cavenley's question.

"If there's nothing else—"

"No, sir. Nothing more. I'll have a word with Mr. Surrell."

Cavenley turned sharply, striding away.

Carris informed MacCurdy he planned to take a stroll about the main deck. What he didn't mention was his plan to pass close to Zorinda and the twins. Shouts and orders to unfurl the royal and studding sails boomed across the deck. The satisfying flap of filling canvas greeted his ears as he neared the impromptu school room.

The children immediately looked up while Zorinda kept her eyes lowered. She'd said little to him since the broken dinner engagement.

He hoped she didn't think he was angry.

"Oncle Carris." Raine smiled, her sweet face reminding him of an angel's. "We've been reading about the South Pole, but Ronnie and I want to know if you've ever been to the North Pole."

Carris couldn't help but chuckle. "I haven't. But maybe one day. What say you, Miss Wemblish?"

Zorinda looked at him, a small smile playing about her lips. "With the right ship and the right captain, I imagine one could sail anywhere."

"Miss Wemblish believes we can." Carris grinned.

"How many days until we reach the South Pole?" Ronnie asked.

"We won't actually sail to the pole, but we'll be very close," Carris said. "If the weather holds, and we suffer no damage, we may round the cape in a little less than six weeks. I expect we'll cross the equator in a few days. We should celebrate the momentous event of your first crossing. Would you be agreeable to a small celebration, Miss Wemblish?"

"This is your ship, Captain. If you wish to celebrate, we will celebrate."

"Very good." He gave Zorinda a close inspection, her eyes now reflecting another emotion—approval, perhaps? A good sign? Or should he be worried? "Don't forget your duties after completing your lessons."

Raine and Ronnie nodded solemnly.

Though his punishment was intended to teach them a lesson, he hoped their new responsibilities became more fun than trial.

"As you are expecting them later, Captain, may I continue with their studies?" Zorinda's voice was pleasant, but far too governess-y for his liking.

"By all means. I apologize for the interruption. Good day." He strode off, his collar uncomfortably tight, his face burning from his dismissal. Something made him slow and peer over his shoulder.

Zorinda watched him. Hastily, she looked away, but she'd been caught. Dare he be encouraged?

The following day, ominous clouds gathered in the east, and as Zorinda and the children reviewed their mathematic equations for the day on deck, her concern mounted. She could tell by Carris's grim expression and those of his men, something serious threatened. Though the crew went about their usual tasks, the tension was palpable.

After luncheon, the twins scurried off to fulfill their work assignments, so Zorinda took advantage of the break to seek Carris. She needed confirmation of her suspicions for she wanted no surprises. Zorinda found him conversing with Mr. Surrell, but when Carris noticed her, he ended his discussion.

"Have I interrupted?"

"Not at all. Mr. Surrell and I were done. You have my complete attention."

Do I see a bit of a smile lurking about his lips? Hastily, she lowered her eyes.

"I'm sorry I couldn't have dinner with you the other night. The children were terribly upset."

"I was disappointed, but I understood. Mayhap there will be another opportunity?" Carris's voice held a note of hope.

She couldn't help but smile. "Certainly." Zorinda dared to meet his amazing aqua eyes.

"I look forward to the occasion." He reached out and captured her hand, touching his lips lightly to the back.

Heat spiraled within her leaving her flushed and flustered—sensations which occurred with alarming frequency. Zorinda reluctantly freed her hand and looked skyward. The thickening clouds reminded her of her initial concern. "How serious will the storm be?"

"We're taking precautions. The barometer drop is significant. For once, I wish we were in the doldrums.

Zorinda had often heard her father complain about the effects of the doldrums. The northeasterly trade winds of the North Atlantic and the southeasterly trades below the Equator created a phenomenon rendering a ship nearly motionless from lack of wind. "If we were closer to Cape São Roque, we could take advantage of the westerly winds and the favorable currents near the coast and outrun the storm."

"Is this storm of more concern than the others?" Zorinda hoped there was no trace of fear in her voice.

Carris looked up at the rigging, as though he hadn't heard her question.

And honestly, she wasn't sure she wanted an answer. The mounting breeze snapped the sails, chilling Zorinda, though the air was heavy and humid. Carris's uncharacteristic distraction was frightening, but she vowed not to alarm the children. *Lord, please bring us safely through another storm.*

Chapter 17

A furious thunderstorm encompassed the *Paradise* within an hour, and the hammering waves coalesced with the raging wind. Carris sensed the disturbance tropical in nature, conditions ripe for intensification. As he shared his premonition with Cavenley, the ship careened violently. Men scurried across the deck furling skysails, reefing the topsails, royals, and topgallants. The rain pelted every man and everything, adding to the difficulty of being heard above the roar of wind and wave.

"Topsails have been double-reefed and surface exposure reduced by at least a third," Cavenley reported, rain cascading over the brim of his hat.

"Good. We'll run her before the storm, and if need be, we'll shorten the topsails to their last row of reef points. Let the staysails remain to steady her."

"Should the gusts strengthen," Cavenley turned up the collar of his coat, "we'll be reduced to trial and error."

Carris nodded, his eyes fixed on the seething heavens, hurling macabre darts at the ocean, the lightning illuminating the tumultuous black sea as dark and endless as time itself. But not so dark God couldn't see through. To him. To his soul. To the woman and two children under his care.

"But the Lord sent out a great wind into the sea, and there was a mighty tempest in the sea, so that the ship was like to be broken."

Why would a verse from the book of Jonah return to haunt him now?

Because Jonah was running from God. And he too was running from God.

Howling bursts shook the *Paradise*. Reducing sail wouldn't pull the ship through the storm. Bands of squalls pummeled mercilessly while Carris staggered between Cavenley and Surrell, shouting orders he wasn't sure they heard.

Unexpectedly, the ship lifted, tossing Carris to the deck. A mountainous swell went under the ship then sluiced downhill as waves rose astern. The clipper tottered and pitched as the sea smashed against the hull. As Carris regained his feet, Cavenley reached him, the man ashen of face and breathing raggedly. Rain ran off his nose like a small waterfall.

"The spars are weakening, Captain—I'm afraid the ship will roll leeward, and the tips of the yardarms will go into the sea."

Before Carris could reply, a horrific sundering rose above the chaos, the sound chilling him to the bone. A chorus of wild shouts and yells greeted the disaster. Carris ran towards the main royal staysail, Surrell already there, issuing orders and bellowing instructions. The staysail had split.

"Bristow," Surrell yelled, "go aloft and reef the torn sail. Keep yourself on the weather side or you'll blow off."

One of the younger men emerged from the huddle and grasped the ropes, swinging himself up on the ratlines.

Carris grasped Surrell's arm. "Has he experience aloft?" he yelled.

"He's been up there before."

"But not in a storm."

"Ashby's the most experienced, but he broke his arm during the storm along the Eastern Shore."

Alternatives were nonexistent. Still, Carris was uneasy as he watched Bristow climb. The man seemed to know what he was about even though the wind snatched at the staysail, flapping so forcefully the mast creaked and groaned. Bristow's climb slowed as his feet began to slip on the thin ropes.

"Surrell, he's slipping."

"Cap'n, he's almost there."

Just as Surrell said, Bristow was within reach of the shredded sail. The *Paradise* heeled precariously as another wave battered. Bristow fell. Somehow the man caught a length of the canvas avoiding certain death. Pulling himself up, he recovered his lost position then latched on to the tattered sail. The whipping wind punched, jerking the canvas from his grasp, striking him in the chest. Bristow lost his hold, his piercing scream rising above the shattering din of the storm. The merciless waves swallowed him.

Tearing off his coat and shirt, Carris raced starboard. "Give me a rope. Now!" He had no idea who met his request, but with swiftness born of desperation, Carris quickly tied the rope around his waist. Climbing up to the rail, he hesitated for a second then leaped into the water.

Another scream rose above the terrifying din. A woman's scream. *Zorinda*. He hit the water. Hard.

Carris instantly sank below the crushing waves. He kicked his legs, holding his breath as he propelled upward.

He resurfaced and scanned the churning waves, searching for a sign of Bristow. Fortunately, the man hadn't lost consciousness when he'd hit the water. He thrashed and bobbed about twenty feet away.

Carris fought against the waves swimming to the man. Once he reached him, the panicked sailor refused to calm enough for Carris to take hold. He refused to lose Bristow and did the only thing he could to give them a chance. He thrust his fist under the man's jaw, and Bristow went limp. Carris hooked his arm around the sailor's upper chest then yanked on the rope about his waist as a signal to be hoisted. Relief inflated his aching lungs when he felt an answering tug. An eternity passed before the side of the *Paradise* came into view, the minutes ticking by with agonizing slowness. Finally, they were pulled out of the mounting swells. Carris's arms burned from supporting Bristow's dead weight.

Dozens of hands reached out to pull them over the side. Surrell and two other men relieved Carris of Bristow, and Cavenley helped him over to a wooden seat. Dropping down, Carris rubbed his hands over his face, drawing an unsteady breath. He could've died out there, and Zorinda lost to him forever.

"Sir, you don't look well. I can help you to your cabin."

"While a storm rages? I think not, Mr. Cavenley." Carris stood though his legs were weak, and his lungs burned from the salty sea water. He caught sight of a mystical wraith hovering on the fringes of his vision. She was floating toward him ... she had no business being on deck. Dangerous—foolish—maddening.

His legs buckled, and the flooded deck rose up to meet him.

Zorinda should never have ventured from the twins' cabin, but her unreasoning fear for Carris had proven too powerful. The children were frightened for him, as well. They begged Zorinda to sneak on deck for a look. Now, she knew why she'd been compelled to disobey. Concern for her safety faded into insignificance as Zorinda rushed toward Carris, sprawled face first on the wooden planks while his crew stared disbelieving at his prone form. As soon as she dropped beside him, Den Cavenley sprang into action.

"Help me lift him." He ordered several men who immediately complied, turning him over then heaving him up from the treacherous planks.

She followed them to Carris's cabin, silently daring any man to tell her she had no business being there.

But if Mr. Cavenley had a problem with her presence, he said nothing. When he spoke, he asked for her help. "Miss Wemblish, would you assist Mr. Rollins with the captain? I need to return to the deck with all haste."

"Of course." Zorinda hurried forward, clutching her shawl close about her neck.

Cavenley nodded, then he and the other men rushed out.

Zorinda turned to Mr. Rollins who seemed unfazed by Carris's collapse. The steward's manner calmed her. Of one thing she was certain—he was flawless in the execution of his duties.

"The captain could have lost his life jumping into the ocean." Rollins shook his head as he brought over a bowl of water and a cloth, placing both items on a table near Carris's bunk. The water sloshed over the sides as the ship pitched and rolled.

Fear slid insidious fingers along Zorinda's arms centering in her chest. She looked down at Carris, still unconscious, the natural bronze of his face now a sickly hue darkened by a stubble of beard. Even so, he was every inch the Poseidon of her fantasies. Rollins dragged a stool to her where she settled. Hopefully, she wouldn't fall off.

"Typical of the captain to save one of his men. Such a stunt I've never heard of nor seen. Now, look at him."

"How long have you known the captain?" Zorinda dipped the cloth in the water then sponged Carris's face and neck. She took extra care to avoid gaping at his exposed chest fearing she might be the next to swoon.

"Ten years have passed since he pulled me out of a terrible spot." A haunted look filled the man's eyes. "I'd recently been released from service—I was a surgeon's assistant in Her Majesty's Navy. And, previously, a purser."

Which explained the man's circumspect manner and competence.

"Unfortunately, I almost lost my leg in the late Opium War when our ship came under attack. Thus, I found myself hobbling about Plymouth, looking for work on any vessel that would have me. I was quite alone in the world. No family to speak of. The sea had been my life for nearly twenty years. I was set upon by a group of miscreants bent on taking what little bit of coin I had left. The captain, about a score and five at the time, witnessed the attempted theft. He and his companion, our Mr. Surrell, scattered the ne'er-do-wells. But the captain took the worse of the fracas and carries a scar to this day."

Zorinda uttered a tiny gasp, pausing momentarily with her sponging of Carris's face, the dripping cloth in her grip. She'd often wondered what had caused Carris's scar but had refrained from asking. She looked at his face now, her artist's eye memorizing the angles and planes, the firm jaw, the corded muscle thickening his neck. Then dared to trace his scar. When his eyes snapped open, she shrieked and reared back.

His hand came around her wrist, steadying her. "What happened? Why am I here?"

Zorinda couldn't find her voice, but Mr. Rollins quickly joined her, explaining the situation to Carris. Carris released her and tried to rise, but the steward pushed him down, ordering him to remain where he lay explaining he needed to attend to Bristow's more serious injuries.

Zorinda chose the distraction to slip away and rejoin the children in their cabin, letting them know their uncle was safe. What if Carris had died trying to save his crewman? She trembled as she gathered Raine and Ronnie close.

Carris's memories of the events following his rescue of Bristow were fuzzy save one. While he traversed the length of the deck mentally assessing the storm's damage, he clearly recalled Zorinda's face and her beautiful eyes when he'd roused from what he preferred to call a dizzy spell. He knew his men whispered about his faint.

Zorinda had seemed a divine creature, and for a moment he'd thought he'd died and somehow, miraculously, entered Heaven. But her cry of fright had been real and earthbound, shaking him free of the fantasy.

"Captain Trewellyn, sir." Rollins had joined him without making a sound. "I must remind you not to overdo. Bristow broke his collar bone, and he's still suffering from his time spent in the water. I wouldn't be surprised if you fall prey to additional distress."

"I'm sorry for Bristow, but I'm hale and hearty, Rollins."

"Even so, sir, I would recommend you curtail your normal activities, at least for the day."

Carris looked about. Broken yards, a cracked mizzenmast listing at a forty-five-degree angle, tangled webs of rigging—limp and useless. A tattered staysail. Walking the deck was hazardous at best. "I'll think on your suggestion. Would you check on Miss Wemblish and the children? Please instruct them—per my orders—to remain below deck until further notice. I'll not have them scampering about and risking injury."

"Of course, sir. I have to say Miss Wemblish is quite the brave lass." Rollins walked on, unruffled and unperturbed.

Had the man any idea what his words had done to him? Angry and frustrated, Carris slammed his fist on the top of a barrel. The action did nothing to resolve his emotional tangle, snarled worse than the rigging. But the hit managed to bruise his knuckles.

Two days after the storm, Zorinda and the twins were allowed to leave their cabins. Evidence of the storm's wrath littered the deck although men were in the rigging repairing what they could while under sail. Zorinda scanned the faces of those so hard at work, the sight of one heating her uncomfortably. Stripped to the waist and drenched with the sweat of his labor, Carris worked beside two sailors and Mr. Tenney, the bosun, a bearded, angular fellow. Carris's hair seemed afire, the sun picking out the copper strands. He had no right to look as he did, his muscular chest and arms rippling and tensing as he lifted and strained.

A tug on her skirt brought her back to reality though she feared she was flushed. She looked down at Raine and Ronnie.

"Did you hear us?"

"I ... uh, no children, I didn't. I was watching the men in the rigging."

"Mr. Surrell said we can return to our jobs today. Shouldn't we begin our lessons?"

Their expressions told Zorinda they were more interested in making money than studying.

"We can. Why don't we look through our nautical book and review the instruments needed for celestial navigation. In the event one of you decides to be a captain like your uncle."

"I could be a captain?" Raine asked.

"Why not?" Zorinda smiled. "But you'd better learn to swim as well as Captain Trewellyn. You might have to jump overboard and save someone."

Raine scrunched her face. "I'd rather be a painter like you."

Zorinda laughed as she guided the children toward the steps leading down to their quarters. Something caused her to turn, her gaze colliding with Carris's. The terrifying thought he might have died confirmed her growing attachment. *Lord, help me.*

Zorinda shared the evening meal with the twins even though Tate had delivered an invitation to dine with Carris and his officers. Raine and Ronnie eagerly related their work adventures, Ronnie was especially proud he'd been tasked with carrying messages to and fro—bow to stern and poop deck to the hold. Raine had learned what ingredients were needed to make biscuits. Both declared they could hardly wait for the morrow.

A copy of *Gulliver's Travels* had mysteriously appeared in the children's cabin. After eating together, Zorinda read from the new book then tucked them into their bunks. Once back in her cabin, she'd hoped to sketch a little, but as soon as she put charcoal to paper, the image taking shape was Carris, garbed as if he were Poseidon. *This will never do.*

Standing, she took up her shawl and slipped out, certain the sea air would clear her head. Unfortunately, she encountered Carris on the main deck. They stood facing one another, and she was powerless to look away. A shirt, waistcoat, and loosely tied cravat now adequately covered his upper torso. Unfortunately, her memory easily sketched what lay beneath his shirt. The breeze rustled his dark hair. *Confound his enticing lock of hair.*

"I missed you at the meal."

Her heart thumped painfully.

"Thank you for your assistance the night of the storm. My, uh, swim took more out of me than I realized."

"You were incredibly brave." The words seemed to burst from someplace other than her mouth. Carris stepped nearer, but she remained where she stood.

Reaching out, he lifted a curl which had loosened.

"Not really."

Zorinda noticed the uneasiness in his voice.

"I only did what was necessary."

"You saved a man's life." An awkward silence slipped between them, her heart hammering, discomfort forcing words to tumble forth. "Sometimes, I fear I'm not your best choice of governess."

"Really? Where would I find another so open and frank when assessing my character?"

Zorinda's eyes widened. There was no jest to his words, and she wasn't sure how to respond.

He stepped back as something changed in his eyes, in his manner.

"I've no right to assess your character."

"No? Haven't you disparaged my character since our first meeting? You accused me of abusing the children. You've accused me of misjudging my brother. You've accused me of intolerance." His breathing was uneven, his muscled shoulders rising and falling, his solid chest expanding and contracting. She'd never seen him in so foul a mood.

Once again, the memory of him lacking his shirt returned to taunt, and the heat in her face intensified. Here was a man to be reckoned with—one who exacted and demanded the best from those under his command. What chance did she stand in fighting an attraction bordering on insanity?

"Are you determined to rank me as another Goodwell?"

Zorinda's heart threatened to burst from her corseted chest, his words accusatory and inflaming. She should leave now before matters escalated. Against her better judgment, she answered. "You've done little to convince me otherwise."

His arm of steel banded about her while he cupped the side of her face, his fierceness rendering her immobile. His eyes were nearly black with anger.

I can't faint. I have to keep my wits about me. I can't let this happen. He pressed his brow to hers opening his mouth as though to speak. There was only silence, then ...

"Why can't you see what's right before you?"

Carris released her leaving her stunned. After turning, he strode toward the shadows enveloping the deck. Zorinda raced over to the starboard side of the ship and clutched the rail as though a lifeline. *God, don't let me care for him.* But her petition rang hollow because she knew there'd be no ignoring her foolish desire.

Chapter 18

When the *Paradise* crossed the equator, Carris held the promised celebration for Raine and Ronnie. All assembled on the quarterdeck where his men entertained them with singing, jigs, and general silliness. Amos, the cook, provided a special meal and fancy cake.

Carris invited Zorinda to dine with him and his officers in the evening after the twins had settled in their cabin. She avoided speaking to him throughout the meal while holding her queenly court and charming his men. He didn't deserve her attention given his recent irrational behavior. There was no excuse for his argumentative mood when they'd last conversed on deck. Carris had no right to take out his frustration on Zorinda as though she'd calculatingly bewitched him. He was solely responsible for his current miasma.

As the *Paradise* neared Cape São Roque, Carris received the wish he'd made the evening of the last storm. The ship slipped into the doldrums and progress nearly halted. He knew the best way to push through was to follow Maury's charts—head due south and make use of the land breeze off Brazil. They lost a day—hardly noteworthy given the condition of the ship. When the *Paradise* reached Rio, he'd make sure she was returned to her original seaworthy status, even if he lost time. He'd promised Sharp and the Darrows he'd have their cargo in San Francisco by September fifteenth. If the rounding of the Horn went smoothly, there'd be no reason he wouldn't meet the deadline.

Thirty-five days out of Norfolk, the *Paradise* sailed into Guanabara Bay, Rio de Janeiro, situated on the jutting peninsula like a sparkling gem, nestled in the shadow of a mountain towering majestically over the city. Carris stood beside Cavenley as Mr. MacCurdy guided the ship into port with the assistance of the Portuguese harbor pilot.

"We've made good time," Cavenley said, "even though you weren't pushing her."

"I'm satisfied. And with the exception of this last storm, we've had fairly good weather."

"Mr. Sharp will be extremely happy if we arrive in San Francisco sooner than estimated."

"I'm not running a race, Mr. Cavenley. No matter when the cotton arrives, the banker stands to make a tidy sum." *As do I and the crew.* Guilt hammered Carris, causing him to swallow with some difficulty.

"Then there's the bonus provided by the Darrow brothers for transporting those crates."

Cavenley's reminder nearly sent him into a coughing spasm, which he covered with a raspy grunt. How could he justify taking the ship chandlers' money then spend funds on a frivolity—of all things, a painting—when there were so many who could have benefitted from the sum he'd impulsively spent? He'd never considered what others lived without, often through no fault of their own. But the ship in the painting seemed more a living soul than a manmade vessel. With the scene residing over his bed, he was profoundly stirred whenever he looked up. Ridiculous, to be sure. And its existence was a condemnation of sorts. He was seriously considering returning some of the Darrows' money.

Laughter and chatter drew Carris's eyes to the open deck below where Raine and Ronnie chased each other. Zorinda followed sedately, her gown of lemon yellow and pale peach as inviting as ice cream. Her gentle laugh floated to his ears, setting his heart afire. He loved her. And he had since the moment he'd confronted her on the Norfolk waterfront. The realization abruptly altered his mood. He was unforgivably close to forgetting what mattered. Ships. Business. Making Trewellyn Shipping a name commanding respect around the world.

Zorinda wouldn't let herself love him. She was a woman of deep faith, devoted to good works and charity. Her love for God was real and tangible. His feelings on the matter were divided. Part of him yearned for the faith of his childhood. The cynical, embittered side of him chose to believe a man made his own destiny through his choices and actions.

"The children are quite fond of Miss Wemblish," Cavenley said, forcing Carris to look away from the pleasant scene on the lower deck.

"Unfortunately," he retorted gruffly. "At some point, they will be separated. At least they won't miss me."

"I believe you're making progress, sir. They're more comfortable around you."

"You mean they no longer quake in terror when they see me."

"Well," Cavenley hedged, "you were somewhat impatient."

Carris fought back an angry retort.

"Children are spontaneous, energetic. Miss Wemblish understands them."

"Whereas I am locked in a rigid, unyielding persona where all things conform and nothing left to chance."

"Those are not my words, sir." Cavenley appeared genuinely distressed.

Carris shook his head. "No. But others have mentioned those traits. Please see Miss Wemblish and the twins escorted ashore with appropriate attendants once the ship is secure and watches in place."

"Wouldn't you prefer to accompany them?"

"I wouldn't be welcomed." Carris turned away, unable to tolerate the silent censure of his first mate or the sight of Zorinda and the children.

The water of the bay was identical to the color of Carris's eyes, and Zorinda yearned for a canvas, paints, and brushes. A charcoal sketch seemed so inadequate when presented with spectacular color. But there was no opportunity for artistic endeavors, as she and the twins were allowed but a short time on deck. The ship, Mr. Surrell explained, was being secured, requiring she and the children return to their cabins. Even so, the children were so distracted they raced to the porthole at every noise, bump, or jolt. Exasperated, Zorinda loudly cleared her throat forcing Raine and Ronnie to face her with guilty expressions.

"We are sorry, mademoiselle. But we want to know what's happening," Raine said.

"Can't we go back on deck?" Ronnie asked.

"I promised Mr. Surrell we'd stay in our cabin until the ship moored. We should be discussing geography"

Raine and Ronnie sighed. They moved from the porthole and dutifully returned to their seats. Their disappointment was unbearable, and Zorinda was about to disregard her promise to the second mate when a knock sounded on the door.

Raine and Ronnie jumped up and rushed to open it.

Mr. Cavenley stood there grinning. "Permission granted to come on deck. Mr. Sanders and Mr. Doherty will escort you from the ship for a brief sightseeing excursion. However, the captain requests you be back on board before dark."

Pandemonium erupted as the children hugged each other and danced about their small space. Their excitement was contagious, and were Zorinda completely honest with herself, she too was thrilled. Rio de Janeiro! How long had she dreamed of visiting the Brazilian city her father had so vividly painted in words? But she was the adult, and in view of her position, she cautioned the children to remain calm so they could stack their books and tidy up. Mr. Cavenley slipped away, and as soon as he was gone, Raine and Ronnie picked up and put things away as quickly as she'd ever seen.

Carris watched Zorinda and the children leave with Sanders and Doherty. Raine and Ronnie, in their lighter clothing, skipped while Zorinda cautioned them to be careful as they navigated the gangplank. He couldn't help but smile at the sight, wishing he could be as carefree and excited as his niece and nephew. He'd once been so a very long time ago.

Rather than brood on the past, he looked at the *Pão de Açúcar*—Sugarloaf Mountain—and the *Corcovado*—Hunchback Mountain—looming over the bay. The harbor teemed with all manner of vessels, the majority at anchor, and clippers likely headed to San Francisco. Carris shook his head knowing many on those ships would never realize their dreams of gold.

"Sir, Miss Wemblish and the children have left," Mr. Cavenley interrupted his thoughts. "I instructed Mr. Sanders and Mr. Doherty to keep them in sight at all times. They've also coin enough to purchase a meal."

"Thank you, Mr. Cavenley. Now, we get down to business. Send the men up in the rigging to assess the damage and needed repairs. Take inventory of the extra spars. The trip around the Horn will prove arduous at best, and we can't take any chances."

"We'll make sure the cargo arrives safely."

Carris realized his first officer had misunderstood his concern. "Not the cargo. My passengers. And my crew."

Turning away, Carris sought the three who had suddenly become more important to him than anything else. But there was no sign of Zorinda or the twins. Uneasiness settled over him, which he immediately dismissed. The two seamen were more than capable of taking care of them.

After a simple lunch ordered by Mr. Sanders, who could speak passable Portuguese, they made their way to the *Passeio Público*. The park was magnificent, and Zorinda so wished she'd brought her pad and charcoal. The formal, hexagonal gardens were magnificently arrayed with amazing, fragrant blooms, and a terrace overlooked the sea. Raine and Ronnie gave her little time to absorb the breathtaking view as they pulled her first one way then another.

Mr. Sanders and Mr. Doherty followed discreetly and seemed to enjoy their assignment especially when she noticed several young women had captured their attention. At one point, a group of children, shepherded by black robed nuns, passed before her and the twins. Zorinda lost sight of the sailors, but Raine and Ronnie scampered forward leaving her no choice but to follow them. The two men were sure to catch up.

They passed fountains and stunning statues—one was of a little boy holding a turtle, Ronnie insisting the boy looked like him.

Zorinda discovered beauty with every step. Beyond the granite pyramids adorned with amazing medallions, she came upon a pavilion covered with oval paintings of the bay.

Raine's and Ronnie's giggles floated on the air as they chased one another out of her immediate sight, but not beyond her hearing. Zorinda wasn't sure how long she stood looking at the beautiful display when she sensed someone to her left.

When she glanced to her side, a man stood within a few feet of her, possessed of russet hair and a full beard. His garb and cap marked him a seaman, perhaps an officer. He studied the paintings, his hands clasped behind him. Glancing over at her, he smiled. Nice but not Carris's smile. Of late, she hadn't received so much as a twitch of Carris's lips.

"Good afternoon."

British. Attractive. Zorinda smiled politely. "Good afternoon," she replied, self-conscious. Zorinda turned, intending to join the children.

"This is fascinating." The seaman's deep voice held a timbre reminiscent of Carris's.

Zorinda looked back at the seaman. He had green eyes but a far cry from the pure aqua of Carris's. Aware she was making pointless comparisons, she wanted to stomp her foot and scream. Sanity won out, and she did neither. Instead, Zorinda silently surveyed the man. Close to six feet in height—a slim build masking what she imagined to be deceptive strength. A cocky, authoritative air about him. She suddenly realized he awaited a reply. "I've never seen anything so amazing," she said.

"I'm intrigued." His eyes conveyed an uncomfortable something. Nothing threatening, but he seemed to appraise her, outwardly and inwardly. Reminded her of the poor horses at an auction. She hoped he didn't ask to see her teeth.

"I'm sorry. Where are my manners? Arthur Wells, at your service." He removed his hat and bowed.

"A pleasure to meet you, Mr. Wells. You're here on business?" She was hesitant to return his pleasantry by revealing her name, not sure what to make of him.

"I'm the captain of the *Falcon's Wing*, bound for—"

"San Francisco?" Zorinda asked.

When his brows quirked upward, she laughed. "Isn't every ship in the world bound for San Francisco loaded with gold-mad miners?"

"Unfortunately," Captain Wells said. "For a moment, I thought you might be a diviner."

"Nothing of the sort," she said. "I too am headed to San Francisco." Zorinda dared a closer look at him. There was no ignoring the chiseled planes of his face, though partially hidden by his thick beard. Captain Wells exuded charisma, and she sensed he knew his way around women. Another Wil, perhaps?

"I believe you're American, yet you have a whisper of an accent. French perhaps?" Captain Wells's comment drew her back into the conversation

"I speak fluent French thanks to my mother." Disquiet settled upon her, which she shoved aside.

"What takes you to San Francisco?" the captain asked.

Raine and Ronnie's laughter moved closer. She wondered briefly what had become of Carris's crewmen.

Captain Wells inclined his head at the sound of the twins' merriment, his brow furrowing.

"San Francisco is only the first stop of my voyage," Zorinda said. "I'm temporarily caring for two children until they are delivered to their guardian. Their uncle, captain of the clipper, *Bird of Paradise*, is taking them to live with a relative."

A shutter slipped over the man's face, and he stiffened. His flirtatiousness vanished. But his shift in mood was temporary. Within a heartbeat, Arthur Wells's roguish smile reappeared in full force as though she'd imagined the alteration.

"I was afraid you were planning to seek your fortune in San Francisco. Somehow, I can't imagine you panning for gold." A hint of teasing was in his voice and eyes.

"If I were of a mind to pan for gold, I assure you, I'd manage." Zorinda mirrored his humor. "A woman's ability should never be underestimated."

"Touché. I only meant a woman as engaging and as beautiful as you would hardly need to pan for gold when there would be dozens of men willing to assist you."

"Thank you for the compliment, Captain Wells," she said wryly. "Your velvet tongue must garner you many admirers."

"Not always." His eyes dimmed for a second.

"If you'll excuse me, I must locate my charges. I hear them, but I can't see them. Which gives cause for worry."

"I understand. But I'm sure they are in capable hands." A shadow of sadness filled his eyes, so contradictory to his earlier conviviality "I have two children whom I miss very much. And a wife I've egregiously neglected. I haven't been a proper father or husband."

"The seafaring life is difficult. My father is a ship's captain." She spoke as though her father was very much alive. In her heart he was. "Thaddeous Wemblish."

There was no mistaking the physical jolt when Captain Wells stepped back.

Her heart raced. "Do you know him?"

"I know of him. I heard he and his crew went missing somewhere in the South Pacific. Most tragic."

Zorinda's heart lurched, her tiny hope dashed.

"So, you are Miss Wemblish?" His question hung between them.

Zorinda managed an answer. "Zorinda Wemblish."

"Though I never met the man, I can say his daughter is beyond compare." The captain was a master of recovering his equilibrium, and she envied him his ability. A ready jest and suavity were his trademark.

The time arrived for her to gather the children and return to the ship. Something about the captain unsettled her. "Your flattery knows no bounds, Captain. Good day." Zorinda walked away in search of the unseen children whose chatter increased in volume. At least they weren't far away.

"Miss Wemblish." She slowed her steps and looked back at Captain Wells. "Your charges—they are well?"

"Very much so, and full of energy. How fare your children?"

"I've been assured they are in good hands. Should you ever need anything, please don't hesitate to look me up."

"I doubt I would find myself in such a position, Captain."

"You never know. Actually, I wouldn't mind a race with this *Bird of Paradise.*" He flashed a wicked grin. "Most likely the *Falcon* would beat the ship as she's more streamlined than a typical clipper. I'm not afraid to raise as much canvas as she carries—without capsizing, of course." The man chuckled.

"Captain Trewellyn will not accommodate you. He has no desire to subject his crew and ship to the whims of time and nature." *Why the need to defend Carris?*

Captain Wells's right brow raised.

Let him think whatever he wishes.

"I'm not surprised," he said.

Zorinda wasn't sure she'd heard correctly. "I beg your pardon?"

The man cleared his throat then showered her with his roguish smile.

"I'm not surprised he'd be cautious with a woman and children on his ship. This captain of yours would undoubtedly be practical and conscientious."

"He is, but he's not my captain. He's my employer."

"You don't say?" The captain's eyes reflected skepticism. "He may be cautious, but he has no sense."

Zorinda was about to remand him for his misconception when he spoke again.

"Miss Wemblish, I would be remiss if I were not honest with you."

His words startled her. Somber, lacking all trace of teasing or humor, the captain continued, "Hostilities still exist between England and China, and to some extent, France, over the trading of opium. Smuggling is rampant and encourages extreme measures and little value for human life. I know you would not want to place your charges in danger. Nor yourself." Captain Wells turned abruptly and strode away.

Zorinda struggled for understanding. Was the man insinuating the *Paradise* was transporting opium? Carris would never engage in opium smuggling.

Raine and Ronnie chose to appear along with Sanders and Doherty who profusely apologized for losing them.

As Zorinda gathered the children close, listening to their adventures, she looked over their heads to see Captain Wells watching them from afar. With an unnerving intensity.

Chapter 19

Carris wasn't consciously aware he'd been listening for the return of the twins and Zorinda. But as soon as he heard the banter and laughter, he immediately stopped what he was doing. He'd struggled so long with the steering gears, which had somehow misaligned, he'd lost track of the time. Though he was sweaty and dirty, he gave no thought to his unseemly appearance as he came to stand at the gangway. All he cared about was the return of the three.

Raine and Ronnie raced up the gangplank, and when they reached him, they threw their arms around him. He was beyond amazed by their greeting.

"We had such fun, Oncle."

"We saw fountains, and there were birds we've never seen before. And a little stone boy with a turtle."

"There were pyramids too. And pretty paintings. But not as pretty as the ones Mademoiselle makes."

The children's rambling blended, and he hardly knew who was saying what. He looked over their heads to see Zorinda. She seemed distracted. "What did you think of the city, Miss Wemblish?"

"The children described our visit perfectly. If you'll excuse me. I'll await them in their cabin." Zorinda walked past without another word while Raine and Ronnie continued their excited recitation. By now Doherty and Sanders had boarded.

"Did something happen?" Carris asked.

"Happen?" Sanders appeared confused. "After lunch, we went to the park, but nothing happened. Jep and I lost sight of Miss Wemblish and the children for a short while when several nuns brought along a large group of children. But we met back up a few minutes later."

"I see. Thank you for watching them."

"Our pleasure, sir," both men replied in unison before moving on.

Carris took the hand of each child. "Did somebody upset Miss Wemblish?"

"I don't think so," Ronnie replied. "There was a man speaking to her."

"He had a beard," Raine said. "But then he walked away."

"Nothing more?"

The twins simultaneously said no, then resumed their tales. Eventually, they expounded upon everything they'd seen and done and expended what was left of their energy.

Carris directed them to their cabin and returned to his labor. Yet Zorinda's manner was disturbing, and he wondered what she'd encountered no one had witnessed. Could the bearded man be the source of her unnatural reticence?

Unable to dismiss the conversation with Captain Wells, sleep eluded Zorinda. He'd stirred her curiosity. Though a charming rogue, a shadowy sadness lurked beneath the surface. She'd felt no personal attraction yet sensed a kindred soul for he seemed to be searching for something.

His warning words to her conveyed unknown menace. Those words, more than anything, kept her awake.

"Nonsense," Zorinda spoke into the darkness. She threw off the coverlet and lit the lamp nearest her bunk. After removing her nightdress, she hastily slipped on the gown she'd worn earlier. A walk on deck in the cooling bay breeze might prove restful.

Once there, she made her way to the starboard rail searching for a place to sit. The men at watch nodded and called out soft greetings as though afraid of disturbing the night. She was surprised to see a lantern resting on a barrel and changed direction then realized someone sat there.

"Zorinda?"

She was close enough now to see Carris with a book in his lap. A Bible.

"Is something amiss?"

"I couldn't sleep so I came up seeking the breeze."

"Join me." He indicated the space beside him.

Seeing no way to decline without being rude, she did so, smoothing out her skirt. Clasping her hands in her lap, she drew in of the air, an amazing blend of flowers and sea and—Carris. The essence of the man mingled with the sandalwood and citrus he favored. Masculine and intoxicating.

"What are you reading?" she asked, hoping to alter the uncomfortable direction of her thoughts.

"Psalms. This Bible belonged to my mother." Carris shut the book which he placed beside him. "I realize I may have been wrong."

"About what?"

Raw vulnerability flickered in his eyes, taking Zorinda by surprise. His unguarded emotion tugged at her heart.

"About Lance. I wish I was delivering Raine and Ronnie to him rather than their grandfather. There is good in Lance. I've chosen to remember all the bad—the things I've said." Carris paused and swallowed visibly. "In the New Testament, James compares a thoughtless tongue to a horse's bit in that both are small but can effect great change. The same of a ship. 'Behold also the ships, which though they be so great, and are driven of fierce winds yet are they turned about with a very small helm.'" Several seconds of silence passed before he spoke again.

"I know nothing about their grandfather. I sent Montagne a letter from Marseille, but I have no way of knowing if delivered. I informed him of the children's plight and their impending arrival. I don't know if he'll take the children, considering their mother ran away from him."

"They've wiggled their way into your heart." Zorinda couldn't keep the joy from her voice. "I have prayed daily they'd be welcomed. But you doubt Lance is alive."

"My solicitor is a levelheaded man, not given to fancy. I've never known him to steer me wrong. If Truesdale is right, how do I find Lance?" Carris leaned forward, resting his arms on his knees. "Sometimes I wonder if the sea is my true path. I always assumed as much. Only recently, since meeting you," he turned and gave her a lopsided smile, "I've begun to question my direction. I've never asked God what he has planned for me. Mayhap too late to ask now."

"Never too late. God expects us to rely on him. Not on ourselves. As for finding Lance, perhaps God will place your brother on the path he's created for you."

"If so, he needs to do so quickly. Once we round the Horn and complete business in San Francisco, we'll sail to Bora Bora. So, tell me about this bearded man."

An annoying flutter commenced in her stomach, and she pressed her hand there. How could he have known? Sanders and Doherty? Something within her wanted to share the captain's message with him. Until she cautioned herself not to make too much of the man's ridiculous warning.

"Ronnie mentioned a man was speaking to you in the park."

"Ronnie is most observant." *Too observant.* "I was looking at the paintings on a pavilion when I noticed a man standing near me. He too is a captain, far from home, missing his family, especially his children. He was annoyingly flirtatious."

"Really? Annoyance is often the prelude to an attraction."

"I ... I don't understand." Zorinda debated the possibility of fleeing until Carris placed his rough palm against her cheek.

"Today, when you were away, I could think of nothing but you and the children."

"What are you saying?" Her words came out breathlessly.

"I desperately wish your annoyance with me might soften to a congenial tolerance. I have no right to ask anything of you, but I have this hope—"

"Captain, I hate to disturb you." The bosun, twisting his cap nervously, seemed embarrassed to have interrupted them. "Cook's cat was chasin' a rat and has gotten himself caught in one o' them crates in the hold—one with a loose board. I wanted to let you know we had to pry open a slat to rescue the rascal."

Zorinda could tell Carris was trying hard not to laugh.

"Quite all right, Mr. Tenney. No harm done."

Mumbling his thanks, the bosun quickly turned and hurried off. Carris sighed, running a hand through his unruly hair.

"I never realized a captain's duties were so unusual." Zorinda grinned. "I should leave you to your reading. Good night." Reluctantly, she stood and walked away, wondering what Carris had been about to say. One could never be sure with him. When she reached the steps, she heard Carris chuckle. Her heart lightened.

Seaman Bristow, his arm in a sling to stabilize his broken collar bone, was assigned to accompany Zorinda and the children back to the park the following morning, Plans were to hold the day's class there with the promise of a treat when lessons were completed. The twins proved most attentive, and in short time, were in possession of two *pasteis de nata*—a crispy, egg custard tart. Right before the noon hour, after helping Zorinda post a letter to Sarah, Bristow returned them to the ship.

Four bells sounded when Zorinda returned to her cabin, the children tidying up before reporting for afternoon chores. She'd taken but a step within when she noticed a folded note on the floor, apparently slipped under the door. Once unfolded, she read aloud.

> Zorinda,
> I'm sorry we were interrupted last evening, for there is much I want to say. I'm hoping to convince you to dine with me in the city this evening. I deeply regret mishandling matters between us. As our Lord instructed, we should be honest in all things. I await your reply.
> Affectionately yours,
> Carris

Carris had invited her to dine with him.

"I knew it," Raine said excitedly.

Zorinda gasped and looked at the open doorway filled with two impish faces.

"We knew he liked you. When you marry, Ronnie and I will be your little boy and girl. Then we won't have to live with our grandfather."

A lump lodged in Zorinda's throat, and she knelt, taking hold of Raine's hands. How to explain the truth of the matter to an eight-year-old? She sighed. "Raine, the captain and I are friends. I'm sure you'll love your grandfather, and he will love both of you. You and Ronnie and your grandfather will be a family soon."

Tears glistened in Raine's eyes. Ronnie sniffed suspiciously. Zorinda wanted to cry, but she couldn't.

"Your uncle and I will always love you. You will live in our hearts. Even when we're not together."

Unexpectedly, both children threw their arms around her and hugged her as though they would never let go.

Zorinda lost her battle with tears, and cried with them, wishing, somehow, their dream could come true. Because then her dream would as well.

Carris had hoped to receive an answer to his invitation by now. Impatient and nervous, pacing the deck, he was about to go in search of Zorinda when he saw her heading his way. Endless seconds passed before she reached him.

"I was hoping you'd seen my note." He nodded at the folded paper she held.

"I did." She too seemed nervous. "I ..." Her hesitation knotted his nerves. "... would enjoy dining with you. At what time?"

"Six bells."

A silence slipped between them, and he simply stood, mesmerized by the shimmer lighting her eyes. Had she been crying? She didn't seem upset, but her lower lip trembled slightly.

"I'll have time to settle Raine and Ronnie."

"Of course. I look forward to our outing." He gave her a slight bow then turned, walking away until he heard steps behind him. Halting, he pivoted, surprised to see Zorinda, a gentle smile curving her perfect lips. Lifting on her toes, she brushed a quick kiss on his cheek. Before he could process what had happened, she moved away, escaping down the companionway stairs. Surviving Zorinda's departure at the end of the voyage was no longer a concern. His concern now was to make sure she didn't leave.

Why had she kissed Carris Trewellyn?

Seated at the small desk in her cabin, Zorinda pondered her rash behavior. She could only attribute her insanity to Carris's kind manner with the children. He seemed a different man.

But the fact remained he was still the Carris Trewellyn who couldn't forgive his brother, who resented his father, and had relegated his faith to a distant memory. Rising from the seat, she paced the cabin, wondering if she should cancel her acceptance. Her heart had already taken her to a place she shouldn't be. To attempt another evening with Carris could end in more broken dreams. Then why had she spent overlong on her bathing and toilette? And wasted an inordinate amount of time styling her hair?

The ship's bell ended her vacillation. Either she presented herself on deck or sent a note declining his invitation—nothing short of cowardly. She was tired of running. Tired of fearing Carris would become another Wil.

She was making far too much of this evening, which likely meant little to him. But meant everything to her.

A knock on her door set her heart pounding. She stared at the door, certain Carris was on the other side.

"Zorinda?"

Never in her life had she been so uncertain. She wanted to be with him, but something deep within her warned her not to yield to her weakness.

Her legs wobbled as she walked to the door and, once opened, revealed Carris formally attired, much as he'd been the night he'd escorted her to the mayor's home. And there she stood in the same gown she'd worn the same evening.

His smile drew her eyes to his mouth.

"I was afraid you'd changed your mind."

"I ... I'm sorry to be tardy. Let me get my wrap, and ... I." Her voice faltered when she realized *his* eyes now fixed on *her* lips. Self-conscious she pressed her fingertips to them.

Suddenly, Carris roused himself.

Lost and confused by her betraying thoughts, Zorinda hastily turned aside and took up her gossamer wrap.

Moving a few steps within the cabin, he took the gauze fabric, placing the length about her shoulders. His hands lingered on her flesh for several breathless seconds.

Did Carris gently caress her shoulder before stepping back through the open door? She couldn't be sure, but there was no dismissing his open admiration. The realization jolted her, as did the unnerving depths of his eyes. After drawing on her gloves, she laid her hand upon his offered arm, knowing full well she was both terrified and excited. And for the life of her, she couldn't run. She wouldn't run. Come what may.

Chapter 20

The hired carriage delivered Zorinda and Carris to an establishment proclaiming to be the *Café o Sol na Baia*. Situated on Guanabara Bay, hundreds of lights danced across the water as twilight heralded the approaching night. Zorinda waited for Carris to alight then grasped his extended hand as he assisted her. After gaining the oyster shell walkway, she paused for an unobstructed look.

"How beautiful," she whispered.

"But falls far short of the beauty at my side."

Zorinda looked up at him, startled. "Are you merely being polite?"

"I'm speaking the truth." Charged silence slipped between them for several seconds until Carris spoke again. "I want to introduce you to *Senhor Gabriel,* who has promised me his finest table."

"You've dined here before?" Zorinda asked as they resumed their walk, the shells crunching beneath their heels.

"A few times. And I've never forgotten the *feijoada*. You'll understand when you have a taste."

Greeted at the door by the proprietor, Sr. Gabriel was clearly delighted Carris had brought, in Sr. Gabrielle's words—*uma mulher bela,* with him. Zorinda, certain bela was the equivalent of beautiful, blushed.

Sr. Gabrielle led them to a table with a splendid view of the bay, the candlelight bathing the intimate corner with a muted glow. After being seated, Zorinda politely asked Carris to order for her. His eyes darkened with confusion, and she realized she'd never asked nor permitted him to decide for her. She confirmed with a nod, and after a slight hesitation, Carris turned his attention to Sr. Gabrielle. The proprietor and Carris proceeded, employing a mix of English and Portuguese with Carris nodding from time to time. Zorinda, bewildered by the serious exchange, was suddenly eager to view the selections. *Vai ser magnifico* were Sr. Gabrielle's parting words.

In a short time, a woman of middle years delivered two steaming bowls of *caldo verde* and warm bread. After ensuring their satisfaction, the pleasant woman moved to another table where two couples sat. Zorinda eagerly dipped her spoon into the soup of potatoes, kale and sausage. One taste sent her on a savory culinary adventure. When the main courses arrived, Zorinda wasn't sure the table would hold the bounty. Carris assured her they would be sharing the entrees, much to her relief.

The feijoada was a savory stew of black turtle beans, smoked sausage, and beef served with rice and as delicious as Carris had promised. The entrée of dried, salted codfish completed the flavorful and unsurpassed Brazilian feast. Dessert was an enticing array of small cakes possessed of a blend of coconut, cheese, and cinnamon. Amazing how flavors could paint pictures and inspire the imagination.

After leaving the café, Carris suggested they visit the terraced garden behind the establishment. A couple strolled through but as Carris led her higher, they moved beyond sight.

Reaching the top, Zorinda could do little but take in the beauty of the city below, the bay, and the tiny ships more resembling toys than conquerors of the sea. "I wish I had my paints and a canvas at this very moment."

"We could return tomorrow."

"I've nothing to work with. Though Ronnie and Raine assure me my items will soon be replaced. Could someone be overpaying them?" Zorinda turned to Carris who displayed a hint of guilt.

"They are learning about consequences. A lesson we all learn—sometimes in ways we'd rather not."

His words held a wounded note, and without thinking, Zorinda instinctively reached up touching his scarred jaw. Carris clasped her searching fingers then shifted them to his lips, brushing a burning kiss across her glove. An unruly warmth raced up her arm and her breath caught. Releasing her, Carris cupped her face with his strong, callused hands, tilting her face up to his.

Would Carris know his kiss would be her first? She'd frequently angered Wil by avoiding his overbearing attempts. Carris's thumb brushed her lips, then he lowered his mouth to hers. *Great stars above.*

Carris gently feathered kisses against Zorinda's motionless lips, sensing her reticence, hoping to convey he'd make no unwelcome demands. His exquisite exploration awakened a connection he'd never believed possible. When Carris raised his head, he savored the shy ardor in her eyes, shaking him with humbling bliss. He hesitated, silently awaiting her permission.

Unexpectedly, she lifted up on her toes in a wordless invitation Carris hadn't the strength to decline.

Her lashes lowered as he captured her mouth, this kiss breaching whatever walls had existed between them and dissolved rational thought. She pressed her hands to his chest, and he was certain he heard the pounding of her heart matching his. Thunder, a shattering rumble in the distance, perfectly mirrored his current state of mind.

Reluctantly ending their kiss, Carris lowered his hands and wrapped his arms about her, drawing her against him. When she clutched his arms, he willed his strength to flow through and around her, a silent promise he would shield her from the storms of life.

When she looked up at him, Zorinda raised her hand and brushed back his lock of hair which never remained in place.

Grasping her soothing hand, Carris slowly removed her glove then kissed each finger. *Utter madness ... merciless pleasure.*

"Zorinda."

His rough utterance left Zorinda reeling. Followed by his consuming kiss. She should have been frightened, but Carris was her anchor in this churning sea in which she'd fallen. Heaven help her, but this man's embrace was nothing short of magnificent. *I love him.* The words beat in time to her racing heart. How could she survive the day they parted? How could she say goodbye to Raine and Ronnie when she loved them as though they were hers? How could she ever be content at home when she'd seen something of the world and tasted adventure and excitement? And love.

Zorinda quickly turned her face aside, caution warring with her wayward thoughts. She dared not look at Carris, aware of his harsh breaths fanning her heated brow. The feel of his arms, the taste of his lips, the caress of his hands thrilled her. But this exhilaration might quickly lead them down a treacherous path. As though his mind mirrored her thoughts, he released her and put a small space between them though he reclaimed her hands.

"I've frightened you."

"I've frightened myself." Zorinda uttered a shaky laugh. "You must think me unprincipled."

"I could live with so serious a failing." A flash of lightning revealed his grin. Would there soon be a storm? Or was the real storm within her?

"You are incorrigible."

"And you are irresistible." A charged silence slipped between them while thunder shook the earth and the lightning slashed. "If I've been too forward ..."

She shook her head no.

Carris traced her jaw with his thumb, erasing the last remnant of Wil's betrayal—the sensation so overwhelming she closed her eyes, a frantic breath escaping. Slowly, purposefully, Carris kissed her lids, her cheeks, and then her lips. But these kisses were whisper-like and abbreviated. Was she disappointed?

"Look at me."

Zorinda forced herself to comply, her entire body shuddering as heat and ice coursed her. Had she taken ill?

"This voyage can be our beginning. Once the children have been safely settled, the world is ours. No constraints, no limitations." He leaned close for another kiss, but she averted her head, his words striking a discordant note.

Captain Wells's odd warning intruded, even though she was certain Carris would never be part of anything so terrible. "Carris, petition for guardianship of Raine and Ronnie."

"They wouldn't be any happier with me." Carris's mocking tone dimmed her euphoria.

"Things are different. You're different. All Ronnie can talk about is being a captain. And Raine thinks you most brave."

"We'll speak of this another time." He caught her close, but she pulled back.

"Consider what's best for them. They're fond of you."

"Hardly. They're fond of you and have been from the moment they attached themselves to you on the wharf."

"They do hold you in affection, Carris. They needn't live with their grandfather." Zorinda couldn't let him push the matter aside.

"I promise we'll discuss this. But not tonight. We should return to the ship before the rain begins." The thunder did seem closer. As did the slashes of lightning.

Zorinda nodded, not entirely convinced the fate of Raine and Ronnie should be postponed, but pressing for a decision now might not be the best course. She wasn't ready to dispel the magic. After she nodded, Carris returned her glove then tucked her arm within his as he led her from the terraced overlook.

But the spell broke, and the ride back to the ship quiet, the only noise the patter of light rain. As they made their way aboard the *Paradise*, Zorinda feared she'd allowed Carris to assume she'd consented to a personal understanding. The men on watch greeted them, redirecting her minor panic as she returned their goodnights. Carris paused by the companionway stairs leading up to his cabin.

"I asked Rollins to have tea set up in my cabin for our return, and he'll be within hearing distance in his quarters adjacent to my cabin."

Zorinda had to admit she was in no hurry to end the evening though comforted knowing Rollins would be near at hand.

"How thoughtful," she said softly.

Carris's smile sent her heart soaring.

Mr. Rollins met them at Carris's cabin with a formal greeting and a table laden with much more than a pot of tea and cups. As she moved within the space, she wondered once more if she was risking disaster. Carris had been lured to the sea as so many men before him, willing to accept the risks and rewards. She had vowed not to meet the same fate as her mother.

Carris walked over to the small table where Rollins poured tea into china cups, the aroma exotic. The man then fussed over the tiny sandwiches and cakes before deciding all was in order.

Zorinda moved toward the desk littered with Carris's instruments while removing her other glove.

Carris joined her as Rollins quietly slipped out.

"Still dreaming of your own ship?" Carris leaned close as he placed a hand on her shoulder.

A tiny laugh escaped her lips as she reached up and covered his hand. "Perhaps. I was wondering, if time permits, you might instruct Ronnie, Raine, and me on the finer points of celestial navigation. I've touched on the subject, but I know you'd do a much better job than I.

"Not necessarily," Carris said softly, turning her gently until she faced him. She instinctively angled her head, allowing his lips to press perfectly to hers while she threaded her fingers through the hair at his nape. This kiss burned through her, down to the tips of her toes. When they parted, she sighed and gave in to the need to rest her head on his chest.

He lightly stroked her cheek with his knuckles. "You love those children."

"I do. I dread the day they reach their grandfather." Tears burned behind her eyes, but Zorinda refused to shed them. "I've sadly learned we form attachments, and then the person—or persons—slips from our lives."

"Not for us."

If she remained in his arms, she could believe there would be a future for them. She couldn't think clearly, terrified by this consuming emotion. Her breathing unsteady, she turned within the circle of his arms until she faced his bunk, heat assailing her as she contemplated sharing life with the man who held her. She raised her eyes higher, a painting positioned prominently above the headboard. There was something terribly familiar about the scene portraying a ship at anchor in a tropical setting.

She gasped, trembling as realization dawned. Her painting. The last one she'd delivered to Mr. Arnell. The one he'd sold for more than enough to pay for the orphanage windows. How was *Promise of Paradise* hanging on Carris's wall? Could he have ... had Carris stolen the painting from the buyer?

Suspicion and doubt converged, nearly choking her, and she turned back to face him.

"Why is that painting in your cabin?"

Chapter 21

A premonition of disaster choked Carris as though a hangman's noose encircled his neck. Zorinda's tone was more accusatory than questioning, and when she turned within his arms, her face so close to his, her pallor unnerved him. There was no mistaking the mistiness in her eyes, as though she was fighting tears. Several seconds elapsed before he realized he should answer.

"I came across the work in Norfolk displayed in the window of a small art gallery. And is by the same artist who painted your father's ship. Spectacular, I'd say." He prayed she would agree.

"I … I." She fell silent as though gathering her thoughts, quaking within his arms. "Joseph Arnell was the proprietor?"

Zorinda broke his embrace, leaving him chilled and bereft. Her tortured eyes seared his soul, the painting somehow the cause of her distress. "I believe so. Zorinda, what's wrong?"

Tears spilled down her cheeks as she visibly swallowed. "I'm the artist. And I also painted the one in my home."

"But the initials are *R.I.N.*" As soon as Carris spoke, he realized he was the ultimate dullard. Zo-RIN-da. She was the artist. An amazing artist with the rare ability to capture the intricacies of a ship with amazing detail. "You should have told me. Why initials? Why didn't you use your last name?"

"Because no one would ever purchase art painted by a woman and a social outcast." Her eyes burned brightly through her tears while her posture stiffened.

"What are you trying to tell me?"

"I told you Banker Sharp denied me access to Papa's funds when I refused to have him declared dead. I've taken several of my paintings to Mr. Arnell for nearly two years to sell, and when sold, I donate the additional income to the Female Orphanage and other charities." She paused, drawing a deep breath while wiping the moisture from her eyes. "This painting was my most recent one. Before I left, Mr. Arnell gave me the funds from the sale, which I delivered to the orphanage."

Zorinda's eyes suddenly widened, the red flush of anger suffusing her neck. She seemed to have realized something which filled her with righteous indignation. "All the ships in port bound for San Francisco," she said. Her eyes narrowed suspiciously as she pressed her hand to her throat.

What on earth was wrong?

"Are you the captain the Darrow brothers paid to deliver the mission society's supplies?" Her abrupt conversational shift disconcerted.

"I … I am."

Zorinda's eyes burned.

He nearly stepped back until he reminded himself he'd done nothing wrong.

"Why would you charge to take those items? I visited Mr. Darrow to discuss funding for the orphanage windows, and he told me he'd used all available mission reserves to ship those supplies. Money paid to you."

Carris remained silent, absorbing her words. She deserved an explanation. But how did he make her understand? "Darrow did pay me a partial sum. I believed he was compensating me with his company's funds. He made no mention of mission money. But my purchase of your painting enabled you to aid the orphanage. Matters worked out."

Zorinda fisted her hands.

Carris nearly groaned. If he'd been tied to a stake, he would have felt the flames lapping about his legs.

"Those boxes and crates are filled with items intended for mining families and a charity in San Francisco. They couldn't have taken up much space in the hold."

Though her words carried truth, he bristled. "Zorinda, I own a merchant fleet—not only the *Paradise*. I have a duty to make a profit for the company and pay salaries. The Darrow brothers understood and were not offended by the financial arrangement."

"You are a cold, calculating, heartless soul. How much would you have lost by agreeing to carry the supplies gratis? Then the mission funds could have been used locally in Norfolk, not only for the orphanage, but for those not so blessed as to own a merchant fleet."

"I didn't know they were mission funds. I'm not your enemy. Or the orphanage's enemy."

"You are the horrible man the children ran from. You've no thought for anyone but yourself with no tolerance of inconvenience. I understand why Lance cut ties with you. If I were him, I would never want to see you again."

Zorinda's words drove a knife into his heart. But the pain produced anger.

"You have no idea what my brother is capable of."

"I doubt he's done worse than you."

"He's a lying, self-centered scoundrel."

"You should recognize those traits."

Zorinda's words stung. His tongue sharpened when he should have remained silent. "And you, hiding from your life in a town faulting you for being different, dare point out my shortcomings?" His heart twisted, but he was committed to this disastrous turn in the conversation.

"You count the days until the children are delivered to a stranger. You only agreed to take me on this voyage to keep the children out of your way."

"You're wrong." Carris knew his tone was intentionally savage and intimidating. He'd not tolerate another word from her until she listened to reason. He took hold of her arms, drawing her against him.

Her eyes widened. Her lips parted. "Then why did you change your mind?"

Her demand shredded his last thread of composure. "I couldn't let you go."

She blinked in confusion, new tears slipping along her jaw. "What?"

"The other ship in Hampton—I couldn't let you sail not knowing how you would fare. Fearful someone might avail themselves of your company and claim something I so desperately wanted."

Zorinda gasped, horror etched in her eyes. "What could you have possibly wanted from me?"

Dear God, I know what she's thinking—not what I meant.

"Did you think I would willingly give you what Wil asked of me?"

"No, Zorinda. Never."

"Then explain yourself."

Somewhere deep inside him, the truth roared for release. He loved her. But her accusatory glare, the angry tension in her arms, silenced his tongue. "I've nothing to explain. Whatever you're thinking, you're wrong. You're searching for a man most likely dead. Don't condemn me for conducting legitimate business when you're wasting your time. And mine."

"Forgive me for wasting *your* time." Zorinda retorted sarcastically, her tears now slowing.

How, at this moment, while everything was crashing down, he was consumed by her heart-stopping beauty?

"You knew I planned to search for my father. But you also knew I would see to the children's welfare, something you sorely neglected. This was nothing more than one of your advantageous business arrangements."

"Take the painting." Carris released her. With forceful strides, he reached the gallery, grasped the painting and ripped downward leaving a splintery hole in the polished wood. "This means nothing to me." He held the painting out to her.

A ragged cry escaped Zorinda's lips.

"Sell the thing again and give those funds to the orphanage. For some reason, the place holds an irrational significance for you." The stricken look on her face tore at his heart making him wish he could swallow all the words he'd so scathingly uttered.

"The Female Orphanage was the only institution educating children of mixed blood. Papa spoke to the directress, and she granted special permission allowing me to study with the girls who lived there."

Carris's gut clenched, and he thought he might lose his meal. How could anyone be so cruel to a beautiful and intelligent child? And how cruel was he forcing her to relive painful memories? He was the worst cad alive.

"I was welcomed and encouraged in that orphanage for which you have so little regard."

"Zorinda, I'm sorry. I had no idea."

Pressing her hand to her lips, Zorinda turned and fled, the door slamming behind her after her departure.

Carris stood, shaking with anger and bewilderment. And guilt. *Lord, please help me fix this.*

The side door slowly opened, and Rollins stood there, his expression sympathetic.

Carris couldn't bear any more. "I've no further need of you this evening, Rollins." Carris tossed the painting on his bed.

Rollins nodded. Walking solemnly to the door, he paused before leaving. "Sir, if I may give voice to an observation?"

Carris looked over at his steward and nodded. Reluctantly.

"There comes a time in every man's life when he has to look at his priorities. Will it be business and the accumulation of the material? Or will it be cultivating familial ties and bonds lasting beyond one's existence on earth. Trewellyn Shipping, this ship—all your ships, your success—vanishes in but a wink. Love remains with you for eternity. Good night, sir."

The wise steward had spoken words guaranteeing Carris's night would be anything but good.

Once within the bolted door of her cabin, Zorinda dropped on her bunk and sobbed into her pillow. The tears flowed, and she made no effort to stop them. She wasn't sure how long she cried but finally spent, she pushed herself up and looked around. There was the barely begun portrait of the twins, the partially finished painting of Havana's Morro

Castle, and several sketches of Carris, one of which she'd planned to transfer to canvas. And resting on the small desk was a box she hadn't noticed earlier. A teakwood box, the lid inlaid with ivory looking suspiciously like the one she'd lost.

Coming to her feet, she walked to the desk and ran her hands along the satiny top afraid to look inside. Summoning the courage, she managed to lift the clasp and pushed up the lid, confirming new tubes of paint and brushes within. A note rested inside the lid. With shaking fingers, she broke Carris's identifying seal and unfolded the fine vellum.

> I know the children are earning money to replace your lost items, but in view of the fact such might take a while, I took the liberty of replacing your paints. The children will continue with their duties until they've paid me back. Now you can resume painting and gift us all with your exceptional talent. Yours affectionately, Carris.

She turned away from the generous gift, her heart shattered. How could she even consider keeping this? She couldn't stay on the ship. As much as she hated to leave Raine and Ronnie, she had to return home. Her dreams had dropped into the deepest part of the ocean. And Carris was right. Her father was dead. In Norfolk, she would face Wil and any others who wished to disparage her. Those trials would be less painful than having her heart broken by a man whose only concerns were his ships and money. A man who wanted her as Wil wanted her?

Zorinda looked around locating her empty trunks. She could pack quickly and have her things removed before the children awoke. Captain Wells of the *Falcon's Wing* had promised to aid her if she should need anything. Surely, he could direct her to a northbound ship. But first, she needed to write a letter to the twins. She wanted them to know she would always be with them in heart and memory. Then why did she feel as though she was abandoning them?

Carris fell into a fitful sleep punctuated by nightmares. He was running through fog calling for Zorinda, unable to find her. Then a ship appeared in the mist—not the *Paradise*—and there was no one on board. A shrouded figure emerged. When Carris neared the ship's bow, he realized another person was with the unrecognizable figure. The cloaking shadows dispersed revealing Zorinda, the cold glint of a blade pressed to her slender neck.

Terror clutched his heart, forcing his eyes open, his breathing ragged. Dawn was at hand, which meant he should already be on deck. Throwing off the coverlet, Carris hastily performed his ablutions, dressed, and presented himself in record time. If he threw himself into his work, he couldn't think about Zorinda or her accusations of heartless greed. And immoral intentions.

To his surprise, Doherty and Sanders were walking up the gangplank. Had they been out all night? If there were spirits on their breath, he had half a mind to ... "Where have you been?" Carris bellowed.

Panic spread over each man's face.

"They were assisting Miss Wemblish, sir." Cavenley spoke from somewhere behind him. Carris wheeled about to face his first officer.

"What do you mean?" A hard knot lodged near his heart as he awaited the man's words.

"She asked for help transporting her trunks to the *Falcon's Wing*. I believe her intent is to find a ship sailing north so she can return to Norfolk." Cavenley's expression conveyed condemnation.

Breathing nearly ceased, and Carris knew his heart had broken. He couldn't speak or move. His head pounded. The woman who had become as one with his soul had left. The paralyzing sensation threatened to cripple his control. His arms ached with the memory of holding her—the remnants of her warmth rekindled to torture him. Images of Zorinda flashed relentlessly—her kisses, her touch, her beauty, which transcended the physical. He suddenly realized Cavenley awaited his response.

"Why of all the ridiculous, irrational things she could have considered did she do something so foolish?" Carris's voice cracked. He mustn't show emotion. He had to right his exploding world.

"Miss Wemblish says she's no longer needed and wishes to return home. She said you would understand. She left a note for the twins."

But not for me?

She'd left. All because he'd agreed to carry missionary supplies for a reasonable fee. When had earning a living become a sin?

For what is a man profited, if he should gain the whole world, and lose his own soul? The words from Matthew struck powerfully. Carris's head resumed throbbing at the enormity of his loss. He couldn't let Zorinda leave. He had to convince her to return, if not for his sake, for the twins. And his dream haunted him. What if she unknowingly placed herself in danger?

"Where can I find the *Falcon's Wing*?"

Doherty replied. "She's a streamlined clipper, some distance from here, at a berth near Sugar Loaf and flying the French flag. The ship is sailing sometime this morning according to Jep." Sanders nodded his head in confirmation.

"And this captain is going to find her passage on a ship north?"

"Aye, sir," Sanders answered. "One returning to or near Virginia."

Carris knew what he had to do. Her departure was not an option.

"Sir," Cavenley said, "If you are hoping to speak with her, now might be a good time to do so."

"Cavenley, you're in charge until I return."

"Of course, sir. Are you taking someone with you?"

"No. I've caused this. I'll resolve the matter. Carry on."

Carris raced down the gangplank and set off at a run toward Sugar Loaf Mountain. Desperation mounted beneath his breast. The *Falcon's Wing*—a very British name for a French ship—could not take the woman who'd restored his hope.

The ship—the name of little consequence at the moment—came into view. Though breathing was painful, he ran faster.

Chapter 22

"The *Blue Dolphin* is bound for Baltimore."

Zorinda watched Captain Wells stroke his beard, surveying the deck activity on the *Falcon's Wing*.

The ship would leave within the hour, and she knew the man had many issues claiming his attention. Even so, he'd agreed to help her.

"She's out in the harbor," he said. "I'll pen a letter to the captain explaining your situation, and I can have two of my men row you there."

"Thank you so much. I had no idea how to find a ship traveling north." Zorinda allowed herself to draw a steadying breath.

"I can't help but wonder why you've suddenly decided to end your voyage. Your charges seemed most fond of you. I hope they haven't taken to putting frogs in your bed or spiders in your garments."

"Nothing of the kind. Their uncle and I had a disagreement. He'd be much happier replacing me." Zorinda hoped her distress didn't show on her face.

"Um ... unlikely. But I must express some worry on behalf of the children."

His serious expression alarmed her. "The captain will see to their welfare. I know Car ... Captain Trewellyn will do everything in his power to keep them safe."

"Perhaps." Captain Wells wrestled with ... what? Disapproval over her desertion of the twins? Unexpectedly, his countenance brightened. "But where will he find another so accomplished as you?"

The captain's trademark insouciance had returned, yet he held himself stiffly, his eyes roving over the nearby mountain, not far from where the *Paradise* berthed. The crew studied her intently, their brazen looks making her skin crawl and stomach clench. Captain Wells's crew in no way resembled the *Paradise's* attentive, orderly seamen. And none gave her a cheery smile or pleasant greeting. Maybe she'd overreacted.

Of course, she'd overreacted.

Zorinda had refused to hear Carris's side. She'd been too busy detailing his shortcomings. Telling him why he'd acted as he had. Accusing him of lewd intentions. Practically blaming him for the fact she'd been forced to attend school with the orphan girls. A sob threatened, but she managed a quivery smile. "He'll find someone more suitable."

Before Captain Wells could reply, one of the sailors rushed over to him, whispering something in his ear. Captain Wells frowned, then turned to her, replacing the frown with a tight smile. Had something happened? "If you'll excuse me, Miss Wemblish. A matter requires my attention, but I won't be long."

Zorinda nodded, watching Captain Wells stride fiercely across the deck, taking the companionway most likely leading to his personal quarters. Ill at ease and aware of the unwelcome notice, she drifted to the starboard side and looked down at the dock teeming with activity. The men seemed to increase their pace as the sun slipped into view in the east. She was about to turn away when she heard her name. Leaning over for a better look, her heart pounded when she recognized Carris.

Frantic, she turned away. Had he come for her? She shouldn't have been so condemning and accusatory. Rather than let him explain, she'd concentrated on her own hurt. Zorinda turned back and waved frantically. "Carris, Carris!"

He turned. He saw her. He ran toward the gangplank.

"I'm going to tell Captain Wells I've changed my mind. Stay there." Zorinda didn't wait to see if Carris complied. She would find Captain Wells and let him know she was returning to the children. Surely, he would understand.

Hoisting her skirts and petticoats, she headed in the direction Captain Wells had taken. Passing through the hooded opening, she rushed through the narrow space until she reached what looked impressive enough to be the door to the captain's cabin. Hesitating, she prayed Captain Wells would be on the other side. She raised her hand to knock when harsh, angry words from within the cabin assaulted her ears.

"If he discovers what you're about, he'll kill you," said an unknown male.

"Something you and the crew are paid royally to prevent. My delivery of the opium will guarantee his welcome." She recognized Captain Wells's voice.

"I'm not so sure. If he suspects a double cross—"

"I don't need your warnings," the captain snapped. Sounds of his pacing heightened her alarm. "Is your source reliable?"

"He's known to have certain connections. I'm not sure—"

"This isn't the time to be unsure!" Captain Wells thundered so loudly Zorinda was certain the ship shook.

"This has to work. I won't allow anything to compromise the plan. There aren't any second chances for me. Either I pull this off, or my head will be delivered to Yizhu. You're spouting hearsay. I won't—"

An uproar on the stairs drowned out the rest of Captain Wells's comments. Zorinda looked up to see Carris striding toward her while several seamen attempted to subdue him.

The door to Wells's cabin flew open forcing Zorinda to jump back. In the process, she stepped on her hem, tripped and ingloriously fell on her bottom. She struggled to her feet only to see Captain Wells and Carris, eye to eye, staring at each other as though facing an apparition. The conversation she'd overheard reminded Zorinda she, and now Carris, were in danger. The *Falcon's Wing* was the ship transporting opium—a source of deadly contention between England and China and frowned upon by the United States and several other countries.

"What a surprise." Captain Wells's sarcasm broke the unnerving silence.

"I'd say so." Carris's voice was clipped. Terse.

Zorinda inched closer to Carris and clasped his arm.

"Captain Trewellyn, might we speak on deck?"

Carris looked over at her as though he'd suddenly recalled she was there.

"We should probably return to the *Paradise*. *Now*," Zorinda urged.

"Miss Wemblish," Captain Wells said, his eyes radiating fury. "You haven't changed your mind because you eavesdropped outside my cabin?"

Dear God, Captain Wells knows. He's certain to kill us. This is my fault. What will the children do if they lose Carris? Please help ... please help. "What do you mean?" Zorinda tightened her hold on Carris.

Captain Wells advanced. Gone was the silver-tongued Lothario she'd met in the park. "You understand perfectly. You surely possess a modicum of intelligence, or my brother wouldn't have taken you to his bed. Though he did make an exception for Ivy. Much to his sorrow."

Carris's arm tensed beneath her grip. When she looked at him, his jaw twitched. Who was Ivy? Why did Captain Wells assume she was—heaven help her—Carris's mistress? Why did the captain call Carris his brother? How could ...?

"Lance Trewellyn?" Her words echoed in the narrow space.

Carris broke her hold and lunged at his brother—ramming his fist into the man's midsection.

Wells—Lance—groaned and sank to his knees, but five men surrounded Carris, forcing him down with battering blows then wrenched his arms behind his back.

Zorinda cried in protest, unable to reach Carris. A cut on his temple bled and drops splattered the collar of his white shirt. Never had she seen such looks of hatred pass between two men.

Lance regained his feet, wrapped his arm around his middle, and snarled at Carris.

"The *Falcon's Wing* has acquired two passengers. Both of you are sailing with me. And Miss Wemblish, for your information, I'm not bound for San Francisco. I'm headed to Bora Bora and the home of my father-in-law."

Carris lumbered to his feet with a savage yell, hurling himself at his brother. Both men went down, but the man who'd been speaking with Lance earlier freed his pistol, slamming Carris's already bleeding temple. Carris released Lance and dropped to the floor.

Zorinda rushed over and knelt beside him, his face chalky, his eyes closed.

Looking up at Lance, words tumbled free. "How could you do this to your brother? If you keep him a prisoner, who will watch over the twi ... your children? How can you be so cruel?"

"No more so than he," Lance uttered gruffly. "Take him to the hold." He looked directly at Zorinda. "Put her in the storage cabin. And be sure to bolt the door."

When Carris regained consciousness, he was sprawled atop a layer of moldy straw. Skitterings and squeaks in the darkness told him he wasn't alone. His temple throbbed, and when he managed to lift an uncooperative arm, his fingers encountered what he was certain was dried blood from the blow he'd received. The motion of his prison indicated the ship was under sail, which meant ... his bellow of rage drowned out the noise of his disease-carrying cell mates.

Carris nearly lost his balance when he lurched to his feet, grasping a splintery beam to remain steady. Nausea threatened to send him back to his knees. His head swam and his gut roiled. Fighting the sensation, he managed to steady his breathing.

Of all the men in the world Zorinda could have sought for help, how did she pick Lance? From what he recalled, she hadn't known the *Falcon's* captain was Lance—she'd been as shocked as he. He hadn't recognized his half-brother at first, hiding behind a beard with hair much longer than Carris had ever seen on him. This was beyond the realm of possibility.

Carris took a step, then another, eventually crossing the dim space to the door. When he grasped the latch, he realized the door was bolted from the outside. Rancid odors surrounded him without so much as a hint of pure air. Throwing his shoulder against the oak door, he gained a burning bruise and but a minor rattle of the thick, impenetrable slab. If he was given to bouts of profanity, this might be the time to employee those words. Instead, he sank down, draping his arms over his bent knees, his head hanging. He had no one to blame but himself. He'd alienated Lance years ago. And Zorinda would never have left had he been honest with her. The twins—they'd borne the brunt of his ill-temper during the crossing from France to America. His fury over Lance's irresponsibility had made him unreasonable and gruff. What a blessing they'd run away and found Zorinda—for God had surely placed her in their path.

Lord, I have no idea what Lance has done, but he was furious Zorinda had listened outside his door. Please spare her—help me to get her to safety. Watch over the children. Please, God.

"Carris?"

A familiar, feminine voice whispered his name, and he stood, relieved the world had stopped spinning, relieved Zorinda was well. Making his way to the door, he leaned close, pressing his ear to the wood. He rasped her name. "Zorinda?"

No answer, but there was a harsh grating as the bolt was maneuvered. Carris moved back when the door swung open.

Zorinda stood there, looking like an angel in a mussed gown, her hair loosened from the usual tidy coils and braids. Fear and uncertainty widened her eyes.

A man loomed over Zorinda, pushing her aside. "Come on—the captain wants a word with you both. Now."

The rough voice turned Carris's attention to Zorinda's companion. He recognized him as the man who'd been with Lance when he'd entered Lance's cabin. Now Carris had the time to take a good look. There was something familiar about him.

"Rafe? Rafe Henderson?"

The man scowled then surprised him by grinning.

"Aye. And dratted awkward to be angry with the man who taught me everything about sailing. Welcome aboard, Carris."

"Welcome? Why did you hit me with your pistol?"

"I didn't have much choice. Either I interfered or watch the two of you kill each other."

"What has Lance involved you in now?"

"Not for me to say. Let's go." Steel laced Henderson's tone, and Carris was in no position to protest.

Reluctantly, Carris stepped through the open door. Henderson, once his brother's childhood playmate and best friend—the son of the Trewellyn's cook—preceded them as they made their way out of the bowels of the ship.

Zorinda failed to hide a sniff—had she been crying?

Carris ached to comfort her. If he'd had the sense to contain his pride-induced rage last evening, neither of them would be standing here. They were at the mercy of his brother, and eventually Montagne, both involved in some twisted scheme. Zorinda's steps had slowed, allowing the distance between them and Henderson to increase.

"Your brother is transporting opium," Zorinda whispered as though reading his mind.

Carris forced back a groan. *Of all the idiotic, dangerous, immoral things Lance could do, he had to pick opium smuggling? Bad enough he deserted Amalie and the children. Now, he's going to be hunted by the Chinese. Lance, you'd better start praying.*

They covered the remaining distance in silence until they reached Lance's cabin. After they entered, Lance remained seated at his desk examining paperwork and ignoring them until Henderson departed and closed the door behind him. Lance looked up. "Sit."

Two chairs were positioned before his desk, a much more elaborate one than Carris's. Zorinda complied, but Carris remained standing.

Lance met his glare. "I said sit."

"I'll stand."

Lance shrugged indifferently. "You've a nasty cut. Have Henderson take a look. He serves as the ship's surgeon. And doesn't butcher too many men."

"The only items I recall him capable of butchering were hogs. For his mother to roast for our table."

"He's picked up a few skills since then."

A corner of Lance's mouth quirked, but his humor was lost on Carris. In fact, Carris's blood boiled.

Lance rose from his seat and paced, his hands thrust in his pockets. "The two of you are a problem. Miss Wemblish—might I call you Zorinda?" He didn't wait for an answer before continuing. "I regret this situation, but your curiosity forced me to withdraw my offer of help. As for you, Carris"—Lance turned and faced him—"as usual, you've intruded where you weren't needed. Hence, your presence on the *Falcon's Wing.*"

"Have you any idea what you've done?" Carris demanded. "Your children are on my ship with no guardian."

"Is your concern for them, or are you worried your lucrative cargo won't reach San Francisco?" Lance's tone was icy and soulless.

"Your children are my concern because of you." Carris clenched his fists at his side certain he would attempt to wipe the smugness from Lance's face. Common sense prevailed. "Why don't you tell me about the *cargo* on this ship?"

"I'm not discussing my cargo."

"I already know." Carris's common sense snapped. "Who lured you into this?"

Lance shook his head and laughed humorlessly. "A man with a great deal of money. Rather like the businessmen who keep you in fine clothes and enable your various pleasures." Lance's eyes cut salaciously to Zorinda.

Fury heated Carris's veins, but he knew he'd never come out the winner if he rushed Lance.

"If you must know ..." Lance looked at Carris. "... Montagne. And don't insult me by thinking I'm planning a cordial visit to my father-in-law. He's become something of an intermediary in the opium trade. Montagne takes delivery of the opium, then is sufficiently reimbursed to deliver to those willing to take the risk."

Several seconds of absolute silence consumed the cabin as the implications of Lance's revelation sank in. Zorinda covered her mouth with shaking hands. Carris had never known such hate and rage. Imaginary flames licked mercilessly, threatening to consume him.

Lance ignored him as he continued, unconcerned his words had flipped the world upside down. "I had you brought here in order to share my expectations regarding your conduct until I'm able to rid myself of both of you." Lance paused then pointed a finger at Zorinda. "You will refrain from telling me or my men what we should or shouldn't do. Any demands you make on behalf of my brother"—Lance's green glare encompassed Carris—"will fall on deaf ears. I only relented to his release from the hold because my men were tired of your condemnations of their character. My third mate didn't appreciate the black eye you gave him when you hit him with the lamp in your quarters."

Carris wanted to laugh. His Zorinda was feisty. *His Zorinda? I've no right to lay claim to her after making her think the worst of me.*

"You knew I would try to help Carris. You can't do this."

Lance glared.

Biting her lip, Zorinda clasped her hands in her lap.

"Would you care to join him in the hold?"

"What insanity do you intend?" Carris demanded, angered by Lance's bullying. "You're going to end up dead."

"Which would be fine with you. I see you're wearing the ring Father gave me."

"Which you lost gambling in Madagascar." Carris wished he hadn't decided to wear his father's ring last night when he'd dined with Zorinda. He should have thrown the ring into the sea. Why keep a token of a man who couldn't gaze upon his firstborn without disdain—as though Carris had caused the death of his two wives. Carris Sr. lived his remaining twelve years bitter and angry.

"It didn't mean anything to you then. Why would you feel differently now?"

"Therein lies the problem, Carris. You're so busy condemning me you've no idea what does or doesn't matter to me. You and Zorinda ..." Lance's attention swiveled to Zorinda.

Carris curled his right hand into a fist. *I will thrash him if he so much as lays a hand on her.*

"Are uninvited guests. If either of you give me or my men any trouble, I will tie you up and secure you in the hold. Carris, you already know how unpleasant the place is."

Carris gritted his teeth to keep from saying something to make matters worse for Zorinda. As for himself, he hardly cared about Lance's threats. His younger brother had finally stooped lower than Carris had imagined possible.

"Let Zorinda return to the *Paradise*. The children need her."

"No."

Lance lowered his eyes while pretending to study his desk. He swallowed noticeably before looking at him. "Rafe will show you to the new quarters Zorinda insisted were your due as she believes the hold beneath your esteemed status. We're done here."

His arrogant dismissal fueled Carris's simmering rage. A few short, angry strides brought him up to his brother. Flattening his palms on the desk, he leaned close.

"If anything happens to Zorinda—"

Lance's brows lifted. "Have you actually fallen in love? I never thought I'd see the day." Lance snorted in derision. "When Ivy left you for Mayes, you swore you'd never bother with another woman. What a shame when your best friend steals your fiancée out from under your nose."

Carris beat down his consuming fury before responding. "I've warned you." Carris looked over at Zorinda, his gut clenching at the look in her eyes.

"I've warned you as well. Get out."

Carris wanted to smash his fist in Lance's face but took Zorinda's hand instead, hoping to convey assurance.

She immediately pulled free.

His heart ached. She still believed he'd planned to ill-use her.

"Henderson!" At Lance's bellow, the door opened, and the first mate entered. "Take a look at Carris's cut."

As Rafe Henderson shoved Carris from the cabin with Zorinda behind them, Carris silently vowed, with God's help, he would find a way to keep Lance from making the worst mistake of his life.

Chapter 23

Agony had been Zorinda's constant companion in the two weeks since Lance Trewellyn had summoned her and Carris to his cabin. Lance, transporting opium to François Montagne, was risking everything, including the safety of his children—for what? Had he no qualms engaging in treachery and human suffering? No reason or excuse could justify Lance's reprehensible actions. Although Carris had been removed from the ship's hold, she feared for his wellbeing. She'd been allowed free access to the upper decks though restricted to short visits. But she hadn't seen Carris since their imprisonment on the *Falcon*.

Her part in the cataclysmic disaster kept her awake at night, and rather than toss and turn, she'd resumed painting, using the lovely carved box of paints Carris had given her. Though furious with him, she'd packed his gift with her belongings, unable to ignore his gesture. What a blessing she had, for painting helped her endure the living nightmare she'd created. And having been moved to a cabin with a small porthole, when opened, allowed the chemical smell of her paints and cleaners to escape. Zorinda tried to defend her anger with Carris in Rio de Janeiro. Her parents had encouraged her to be generous and giving, and she'd always assumed others would be willing to share of their blessings. She reasoned Carris should have transported the mission supplies without charge. But how would her father's income have suffered if he'd shipped cargo for free? There had to be a balance somehow.

Zorinda pushed aside the tasteless porridge delivered earlier to her cabin prison and decided to visit the main deck. She saw Lance, his first mate, Henderson, and several others huddled near the poop deck. And Carris—*Thank you, Lord*—sitting on a crate, one booted foot propped on the ship's rail, his hands bound before him. Zorinda hadn't forgotten his unseemly declaration the night of their argument but was so relieved to see him. He looked up at her approach and gave her a tired smile. "The next time you intercede on my behalf, please be certain doing so improves my lot."

Good morning to you, too. "What do you mean?" Zorinda stiffened. *The ungrateful—*

"I'm now sharing tight quarters with the bosun, ship's carpenter, and the malodorous helmsman who hasn't bathed since his twelfth birthday, and he's at least two score and ten."

Her ire drained. "I'm sorry, Carris." She didn't want him to suffer.

"No apology needed. I've been so obsessed with proving myself the worthier son, I've forgotten what's important. Which is my fault, not Lance's." Carris shook his head in defeat.

Zorinda settled beside him and folded her hand over one of his. Why did she have this need to comfort him? "When I saw you on the pier, I had already decided to return to the *Paradise*."

Carris's brows lowered.

"I went in search of Lance—Wells—to tell him, which is how I came to be outside his cabin when I overheard." Pausing, she drew a deep breath. "I don't believe the hard, determined exterior you show the world is truly what's inside you. You have a need to rescue." She recalled Rollins's story and how Carris had saved Bristow from the sea. "To rescue not only me, but others who've been hurt, or lost, or seeking something they may not realize. What you said to me in your cabin—all I could think of was Wil."

"I'm not Goodwell."

"I've been unfair," she whispered. "The Bible admonishes us to let God judge. And I've been wrong—about so many things."

"Your friendship has been a blessing."

Zorinda absorbed Carris's words silently, the wind and the undulating crash of the waves filling the air. They were kind words, but not heart-fluttering. She almost felt foolish assuming Carris harbored indecent intentions. She looked around her noting Lance's ship lacked the grace and beauty of the *Paradise*. Was the *Paradise* still in Rio, or had Den Cavenley sailed in pursuit? If he had, she feared for the safety of the crew and the twins. Lance had endangered his children and many others.

"When were you pledged to Ivy?" Zorinda removed her hand from his. At first she wondered if Carris had heard her softly spoken question. But the tic in his scared jaw told her he had.

"Nearly fifteen years ago. She was the daughter of the local doctor in our shire. Pretty and congenial and seemingly fond of me."

Zorinda swallowed a lump. She feared she wasn't anything like Ivy.

"I fancied myself in love with her. Not long after our betrothal, I was captaining one of my father's ships. During my absence, my best friend, and son of an earl, showered Ivy with attention and affection. Needless to say, the engagement ended when the lure of a titled, land-bound beau negated our commitment."

"How cruel."

Carris shook his head. "My pride was wounded. When I look back, I know I was far too content when at sea. When one truly loves, separation is agonizing."

"I believe my mother died from missing my father. Not from the fever the doctor diagnosed. If I could find Papa ..." Tears formed in her eyes, and she turned her face aside, wiping at the moisture with the tip of her index finger.

"I pray you do."

"But you said I'm wasting my time." *And yours.*

"If God wills, you'll find him."

"You're right." Zorinda idly smoothed her skirt. "Thank you for the paints. The box is beautiful."

"I may have helped, but they're officially from the twins."

Zorinda dared to look at Carris. "I told myself I should return the gift, but I couldn't. So, I brought the box. I've plenty of time to paint as I've little else to do."

"You could help me improve my French."

"If you insist." Zorinda rubbed her arms. Thick clouds had formed overhead making her wish she'd worn her shawl. "The temperature seems to have dropped since I came on deck."

"As we near the Cape, you'll think winter has arrived."

"Do you believe Mr. Cavenley has the *Paradise* following?"

"Most certainly. Though he hasn't been around the Horn, he knows what he's doing. But the children ..."

"I'm afraid for them, Carris." Zorinda shivered, thinking of what lay ahead, so many things uncertain.

"You should return to your cabin. I can't have you taking sick."

Zorinda stood then looked down at him. "I wish I could change what's happened."

"If you could, then I wouldn't be enjoying this unexpected holiday. I can't remember the last time I was a passenger—albeit against my will—on a ship. No cares, no responsibilities. And sharing a cabin with an assortment of interesting blokes."

Zorinda tried to smile but only managed a grimace. "Carris, if we come through this, what of Raine and Ronnie?"

Carris sighed. "I'm ultimately responsible for their welfare. But there's little to be done as long as I'm Lance's prisoner. The Chinese are certainly hunting him and Montagne."

"Please be careful around Lance."

Carris's brows lifted, but Zorinda quickly turned and walked away, determined he not see her love for him in her eyes. One brother had stolen her heart—the other threatened to break it.

As the days turned into weeks, Carris's prediction became reality, and Zorinda shortened her walks. And fate—perhaps aided by Lance—arranged her walks when Carris was absent. Spending most of her time in her cabin, she painted to ease her guilt and boredom.

With the passage around Cape Horn less than a week away, she prayed the *Falcon*, and the *Paradise*, assuming she followed, would navigate the dangerous route safely. Whenever she looked in her small hand mirror, she saw a stranger. Gone was the Zorinda Wemblish who'd once dreamed of faraway places. Now she saw a woman who'd fallen in love and was about to lose the one man far grander than any imagined paradise. How could she and Carris ever move beyond this disaster? And if harm befell the twins—she couldn't consider such a possibility, or she would fall apart.

As Zorinda stepped out on deck a few days later, having endured another tasteless bowl of porridge, there was no sign of Lance. But Carris stood at the starboard side looking toward the bow of the ship, his hands once again bound before him. Someone must have taken pity on him, for he now wore a change of clothing under his coat. She was happy to see him, but when he turned and looked at her, his eyes were fierce.

Zorinda forced herself forward. "I hadn't seen you in so long I feared something had happened."

The cut to his forehead was nearly healed with no sign of redness. Apparently, Rafe Henderson had taken proper care of his wound.

"Lance shortened my visits on deck fearing I would instigate a mutiny. Not every crewmember is comfortable transporting something the Chinese have banned and the United States has deemed illegal."

"But the British defeated the Chinese in the Opium War."

"An incentive for the Chinese to take matters into their own hands."

"Why is the *Falcon* flying the French flag rather than the British?" Zorinda asked.

"The *Falcon* is likely owned by Montagne, and for the most part, France has remained neutral. Neither the British nor French would be concerned with his activities, allowing Montagne to smuggle to his heart's content. That is where Lance comes in." There was a grim set to Carris's lips.

"If Lance is caught by the Chinese?"

"He'll be at their mercy."

There was no satisfaction in Carris's words. Zorinda knew he didn't want Lance executed, regardless of the differences between them. Pulling her shawl closer, she looked out over the ocean.

"We're about four days from the Horn," Carris said.

Zorinda looked above the sails. "Those clouds look as though they could release snow any second."

"I predict a full-blown blizzard by tomorrow. The sails should be reduced."

"But they aren't going to be. Not yet."

Both of them turned. Lance had slipped up behind them. His steely glare met Carris's.

"In fact, I've given the order to raise them all. The ship will need to reach twenty knots if we're to outrun the ship following us."

"There's a ship?" Zorinda asked. The *Paradise?* She looked at Carris, his expression unreadable. Carris believed Cavenley had the ability to bring the ship around the treacherous Horn though his first time. *God, help Mr. Cavenley* "Not close enough to identify." Lance spoke as though reading her mind, his glare fixed on Carris. "But I'm not taking any chances."

"Why would you endanger your children to punish Carris? Have you no conscience?"

At Zorinda's words, a shutter slipped over Lance's eyes as though blocking any emotion she might stir. "You can thank yourself and Carris for the current situation. But if the ship is the *Paradise*, once we've rounded the Horn, we'll lose them. The *Falcon* will easily outdistance her."

Lance prudently moved on, but Zorinda saw Carris's fists. She knew he would give anything to be rid of the ropes rubbing his wrists raw enabling him to punish Lance physically.

"We put them in God's hands," she whispered. Raising up on her toes, she pressed a kiss to his cold, beard-stubbled jaw.

He looked aside, but she saw a lone tear slide down the side of his nose. As though accepting the inevitability of the unknown, he drew a deep breath, his face still averted. "You believe this is the path God has planned for me? I found Lance, but at what cost?"

Knowing he wasn't ready to hear her answer, she silently walked away. Praying God would heal the inner wounds burning within Carris.

Chapter 24

With instinct born from years at sea, Carris knew trouble brewed for his brother's ship as a washed-out sun rose four days later. Allowed on deck after his meager meal of stale bread and moldy cheese, Carris almost wished he'd remained in the cramped, odiferous cabin. The feverish glaze in many of the sailors' eyes assured him some malady ran rampant through the crew, and had, apparently, affected his brother.

Lance was noticeably pale and unsteady on his feet when he passed Carris without a glance. Voices were hushed. There was more whispering than shouting, unnatural on any ship. Icy flakes swirled, escalating quickly into blinding snow.

Carris prayed Zorinda wouldn't come into contact with the men lest she become ill. As for himself, he'd weathered his share of fevers. Given the deplorable food served to the men, and of which he'd eaten little, Carris had a suspicion they could be suffering from a meal of spoiled meat or fish.

A commotion on the poop deck claimed Carris's attention. From his vantage point on the main deck, he couldn't tell what was happening. Sensing a presence behind him, he turned. Zorinda, clad in a woolen, fur lined cape joined him, shivering, while snow dusted her dark lashes and her outer garment.

"You shouldn't be here," he said.

"Something's wrong with Lance. Henderson told Lance he looked ill, but Lance claimed he was fine. Henderson doesn't look himself, either."

"They may be suffering from a fever or the effects of contaminated food or water. And making the rounds of the crew."

"Do you feel ill?"

"I've eaten very little and limit myself to small sips of water. But you shouldn't get close to anyone. Watch what you eat or drink."

"Aye, Captain." Zorinda managed a half smile then resumed shaking.

"Go below, Zorinda."

She instantly bristled while brushing snow from her lashes. "You should too."

"I'm used to this."

"You're not invincible. I hope Mr. Cavenley, or Mr. Surrell, has made sure the children are warmly dressed. Do you think the ship following is the *Paradise*?"

"Lance was right—no way to be certain." Carris looked up at the leaden heavens. The williwaw winds churned the waves and bobbed the ship as though a toy. If Lance and Rafe were unwell, the second mate, Marlson, would be the one commanding the ship. The young man had admitted to Carris a few days ago this was his first voyage past the Cape. The time had come for Carris to actively involve himself in what was happening. He had no wish to meet his end in the frigid waters. More concerning was Zorinda's safety. "I should have a word with my brother. You go below deck."

A hint of the old challenge darkened her eyes, but she nodded stiffly and headed away. Carris tightened his lips as he made his way across the main deck, taking the steps to the helm. Upon reaching the cluster he believed Lance part of, he noticed several men kneeling. Looking between them, he saw Lance, prone and moaning, his eyes shut.

"What's wrong?" Carris's innate sense of leadership surfaced, but no one uttered a reprimand. Those gathered looked pale around the gills. Especially Rafe Henderson.

"The captain passed out. He's burning up with fever. Every time we try to haul him up, he curses and tells us to leave him be so he can die."

"Cut these ropes."

No one acknowledged Carris's demand. Finally, Rafe nodded at the second mate who quickly complied. With his hands freed, Carris knelt beside Lance, feeling his forehead and checking his pulse. Carris was no doctor, but Lance was gravely ill. "Take him to his cabin before he gets his wish. Now."

Four men lifted Lance who still managed to thrash and writhe.

Carris followed them to his brother's cabin, and after what seemed ages, Lance's frame filled his bunk as he muttered something about the "mission." The opium smuggling?

"Henderson, ask Miss Wemblish to join me."

Rafe nodded, took two steps then stumbled, grabbing the back of a chair as he retched on the floor. Henderson was too sick to go to Zorinda's cabin.

"Captain." The second mate, Marlson, now looked close to fainting. "The helmsman took ill yesterday. I'm not sure what to do. I know you're the captain of a clipper. Do you think ... might you ...? I need help."

A tense silence accompanied by the roar of the mounting wind surrounded all. Carris finally nodded. A sigh of relief filled the cabin. He might have laughed had he not been facing catastrophe.

"Mr. Marlson, find Miss Wemblish and tell her I need her to aid Lance and Henderson." Rafe's groans punctuated his comment. "Then meet me at the helm. The sails have been spliced, tarred and resurfaced?"

"Aye, sir," the curiously scented bosun replied.

"Take down the fair-weather sails. Roll them tightly for stowing below deck. Have all able-bodied men up in the rigging. We've no time to lose before this storm worsens."

The men simply stood and stared. Marlson visibly trembled.

"Move."

They obeyed.

Lance slipped in and out of lucidity while Zorinda sponged his burning forehead. Rafe Henderson moaned and prayed from a pallet on the floor of the wildly pitching ship, still conscious enough to be utterly miserable. Since her summons by Carris, she'd been with the two men, praying God would lead Carris and the crew as they battled the frightening elements. She also prayed for Den Cavenley and the twins and all the men of the *Paradise.*

The wind screamed and howled like a hoard of banshees, and Zorinda wanted to put her hands over her ears, but her nursing duties required she use her hands. Lance continuously muttered as he tossed and turned. His rambling declarations concerning the 'jeopardized mission' mingled with repetitions of the name Amalie, the twins' mother. Had Lance truly loved her?

After endless hours, both men finally drifted to sleep. The lurching and belly flopping plunges told Zorinda the ship was in the throes of a merciless storm. Fear and worry over Carris urged her to action, and Zorinda located Lance's oil-coated rain garments. She struggled into the uncomfortable coat which fell below her knees and rolled-up sleeves dangled inches beyond her fingertips. She left the sick cabin and made her way on deck knowing, when Carris saw her, he'd likely produce the cat-o'-nine-tails the twins had fabricated. But at the moment nothing mattered but seeing him.

Once on deck, Zorinda staggered, her vision blurred, and her senses reeled. Snow and ice coated the ship and rigging as the *Falcon* ploughed fiercely through a blizzard. Visibility was non-existent though Zorinda believed the time to be mid-afternoon.

She slid and careened from one stationary object to the next, praying she'd remain upright. Carris was easy to locate. He stood in the middle of an icy purgatory, bellowing at the top of his lungs and so preoccupied he didn't see her. Stinging snow pelted her, and she knew she should return to the cabin. Yet something kept her where she was. Morbid fascination? A need to see Carris one last time? Hoping to apologize for believing him another Wil? She moved closer to where Carris stood with legs spread, his booted feet braced on the icy deck.

"We're sailing blind," the young second mate, Marlson, yelled at Carris. "But, my calculations say Tierra del Fuego and Cape San Diego lie dead ahead."

"Turn her away from the Cape," Carris ordered. "Close reef the topsails so we can retain control."

Marlson lurched away, while another man headed in an opposite direction. A new group besieged Carris.

Overwhelmed by the enormity and inevitableness of the unfolding tragedy, Zorinda's eyes filled. She was the reason Carris commanded a ship other than his own, Den Cavenley guided the *Paradise* without Carris's expertise, and the feud had resumed between two brothers. Two ships punished beyond the strength of wood, canvas, and rope. Brothers caught in a web of deceit and crippling hatred. Amidst a world frozen and harsh.

A horrific splintering rent the air, piercing the ferocious roar of the wind and waves. Zorinda looked up—the mizzenmast had snapped.

Carris shouted for all to clear as the mast's remaining connection severed. Men scattered with screams of terror as the mast plummeted toward the deck.

Zorinda added her own shrill cry. "Carris!"

A prayer erratically danced in her head as she pleaded to God to spare Carris while she stumbled and slid toward the broken mast and the last place he'd been standing.

Men were already pulling each other from the calamitous tangle. A man staggered away from the debris, dragging an unconscious man. The man upright was Carris. The man he held was Marlson.

Two men grabbed Marlson and hauled him away. The sick and injured men on the ship far exceeded those possessed of their senses and working limbs. Now Carris had lost the second mate. Could she help?

Without another thought, Zorinda skidded toward Carris. A cut near his eye bled but didn't look serious. Upon sighting her, he opened his mouth, but having reached him, Zorinda slapped her hand over his parted lips. "Listen to me. You need me. Half of your crew is incapacitated. There's nothing more I can do for Lance or Rafe. Let me help."

“Captain,” the helmsman said, his colorless face telling Zorinda he was still suffering from the mysterious fever. “We can’t let out any more sail or the remaining masts will come down.”

“Reef the sails,” Carris boomed as though he’d forgotten her. Which was fine. “We’re running close to Staten Island. Leave the topsails as they are. Lower the top gallant and royal yards before we enter the Le Maire. Once in the straight, we’ll have to pray nature cooperates.”

“What if we get caught in the rip tide? We’ll be hurled against the rocks. There’ll be no way to avoid them,” the helmsman cried.

“We pray harder,” was Carris’s clipped response.

Zorinda thought for the briefest second the helmsman was about to tell Carris he was crazy, but he must have realized Carris was the ship’s only hope. Nodding, he disappeared into the driving snow.

Other men surrounded Carris while the ship shuddered and quaked, sinking into valleys between the huge waves then rising as those same waves passed under. Even in the midst of such panic, an unexpected calm flooded Zorinda clearing her mind and firming her resolve. She managed to present herself before Carris once again. He looked at her, opened his mouth as if to rage at her. Closed his mouth. Swallowed.

“Dead reckoning,” he said. His storm-green eyes fastened on hers. He handed her the compass.

She folded her frozen fingers about the instrument with a nod then caught sight of two men—actually boys—attempting to uncoil the leadline. There was no choice but to cross the icy deck, praying she would reach them without taking a tumble. Though struggling with the line of evenly spaced red and white rags denoting fathoms, they stilled at her appearance. Zorinda issued instructions with rapid precision, earning their shrugs and bewildered looks. Fortunately, the lads immediately complied, assuring her they'd present no problem. Zorinda dared to pause to search for Carris finding him surrounded by snow, ice, questioning men, and chaos.

Time stalled. Zorinda's fingers stiffened as she assisted the boys and made notations on a pad held by one of them, her concentration fixed on the compass. Then the call rose from the crow's nest, lifting above the din.

"Cape San Diego! Dead ahead."

Zorinda straightened. Even through the merciless sheet of snow, she was able to make out the formidable mountains hugging the coast. Loud whoops issued from bodies too tired to so much as lift a rope, and she cried out in relief.

"Run up the sails," Carris commanded. "All of them."

"The current's tricky here."

Zorinda couldn't tell who'd spoken.

"The sails—now!" Carris's roar rose above all else.

The sails quickly billowed white and full as the ship shook viciously, suddenly enveloped by an unseen whirlpool. As the ship spun wildly, Zorinda lost her balance and hit the deck hard.

"Pull the ship out!" Another order from Carris to the ill helmsman positioned at the wheel.

Suddenly righting, the *Falcon's Wing* moved out of the tempest, the tide pulling them northward. Zorinda rushed aft, surprised to see the snow abating and improving visibility. Behind them, another ship struggled in the area where they'd nearly lost their battle. The *Paradise?* In the early twilight, could Carris now identify the vessel following?

The entrapping current caught the unknown ship, sending the vessel toward Cape San Diego. Lifted on a wave, she hurled toward the granite outcropping. Zorinda screamed as the wooden sides splintered, the ship breaking in two. Grasping the rail, her cry rose above the wind.

"No. Dear Lord, no. Raine—Ronnie. No-o-o-o!"

Arms folded her close as she buried her face in her hands. The children ... how could this be? If Carris had been on the ship, he'd have steered through the treacherous straight. How could she endure this nightmare? "I wish to God, I could help them. But I have to keep this one afloat. I'm almost certain she's not the *Paradise*."

Zorinda managed to look up at Carris, her head swirling.

"Praise God." Then the swirling dissolved into blackness, and she slipped down ... until Poseidon lifted her in his arms.

Chapter 25

Carris cradled Zorinda against his chest intending to take her to her cabin. Until she grasped the collar of his coat, her eyes fastened on him.

"That wasn't the *Paradise*?"

He nodded. "I'm taking you below, and you're not—"

"Put me down. We have to help them." Zorinda managed to wriggle free of his arms although she still clutched his icy coat as her feet found the deck.

Carris covered her frigid hand with his. "I can't simply turn the ship around and sail back. And the water is too rough for me to send a rescue boat. Their best chance now lies with the *Paradise*."

"What if the *Paradise* isn't following?" Zorinda bit her quavering lower lip.

"Listen to me." Carris clasped her arms. "This is beyond our control. You've convinced me God hears us." Releasing her arms, he cupped her chin and tipped her face, her beautiful, dark eyes crystal rimmed. She needed to understand.

"I'm not going below."

Persistent, infuriating woman. "You're soaked and shivering. If you don't go to your cabin and get out of these things," he plucked at what looked like Lance's coat, "you'll catch winter fever. And I refuse to lose you after all the trouble you've caused me. Do as I ask." Carris could see defiance surfacing in Zorinda's eyes. Then the emotion vanished.

"When I've changed, I'll be back."

Thrusting the compass into his hand, she shot him a fierce look then turned away, walking unsteadily to the stairs to the lower decks. One of Lance's men, having overheard, raised bushy brows.

Carris gripped the compass.

"She be a handful."

Carris sighed shaking his head. An understatement if he'd ever heard one.

Zorinda's eyes snapped open. She gasped, the sort of gasp one makes when they've overslept. She recalled disrobing in the tiny cabin and pulling on woolen undergarments. She'd sat on the bunk and drawn a blanket around her with the intention of resting for a moment. This uneasy sensation suggested she'd rested for much longer than a moment. She tossed the blanket aside and hurriedly dressed, chastising herself for lazing in the cabin. The ship wasn't moving nearly as erratically, and Zorinda prayed the worst was behind. After wrapping a dry cloak about her shoulders, she left the cabin and made her way on deck. Mist swirled, and she could make out snowflakes coiling about the gray tendrils of a frozen dawn. Spotting Carris with the helmsman at the wheel, she headed toward the bridge. Before she reached him, a shout rose above the wind and flap of the sails.

"Cap'n, the Horn! The Horn's been sighted. We're nearly there."

Zorinda rushed forward, forgetting everything but the fact she was about to see Cape Horn. Unexpectedly, a hand fastened on her arm, hauling her back. Carris's eyes met hers, and she wrapped her arms around him, breathless at the unfolding spectacle.

The Cape rose up on the starboard side, its spiked peaks extending hundreds of feet into the air. An albatross soared over the top, winging down and diving close to the water near the monolithic rock encompassed by cloying black clouds. The stiff breeze blew flurries across the deck and through the sails, momentarily obscuring her view. Then unexpectedly, the squall cleared, and the Horn was again visible. Amazement and wonder filled Zorinda witnessing the breathtaking handiwork of the Creator.

Carris hugged her close, his chin resting atop her head.

An aching desire to be treasured by this man overwhelmed her. *I love him, Lord. Is this your will? Or mine?*

I love her, Lord. Please end my agony.

"I hate to shatter this moment of bliss, but I'd like to reclaim my position on this ship."

Carris turned to see Lance supported by two of his men.

Zorinda clutched Carris's arm.

"You're in no condition to command so much as a dinghy," Carris snapped.

"I know you too well, brother," Lance growled, shoving away the supporting hands of the two sailors. "You'll hand me over to the American authorities in San Francisco."

"There's damage enough to keep the *Falcon* from sailing the rest of this day, much less to San Francisco."

"You hope." Lance snorted, then convulsed with coughing.

Carris didn't like the pallor of his brother's face or the brightness of his eyes. He was still sick and bordering on insanity. "What I like doesn't matter. You won't live long enough to see San Francisco, Bora Bora, or anywhere if you don't recover."

"You don't understand. I have to do this. My only choice—" Lance's words were interrupted by racking barks as though his throat was ripping apart.

"Go back to your quarters," Carris said as he released Zorinda and grabbed his brother's coat sleeve.

His brother's fingers curled about his arm with surprising strength.

"There's something you should know," Lance said, struggling to keep his eyes open. He looked close to fainting.

Alarm fanned a flame within Carris, and he broke out in an unnatural sweat.

Lance shut his eyes and swallowed hard, struggling to remain conscious. Finally, with great effort, he opened his eyes.

"I'm working for the Chinese. Got myself into some trouble so I promised to help ... find ... opium smugglers. Montagne ... a man the Chinese want. I promised to bring him to them. I don't want to die, Carris. Help."

Stunned by Lance's words, Carris forgot to keep Lance from hitting the deck. The thud roused Carris from his shock, and he quickly hauled his brother up. With the two men who'd brought Lance from his cabin, he managed to get his brother back to his bed.

Zorinda had followed. Looking up at him, her eyes were wide with fright. "Carris, what did Lance mean?"

"Only God knows."

Carris watched a haggard Lance manage a wobbly turnabout deck two days later, saying little while surveying the damaged mizenmast and top hamper. After asking a few terse questions, he headed back to his cabin but not before asking Carris to join him.

About time, Carris thought as he complied. Since Lance had uttered his cryptic confession, Carris had redefined frustration as the state of being angry and hopeless simultaneously. Now as the confrontation loomed, Carris prayed he could contain his anger and conquer his hopelessness.

After Carris took a seat before Lance, the door opened, and Zorinda entered. At least she looked more like herself, though pale and subdued. He missed the fire snapping in those dark eyes and the lift of her delicate, defiant chin.

Zorinda sat in the battered and marred leather chair next to him, her reddened eyes tugging at Carris. Reluctantly, he looked at Lance, his impulsive, *bon vivant* brother strangely silent. Causing him worry.

Lance steepled his fingers, his eyes lowered. "I'm not proud of my past, which, unfortunately caught up to me several months ago in Canton. I was a free trader, part of a British smuggling ring exporting Indian opium to China. Since the war with England and the monopoly of Matheson and Jardine—"

Carris recognized the names as the two Scotsmen who controlled the opium trade from their headquarters in Hong Kong.

"The Chinese have prioritized ending importation of the drug. In an effort to save my neck." Lance paused and actually ran a hand around his nape, "I gave them the name of a middleman, who happens to be Amalie's father. There's no love lost between me and Montagne, and I jumped at the chance to betray him. Unfortunately, the Chinese government decided I should be the one to capture and bring him to them. Alive. Otherwise, I would be dealt the punishment they planned for Montagne. I'm sure you know what they intend. This ship actually belongs to Montagne—the *Aile de Faucon*—the *Falcon's Wing*. I convinced Montagne to take me on as a partner, promising I'd make sure he was graciously rewarded. I rendezvoused with my British contact in St. George two months ago to accept delivery of the goods. Then continued along the South American coast. Putting me on the same route as yours with no knowledge the *Paradise* was sailing to San Francisco." Lance drew a deep breath. "And I certainly didn't know the children were with you. My Rio encounter with you, Zorinda, was an ironic coincidence."

Carris looked at Zorinda. Lance was the man seen speaking to her in the park. And why she'd had no reason to connect Captain Wells to Lance. If only he'd accompanied her and the children.

"Why seek Montagne or return to Canton?" Zorinda asked.

"Because if I don't, the Chinese will find me. I'm not living my life looking over my shoulder."

"Until a few weeks ago, I didn't know you had a life to live." Carris's comments were intentionally sarcastic. He idly rubbed his thumb over his father's ring.

Lance's eyes fastened on the movement of his thumb. Carris bristled.

"I decided to allow my "death" to circulate. I knew you'd take care of Amalie and the twins. I assume Amalie refused to leave Marseille, but why would she have allowed you to take Raine and Ronnie to her father? She hates him."

"Amalie is dead. The nuns said she died of consumption. Your children were residents of a Catholic orphanage in Marseille. Letters from you to Amalie were found in the flat where they lived, and the local authorities gleaned enough information to locate me."

The silence following Carris's words echoed and throbbed. *Lance—irresponsible, selfish, unconcerned, self-absorbed.* Carris looked at Lance. His brother was stunned.

"But the twins are fine." Count upon Zorinda to find the bright spot in this deplorable situation.

Carris wanted Lance to feel something—remorse—guilt—pain.

"They are intelligent and bright," Zorinda said. "Raine excels in mathematics, and Ronnie wants to be a sailor. And they are natural artists."

"Thank God they have you." Lance's eyes filled with regret.

"What do you want with us?" Carris leaned forward, clasping his hands until they ached.

Lance sighed as he picked up a ruler and tapped the desk's surface. The sound annoyed, but Carris clamped down on his mounting anger.

"I have to reach Bora Bora without delay."

"You plan to arrive on Montagne's doorstep and tell him you're taking him to Canton to be executed? You wouldn't survive five minutes."

"He's expecting my delivery, so my arrival won't be a surprise, only the timing. I told Montagne I'd have a short layover in San Francisco before sailing to the island delaying my arrival about one week. But I've no intention of visiting San Francisco as I might be of undue interest to certain town authorities—some nonsense about shanghaiing and other unpleasantness. There may also be a French naval officer looking for me in connection with a theft."

British captain commanding a French ship. Shanghaied some of Wemblish's men. Carris vividly recalled Witherspoon's words. What if Lance ... n*ot now. Now is not the time. Be patient.* His thought or someone's divine caution? The last thing he wanted to do was alarm Zorinda by asking more questions. Lance was his priority now.

"When you reach Bora Bora, then what?" Zorinda asked.

Carris reached out and grasped her hand, his fingers lacing with hers. Lance frowned at the physical display. Carris wondered if Lance had ever given Amalie any comfort.

"A warship from Canton will rendezvous with the *Falcon* near the island the first full moon after the autumnal equinox. Then we join forces to attack Montagne."

"At his home?" Carris asked.

Lance gave them a humorless grin. "The man hasn't survived this long without protection. Trained guards patrol the grounds and the perimeter of his estate. He even has a prison on his property filled with those who have crossed or threatened him. Many awaiting execution."

"No wonder Amalie ran away." Carris shook his head.

"Poor girl." Zorinda's voice was filled with sadness. "She would have left with any man who offered escape."

"Amalie sought love from the wrong men. Including me. I wasn't meant to be a husband or a father," Lance said. "When I discovered she was with child, I wanted to do the right thing, even though I knew I wouldn't be faithful or settle down. I was never the husband she needed." Lance squeezed the bridge of his nose while shutting his eyes. Gathering his composure, he looked at Carris.

"I'm telling you," Lance captured both of them with his eyes, "I won't allow anything to compromise this voyage. If I have to, I'll imprison the two of you. In all honesty, Carris, I could use your help. Rafe is good, but I know you're the best. Working together, we should make excellent time."

Lance now looked at Zorinda. "I'm sorry I separated you from the children. But I'm keeping my end of this bargain."

"And afterward, what will be different?" Zorinda tugged her hand from Carris's. She stood, glaring down at Lance. "Will you make a home for your children? Will you give up your wanderlust and entanglements and be a father?"

Lance lowered his eyes, a sure sign he was uncomfortable.

Little brother, you'll never change.

"I don't know. I can't change what's happened."

"No, but you can be a father. Stop chasing the impossible. Thank God for the blessing of two beautiful children many childless couples would love to have in their lives. If you will excuse me." Zorinda turned and marched toward the door, quickly letting herself out. Silence slipped around Carris and Lance.

Lance finally spoke. "She would make a good mother. And a fine wife if one can overlook the shrewish tongue."

Carris stood, his turn to look down at his brother. "Yes."

Lance's brows furrowed in uncertainty. "Yes, what?"

"I'll help you make all haste to Bora Bora. But if your mission brings harm to Zorinda, I'll deal with you in ways shocking to the Chinese. And you'd best pray Cavenley gets the *Paradise*, her crew and passengers—your children—to San Francisco. Safely."

Carris strode forcefully across the cabin and entered the companionway, allowing the door to slam behind him.

Aware of where Zorinda had been installed, he made his way to a lower deck and her tiny cabin. As he stood outside the partially open door, he heard what sounded like muffled sobbing. He widened the opening and found Zorinda lying face down in her berth.

At his entrance, she sat up, brushing at her damp cheeks. Carris ignored propriety and sat on the edge of the unyielding bunk, absorbing her shudders as he wrapped his arms around her. She quickly composed herself and managed to speak.

"Raine and Ronnie must be terrified. And we've no choice but to sail with Lance to this monster who destroys people with a terrible drug, which—"

Carris silenced Zorinda with his lips, hers unmoving beneath his. Then suddenly, her arms encircled his neck, and she returned his kiss. The love he'd struggled to contain for weeks eluded caution, the taste of her sweet surrender filling him with breathless wonder. Zorinda's acceptance of him eased his losses and disappointments, reviving his empty soul with her beauty and compassion. As Carris slid his fingers through her hair, he made a tangled mess of her braids and coils, several strands of silken midnight cascading over her shoulders.

His life had begun the first moment he saw her. Life would be unbearable without her. Did she realize what she meant to him? Honor and desire warred within Carris, but sanity prevailed, and he eased his hold. Zorinda pulled back, her beautiful eyes wide with uncertainty. His pulse raced and his thoughts ran riot. Now was the time to tell her. Grasping her hand, he brought it to his lips.

"I was so very wrong," Zorinda said. "I expected God to provide the money for the orphanage according to my plan.

I should have trusted his wisdom much more than my own. I have been unreasonable and censorious and—"

"Why ever would you think so?" Carris asked with gentle teasing, brushing back a wayward tendril of her glossy black hair before running his fingertips over her lips, still soft and rosy from their kiss. Rather than answer, she shut her eyes as though savoring his touch. "I also have many flaws requiring correction," he said. "Perhaps we could work together on improving one another's foibles."

Zorinda's eyes opened. And she smiled, making him want to kiss her again. Then the smile vanished. "When I left the *Paradise*, why did you come for me?"

"Because you are my life. My destiny."

Suddenly, Zorinda claimed his lips, stoking his internal fire. When he reluctantly raised his head, her eyes fixed on his. Now was the time to be honest. "You asked me once what I wanted from you. I wanted ... I want you to be—"

"Am I interrupting?"

Lance stood at the open door.

Zorinda released a tiny cry.

"Not at all, Brother," Carris replied. Would he ever have a chance to tell Zorinda he loved her and wanted to marry her? "Did you need something?"

"I thought Zorinda would enjoy a look at the Southern Lights. The seas have roughened, and there's certain to be more snow. Best come along now before you miss them." Lance looked directly at Zorinda.

"I'll be there shortly. Thank you."

Accepting Zorinda's dismissal, Lance walked on. She looked up at Carris, resting her hand on his bristled jaw, her thumb idly tracing his scar. "Shall we view the Southern Lights?"

"Of course," he said, inwardly aggravated how, once again, his timing was terrible. Or had Lance intentionally ruined his opportunity?

Chapter 26

With the treacherous Horn behind them, the trek northward began. Zorinda battled consuming dread as she prayed for the safety of Raine and Ronnie, the *Paradise*, and crew. But though her heart ached with sadness, Zorinda couldn't deny the insatiable curiosity prodding her on deck, even when Carris cast her frowns. There was a change among the crew as the men now politely greeted her. When weather permitted, she would sketch. And somehow, she always completed at least one drawing of Carris. She was in the process of doing so when Lance came upon her several days after issuing his warning to her and Carris. He looked as hearty as he had before his illness during the rounding of the Horn, as did his first mate and the rest of the crew.

"A picture is indeed worth a thousand words," Lance said. "Only a woman in love with my brother could depict him so attractively."

"Carris is most fine of form." Zorinda remained focused on her subject who was unaware of her close scrutiny and currently in discussion with Mr. Marlson.

"But so am I."

Zorinda looked up at Lance hovering over her shoulder. “I’ll not confirm what you already know. Too many women have done so.”

“You won’t fall prey to my charms, will you, Zorinda? You see into my black heart.”

“Your heart is perfectly red, and you are more than capable of goodness. Look at how well you and Carris are working together.”

“Only because I need him to get as much speed as possible from the ship, given the battering she took. I’m allowing him to put into port at Valparaiso for repairs as I’m tired of his reminders one more storm could sink the girl. Though we’re eager to be rid of one another, neither of us wants to meet our end at the bottom of the Pacific. Our truce is a necessity of survival.”

“Whatever the reason, matters have improved. Now, if you don’t mind—”

“He’ll never settle. The sea’s in his blood. Same with me.”

“I hold no illusions.”

“However, you might be the one woman who could tie him down. He’s obviously in love with you.”

“Even if what you say were true, love alone won’t resolve our differences.”

“Then he’s an idiot. I’ve a mind to toss my hat in the ring. From what I’ve gathered, my children adore you. You’re a fine navigator—don’t look surprised. I know what you did for Carris when I was, um, laid up. And I’ve seen the fire you try to hide.”

Before Zorinda could respond to his outlandish comments, a loud clearing of a throat forced her to look up. Carris stood before them looking most displeased. “Might I have a word with you, Miss Wemblish?” Carris looked over at Lance. “Alone.”

Lance chuckled, then moved on, heading to the spot Carris had recently vacated.

"His pretty words are meaningless."

"I know a rogue when I see one. Have you forgotten Mr. Goodwell?" Flipping her sketch pad closed, she quickly stood in preparation of leaving, but Carris caught her arm.

"I'm sorry, but I ..." He faltered as though hesitant to continue.

"But what?" Zorinda asked, fighting a simmering irritation. "Your brother was goading me, but I put him in his place. I have accepted your kisses, but I can still speak to another man if I so choose. Now, if you'll excuse me." Carris released her, and she stepped back. Yet, something urged her not to leave without settling this ridiculous spat.

"I'm sorry." Carris said.

Her heart raced at his apology, and she took a step closer. Waiting.

"I've lost my direction."

What did he mean? Even though she loved Carris, she would not succumb to vulnerability. Disaster resulted when love was one-sided. Carris was nothing like Wil. But the sea was his life, leaving little room for her. Though disappointed, she placed her hand on his arm, which he covered with his.

"Find your North Star, Carris." Pulling her hand from under his, she turned, quickly crossing the deck. Otherwise, Carris might realize how deeply she loved him.

The layover at Valparaiso was productive, and though patched and jury-rigged in places, Carris was confident the *Falcon's Wing* would reach Bora Bora.

But his conversation with Zorinda days earlier constantly replayed in his mind. Standing at the *Falcon's* helm, he fixed on the gentle swells while a solid breeze pushed the ship at a satisfactory clip. The *Falcon* seemed to fly along the western coast of South America, rapidly closing the distance before veering farther west to the Society Islands.

Releasing one hand, he rubbed his face. His calloused fingers grazed the scar he'd received when he'd first encountered John Rollins ten years ago. Carris hadn't thought of their meeting in years. A young captain, at the time, he and Surrell had come upon Rollins in the grip of three thieves who'd most likely never worked an honest day in their lives.

If only he had the power to protect the two children who had been placed in his care. Daily what-ifs tortured constantly. Cavenley, level-headed, calm in crisis, and a seaman through and through, was one of the few Carris would have trusted to care for the children. If God had brought the *Paradise* around the Horn.

"Mornin', Captain," Marlson said then joined him at the helm. Carris and the man had bonded during the harrowing passage around the Cape. Even though Carris reminded Marlson numerous times he wasn't the captain, Lance's second mate insisted on calling him thus.

"Good morning, Mr. Marlson. The *Falcon's* making good time. The weather should remain favorable today—the sun set red last evening."

"Aye, it did. Maybe the *Falcon* will break her old record of two hundred seventy knots in a day. Might come close to three hundred."

"Not bad," Carris said. "However, the *Paradise* covered three hundred and fifty nautical miles in the run between Boston and Baltimore in one day."

Marlson whistled appreciatively. "Now you're stuck on this slow barge."

"Not much longer." Carris gave the man a half grin. "I wouldn't want to overstay my welcome."

"A bit ago, I overheard Miss Wemblish sayin' nice things about you to the captain."

For a span of seconds Carris wasn't sure he'd heard correctly. "What did Miss Wemblish say?" Carris hoped he sounded mildly curious. And not desperate to know—which he was.

"She said you were very brave when you took the *Falcon* around the Horn. She told Captain Wells, or rather Trewellyn, his little ones are lucky to have you for an uncle."

"Did she?"

"Miss Wemblish said things were kinda hard at first, but then everything turned around. She says you set a fine example."

"I'll have to thank her for her kind words."

"You can right now—there she is." Marlson pointed to the opposite side of the main deck. Zorinda was there, walking with Lance. A crewman hailed Marlson, and the man hurried off, leaving Carris to watch his brother smiling at the woman who meant everything to him.

Was this part of God's indecipherable plan? Having read the Bible more in the weeks before his "abduction" than he had in twenty years, he'd been reminded life often worked out much differently than mortal man anticipated. How could he give God all control and allow him to work his will? Who was he to expect the Father to suddenly gift him the love of a wonderful woman when he'd so long ignored him?

Carris turned away from the sight, tightening his grip on the wheel. With his eyes on the water, he concentrated on the white caps careening haphazardly while salt spray misted his face.

"Good morning."

Carris's heart lurched at Zorinda's voice. She hadn't spoken to him in days.

"Good morning." He stared straight ahead.

"What a beautiful day. Lance says we may make close to three hundred nautical miles."

He silently objected to her casual reference to his brother. She continued.

"And we should reach Bora Bora in a few weeks."

Carris forced himself to turn and look at her, her dark eyes tugging him mercilessly. Unexpectedly, he found himself smiling. One look at her and what seemed insurmountable suddenly resolved.

"I haven't properly thanked you for what you did and how well you did so when we reached the Horn. You were a marvel."

"I did what I could." She paused. "Carris, we've no need to suffer misunderstandings."

Carris's heart leapt then thudded.

She gave him a tentative smile. "I too should have apologized when we last spoke. May I do so now?"

Carris wanted to pull her to him, to tell her he loved her and wanted to marry her, he wanted—glancing up, he saw Lance taking the stairs to the poop deck, watching. Frowning.

"Zorinda, Lance may be falling in love with you."

She laughed—an angel's sweet laugh. "Lance is in love with a challenge. Besides, you're, ah, finely formed." A teasing light danced in her eyes.

"I'm serious, Zorinda."

Her merriment vanished. "You can't be," Zorinda said then looked away, clasping her hands tightly. Drawing an unsteady breath, she continued. "Lance loves his freedom."

"Raine and Ronnie love you, Zorinda." *As do I.*

"Only Raine and Ronnie? Is there anyone else? Someone you were about to mention when Lance interrupted us."

Carris knew she referred to the time in her cabin when he'd tried to tell her he wanted to marry her. Zorinda looked at him hopefully. *Tell her, man.*

Lance descended the steps to the quarterdeck, scowling.

Could his love be enough for Zorinda? Nothing he'd offered Ivy had been enough.

Zorinda's sigh chased his hope into a dark corner. Another chance wasted. Could he explain his sense of inadequacy? "I fear I'm not the man you deserve."

The tightening of her lips sliced his heart.

"Who do I deserve?" Zorinda's voice trembled slightly. "If I've led you to believe I expect a declaration of commitment, I owe you another apology. I appreciate your honesty but am saddened by your inability to speak from the heart. You hide what your brother so easily expresses."

Zorinda moved away before Lance reached them. Taking another set of stairs, she descended to the main deck.

Carris's pain intensified making him wonder if a plunge in the icy water off South America's Cape wouldn't be less painful than what he felt. Lance's smirk didn't help.

Chapter 27

Northwest of Tahiti—Early September

Lance stood on the bridge when Carris joined him, the sun disappearing behind streaks of azure, coral, and gold. Carris was scheduled to relieve Lance at the *Falcon's* wheel for the next watch. Weeks had passed since he'd angered Zorinda with his poorly chosen words, leaving him irascible and easily provoked. If Lance dared say or do anything to ignite his temper, heaven help them both.

"I'm not used to this stoic, long-suffering Carris." Lance fired the first volley, his voice laced with sarcasm. His brother had recovered his pre-fever hostility. "I've also noticed our lovely Zorinda is not her usual self. What could have taken the joy from her smile?"

Carris ground his teeth, refusing to look at Lance. *Lord, let me ignore his goading.* "She is neither yours nor mine."

"So you say." Lance leaned against a post and folded his arms. "I've seen Zorinda's sketches—she seems most fascinated with your, ah, physicality."

"How would you know?" Carris grasped Lance's upper arm, tempted to wipe the provoking look from his face.

With a violent jerk, Lance broke free, his face dark with fury. "Let's lay our cards out, brother," Lance snarled.

"I'm tired of living in your shadow, of being constantly reminded I'll never meet your standards. You have no idea what Amalie's death has done to me. I wasn't there when she needed me. My children were living in an orphanage. But you, the shining knight, went to their rescue. I've made mistakes. But you have, as well." Lance paused, but he was far from finished. "When I happened upon Zorinda on deck the day you wanted to speak with her alone, she'd been sketching a portrait of you. Perfectly capturing your arrogance and self-importance. Yet, revealing her heart. You're an imbecile, Carris."

Carris stepped back from Lance, stunned by his words. Could Lance have actually loved Amalie? Did he love his children? Was there more to him than the selfish, egotistical, favored son Carris had always believed. The fire drained from Carris's veins.

"I'd rather stay here," Lance said. "I don't need the sleep."

The resulting silence stretched between them until Lance spoke again. "When we reach the island, be sure Zorinda stays aboard ship and in her cabin. Once the Chinese contingent arrives, I'm counting on the element of surprise, but there's no way of knowing the number of men Montagne has to protect him. There can be no interference from her."

Voices of the sailors rose and fell, accompanied by the flap of sails, and the muffled rush of the waves as the advancing prow gave no quarter. Several minutes passed. Carris sighed, then walked away.

Zorinda sat in the shadows on deck, the breeze gently fanning her face, the blistering tropical sun having set.

Lance had mentioned earlier they could reach Bora Bora at any time. How could the voyage she'd expected to be the grandest thing she'd ever experienced fallen so far short of her expectations? Granted, she'd seen many of the sights her father had often described and marveled at each and every one. Yet, she ached with disappointment.

The *Falcon's* shanty man struck up a tune, "A Bully Ship and a Bully Crew," and the men joined in. Perhaps their enthusiastic singing was inspired by the proximity of their destination. But Zorinda feared their arrival. She'd lost her opportunity to inquire about her father's visits to San Francisco and Papeete because of Lance's urgent rendezvous with the Chinese. She was no closer to finding her father, and she still worried about the children. Could the *Paradise* be following?

Across the deck, Carris leaned on the rail, looking out over the water, the moonlight outlining his broad shoulders, now slumped. In resignation? After their last conversation she'd shoved aside all idiotic dreams she'd foolishly entertained. Her solace resided in her tiny cabin, her renderings of Carris and drawings from memory of the twins. Now, in what the twins' book had described as paradise, she had no desire to draw islands, or paint aqua waters, or sketch shading palms. She could only draw those she loved—Carris, Raine, and Ronnie.

Enthusiastic *Doodahs* shouted by the singing men grabbed her attention, and after two rousing renditions of the ditty, they finally moved on to another. Zorinda lightly tapped her foot in time with the tune. How would Carris have responded if she'd confessed her love? Had lack of courage held her tongue? Or pride? She'd often heard Uncle Teig say pride could strip one of all peace and should be used sparingly. Her misplaced trust in Wil caused her to doubt herself. She often wished she could relive the night in Rio with Carris when she'd imagined herself a different woman. Sadly, the memory was as ethereal as the mist shrouding the Horn.

"I've ruined everything," she whispered aloud, looking down at her folded hands. One of the lanterns hanging near threw a tall shadow across her lap. She feared Lance was standing there until the voice she loved asked, "May I join you?"

Zorinda nodded, and Carris seated himself on the end of the bench, clasping his knees with his hands—those work-hardened hands with the capacity to soothe her fears.

"We're nearing Bora Bora, and honestly, I don't know what to expect. Lance says we wait until the Chinese arrive. But when they do, you must remain on the ship and in your cabin. Lance is hoping the support of the Chinese force will enable a quick capture of Montagne before those at his estate can mount a defense. The last thing I—and Lance—want is for you to be in danger. Will you promise me?"

Zorinda hesitated, then reluctantly nodded.

"You believe there will be violence?"

"I'm certain. Montagne isn't going to give up without a fight. He knows the Chinese will execute him."

Carris laid his large hand over hers. "When we last spoke, I had convinced myself I would be wrong to bring you into my uncertain world. But I'm selfish, Zorinda. The thought of losing the exquisite, maddening joy you've given me is agonizing. I am hoping—no, I am praying—you have retained some bit of feeling for me. And if not, in time, perhaps, I will be given the chance to rekindle those feelings."

"You hurt me." She knew she was trembling. How could she trust him? Should she trust him?

"I hurt myself because I was once more arranging things to fit my plan. Only you can decide if I could make you happy."

"What do you mean?" There was a slight catch to her voice, which she hoped Carris didn't notice.

He gave no indication he did. He leaned closer to her—

"Land! Land ho!"

They rose simultaneously, and Carris accidentally stepped on her skirt causing Zorinda to fall against him. As she looked up, his gaze intense, she knew her heart had decided. But only God could bring them together for a lifetime.

Lance summoned Carris to his cabin shortly after the cry went up. Henderson, Marlson, and the helmsman were already present. Sensing a strategy session, Carris was surprised his brother included him. He reminded himself to be content with any progress.

"After the Chinese arrive, Montagne mustn't have time to react. Rafe, you and Marlson will surround the residence with most of the men. Griffin, you and five others—your choice—will guard the long boat. Montagne will assume I'm there to fulfill our agreement. Carris, I'd like you to accompany me—you know the language better than I. The Chinese force will secure the perimeter of the plantation."

"I sent a letter to Montagne when I left Marseille with the children," Carris said. He may have received it by now and will know Amalie is dead."

Lance refused to look at him.

"Nothing changes."

"Who'll be left on the ship?" Carris asked even though he concurred Lance shouldn't confront Montagne alone. But Zorinda would be on the ship and in need of protection.

"You can add and subtract the number of men." Lance slipped into the arrogant, annoying side of himself.

Carris bit back the retort on the tip of his tongue. Now was not the time to engage in sibling rivalry. "Let me rephrase," Carris managed civilly. "Who, with authority, will remain on the ship?"

"The third mate and the bosun. They're seasoned seamen. Zorinda will be fine."

Carris looked at Lance, surprised by his brother's reassurance.

"What now?" Rafe asked.

"We stay out of sight and wait," Lance said.

"What if the Chinese don't arrive at the agreed upon time?" Carris asked.

The men looked at him. He'd dared ask the one question no one wanted to voice. Lance hesitated a second. "Then we take Montagne. And we follow the same plan. We move swiftly, the element of surprise on our side. I know where Montagne's residence and property are most heavily protected. Admittedly, the risk heightens. There'll be fewer men with Zorinda."

Carris knew Lance had no other choice, but the part of him loving Zorinda raged in protest. Silence, tense and heavy, consumed the cabin. Rafe broke the pall. "Lance, we've been friends a long time. I can't speak for anyone but me, but I'm with you. If things work out, I'll have a chance to be respectable and make something of myself. I'm tired of running. Most of us are."

"Captain, I'm with you," Marlson said.

The helmsman, Griffin, nodded in agreement.

Lance fixed his eyes on Carris.

"I consider this another one of those times I'm forced to pull you out of a scrap. I'm in."

An unspoken alliance forged.

"Some things never change," Lance said as he stood and made eye contact with each man.

Carris saw a different side of Lance. And something shifted within him.

Slightly before dawn, the *Falcon* anchored near an islet outside of the lagoon, where, when the sun rose, the waters would be a perfect shade of aqua and jade. With the main island before her, Zorinda saw two volcanic mountain peaks towering above clustering palms in the faint light. One of the sailors had identified the highest one as Mt. Otemanu and the other, Mt. Pahia, and both volcanoes were inactive thus eliminating a volcanic eruption from her list of worries.

But Zorinda gave no thought to the tropical beauty as she searched for Carris. She would share her heart knowing there was no guarantee either of them would survive what was to come. The Bible instructed Christians to be brave and of good courage. At the moment, she was a quaking coward. Yet, when she located him on deck, and he looked at her, the fear eased. Shoving aside her gnawing uncertainty and ignoring the others surrounding them, she purposefully strode forward. He advanced, and they met. Halfway. A promising sign? Before she could open her mouth, Carris took her face in his hands and pressed his mouth hard to hers. As she returned his kiss, she tried to convey everything she'd been too insecure to admit. Lance bellowed for Carris, but Carris only deepened his kiss. When the second bellow echoed in her ears, Zorinda turned her face aside. Carris persisted, pressing his lips to her brow.

"Lance is calling," she whispered, resting her hands on his chest. Beneath the thin linen, the heat of him invaded her soul.

"I love you, Zorinda. From the very moment I laid eyes on you on Newton Wharf. Can you ever forgive me?"

"There's nothing to forgive. And I fell in love with you the minute I realized you weren't a Captain Bligh."

"Surely another of your father's tales. I've heard the captain's actions were exaggerated."

Zorinda managed a quivery laugh. "Can you forgive me? Here you are, stripped of your ship and all the others who need you because you rescued me. From my own judgmental self."

Carris shook his head. "I'm here because I feared taking an uncharted course. When the Chinese force arrives, you stay below deck."

"But what if—"

"No matter what," Carris said.

"I might be able to ..."

Carris's frown silenced her.

"I promise." To her surprise and horror, he thrust a revolver into her hand. "What?" She looked up at him in confusion.

"Use this if the need arises. You can stop a man by shooting him in the leg."

"I've never fired a weapon."

"Cock the trigger and fire. There are six charges. Lance won five of these playing poker in San Francisco on his last visit. This is a Colt Walker, supposedly one of the finest handguns in the world."

"Have you fired one?"

"Not yet. Lance gave me this one and another I'll use."

"You might need them both."

"I'll manage."

Leaning forward, he kissed her once more. "You told me to find my North Star. Zorinda, you're my North Star."

Lance's roar filled the air.

"See what he wants," Zorinda said though reeling from his words.

Carris nodded then turned away. She stood, stunned, worried, and panicked. What if Carris was wounded—or worse? Yet gentle, comforting words came to her. *My peace I give unto you ... Let not your heart be troubled, neither let it be afraid.*

"Lord, please protect Carris. Keep him safe. Help us find a future together," she whispered. Looking down at her hand, she silently petitioned she'd not be forced to use the revolver. Suddenly, a shout burst from an unseen sailor high in the rigging. Every man—and herself—looked in the direction another seaman pointed. And her heart nearly beat out of her chest.

By the time Carris noticed the Chinese junk entering the lagoon, there was no time to take the *Falcon* out to sea.

Uniformed men rushed to the starboard side of the three-masted vessel armed with carronades, while others similarly attired lined the beach. So much for a surprise raid when the Chinese had beaten Lance to Montagne. And if whoever was in charge didn't believe Lance's tale of aiding Chinese officials in Canton, they would be killed.

"Lance," Carris said as he moved closer to where his brother stood stoically, arms folded, "Is this part of the arrangement?"

"No."

God help us. "Did your Chinese contacts doubt you'd keep your word?"

Lance, having regained his speech, uttered a string of curses.

"You might consider praying. Prayers might accomplish more."

"When did you become so religious?" Lance snapped.

Carris could see the fear in his brother's eyes. If truth be known, Carris felt the same.

"When a very special woman told me I should rely on God. Not myself. I'm about to discover the power of prayer."

He could have sworn Lance sarcastically muttered, "I prefer evening the odds," when a long boat bearing a contingent of Chinese soldiers from the beach reached the *Falcon*. Rafe and Marlson awaited Lance's instructions.

"Do we fight?" Rafe asked, his eyes widening as the Chinese began to board.

"Not now. Now"—Lance looked at Carris—"we pray." Within seconds they were surrounded. Hands grasped Carris's arms shoving him face down on the hard deck. Booted feet kicked him, and those same merciless boots flipped him over. Carris looked up, meeting the cold dark eyes of a blue and green robed warrior, wearing a padded helmet and kerchief. He pressed the tip of his longsword to Carris's heart and took the Colt while the soldier's rapid Cantonese pounded Carris's skull. Blood trickled from his nose as his captor hauled him to his feet, growling in his ear. Carris easily translated.

"Obey or die."

The splashing of untold pounds of opium bricks hit the water, their captors having already discovered the ship's deadly cargo. *God, protect Zorinda.*

The hardest and most terrifying thing Zorinda had ever done was flee the deck after the junk came into view, a miracle she reached her cabin, and an acrobatic achievement she squeezed behind her trunks and bags filling the small space. Shouts and curses assaulted her ears, unmistakable thuds and crashes confirming men were suffering blows—Carris, Lance, and the *Falcon's* crew. Her lips wouldn't move, but her mind screamed for God's deliverance.

She had no idea how long she crouched, quaking at every unnatural sound. Then all fell silent. And the silence was worse than the earlier melee. Zorinda dared to stand, afraid to move, afraid not to move. She considered one course of action, then another. She had to do something. She couldn't hide and let Carris suffer because she'd led him into a trap set for his brother. Zorinda looked at the pistol. *I don't want to use this but if doing so saves Carris ...*

There were voices—English voices. And booted feet thudded above deck.

"Any one on board? Halloo?"

Familiar voices. Zorinda nearly fell over her trunks as she shoved the pistol into the large pocket of her skirt, her destination the door. God had sent deliverance. An eternity passed before she reached the deck. Now early afternoon, she'd been hiding since dawn.

"Mr. Cavenley, Mr. Surrell."

She ran toward the two men she knew could make sense of this nightmare though they stared at her in disbelief. She wrapped her arms around them and hugged them tightly, tossing all propriety overboard. When she at last released both men, she prayed she could speak coherently. "Thank God you're here." Her words miraculously poured out. "They've taken Carris and the entire crew. How are the twins and all of you and the *Paradise* ... where is ...?"

"We weighed anchor near a small island about half o' an hour from here, not certain what we'd be facin' once we arrived. The ship took a bit o' a batterin' round the Horn," Mr. Surrell said, "especially when we rescued those men whose ship busted up on the rocks. But Mr. Cavenley pulled us and the twins through right fine. We knew we had to rescue you and the cap'n, and when we put into port at Valparaiso, we learned you were headed here—not San Francisco. What's this about the cap'n?"

"The Chinese surrounded the *Falcon* at dawn forcing Carris and Lance and ..."

Her voice trailed off as both men's eyes widened with shock. They had no way of knowing Lance was alive and the captain of the *Falcon*. She quickly explained.

"Captain Wells is actually Lance Trewellyn. He's in trouble with the Chinese, but he was offered a pardon if he promised to help them capture an opium smuggler who lives here on the island."

Cavenley's eyes narrowed. "Not the twins' grandfather?"

Zorinda nodded aware precious moments were slipping by. They couldn't waste a second. "Mr. Cavenley, we have to find Montagne's plantation. The Chinese have likely taken the men there."

"The captain would want you on the *Paradise*. He wouldn't—"

"Mr. Cavenley," Seaman Bristow, no longer hindered by a sling, bellowed. "There's a Chinese junk o' war headin' toward us. I'm thinkin' not a friendly visit. They're carryin' what looks like cannons. And she's loaded with fellas wearing helmets."

"We leave. Now." Cavenley said.

"We can't," Zorinda cried. "We have to help Carris."

"Didn't you say Cap'n Trewellyn's brother is workin' for the Chinese? Why are they in danger?" Mr. Surrell asked, clearly confused.

"Something isn't right," Zorinda insisted. "I believe the Chinese planned to trap Lance and have no intention of pardoning him."

"I should take you to the children," Cavenley said, his expression grave. "And the captain's brother kidnapped both of you."

"All a misunderstanding. We were never in any danger."

Cavenley arched a brow in disbelief. But there wasn't time for Zorinda to explain the brothers' horrific reunion.

"Carris and Lance managed to sort through most of their concerns. Since then, Lance has treated us civilly. If he and Carris are in trouble, we can't sail away."

Mr. Cavenley's expression shifted, indecision in his eyes.

"She's got a point," Mr. Surrell said.

Cavenley, visibly torn, released a deep breath, as though reaching a decision.

"Mr. Cavenley," Bristow boomed again, "now two long boats be headin' our way."

Zorinda's eyes met Cavenley's.

Cavenley uttered a mild oath then groaned.

"The children," Zorinda gasped, her blood freezing while an uncontrollable trembling assailed. *God, please help Raine and Ronnie.* They would be terrified if the Chinese took control of the *Paradise*.

"The men will protect them with their lives," Cavenley said.

But Zorinda was far from reassured. Guilt heightened her turmoil as she struggled with the words she'd spoken to Carris—to let God take charge. Squeezing her eyes closed, she lifted up a silent, incoherent prayer. When she once more looked at Cavenley, she still quaked but knew God was their hope. A sudden gust of wind swirled around the furled sails and the ship's timbers creaked. Bristow's third warning carried to all.

"They be boardin'."

Chapter 28

What appeared to be a prison awaited Carris, his brother, and the other men of the *Falcon* as they were herded within one of the smaller volcanic peaks. The prison space exhibited the wear and filth of frequent use accumulated over time. Carris had every reason to suspect this was where Montagne sequestered his unwelcomed guests. His thoughts drifted to Amalie and her life of heartache and tragedy. Carris couldn't ignore Lance's grim expression. Was his brother also thinking of the woman who gave birth to his children and the horrors she likely endured on the island? The barred door was slammed and bolted.

"I'm a fool." Lance shook his head.

Carris wasn't sure what his brother wanted to hear. He waited for Lance to continue.

"What did I expect?"

Carris knew he would likely never see Zorinda or the children again. *Lord, keep Zorinda safe. Bring her and the twins together. She'll take care of them.*

"Why would you take the Chinese at their word?" Carris asked moving over to the one small window overlooking lush vegetation and a narrow strip of the water. What was happening on board the *Falcon?* Would the Chinese set fire to the ship, trapping Zorinda in the inferno? *Dear God, no, please.* They were greatly outnumbered, and his boot-bruised ribs reminded him their guards wouldn't hesitate to use whatever means necessary to subdue. "Most likely Montagne has already been dispatched to the afterlife."

"What happens to anyone who dares defy the Empire?"

Ominous words, spoken in heavily accented, but passable English, brought Carris and Lance to the door of the cell. The other crewmen fell silent while Carris turned his attention to the richly dressed warrior—his silk tunic of red and yellow, feathers of the same colors affixed to his headgear. The door, bolt drawn back with a grating screech, swung open, and the man stepped through. Two others followed with a silk covered throne-like chair, arms carved in the shape of dragon heads. After placing the elaborate seat on the dirt floor, the new arrival sat, examining Carris then Lance. Additional soldiers blocked the opening of the cell. "Which of you is Wells?"

A dormant emotion surfaced within Carris as unwanted memories of his adolescence replayed in his mind. Lancelot Arthur, the miracle son conceived in his father's advancing years. The same son who'd committed and engaged in everything indecent. The brother Carris resented.

"I'm Wells," Carris said stepping forward.

The twins needed their father.

"What are you doing?" Lance ground between clenched teeth. "You're insane."

"Captain Wells," the man addressed Carris, "I am Xing Jung, general in Emperor Xianfeng's army—also addressed as his Imperial Highness, Yizhu. My task these many months has been to curb the unlawful importation of opium into my country."

"I know."

"Then you must also know the Empire frowns heavily upon those making money off the misery of the Chinese people."

"My country's opinion on the matter is mixed. Your country agreed to certain concessions with the British several years ago."

"An unequal treaty, which means we don't have to obey those terms. The emperor is determined to halt British importation of opium."

"Where is Montagne—the man I was sent to find?"

Xing Jung's eyes narrowed.

"He has been dealt with."

"Why was I asked to apprehend him?"

The general rose from his semi-throne and tucked his hands within the folds of his sleeves. "To let the Europeans know we will not sit idly while our nation is destroyed internally. I am afraid, Captain Wells, you will be made an example."

An inhuman yell pierced the air—Lance lunged at the general and was immediately subdued by one of the attending guards. The force of the guard's savage blow snapped Lance's head to the side.

Carris fought the instinct to retaliate.

The guard pushed Lance back, and his brother hit the floor with a jarring thud. Motionless, blood trickled from a cut near Lance's ear.

"Your warriors may be brave but not wise. You will be taken to another cell to await your punishment." Xing Jung nodded at those soldiers surrounding him.

Carris, prodded from the cell, was led deeper within the prison, the air noticeably cold and damp. Shoved into another cell, Carris watched the door shut, wincing as the bolt slid into place. Little light filtered into the space, but he saw what appeared to be a cot, a man sitting on the edge. Before Carris could speak to his cell mate, a terrible coughing spasm consumed the man. Seeing a bucket of water containing a dipper, Carris filled the implement which he handed to the sickly hostage. Carris noticed how badly the prisoner's hand trembled. Once his coughing subsided, he sighed, and handed the dipper back to Carris.

"You don't sound well," Carris said.

The man chuckled hoarsely.

"I'm better than I was six months ago. Half dead I was. Only the grace of God and memory of my little one saved me."

Carris peered more closely at the man, whose wild hair and beard were gray, his tall frame gaunt from malnourishment. His clothing, what was left of the garments, bore the look of a seaman. The tattered fabric offered little warmth in this colder section of Montagne's prison.

"You've a grandchild?" Carris moved closer and squatted before the man.

"Why, I might be a grandfather after all this time."

The man made no sense, his reality understandably rattled.

"My little one might be married and could be a mother since last I saw her. I hope she's found a good man and is happy."

"Your daughter is a grown woman?" Carris asked, unsettled by his cell mate, disturbed by his thinness, his sadness—the memory of a daughter. Logic and reason eluded Carris at the moment. He didn't know what to make of this man who seemed sane but uttered nonsense. "Where is she?"

"Far from here. On the other side of the world. In the United States—Virginia. Have you ever been there?"

Carris grasped the man's bony shoulders, his eyes searching for—for what? Something, anything. The man raised his head and met Carris's penetrating stare.

"Are you badly injured, lad?"

"What—what is your name?" Carris asked, now consumed with greater fear while suspicion and possibility battered his mind.

"Wemblish—Thad Wemblish. What's wrong?"

Carris released him, desperate prayers rising heavenward.

"Lad, you're gravely ill."

"I ..." Carris began, then nearly choked. He tried again. "Your daughter—I—she—she's here. Zorinda has been searching for you."

Zorinda had never imagined merciless evil could be hidden by an earthly paradise. Now a prisoner of the Chinese with Den Cavenley, Mr. Surrell, Bristow, Lem, and Jep, overwhelming anguish stabbed. She'd never appreciated her world in Virginia and the people there who loved her. Now she faced execution or possibly worse and couldn't understand anything being said. Cavenley was frighteningly silent, his lips pulled into a taut line.

The mountain peaks towered above, and beneath the longboat the water mirrored the exact shade of Carris's eyes. Fish scurried out of the path of the oarsmen, all manner of sizes, shapes and colors whipping past. Exactly as described in the twins' book.

"Miss Wemblish?"

At the whispered words, Zorinda turned and realized Cavenley had worked himself closer to her.

"Captain Trewellyn, Carris, taught me Cantonese. These men say we're connected to Captain Wells's—Lance Trewellyn's—smuggling activities. They're assuming you are his woman."

"What should I do?" She spoke breathlessly, panic pounding against her control.

"Nothing. But from what I gather, Lance Trewellyn is in mortal danger. Whatever he did, his offenses are considered unpardonable by the Chinese, and he was lured here intentionally. They plan to demonstrate to the British and other nations they will not tolerate such atrocities. They're angry and humiliated by their defeat in the Opium War."

"No," Zorinda whimpered, sick to her stomach. The children. *Dear God, don't let the* Paradise *be found.*

One of the Chinese soldiers grumbled something at Cavenley then shoved him back to his original place in the boat. Zorinda knew Carris was in as much danger as Lance merely through association.

Carris watched Thad Wemblish's eyes widen.

"What are you saying?" Wemblish's voice cracked. The man's agitation cleared Carris's mind. "How can Rin be here?" Wemblish continued. "Why would you lie?"

"I'm not lying. I made your daughter's acquaintance in Norfolk when I took my ship into port for repairs and to load cotton destined for San Francisco. She befriended my niece and nephew when they became lost in town." *No time to explain the running away debacle.* "When we became better acquainted, she shared how her father—you—was missing, and how she wished she could search for you. When an old friend of yours, Captain Witherspoon—"

"Teig?" Wemblish asked.

Carris nodded. "Captain Witherspoon told Zorinda—Miss Wemblish—he'd heard you'd been seen in San Francisco but planned to travel on to Tahiti to search for several of your crewmen who went missing.

Wemblish sighed and ran his skeletal hands over his bearded face. "Who are you?" he asked.

"Carris Trewellyn of Trewellyn Shipping. Miss Wemblish was determined to follow the lead. As I needed help with my brother's children—"

"Your brother?" Wemblish's eyes narrowed. "Trewellyn—Lance Trewellyn—the smuggler?"

Now was Carris's turn to sigh. "Yes."

"He was behind the shanghaiing of several of the *Scheherazade's* crew. I tracked Trewellyn to Tahiti, where I learned he'd sailed on to Bora Bora. Several islanders suggested I seek François Montagne who owned a large plantation on the island. I literally led my crew and my ship into the lion's den. As soon as I told Montagne who I was looking for and why, he threw me in this prison along with my men. I learned from one of his guards who spoke French my ship was set afire and sunk beyond the lagoon. I also discovered through him Montagne was involved in the opium trade and in some sort of partnership with your brother. Montagne accused me of being sent by the United States to expose his illegal activities."

"So rather than take a chance of exposure, Montagne erased all trace of you and your ship. What a miracle he spared your life." Carris fell silent as he drew a deep breath.

"After he locked us up, I believe he forgot about me and my crew as he had bigger problems. Namely avoiding the Chinese. They found him about two months ago. Montagne was taken away, so my new Chinese guard told me, and was tossed aboard a war junk bound for Canton. Some general and his men occupied the house and are still there far as I know. The Chinese freed my crew. But I was so sick, I believed I was near death. Several of my crew wanted to stay with me, but I knew they had family missing them. I made them promise to tell Rin what happened, and why I couldn't get word to her. After they left, my Chinese guard took pity on me and started bringing me a special tea he said his grandmother would give him for all sorts of sickness. Seems to be working, although I still have this dratted cough. And I'm weak as a babe."

"But you're free to leave?"

Wemblish nodded.

"Yet, the door was locked when they brought me here. Are you sure you could leave if you wished?"

"I've no reason to think otherwise. You're not a prisoner, are you?"

Carris snorted. "Yes and slated for execution."

Wemblish rose shakily to his feet and grasped Carris's arms.

"You say Rin is here? I have to get to her." Wemblish seemed close to tears. "What would the Chinese want with me?"

"I don't know—maybe nothing." Carris gently pushed the man down on his filthy cot. "You sailed here in search of Lance, not Montagne. I wonder if General Jung thinks you're working with my brother. If so, you're in as much trouble as I am."

"You're a smuggler?"

Carris shook his head no.

"But I told the general I'm Lance."

"Why?" Wemblish bellowed then broke into a rattling cough.

"He has children. I've no attachments."

"No wife—no sweetheart?"

Carris's jaw tensed, and he wondered if Wemblish noticed the change in his expression. Should he tell Wemblish of his love for Zorinda? At this point, there was nothing to lose. "I'm in love with your daughter."

Wemblish appeared to ponder his words before finally speaking.

"You're in love with my little girl?" Wemblish's voice broke. "She hasn't married. There are no grandchildren."

"She's not unhappy. But she's missed you. And things haven't been easy for her at home. The banker has given her trouble." Carris left out the information about Wilson Goodwell and the grief he'd caused.

"Sharp's been a thorn in my side since I told him he was no better than a thief charging such high interest rates on his loans. I should have moved all of my money before my last voyage."

Carris was a trifle pleased he'd increased his rates for the banker's cotton. But guilty for having been so all-consumed with profit.

"So, she's struggled since I left."

Carris heard the pain in his voice.

"Zorinda is resourceful. She arranged for a local man to sell her paintings to earn extra funds. But she used the money to help an orphanage and other charities in town. Zorinda is extraordinary."

Wemblish actually smiled.

"My Rin is hardheaded, stubborn, and what a temper. But she's always been generous. I'm glad she's still painting."

"She is amazing. I bought one of her paintings while in port, although Arnell didn't tell me at the time Zorinda was the artist."

"We have to get out of here." Wemblish rose unsteadily but remained standing. A steely determination brightened his tired blue eyes. "A man compassionate enough to take his brother's punishment is the man for my Rin."

"Don't think me good, Captain. I've spent most of my life holding a grudge against Lance. But Zorinda reminded me to let go of the past."

"How does she feel about you?"

"We've been at cross-purposes, but ..." Carris paused. "I truly believe she cares for me."

Wemblish nodded. "I have a sudden need for some of my special tea. Can you speak Cantonese? I can't have a coughing spell and call my guard for help."

"I've sufficient command of the language. You give the performance of your life."

"God, forgive me for my deception," Wemblish prayed.

"I have a feeling he will."

Carris extended his hand to the captain whose grasp was surprisingly strong.

Chapter 29

Though Zorinda's damp garments clung to her, and her feet ached, she managed to take in her surroundings as the Chinese soldiers forced her, Cavenley, Mr. Surrell, and the sailors to walk to what she supposed would be a prison. The cottages were thatched with native palm fronds, and bronzed-skin inhabitants watched them curiously. Had her mother lived in a village like this? Or had her home reflected European construction given her stepfather was French?

They continued to tread the road, a composition of sand and crumbled coral, while the sun burned fiercely. Unexpectedly, they came upon a palm-lined lane wide enough for a carriage to pass. Did this lead to Montagne's residence? When a large, raised cottage came into view, she had her answer.

The residence, painted white, was spacious and rambling. The windows of the basement level peered out from under the gallery, the supports made of brick. Dark green shutters and evenly spaced doors complimented the symmetrical façade, and the myriad flower beds filled with spectacular blooms created a deceptive beauty. As they neared, the central door opened, and several soldiers spread out along the gallery and lawn. Did they really think she or any of the men with her posed a threat? She might have laughed had she not been so sick at heart.

The guards were issued what sounded like a command, followed by the removal of Jep, Lem, and Bristow. Zorinda clasped her shaking hands as an officer, judging by his elaborate tunic and headgear, came to stand before her, Den Cavenley, and Mr. Surrell.

"I am General Jung of the Emperor's army," the man announced in heavily accented English. "Are you with the smugglers?"

Cavenley stepped forward. "No. But we're in search of two men—one is the captain of our ship who was abducted. The other man is his brother. I fear you believe our captain, Carris Trewellyn, is involved in the opium trade. I can verify his ship carries only clothing, household goods, and cotton bound for San Francisco in the United States."

"Where is your captain's ship?"

Zorinda held her breath. Would Cavenley actually divulge the location?

"Nearing Tahiti by now."

She released her breath.

"I and Mr. Surrell," Cavenley nodded at the second mate, "and some of our crew planned to sail on the *Falcon* to Papeete, meet up with the *Paradise* then continue on to San Francisco." A lie, but necessary given the need to protect the twins.

"And this woman?"

Zorinda answered. "I'm in search of my father, a sea captain who disappeared with his crew and ship two years ago. I was told he planned to sail to one of the local islands."

The general frowned, his eyes narrowing before turning to a man standing beside him. They conversed in low tones in their native tongue.

Zorinda cut her eyes to Cavenley, whose jaw twitched. Were their captors discussing their fate?

"The three of you will come inside. There are many pieces to this puzzle I have yet to solve. For your information, my men and I intend to rid this island of those who would further destroy our country. We have already removed the owner of the home," the general gestured around him. "He will be dealt with appropriately."

Raine and Ronnie's grandfather. Thank you, Father, for sparing them a life with such a man. Even so, I ask mercy for Montagne's soul.

"As for your captain," the man pointed at Cavenley, "he may be with the men we took earlier. But the captain who calls himself Arthur Wells will be punished in accordance with his disobedience."

"Captain Wells was working with your country to apprehend the smuggler," Zorinda said.

"After the arrangement was made, we learned from another source where the smuggler could be found, and we no longer needed Captain Wells. In any event, there were no plans to pardon him. He, too, has committed crimes against the empire."

"Have you no honor?" Zorinda demanded even as Cavenley caught her arm and squeezed a warning. "An honorable man follows through on his promises. In your own way, you're as much a criminal as Captain Wells. The Bible tells us honor is to be valued above all things."

"*Chénmò!*" General Jung's command pounded in Zorinda's ears in time with the throbbing in her temple. "Utter another word, and I will see you imprisoned and executed with Captain Wells. Come."

As Zorinda passed through the open double doors, she prayed for forgiveness, for mercy, and for peace. Though this was once her mother's world, and in smaller measure, part of hers, she felt no connection—only terror. There was no joy in this adventure, no magic. Her thirst for excitement had been replaced by choking pain.

They were led to an inner courtyard where two soldiers waited at attention. The general took a seat in a chair appropriately adorned with carved dragon heads. Aides stood on either side, while the general issued what seemed to be commands. Another attendant led Zorinda, Cavenley, and Mr. Surrell to a grouping of red silk ottomans as though they were expected to sit. But they remained standing, Zorinda numb with terror. The woman, once ready to right all imagined wrongs, had vanished. The woman who loved Carris Trewellyn beyond all reason had replaced her.

The general clasped his hands across his wide chest as he leveled his probing glare at them. He tilted his head when a guard came up to him and whispered something. Apparently, whatever the man related displeased him, for the general came to his feet so suddenly he caused the guard to stumble and knock over a vase.

Zorinda flinched as the porcelain crashed and splintered while the general's angry strides brought him to where she stood with Cavenley and Mr. Surrell. Both men moved closer to her, magnifying her alarm. Were they about to be imprisoned? Or executed?

"Captain Wells and Captain Wemblish have escaped. When they are found, they will die."

Zorinda's head pounded as a smoky haze clouded her vision and the acrid scent of burning wood assailed her nostrils. Even so, she understood what the general had said. Captain Wemblish? Zorinda struggled with the release of emotions she'd smothered far too long, her breathing painful as air rushed its way to freedom. Her father was here and a prisoner? This man planned to kill him and Lance?

Her lips parted. How could she be heard over the thundering voice of the general and the booming echo pounding her ears? The man had no right to punish her father who was innocent of any crime. Her father should be freed. Unable to form the words, she screamed.

Carris grasped the edge of the lacquer screen with a white-knuckled grip watching Zorinda, her terrified scream plunging a knife into his heart. Cavenley grasped her arms and shook her, which seemed to banish her shock. He didn't dare reveal himself, or Zorinda might unintentionally alert their captors to his presence. He would have to rely on the chaos Lance and the now freed crew of the *Falcon's Wing* created. The harsh stench of the fires set in various places on the grounds filled the air. One had already been set to the house. Carris prayed Wemblish wouldn't try anything foolish and remain where he'd hidden him near the lagoon. The man could barely walk.

Soldiers swarmed General Jung, confusion rattling the trained warriors unused to the randomness desperate British sailors could employ. The smoke swirled thickly and the crackle of encroaching flame told Carris the residence would soon be engulfed. With the general shouting and gesticulating, Carris acted.

Cavenley saw him first, then Surrell. Zorinda appeared frantic, disoriented by the mayhem. As he loomed over her, she looked up. Her eyes widened, and she covered her mouth as though stifling a sob. Leaning over, Carris gathered her in his arms and whispered. "You're safe."

Zorinda threw her arms around his neck and pressed her face to his shoulder, her heaving tremors telling him she was crying. Cavenley and Surrell lost no time vacating the open space, knowing escape would require reaching the lower level of the plantation house. While the men sprinted toward the central entrance, Carris grasped Zorinda's hand and tugged her into a run. He could taste freedom, which soured on his tongue as six soldiers blocked their way. They would both be killed unless ...

A familiar revolver was thrust in his hand. He looked at Zorinda.

"Don't kill anyone."

Even as he fired, he wasn't sure he'd have a choice.

Zorinda flinched each time he emptied a chamber until he exhausted the rounds.

Jung's soldiers fell back, their swords and lances no match for a man firing a gun. At least two had been wounded from his shots—the rest, frightened by this unexpected development, retreated. Carris and Zorinda raced out on the gallery only to be stopped again. General Jung stood before them, his sword drawn. And Carris's ammunition was spent.

Grasping at any diversion, Carris hurled the revolver at the man. Jung staggered back and lost his hold on his sword. Carris scooped up the weapon, but Jung wasn't done.

The Chinese general kicked him hard in the shin, sending him to his knees.

Carris rolled away as the general aimed a kick at his already aching ribs. Staggering to his feet, Carris lunged at the general, taking his opponent down.

Zorinda screamed—whether from fear or warning, he had no idea.

Suddenly, others grabbed his arms and legs, pain shooting through his body as they forced him on his back. Then a yell rose above the cacophony of fire and fighting.

"Release him! I'm the man you want, the one you call Arthur Wells."

Carris was released, but pushing himself up was agony—-was his shoulder dislocated? The pain intensified as Lance, now in the clutches of the same men who'd seconds ago tried to pull him apart was forced up the steps to the gallery.

General Jung walked up to Lance and slapped him. Blood spurted from a cut on Lance's lip while flames flared grotesquely in the background. The fire hungrily consumed Montagne's once elegant home. Thank God the twins had been spared their fate. But their father was an entirely different matter.

Gaining his feet, Carris stumbled toward Lance. He felt a hand on his arm, knowing Zorinda was beside him. "General Jung, your government promised my brother, Lance Trewellyn—not Arthur Wells—a pardon for his crimes against your country in exchange for his help. In good faith, he carried out your emperor's request. As a general in the army of Emperor Xianfeng, you have pledged to be honorable in performing your duties and in serving China. How can you go back on an agreement made on behalf of your ruler?"

"There is no code of honor when dealing with liars and murderers."

"Opium is a terrible drug. But my brother is a British sea captain, and the British are divided on the matter—thus trading is not illegal. My brother has two children who recently lost their mother. If you kill him, they will be orphans. I believe ..." Here Carris paused for a ragged breath and a look at Lance. "... my brother no longer wishes to profit through the suffering of others."

An eerie silence fell around those gathered, the collapsing timbers behind Carris unnerving. General Jung moved away from Lance and came to stand before Carris, the man nearly as tall as he. Carris prayed he would say the right thing, or Lance could lose his life.

"You lied to protect your brother. Why?"

Jung's glare burned as fiercely as the flames soaring heavenward. The structure could collapse at any moment, destroying the gallery in the process.

"Because my God forgives our sins when he sacrificed his only Son. Sometimes God requires our sacrifice as well. I have condemned my brother for far too many years." Carris paused to steady his voice. Pain racked him as smoky air filled his lungs "I had no right to judge him. I want my brother to know I love him."

The general walked a few steps, stroking his long, braided beard, his tunic no longer pristine and his plumed helmet lost during their fight. Halting, he turned, his eyes fixed on Carris. "You are a foolish but brave man, Captain. Your brother is not worthy of your love, but I'll not deny him your gift. I will release him, not because he no longer deserves punishment, but because I have no wish to bring down the wrath of your God or that of the British. Relations between your country and mine are not good. Unrest is great in China. Our pride has been trampled, and we struggle to make sense of our fate. But hear this, Captain, and know I am most sincere. Should Arthur Wells—or Lance Trewellyn—" Jung glared at Lance. "—ever betray the Empire again, he would do well to look to this God of whom you speak. For he will surely meet him. You and all those with you leave. Immediately. By the time the sun sets, I do not want to see so much as a sail of any ship other than sails belonging to the emperor's fleet."

Carris looked at Lance. Something flickered in his brother's eyes—remorse, regret, gratitude? Lance moved toward him with hand extended. Carris accepted his overture then pulled his brother into a hug. When was the last time they'd hugged? Years ago, when Lance had been a boy of five and his toy sailboat had sunk in the pond beyond the garden. The child had been inconsolable, and Carris had done the only thing a boy of ten and three knew to do. He'd hugged his brother.

When they separated, Carris turned to Zorinda, her lovely hair in total disarray, her dark, expressive eyes red rimmed, her gown ripped and mussed. But she was the loveliest sight he'd ever seen.

She hesitated, and then, as though she'd been freed from shackles, she swayed toward him.

Catching her close, he buried his face in her hair, his fingers slipping through the snarled tresses. Recalling Jung's demand they leave immediately, he ended the embrace. "There's someone you will want to see. We haven't much time so—"

"Papa is here," she whispered, a smile spreading over her face.

"He is. And all he wants is to see you." Pulling her close to his side, he glanced over at Jung.

"General, the other captain Montagne imprisoned has nothing to do with Lance's activities. Two years ago, he came to the island seeking Lance on another matter involving members of his crew. Montagne imprisoned Captain Wemblish, as well as his seamen. When you took Montagne, you released Captain Wemblish's crew, but I fear you assumed he was in league with the Frenchman.

He has been detained as a prisoner and is innocent of any such activity. He wishes to return to his home in the United States, and his daughter has sailed thousands of miles in search of him. We wish to take the captain with us."

Jung hesitated several interminable seconds, then nodded. Carris returned the nod, then gripped Zorinda's hand as he led her to her father.

Chapter 30

Zorinda hardly noticed the trek across the coral outcropping or wading in calf-deep water. All she cared about at the moment was her father who was waiting for her.

Carris told her he'd been ill but was on the mend. He shared what he knew about the captain's misfortune as well as Lance's confession that he'd enlisted the aid of a boarding master in San Francisco when many of the *Falcon's* crew deserted to join the hunt for gold. The boarding master had authorized shanghaiing crewmen from the *Scheherazade*. When her father discovered where his missing men had been taken, he tracked Lance to Tahiti, then to Bora Bora. Unfortunately, when Captain Wemblish arrived at the island, Lance had already come and gone. And François Montagne erroneously assumed her father was there to expose his connection to the opium trade to authorities in the United States. Hence the destruction of the ship and the imprisonment of Wemblish and his remaining crew.

"When the Chinese arrived," Carris said, grasping her arm and hoisting her over a treacherous eddy ...

Where is Papa? Why can't we move faster?

"... Your father was so ill, he made no effort to leave with them. Instead, he urged them to go without him with a pledge they'd get word to you. He didn't realize even if his health improved, he wouldn't be released."

"All this time he's been imprisoned because he put his crew first. Montagne is fortunate he was taken before I arrived because I might have been tempted to shoot him." Carris chuckled.

Zorinda glared.

"We're fortunate General Jung decided we weren't worth the trouble on the off chance he'd incur the wrath of the British."

"As for Lance," Zorinda said, her anger mounting, "he's also responsible for my father's imprisonment because he sanctioned the shanghaiing. Papa knew his men had families who would be devastated if they never returned. Carris, how much farther?"

"We're here."

Drawing a deep breath, Zorinda looked where Carris pointed beyond a thicket of mangroves. A thin man rested against a towering palm, sitting on the sand, his knees bent, and his arms draped over them. He appeared to be sleeping. Could this bearded stranger in the tattered clothing with silver hair be ...?

"Papa—Papa?"

Breaking away from Carris, Zorinda stumbled forward. She dropped down beside her father and reached out a shaking hand.

Familiar blue eyes met hers. He grasped her fingers and squeezed reassuringly.

Zorinda clutched his bony shoulder, appalled by the weight he'd lost. A cry of pain caught in her throat.

"My Rin—my precious Rin. What possessed you to sail so far to find an old salt like me?" He smiled wearily, and she choked on a tearful laugh, wiping at her eyes. His frailty frightened her. Was he truly on the mend as Carris said?

"I would have found a way to the moon if I'd learned you were there. Now, you're going home. Back to Virginia where Sarah and I can spoil and fatten you up."

"I imagined you wouldn't return to Virginia."

"Why ever not?" Zorinda's threatening tears cleared as she pondered her father's odd comment.

"Isn't Captain Trewellyn from England? Once you're married, won't you move to his home?"

Zorinda sucked in a sharp breath at the unexpected mention of marriage, afraid to look up at Carris who hovered nearby. "Don't worry yourself, Papa. I'm taking you to Virginia. Do you think you can stand? The general hasn't given us much time to leave the island."

"I smell smoke. He hasn't burned your ship, has he?" Her father looked up at Carris, concern in his eyes.

"No. But my brother and I had something to do with burning Montagne's home, so the general is going to have to make other sleeping arrangements."

Carris summoned Lance and two others. "We're going to get you on your feet, then carry you to the long boat and on to the *Falcon*. My brother's ship is at anchor in the inlet and has to be at sea within the hour."

"What are we waiting for?"

Carris laughed, and Zorinda's father actually managed a hoarse chuckle, followed by a short bout of coughing. Zorinda watched her father helped up then lifted by the men, all the while wringing her hands. At last, they were on their way, following the arduous path they'd taken earlier. But this time, Zorinda felt as though she floated on air.

"Good to have you back on the lady, sir."

Carris looked over at his first mate who'd joined him at the wheel. The setting sun cast mauve, gold, and blue streaks across the sky. The red orb and its promise of good sailing weather was about to sink out of sight at the stern of the *Paradise* as she followed an easterly direction. They would angle southerly shortly after dawn, heading for Tahiti and the town of Papeete. Both the *Paradise* and the *Falcon's Wing* would take on provisions and fresh water, as well as assess any additional repairs needed before turning north to San Francisco. New faces populated the deck of the *Paradise*—survivors plucked from the wreckage of the *Cloud Burst*, which had crashed on the rocks during the terrible blizzard when navigating the Horn.

"Good to be back."

After delivering Wemblish and Zorinda, along with Lance and his crew, Carris and those from the *Paradise* had rowed on to the clipper's hiding place. How painful to leave Zorinda on the *Falcon* with Lance. But Carris knew the sooner Wemblish was settled and looked after the better.

"You did a fine job bringing the *Paradise* around the Horn, Cavenley."

"Only lost the royal," Cavenley said. "Mr. Tenney believes the repairs can be easily made when we reach San Francisco."

"And the cargo?"

"No problems there."

Carris thought of the crates filled with the missionary society's items. And the sum he'd charged the Darrow brothers. His heart grew heavier. And the pain in his shoulder intensified, making him wonder if he shouldn't have followed Rollins's advice. The man had confirmed

Carris dislocated his shoulder, and with Surrell's help, popped the joint back in place. The steward fashioned him a sling and produced a bottle of laudanum recommending he take a dose. But the last thing Carris wanted was so much as a drop of the dratted stuff considering what opium had nearly cost him. He preferred to suffer. And he had no intention of using the sling beyond one night.

"I never quite understood how you and Captain Wemblish escaped and then set the men from the *Falcon's Wing* free."

Carris glanced at Cavenley. "Captain Wemblish feigned distress along with genuine coughing. When the guard came to our door and stepped in, I tripped him, snatched his keys, knocked the wind from him, and we slipped from the cell. After hiding Wemblish, I managed to locate gunpowder stored in another chamber in Montagne's mountain prison. I set fire to the cache creating enough chaos to cover my search for Lance and his men. Once they were freed, we found Sanders, Doherty, and Bristow who told us the general had taken Zorinda, you, and Surrell to the house. We parted—Lance and the others set fires throughout the estate with the house as their final target. I returned to the cottage for the three of you. You know the rest."

"Oncle, Oncle, you are back." Raine and Ronnie bounded up the steps to the bridge.

"And glad to be back."

Carris squatted as his niece and nephew threw their arms around him and hugged tightly.

"We thought we'd never see you again. Where is Mademoiselle?" Raine asked, worry clouding her green eyes.

"Yes, where is she?" Ronnie echoed.

"Do you remember how worried she was about her papa who was lost somewhere in the South Pacific?"

Both nodded.

"We found him. But he's ill and too weak to move from one ship to another. Children ..." Carris swallowed. "... your father is alive and captains the *Falcon's Wing*."

"Our papa is not dead?" Raine asked. Ronnie's eyes widened.

"No. He was ..." Carris struggled with his words. "... in some trouble and thought best not to involve the two of you or your mother. He didn't know your mother was so ill."

"So, he is captain of the other ship," Ronnie said. Both children turned to face the stern and looked at the ship following.

Carris nodded.

"And our grandpère?" Raine asked.

Carris chose his words carefully. When the twins were older, he would share the truth. But for now, he softened the terrible details. "He made important men in China angry when he did things he shouldn't have. He is to be punished for his misdeeds."

"Will he be whipped with the cat-o'-nine tails? Raine asked, her sweet lips sad.

"I'm not sure what will happen. We can pray for him."

"We will," Ronnie said. "But now we have you and the mademoiselle and a papa."

Carris's heart dropped. He had no idea what role Lance would play in their lives.

"Mademoiselle found her papa too. Will our papa remember us?" Ronnie asked.

"I know he will, and he will be very happy to see you. Mr. Cavenley, Rollins, and Cook have told me you've both been most helpful. Seems to me you've earned the price of Miss Zorinda's paints. I believe you're done with your duties."

“But we don’t want to be,” Raine said. “I like helping in the galley.”

“And I like being a cabin boy. Can’t we continue?”

Carris laughed. “The two of you always amaze me. But if you want to continue ...”

They nodded.

“And we also want Mademoiselle back,” Ronnie said.

“If she doesn’t come back, however will you marry her?” Raine asked.

Carris drew in a shaky breath. Yes, how indeed if Zorinda decided her place was with her father?

A full day had passed since departing Bora Bora, and with darkness descending, Zorinda took a turn about the lantern-lit deck, having left her father sleeping peacefully in Lance’s cabin. She silently offered a prayer to the Almighty for his goodness and mercy. He’d protected her father from enemies, brought him through a serious illness, and placed him where Carris would discover him. God’s unfathomable grace had so blessed her and Thaddeous Wemblish.

“How’s your father?”

Recognizing Lance’s voice, Zorinda halted. Looking up at a clean-shaven Lance, she smiled. He was a handsome man, but he wasn’t Carris.

“Sleeping soundly thanks to your cook’s replication of the tea Papa said the Chinese guard gave him. I’ve written out the ingredients for future use.”

“Has Carris told you he’s in love with you?”

Zorinda’s heart thudded and raced, but she nodded.

“Good. I wondered if he had any sense. Carris isn’t the same man I remember. If someone had told me five years ago he would sacrifice his life for me, I'd have assumed the individual jesting."

"You and Carris remind me of Joseph and his brothers. Jacob's favorite was a younger son—so was your father's."

"Our father gave me his prized ring which should have gone to Carris, and I never lost an opportunity to flaunt the gift. I'm not sure I can be forgiven.

"Ask God for forgiveness."

Lance sighed deeply.

"I was so young when Raine and Ronnie were born. I didn't want to be a father or a husband, and suddenly, I was both. My escape was the sea. Amalie needed me in more ways than I realized. I had no idea what her life had been like on the island. I do now, and I understand why she made certain choices. And she died alone. I'm sick to my soul."

Lance ran a hand over his smooth jaw.

"God has the power to heal."

"I'm unworthy."

"None of us is worthy."

Taking a few steps, she turned so she could see the stern of the *Paradise,* aware the man she loved more with every beat of her heart likely stood at the magnificent ship's wheel.

"Carris is different because of you. When's the wedding?"

"My place is with my father until he's fully recovered. There will be matters to handle—the loss of the ship and the cargo. Insurance filings to submit, contacts made with the merchants whose goods were lost with the burning of the *Scheherazade.*"

"Carris isn't patient."

"He knows I have to consider my father first."

"You should pray on the matter." Lance gave her a teasing wink then walked on, whistling as though he hadn't a care in the world.

The nerve of him. Then another thought surfaced. *Actually, I should pray.*

Zorinda's father had been installed in Lance's cabin, and after departing the deck she made her way there only to find her father sitting at Lance's ornate desk.

He looked up at her entrance, an endearing, guilty look capturing his face. "You caught me."

"Papa, what are you doing?" Zorinda's shock gave way to annoyance, which evolved into anger. "You shouldn't be out of bed." She did have to admit there was more color in his face, and his eyes had a bit of a twinkle to them.

"I refuse to lie around and sleep. I need to be doing something."

"If you have a relapse, I won't pamper you." Zorinda joined him by the desk. "What are you looking at?"

"I was looking at Captain Trewellyn's log—apparently your Carris brought the ship around the Horn. Tell me about this Trewellyn. I hope he's not the scoundrel his brother is."

"You know the answer. Carris shows the world a relentless, determined man. But those who know him see something completely different."

"Exactly how well do you *know* him?"

The heat seeped into Zorinda's cheeks, and she pretended to study something on the desk. "He's a hard man to understand."

"I see," Thad said, a silence slipping between them. "You look so very much like Cappy. You're a beautiful woman, Rin. You deserve a fine man, a man who will appreciate you.

When your mother first arrived in Norfolk, no one would accept her as an equal. I did what I could but was so glad when she found friends at our church. Those people were good to her."

"They've always been accepting and kind. And Miss Redman at the Female Orphanage. There's so much I'd like to help them with. But funds ..." She hesitated to tell her father about Banker Sharp.

"Captain Trewellyn—Carris—told me what you did to make extra money. I'm glad you haven't given up on your painting. And people want your paintings."

"Only because they believe *R.I.N.* are the initials of a man."

"What a surprise for Carris. I gather you've tossed him that one and several more over the last few months."

"Not intentionally." She felt ten years old again being taken to task for tearing a hole in her stockings. "He can be infuriating."

"As can you."

Zorinda lifted her eyes and met her father's knowing look.

"I might be weak, but I'm not blind. Lance Trewellyn paid me a visit earlier today when you were up on deck for some air.

"Why?"

"He wanted to apologize for his misguided actions, which lured me and my men to Montagne."

"An apology can hardly erase two years of imprisonment and illness."

"God will ultimately be Lance's judge."

Shame assailed Zorinda. She was judging Lance, and wasn't she the one who told Carris not to?

"He told me he released my shanghaied men in Algiers because there was an abundance of men there willing to sail rather than dig for gold. I'm sorry no one got word to you."

"Maybe I was meant to leave home and find you."

Thad smiled as he stood, and Zorinda had to press her hands to the desktop to keep from helping him. He managed with a bit of a wobble. "I believe it was God's will. Now, if you don't mind, help me up on deck. This old salt needs a good fill of sea air."

She started to refuse his command, then realized she'd be wasting her time. Her father had made up his mind.

Chapter 31

The arrival of the ships in Papeete generated excitement among the residents of the town considered the hub of the kingdom of Tahiti—a French protectorate. As soon as the anchor dropped, Carris summoned Cavenley, who helped him lower the *Paradise's* dinghy. Once their oars were in the water, the islanders escorted them to shore in their *va'a*—outrigger—canoes.

Once in port, Carris noted Lance and Rafe had arrived, but without Zorinda. Though disappointed, Carris didn't ask her whereabouts. Lance's smirk assured Carris his brother was aware her absence bothered him and a reminder Lance still enjoyed needling him. Carris's inner misery eased when Rafe mentioned Zorinda would arrive later with others from the *Falcon* after seeing her father properly settled. Carris hoped she'd be present when Mr. Surrell delivered the twins. They had been very vocal about missing her. Carris suffered her absence in silent misery.

The previous night Carris had penned missives—one to Barrister Truesdale informing him Lance was very much alive. A second to his managers at Trewellyn Shipping in London, and a third to Banker Sharp informing him of the delay in delivering his cotton. The last letter he composed had been the most important, addressed to the Darrows in Norfolk. Contained in the envelope was a check in the amount he'd accepted as prepayment accompanied by an assurance no further payment was expected upon Carris's return to Norfolk.

Midday fast approached when Carris commenced pacing the waterfront, impatient and anxious to see Zorinda. As though God knew he couldn't stand the uncertainty any longer, the *Falcon's* long boat arrived, bearing Marlson, other crewmen. And ...

"Zorinda!"

Carris wasn't sure how he reached her so quickly, but she'd hardly planted her feet on the pier when he swept her up in his arms. Her laughter was more beautiful than any bird's sweet trills and her lips ...

Surrounded by gaping onlookers, now wasn't the time to explore such a thought. He placed her on her feet then settled for slipping his arm about her waist, basking in her shy smile. The sun shone brighter, and his heart beat wildly. Feeling as though they'd been separated for much longer than two days, he was reluctant to release her. "How is your father?"

Her smile faded a bit.

"He's a terrible patient and angry I wouldn't let him come ashore. But I've tempted him with more freedom in San Francisco."

Carris laughed. "Your cunning ways know no bounds. You are too clever for your own good." Carris lost his battle with propriety and lowered his head for a tempting kiss.

"Mademoiselle. Mademoiselle."

He jerked his head up.

Two children ran down the pier, one with ribbons flying, the other holding down a hat attempting to fly off.

Carris almost missed Surrell following behind, shaking his head over the twins' antics.

Zorinda knelt and gathered them close.

"We've missed you," Raine said.

"We've earned enough for your paints." Ronnie beamed proudly.

"Oncle is helping us with our studies." Raine again.

"When are you coming back to the ship?" Ronnie's turn.

"How is your papa?" Both children asked simultaneously.

The hubbub was maddening, but Carris grinned for no reason other than he was looking at the loveliest woman he'd ever known. And delighted by the excitement of two children he loved.

"Children, have you a hug for your father?"

Lance's voice intruded, forcing Carris to look over at his brother who'd silently slipped up on them. Rising, Zorinda clasped each child's hand as they stared at Lance, uncertainty clouding their expressions. Carris caught Zorinda's attention hoping he could somehow convey the children had been prepared for this moment.

"Raine, Ronnie, this is the man I told you about. You may not remember him, but he is your father, Lance Trewellyn."

The twins' eyes widened, and Carris gave a slight nod, hoping to reassure them Lance presented no threat.

Squatting, Lance held out his arms, but Raine and Ronnie still stared.

"Your beard is gone, but you're the man in the park," Ronnie said. "Why didn't you tell us?"

"I was shocked to see you and your sister. And there were reasons I couldn't tell you who I was."

"Reasons?" Raine asked, pulling free of Zorinda and crossing her arms in censure.

Lance gave them a sad smile. "I was in trouble."

"With the Chinese," Ronnie said. "We know what happened."

Lance glanced accusingly at Carris, then returned his attention to the twins. "You're right. And I knew you were safer with Miss Wemblish and your uncle."

"We were all alone after Maman died."

"We were scared," Ronnie added.

Were Lance's lips trembling? Did his eyes seem unnaturally bright?

The twins looked at one another. Several interminable seconds passed. Then they moved away from Zorinda and walked toward him. Lance folded them in his arms and held them tightly, his eyes closed.

The man needed this time with his children. Carris distanced himself then directed his steps to a tavern, mercifully quiet and nearly empty. Not to drink or eat but to recover his composure. Wondering where this journey would ultimately take him and Lance.

Den Cavenley offered to guide Zorinda and the twins through the town after Carris absented himself during Lance's reunion with the children. After sharing a simple meal at a tavern not far from the waterfront, Carris's first mate took them to a cluster of shops within walking distance. Promising to return for them in two hours, he departed, Ronnie running after the man in an effort to avoid any activity involving *faire des choses de filles*—girl things.

Though concerned for Carris, Zorinda still needed to fulfill her promise to Raine to find the child fabric for a special dress. At the third shop they entered, Raine noticed a lovely coral silk dotted with pink and lavender flowers. Zorinda hadn't planned to purchase anything until a bolt of ivory satin caught her eye. Bird of Paradise flowers, intricately embroidered on the lustrous cloth, were breathtaking. Raine, observing her fascination with the design, innocently mentioned Oncle would *love* to see Zorinda wearing a gown fashioned from the très beau material. Zorinda yielded to temptation.

The remainder of their allotted time passed far too quickly, Mr. Cavenley and Ronnie rejoining them as promised accompanied by Carris—impossibly handsome and wearing a warm smile. Zorinda dreaded their inevitable separation, but she didn't want to put her father through the discomfort of moving him.

"Won't you eat with us tonight?" Ronnie begged, clasping Zorinda's arm, hopping on one foot then another.

Where does his energy come from? "My papa has been alone all day," she said, aware of Carris's intense but silent observation. A clearing of a throat startled her and drew her attention.

Lance and Rafe Henderson had joined them. There was something melancholy in Lance's eyes. "Go with the children," Lance urged her. "I'll look in on the captain personally. I promise not to annoy him overmuch."

"Are you sure?" Zorinda asked, daring to glance at Carris. His expression mirrored his brother's. Both men gave her the impression her decision of where to have supper was of vital importance.

Lance broke the stalemate. "Go before Carris loses his temper. Heaven knows I wouldn't survive."

Now Carris's look darkened with intensity. Her breath hitched, the lure of him—all of him—was more than she could humanly ignore. After their fevered declarations of love before the arrival of the Chinese, she wondered if

Carris might be having second thoughts. She knew she wasn't, but things between them were unsettled. And her father's health was precarious.

Her uncertainty vanished when Carris silently offered his arm while the twins danced about in a circle, Lance unnervingly attentive to the joyous display.

The lively dinner on board the *Paradise* had concluded, and Carris considered the evening a success. With Raine and Ronnie in attendance, Carris, his officers, and Zorinda were able to make sense of the bizarre happenings and their capture by the Chinese. Cavenley supplied the details of the *Paradise's* trip around the Horn, embellished by the twins who eagerly relayed the rescue of the wrecked sailors and their sighting of the Southern Lights.

With the twins now settled in their cabin, Carris stood beside Zorinda, clasping the rail near the bow. The ship gently rocked at anchor in the harbor. His arms ached to hold her, and he did so, turning her gently and capturing her face with both hands. Breathing deeply of her gardenia scent, his eyes lowered to her lips before pressing his mouth to hers, then deepening the kiss. Zorinda responded, intensifying the moment as she caught the lapels of his coat, drawing him closer. Unexpectedly, she shifted her mouth slightly, bestowing a gentle kiss to his scar. He swallowed a groan but managed to speak.

"I've missed you."

Releasing her face, he wrapped his arms around her.

"I've missed you," she whispered then rested her head against his shoulder.

The thought of allowing her to return to the *Falcon* was more than Carris could bear.

"Zorinda, will you marry me?"

She looked up at him, wonder and surprise on her face. "You know Papa needs me. He's far from well, and I can't risk upsetting him."

"Upsetting him?" The words flew from his lips. "He would be upset if you told him you love me?" Had Carris imagined the man's approval of his affection for Zorinda?

"Papa should be greatly improved by the time we reach Norfolk—"

"Four months from now? The distraction will render me useless."

"Distraction?" Zorinda reared back.

Carris instantly regretted his words as anger visibly rippled through Zorinda.

"What have I distracted you from? Your plans—your carefully plotted life?"

"Listen to me." Carris grasped her shoulders. "I love you. I don't want to live my life as I did before I met you." Lantern light reflected off the sheen in her eyes and highlighted the hurt he'd caused. "Let me explain."

"I should return to the *Falcon*."

He'd lost the moment—infinitely worse than a shipwreck. "I'm not the man you met on the Norfolk wharf."

Her eyes softened, and her lower lip trembled.

Taking her hand, Carris kissed each delicate fingertip then turned her palm up. Pressed his lips to her skin bearing faded traces of paint.

Zorinda shuddered—he prayed with pleasure—then, raising his head, dared to kiss her parted lips. Agony as he'd never known consumed him as he moved his mouth from hers then whispered against her silken hair. "May I speak with your father?"

"Be patient, Carris."

How much longer could he wait?

As long as she needed. He wasn't giving up

"Lance tells me we should be in San Francisco around midday tomorrow." Her father took a seat beside Zorinda on the deck of the *Falcon.*

She was inclined to chastise him for not resting as she'd instructed. But healthy color and a welcome fullness was evident in her father's cheeks, his blue eyes no longer haunted. Smiling, she took hold of his sea-roughened hand. A vivid reminder of Carris's, similarly callused and weathered. A dull ache commenced in her chest recalling the night they had shared before sailing from Papeete. His arms. His kisses. His proposal.

"Did I grant you permission to be on deck?" Zorinda teased.

Papa released a gruff chuckle. "No" he replied without remorse, leaning over to lightly pinch her cheek. "I'm the papa in this relationship."

"And I'd not want anyone else. But you should take care—"

"Don't start, Rin." Thaddeous glowered and shook his head. Silence slipped between them, filled with the flap of the sails, the occasional shouts and yells of those in the rigging—all expected sounds accompanying a sailing ship.

"I know of one Trewellyn who'll be glad to see San Francisco Bay."

Zorinda lowered her eyes, afraid of where this topic might lead. When her father sighed, she looked at him.

"What's next?" he asked.

"Next?" Her voice noticeably cracked.

"For you and Carris." Her father's voice boomed, then he mumbled what was most likely a salty saying not fit for her ears.

Zorinda began idly pleating the fabric of her full skirt. "I'm not certain."

"Carris is certain." Her father bellowed. Several crewman halted their activities and glanced at them while Zorinda's face reddened.

"He doesn't waste time on nonsense. He saved his brother's life. Mine. Crews of two ships, two children. And you."

Shaken by her father's forceful words, Zorinda somehow managed to respond. "I will never be able to thank him for what he's done for me. He found you."

Papa shook his head. "Next time I see Witherspoon, I've a good mind to give him a tongue lashing he'll never forget. All of you could have died because of his tale telling. Enough of your nonsense. What have you decided about Carris?"

"The sea is Carris's life. And I have commitments at home."

"Are you telling me you don't want to travel and see the world? I haven't forgotten how you'd hang on my every word when I'd return from a voyage. And your painting. How many times did you say you wished you could see the things you paint—experience them first hand? Where is that Rin?"

"I'm here, Papa. But you need me now. And there are things to see to and help with."

"Which any number of others could. I'm not helpless."

"Can we speak of this later?"

"We're speaking now, Rin. Don't lose something precious. Love is like a first voyage—exciting and scary—robs you of breath and sends your heart soaring. The closest you'll ever be to paradise on earth. Don't waste your time on me. Live your life."

Her father fell silent. Zorinda's heart beat in cadence with the wind and waves. Would this journey lead to Carris? Or to more heartache?

Chapter 32

Carris greeted the semaphore perched atop Goat—more recently named Telegraph—Hill with a prayer of thanksgiving. The windmill-like structure positioned on a pole with two raisable arms signaled the passage and vessel type of the *Paradise* and the *Falcon* as the ships entered San Francisco's Golden Gate. After dropping anchor in the bay of the gold-crazed town, soon to be part of the new state of California, Carris lost no time rowing to the *Falcon*. Lance merely nodded at him when he appeared on deck, but the crew greeted him enthusiastically. After Marlson explained Wemblish was using Lance's cabin, Carris traversed the companionway in record time. Once outside the door, he could hear Wemblish and Zorinda conversing in low tones. Politeness and decorum had no place in this moment. He knocked. Forcefully.

Zorinda opened the door. She looked breathtaking as always, her eyes widening in surprise. She started forward as though to hug him, then halted, seemingly embarrassed at her reaction.

He suffered no such qualms and gathered her close. "No need to hide anything. He already knows." Carris kissed her cheek. Pulling her inside with him, his arm anchored around her waist, he greeted Wemblish. "Afternoon, Captain. I hope I'm not interrupting?" He glanced down at Zorinda who blushed.

Wemblish chuckled. Fully clothed and sitting in a chair, he looked much heartier and healthier than he had two weeks earlier. "Welcome, Carris. All things in order with the *Paradise?*"

"Aye, sir." Carris grinned. "I wonder if I might whisk your daughter away for a short while."

"Carris ..." she began, but after looking at her father, she fell unnaturally silent.

"Actually, I think Zorinda might need to take a turn about the weather deck. Alone. I've a need to speak with you, Trewellyn. Privately."

Zorinda's lips parted as though to protest, but her father's furrowed brow stilled her tongue. "Then I shall take my leave."

Though she gave Carris a pointed glare, he kissed the top of her head before releasing her. The slamming of the door behind her assured him she was displeased. Sensing an unspoken determination in Wemblish, Carris wondered what to expect. He fully intended to tell the man he wished to marry his daughter. If there was something else—well, he'd deal with whatever the man sent his way. He was glad now he'd allowed Rollins to force him into his official captain's garb, including the far too tight black silk cravat.

"Have a seat."

Removing his cap, Carris placed it on Lance's desk, then perched on an old sea chest.

"Amazing what a bath, shave, and clean clothing accomplished for both of us," Wemblish said, then chuckled.

"I'm not the unkempt ruffian with whom you shared a cell. You're looking well. How's the cough?"

"Nearly gone. Carris, I am a blessed man and have thanked the Lord Almighty for your assistance. And for taking care of my little girl. She can be a—"

"Handful?" Carris grinned. "So I've been told. Yet, the experience has given me exquisite pleasure. And I'm thankful to have been the one to find you."

"Which is my dilemma," the captain said, clasping his hands and leaning forward, his elbows braced on his knees. "As I've been pulled from the brink of presumed death, Rin is suffocating me with concern. I was most unwell, but God has brought me back thanks to some Chinese tea and a harebrained rescue by a captain nearly as impulsive as me."

"The safety of Zorinda, my niece and nephew was always my priority," Carris said, a lump lodging in his throat. "Without God's help, we wouldn't be sitting here."

"When are you going to marry my headstrong daughter?"

Wemblish's question caught him off guard, but only momentarily. "As soon as she agrees. I've asked her, and I apologize for not formally requesting your permission. Our unusual situation has necessitated alterations to proper protocol in some matters."

Wemblish arched a graying brow. "She's in love with you. Though she's yet to confess her feelings, there's very little she can hide from me. Have you serious character flaws?" The captain wasn't teasing.

"I'm stubborn, and inflexible. I hate to admit when I'm wrong, but I've learned on this voyage there's no sin in acknowledging one's shortcomings."

"You seem the perfect match for Rin." Wemblish straightened in his chair and directed a look of challenge at Carris.

Carris met his look without flinching.

"Rin is a stronger woman than her mother, God rest her soul. My daughter has a gift, and I want her to keep painting. My late wife always felt an outsider, although she was beautiful outwardly and inwardly. If you love Rin, you will embrace her differences and allow her to thrive."

"Why would I not? She's brought color and beauty into my life. She possesses a uniqueness of mind, soul, and spirit. But we did seriously disagree over a matter."

Another lift of those whiplash brows.

Carris swallowed then continued. "You know of Zorinda's dedication to the Female Orphanage and the Mission Society."

Wemblish nodded.

Silent condemnation beat in rhythm with Carris's heart as the words tumbled from him. The Darrow Brothers' mission crates, his charge to ship them, the orphanage's need for new windows, the lack of funds, Zorinda's compulsive need to assist her former school, his irrational desire to buy a painting she'd given Arnell to sell—unaware she was the artist. The terrible night Zorinda had realized the part he'd played in those matters affecting her so deeply. Their argument. Her departure. His refusal to let her go.

Wemblish nodded, but his eyes glistened with tears.

Carris pressed on. "Though my purchase of the painting provided the funds to assist the orphanage, Zorinda accused me of choosing profit over compassion. Unknown to me, Lance had encountered Zorinda in a public park in Rio, using an assumed name, hiding behind a beard, and offering his services should she ever need help. After our argument, she went in search of him, and I followed her to the *Falcon*, thus becoming trapped in my brother's desperate plan."

Wemblish rubbed his chin while the silence stretched uncomfortably. At last, he spoke. “And now?”

“I can’t change the choices I made. I did send a check by post to the Darrows for the amount they paid my company before the *Paradise* sailed.”

“Does Rin know?”

Carris shook his head.

“Tell her.”

Another silence slipped around them.

“You have hard edges, Trewellyn. Men of the sea often do. But you’ve discovered the balance of responsibility and love. You have my blessing.”

Zorinda didn’t know whether to be angry or worried when she saw Carris leaving the *Falcon* without bidding her goodbye. Had something unpleasant transpired between him and her father? She was glad Lance had departed the ship some time earlier, for if Carris were in high dudgeon, the brothers would certainly have clashed. Rather than imagine disaster, she made her way to Lance’s cabin. She found her father looking out the gallery windows, his fists on his hips. He turned at her entrance, giving her a sad smile. Her heart hitched painfully.

“Did you and Carris have a productive conversation?” Zorinda asked, twisting her clasped hands as she moved toward a chair.

Papa joined her taking a seat in one of the battered leather chairs, looking as though flung about during a particularly vicious storm. “We did. The time has come, Zorinda.”

Startled, Zorinda looked at him, his eyes sending her an unsettling message.

"I loved your mother. But I watched her withdraw from life, little by little. And my fault."

"Papa, Maman understood. She had no regrets because she loved you."

"You're not your mother. You're stronger—more independent. Maybe there's a bit of me in you. Wanderlust and a need to grasp what life offers. Not tomorrow, not in a week, not in six months. Right now."

"What are you saying?"

"There is a man who appreciates you for who you are and who doesn't want you to change." Reaching out, her father took her fidgeting hands and clasped them tightly. "I'm going to be fine, Rin. God pulled me through. He brought us together and for as long as we are on this earth, we'll have each other. Marry Carris."

"I ... I mean, he lives in England." *This excuse sounds ridiculous even to me.*

"Then live in England. We'll be separated by a voyage of less than two weeks on one of Carris's clippers."

"This will never work."

"Why not?"

Zorinda drew a sharp breath at her father's words. She had no choice but to tell him about Wil and what he'd threatened.

"When we reach Norfolk, my reputation will be in shreds."

Thaddeous's brows lowered, but he remained silent awaiting her explanation.

"I thought Banker Sharp's nephew, Wilson Goodwell, was fond of me. When I realized he had dishonorable intentions, I told him I wanted nothing more to do with him. He threatened to spread lies about me."

"Why should you care? I don't. Carris won't."

"Maman always feared she'd do something unacceptable. I fear the same."

"How many times have I told you what's important is what's inside? I love you. God loves you. And one miserable sea captain loves you. End his misery.

Several hours later, gazing across the bay to where the *Paradise* was anchored, Zorinda replayed her father's words. Her heart belonged to Carris. Yet, there was still ambition and drive within him, which attracted and worried her. Closing her eyes, she inhaled the salt scented air and allowed the breeze to loosen the curls on the crown of her head. She prayed for direction—for certainty.

There was no voice whispering to her, yet she felt peace. Her father was right. No more wasting time.

Chapter 33

Midmorning the following day, a talkative Mr. Marlson rowed Zorinda and her father to the *Paradise*. Her father quickly discovered a kindred spirit in the man, and the two of them could speak of nothing other than the wonders of the clippers, and how many were in port.

She had to smile at their enthusiasm while absorbing the excitement of San Francisco.

"I've always known the clippers would be the fastest thing afloat," her father said.

Marlson nodded.

"I heard Henderson say Captain Trewellyn's—Carris, of course—first mate said the *Paradise* ate up the miles once they rounded the Horn. Allowed them to catch up to the *Falcon*."

"Not surprising. I'm looking forward to spending time on the *Paradise*."

Her father's pointed look confirmed he was ready to leave the *Falcon*. Another matter causing elation and distress for Zorinda.

When they arrived, Zorinda noticed Carris in a consuming, heads-together discussion with Den Cavenley and Mr. Tenney, oblivious to the twins' imminent departure. Zorinda asked Mr. Surrell to let Carris know they were going ashore. And her father was accompanying them.

Once installed in the small boat, Raine and Ronnie were so excited at meeting mademoiselle's papa, they plied him with endless questions. Zorinda's father was in his element, thrilling them with his bottomless bag of tales. Making quick work of the row to shore, Marlson was soon bidding them a good day at the pier. As they walked away from the waterfront, Zorinda noticed a decided spring to her father's step.

The town, raw and crude by eastern standards, was the scene of frenzied exuberance. Her father admitted a few landmarks had changed since his last visit but assured Zorinda he could direct them to those areas of greatest interest. And steer them clear of Broadway and Pacific Streets explaining a gang identified as the Sydney Ducks ruled "Sydney-Town."

After two hours on foot, her father confessed he was tiring. Zorinda hired a rig and found the driver most accommodating though expensive. While exploring the safer areas, they neared a residence bearing the sign San Francisco Mission and Orphanage. Certain this was the one supported by the churches at home, Zorinda requested they stop and visit.

Greeted by a plump woman of middle age attired in a black bombazine dress and crisp white pinafore, Zorinda introduced herself explaining her affiliation with the mission society in Norfolk. The woman, Mrs. Klemp, immediately invited them in. She ushered them into a utilitarian parlor, sparsely furnished, but clean and smelling of beeswax. Tea and biscuits with strawberry jam were served while Mrs. Klemp told of the work being done and how badly the mission supplies were needed. Between two to three orphans arrived weekly, and the dorm facilities on the upper floors were stretched to capacity. According to the woman, a larger home had burned in a fire started by the Sidney Ducks the year before.

Zorinda was horrified.

"Thank the Lord for those supplies sent by your local mission. A Captain Trewellyn and his men delivered a bounty of crates about an hour ago. And then, bless that captain's soul, he made a generous financial donation of his own. People like you and the captain and the ones who fund our mission remind me God is watching over us."

"Captain—Carris Trewellyn?" Zorinda glanced at her father who gave her a smug grin and shrug. She frowned.

"You know him?" Mrs. Klemp asked reclaiming her attention.

"Valeraine and Valeron are his niece and nephew." Zorinda gestured at the twins, Ronnie helping himself to a second biscuit. "We're traveling together."

"His generosity is staggering. We'll be able to enlarge our kitchen and dining area now. How long will you be in town?"

"At least a week—perhaps two," Zorinda replied as Marlson had shared the information on the row to the *Paradise*.

"Won't you join us for Sunday services while you're here?"

"May we?" the twins questioned in unison.

Zorinda smiled. "Yes, indeed. Thank you."

After finishing tea and refreshments, Mrs. Klemp gave them a tour, introducing them to several teachers. Time for luncheon when they left, Papa directed their driver to an eatery along the waterfront where they enjoyed seafood stew and freshly baked bread. On the return ride to meet

Marlson, they passed a row of shops, one of which was a modiste's. Tomorrow, Zorinda thought, she and Raine would bring along their fabric purchased in Papeete and see if gowns could be made before they sailed.

When they returned to the pier, several crew members from the *Paradise* and *Falcon's Wing* were there, all calling out greetings. Lem Doherty separated from the others and offered to return Raine and Ronnie to the *Paradise*. A long boat from the *Falcon's Wing* was about to depart, as well, so Zorinda and her father slipped in with the others. As Lance's ship neared, Zorinda recalled Mrs. Klemp's praise for Carris's generosity. What a different man from the one she'd met on Newton Wharf.

After seeing her father settled, Zorinda ventured on deck and noticed Lance looking over the bay. She'd seen little of him since reaching San Francisco and hoped he wasn't in one of his provoking moods.

"I suspect you've had a full day. I was told Carris flew into a rage when he learned you'd gone ashore with the children. Something to do with unsavory characters lurking about."

"My father made sure we remained safe. Our outing was pleasant, and we visited an orphanage supported by the Norfolk churches. The directress invited us to their Sunday service. I'd like to take the children if you've no objection. You could join us."

"What? And incur Carris's wrath? He'll think I'm trying to impress you."

Zorinda laughed. But her laughter faded as she noticed the sadness in Lance's eyes.

"You're a wonderful woman, Zorinda. I hope Carris realizes his good fortune. If only I'd been the husband Amalie needed—"

"I'm sorry, Lance." Zorinda wasn't sure why her eyes watered. Some part of her felt sorry for the man and his poor choices. How hard for Amalie to love him and wonder if she'd ever see him again.

"I'll survive." He gave her a lopsided grin. "Promise me you'll look out for the twins?"

"Of course. But you're back in their lives now."

"Perhaps." Lance's reply was enigmatic. "Anyway," his tone altered, "I've been thinking you and Captain Wemblish might be more comfortable on the *Paradise*."

"Have we become unwelcome?" Zorinda teased, hoping to lighten the moment.

"You would never be unwelcome. But I believe Carris would rest easier knowing you were with him. I'll make arrangements."

"Of course. Lance, the children do need you. But give them time to adjust. When I first met them, they were terrified of Carris. Now they adore him."

"If Carris can get the twins to like him, I should have no problem. After all, I am the more charming." He gave her his roguish grin.

"And more egotistical," she retorted. "Be patient, Lance."

He nodded. "Rest well, Zorinda." Leaning toward her, he chastely kissed her cheek.

There was something almost bittersweet in his gesture, as though he was saying goodbye. After he left, she spent a few more minutes on deck before visiting her father. Later, in her own space, sleep proved elusive. Taking up her sketch book, she began to sketch Lance's face thinking the twins might like to have a portrait of their father.

Rollins surprised Carris by interrupting him at breakfast shortly after dawn to announce Lance was aboard. Carris immediately instructed Rollins to admit his brother and bring in another plate. When Lance entered, Carris rose and went to him, grasping his hand in welcome.

"To what do I owe this pleasure?" Carris asked as he indicated to Lance to pull up a chair and join him at the small, circular table.

"One thing. I spoke to Zorinda last night and suggested she and Wemblish take up residence here."

"I hope you're not in need of your cabin to, ah, entertain?" Carris couldn't keep the note of caution from his voice as he settled back in his chair.

Lance positioned a spindle-backed chair across from him. "Farthest thing from my mind."

Carris gave him a curious look then returned to his meal, lifting a forkful of egg to his mouth. Rollins arrived and deposited a plate and a steaming mug of coffee before Lance.

"And what of your plans, Carris?" Lance asked after Rollins left. "Will your next voyage be down the aisle of matrimony?"

Carris stiffened and lowered his fork. "I've made no secret of my wish to marry Zorinda."

"Ivy truly did you a favor." Lance grasped his mug with both hands, gazing into the dark liquid. "Do you think one woman can truly make a man happy for the rest of his life?"

Carris looked at his brother. The same rascal but with an unmistakable sadness clinging to him.

"I do."

"Then you've proposed?" Lance began shoveling the food into his mouth.

"Yes."

"And?"

Carris sighed, pushing his plate away. "She wants to make sure her father adequately recovers."

"An old salt like Wemblish will probably find another ship and sail off. The sea's in his blood, the same as for us."

"Of late, the sea doesn't have as strong a pull," Carris said. "Remaining in one place for longer than a month or two holds great promise."

"You are in love."

"I am, and I see things differently. Lance, you could join me at the company. A second clipper should be completed by next summer. She's yours to captain."

"An interesting offer, I'll admit. But there are things I need to settle."

"What other countries are looking for you?"

Lance's laughter was brittle.

Carris inwardly groaned.

"Honestly, I'm not sure."

Carris feared there was too much truth to his words. "There's plenty of time to think about the possibility on the voyage back."

As Lance concentrated on chewing and swallowing, Carris flicked a glance at his brother's face, his expression unreadable.

"I have something of yours." Lifting his right hand, Carris removed his father's ring, the one he'd worn since the unforgettable night in Rio. But the ring belonged to Lance.

After taking the ring, Lance rolled the embellished band in his palm. Carris closely watched his brother's face.

"As the eldest son, this should have been yours."

"But Father wanted you to have his ring."

"Which was wrong. So many things were wrong. Once, when Father was in his cups, he told me how you'd cried and cried when your mother died. Your tears frightened him, so he chose to ignore you. He said when I was born, he poured all his hopes into me. What a waste." Lance shook his head. "I was the prodigal son and you, the dedicated, faithful son. You kept things together while I cavorted with every maid along the Spanish Main. You rescued my children when I wasn't there for them. My wife died believing I'd deserted her."

"Why didn't you get word to me?"

"I couldn't handle your justified condemnation. But the Chinese revealed my sins in all their hideous glory. By the way, thank you for saving my hide."

"You're welcome. Shall I have Rollins bring you another plate?" Carris pointed at Lance's empty one.

"No. There's lots to do—moving your lady and her father back where they belong. Now you can keep a closer eye on Zorinda."

Carris was fairly certain Lance was aware of his verbal explosion when he'd been informed Zorinda had gone into town with the children. His tirade ended when Surrell told him Wemblish was with them. A woman and children roaming through Sydney-Town would have ended badly.

"I plan to. Come for supper this evening?"

"I'm not sure." Lance stood and held out Carris Sr.'s ring. "This is truly yours. Besides, I might lose it again."

Carris frowned as he accepted the ring from Lance.

"Only to provide safekeeping. Whenever you ask—"

"I know." Lance lifted his head, looking at the gallery. "How did you come by the ship painting?" Zorinda's creation once more graced his cabin.

"I bought it in Norfolk. At the time, I had no idea Zorinda was the artist."

"I shouldn't be surprised. The ship seems to leap from the canvas. I can almost feel the breeze fanning my face and smell the salt air. I knew she could draw, but this ..."

"She began painting a portrait of the children and several landscapes of the locations we've visited."

"I envy you, Carris. Zorinda is a rare treasure."

A short silence slipped between them. Lance's words aroused Carris's seafarer intuition. Was there more to this moment than what appeared on the surface? Lance strode toward the open door, and Carris joined him.

"Thank you for caring for Raine and Ronnie."

"Zorinda has done more for them than I. Before she came into our lives, the three of us were at loggerheads."

"I would say God brought all of you together. Take care, Carris." Lance walked out, his booted feet thudding down the wooden companionway.

His brother's parting words disturbed, but before Carris could ponder the implications, footsteps alerted him to the arrival of another. Den Cavenley poked his head in, requesting his assistance. Thoughts of Lance departed.

Carris hadn't planned to spend most of the day at a dressmaker's shop. But Zorinda, having been delivered to the *Paradise* along with her father not long after Lance's departure, informed him she planned to have gowns made—one for her and one for Raine. Given her determination and his concern for her and the children's wellbeing, he invited himself on the outing.

Wemblish begged off from going explaining he and Pete Surrell had much catching up to do.

Ronnie announced he wanted to do "sailor things" so he wasn't going, either.

So here Carris sat in what was designated as the gentlemen's parlor listening to the modiste, Zorinda, and Raine in an adjacent room discuss the latest styles. Nearing the point where another word about lace and ribbons would push him to madness, the two most important females in his life appeared.

"They'll be ready in a week," Zorinda said. "We will be here for another week, won't we?"

"I've no choice but to say yes. Otherwise, I would be lashed to the bowsprit."

"Oncle Carris, you're funny," Raine said and laughed throwing her arms around his neck. "Wait until you see mademoiselle's gown. Lovely enough to be married in."

Carris looked at Zorinda, her face red, her manner flustered.

"Raine, don't be silly. We need to go. We've kept the captain from his duties long enough."

"There's no need to return immediately. Why don't we go for a ride?"

Raine bobbed her curls in agreement, and Zorinda smiled, sending his heart heavenward. If she only knew what she did to him. And Raine's impish mention of marriage. Tonight, after the evening meal, he would speak to Zorinda again. She couldn't use her father forever to delay a decision. He needed to know where he stood as torturing what-ifs plagued his every waking moment. *Lord, please convince her of my love.*

Within a few minutes, Carris guided the rig he'd rented for their outing along Broadway, making the turn before reaching Pacific Street.

"*Capitaine* Wemblish told us yesterday this is the bad place," Raine said."

"Not all the people who live here are bad. Some are like you and Miss Wemblish and me—they try to live right, keep a roof over their heads, and food on their tables. Then there are others who think they can frighten, thieve, and cheat."

"Are there orphans there?"

Carris nodded at Raine's question, thinking back on yesterday's delivery to Mrs. Klemp at the San Francisco Mission and Orphanage. How he wished he'd handled the situation with the Darrows differently. Would his efforts to correct matters lessen his mistake? Never again would he trivialize the needs of the poor and destitute. Or put business before charity.

"I'm afraid so. They try to look out for one another. Even so, they're forced into crime to survive."

"If you hadn't come for us, we might be like them."

"These children could seek aid at the orphanage but often choose not to. We can pray they will accept the help they're offered." Carris hoped his words would ease Raine's fears.

"*Ma chère*," Zorinda added, "you and Ronnie don't have to worry about being alone. You have your uncle and me and your father. We all love you."

Raine remained unnaturally quiet after their conversation but seemed fully recovered back on the ship.

Supper was lively. Wemblish shared a fanciful tale of Poseidon, bringing the twins to wide-eyed wonder. Carris admired Zorinda's gown of indigo silk and its distracting fit. Had she given any thought to their situation? Lance's absence at the meal prickled, although Carris knew his brother was in God's hands, even if that meant Lance would always be ... Lance.

After seeing the children tucked into their bunks, Zorinda joined him on deck. Carris held out his hands, and she slipped hers within his. Drawing her close, he pressed his lips to her forehead then wrapped his arms around her. “How terribly long since I’ve held you.”

“Not really.”

“One minute is too long.” His voice betrayed his emotions. Now was the time for answers. And promises.

“Captain, if I could have a word.”

Looking up, Carris inwardly fumed as Cavenley approached. Did the man have to choose this moment to speak with him?

“I’ll be but a second,” Carris whispered then joined Cavenley. The man’s expression foretold unpleasantness. With the ship? With his crew? Had they decided to search for gold?

“The *Falcon’s Wing* is gone. I believe she sailed shortly after sunset.”

“What? Was she moved?”

Cavenley shook his head. “Word is French officials in town were looking for an English captain who robbed a Le Havre merchant of silver and a small fortune in gold about a year ago.”

“Lance,” Carris muttered through clenched teeth. *Lord, help him. He will never learn.*

“Carris, what’s happened?”

Looking to his side, he saw Zorinda had joined them.

“Lance has ... left,” Carris managed, aware of the tic in his jaw.

“One more thing, Captain,” Cavenley continued, looking uncertainly at Zorinda. Carris nodded for him to go on. Zorinda would soon know all. “He didn’t pay for the supplies loaded on his ship today.”

Anger threatened to choke him, until Carris remembered to pray. *Help me, Lord.*

"I'll address the matter. Thank you, Cavenley."

The first mate nodded, his lips pressed tightly before striding away.

"What has he done?" Zorinda asked, the lantern light illuminating the worry in her eyes.

"Apparently, he's in trouble with the French over a robbery they believe he committed in Le Havre. Cavenley said French officials were making inquiries. Lance must have discovered as much and put the *Falcon* to sea rather than chance arrest."

"I thought he might want a different life," Zorinda whispered, laying her hand on his arm.

Carris pulled away and paced, words pouring out of him.

"I thought we'd reached an understanding. I offered him the new clipper to be finished next summer. What does he do? He runs rather than face his problems. He did so with Amalie. And the twins. He let everyone believe he was dead so he wouldn't have to be a husband or father. Or answer for his past. And who picks up the pieces? Me. Always me. Now I'm to raise his children.

"But you love them."

There was no denying Zorinda's words.

"I'm sorry." Carris turned back to her. "What you must think of me. I sound like a petulant child whose prized toy has been taken. But I had hope and expectations. Once more I forgot my plans weren't Lance's plans. And they weren't God's plans. I have so much to be thankful for. God is part of my life again. And I've found love because I found you."

Chapter 34

Carris pulled Zorinda to him, and she slipped her arms around his waist, releasing a sad sigh. Why would Lance do this? With his departure, there went the children's chance of regaining their father. But Carris loved the children, and they loved him. Surely something good could come from this heartbreak. She and Carris would make sure the twins never lacked affection. A clattering sound momentarily distracted her until she considered a pail or mop must have toppled. She gave him a tremulous smile. "I love you, Carris. You'll be the father the children need."

"I'm sadly lacking in parenting skills." There was a hint of teasing in his unsteady voice.

"Because you didn't have any—until now."

"Do you still believe me to be the mercenary captain?"

Zorinda shook her head. "Yesterday, when the twins and I visited the mission orphanage with Papa, Mrs. Klemp told us you made a generous donation."

"I thought I'd found God's path and knew where I was headed. But now, with Lance's defection," Carris shook his head then suddenly stilled. "No. I'm not going back. I'm moving forward with God. With you."

He kissed her as though sealing a pledge. Carris was offering her a precious gift, one she had so many times prayed for. Why now did the doubts resurface? How would his world react to her? She couldn't forget her mother's suffering. Would Society look unfavorably upon the children she and Carris might have? Raising his head, Carris grasped her hands with his strong, rough ones.

"Zorinda?"

"I can't help but fear wherever we are—Virginia or England—I'll always be the different one. And should we have children will they suffer because of me?"

"What matters is our love."

"How can you be certain?" Withdrawing one hand, she pressed her throat.

"I am," he insisted, though the pain in his voice scraped her heart. "I promise you my love and protection. You're not the woman your mother was. I won't allow old memories dictate your choices."

Something uncomfortable stirred within Zorinda. Carris's words reminded her of a distant day in May when she'd decided she'd had her fill of men telling her what she had to do and what she couldn't do. She pulled her other hand free.

"What ...?"

"I can't do this," she said, shaking her head. "No matter how much I love you, there can't be anything more for us when you tell me what to think and what to do."

"I love you."

"You love to command and control. But I'm not your crewman nor the ship's wheel. I have to find my way and make my own decisions. You, of all people, should understand." Zorinda held her breath, fully expecting him to summon the old Carris. She was shocked when he didn't.

He sighed. "You are my dream. My life. I don't want a future without you."

"I have to be sure."

"Then be sure. You are intelligent, compassionate, filled with purpose. I can no more control you than the wind and sea."

Zorinda felt a wobbly smile tip her lips. "I do love you." After Carris pressed a kiss to her brow, she looked up at him. "I should check on the children. We have to tell them about Lance."

"I know. Zorinda, we've been given a gift. I'm not giving up."

The air whooshed from her lungs as she contemplated all Carris said, deeply stirred by his words. If she'd only known at their first encounter he was concealing a lifetime of hurt and disappointment.

Making their way down the narrow stairs of the companionway, they walked single file halting at the door to the cabin the twins shared. Carris carefully opened the door and slipped within. Zorinda followed on his heels. Suddenly, Carris stopped, and Zorinda moved up beside him. Even in the darkness, she could tell there was no one in either of the bunks, the covers thrown back and night clothing discarded haphazardly on the floor.

"Carris?"

"They're not here."

Carris lost no time in commanding every inch of the ship be searched, his crew doing so within a quarter of an hour of the discovery Raine and Ronnie weren't in their cabin. Zorinda searched along with the men, and Wemblish, roused by the commotion, insisted on doing his share. But all came up empty handed. As dawn approached, a crew member realized one of the ship's dinghies was missing. Carris prepared to go into San Francisco, taking Surrell and six men. When Zorinda approached, he knew her intent before she spoke.

"Zorinda, no. I don't want to worry about you."

Her glare warned him before she spoke. "I love Raine and Ronnie. Don't force me to stay on the ship."

"Wemblish will gut me if anything happens to you."

"I make my own decisions. As do you."

Carris clamped his lips tightly as he took in the rigid set of her shoulders, the tilt of her chin, and the defiance in her eyes. He'd waste no time arguing.

"This may be your decision, but I have the right to make a demand. You'll heed my cautions."

Zorinda nodded though her lower lip trembled. Overwhelmed by the seriousness of the situation, he caught her close, hoping to reassure her. If anything happened to the children—no, he couldn't go there. *The Lord on high is mightier than the mighty waves of the sea. Lord, lead me to the children. Help me find them safe.* "We need to go."

Zorinda pulled away and nodded, ready to turn.

Carris grasped her arm and held out a revolver. "You may need this."

As Carris urged the horse of the rented rig into motion, Zorinda looked down at the weapon in her lap. She'd never considered seeking adventure might necessitate the use of guns. Once more, bloodshed was a frightening possibility. Why had Raine and Ronnie run away? Had they somehow learned of their father's departure? Where could they be? If they'd drifted into Sydney-Town ...

The Lord is my light and my salvation; whom shall I fear? The words from Psalms soothed, and Zorinda reminded herself God was with the children. "Please protect them," she whispered aloud.

"Amen," Carris breathed. "We'll find them."

"Raine was asking a lot of questions about the orphans in Sydney-Town," she said.

"She couldn't possibly think she and Ronnie would be better off with them."

"But you're heading toward the area," Zorinda pointed out.

"I'm ruling out the worst, before I search elsewhere. Surrell and the others are covering several streets near the business district. Cavenley, Tenney, and MacCurdy are making inquiries along the waterfront with those ships at berth and anchored in the bay."

"Could Lance have taken them?" Zorinda asked.

"I don't see how. If he left around sunset, the twins were with us."

"Why would they leave?"

Carris considered her question. "What if they overheard what I said about Lance? They would believe I don't want them."

"Carris," she said softly, taking hold of his arm, "surely, they couldn't think so."

Silence slipped between them, Zorinda fearfully aware they had entered the section ruled by the Sydney Ducks. But as the eastern sky brightened, all was quiet. Wagons rattled past. A few travelers were on horseback—others were on foot. Hollow-eyed men watched, and Zorinda could see children peeking out from under a set of sagging steps. Such sadness and need already in a town so new. Zorinda prayed she'd not need the revolver, placing the weapon between her and Carris. Carris's pistol lay in his lap.

Two hours passed swiftly. Carris stopped anytime they chanced upon children asking if they had seen the twins, describing them and their noticeable accent. Failure bred hopelessness within Zorinda, but Carris pressed on. There was no doubting his devotion and love.

By noon, Zorinda was frantic

"Where could they be? What if they've been kidnapped? Ronnie shanghaied, and Raine ..." Zorinda couldn't finish, terrifyingly aware of Raine's fate given the number of local establishments catering to the baser instincts of man.

"There's one more street to search. Then we'll meet up with the others at the Presidio and alert the authorities." Carris urged the horse to a faster pace, his lips tightening.

Rounding a corner, they nearly hit a cluster of children in the company of an older, gangly lad.

"Carris!"

Carris was already slowing, guiding the horse around the startled group. The boy walked up to them. He looked to be about twelve or thirteen but his eyes reflected years far beyond his age. Tousled hair, the shade of wheat, hung in his eyes, but didn't obscure their clear blue. His clothing was hardly more than rags and the smells emanating from him defied identification.

"Hey, mister, why sich a hurry?" The brrr of a Scot rolled off his tongue.

"My apologies. But we're in search of a boy and girl. They have red, curly hair and are French."

The boy looked down, scuffing his bare toes in the dirt. He looked over at the children huddled together. Zorinda wondered if they were somehow related. The boy finally spoke.

"Me *màthair* would be tannin' me if she knew what I'm doin'. She's sick, and there's six mouths to feed."

He gestured at the two boys and two girls, thin, poorly dressed, and greatly in need.

Zorinda's heart broke.

"I'm not so proud I won't ask ye for a coin."

"A gold piece is yours if you can tell me where they are."

The boy stared at Carris.

Zorinda silently prayed. *Lord, let the boy give us the truth.*

"Afore sunrise me little brither and I found them wanderin' around, scared and lost. Said they had no *athair* or *màthair*. We told them this was nae place for the likes o' them—wha' with their fancy clothes and funny speakin'. I took them to the mission orphanage. 'Bout three hours ago. I'm sure they be there still."

Carris produced the promised coin, which the boy accepted, looking as though he'd never seen anything so marvelous.

Of course he hadn't, Zorinda thought.

"What's your name, lad?"

"McKittrick, Tiernan McKittrick of Clan McKittrick of West Galloway. Me *màthair* calls me Ty."

"Mr. McKittrick, thank you for your help. If you ever decide to try the seafaring life, look me up. Carris Trewellyn of Trewellyn Shipping in London."

"Trewellyn," the boy repeated. "I'll remember. Thank ye, sir."

Then he was off herding his flock in a different direction.

Zorinda looked at Carris, not sure if she should laugh or cry. She did neither as he urged the horse into a near gallop.

An hour later, Carris found himself pacing the small parlor of the mission orphanage while Zorinda sat, her hands clenched in her lap. A Miss Fanning had greeted them explaining Mrs. Klemp was away nursing an ailing relative. Miss Fanning was on duty when Raine and Ronnie arrived an hour before dawn. The twins had claimed to be orphans with no one to care for them. When Miss Fanning questioned them further, they'd begun speaking in French.

What do I say to them, Lord? They need to know I love them.

Footsteps approached and Carris turned, seeing Miss Fanning, Raine, and Ronnie, seemingly unharmed and sad of face, on either side of her. Miss Fanning prodded the twins forward, backed away and shut the door behind her.

Carris felt frozen until he sensed a prod—a heavenly prod? He walked slowly to the children, dropped to one knee and held out his arms. They ran to him, burying their heads, one on each shoulder. Then Zorinda was there, kneeling beside him, wrapping her arms around the children. And they cried. For what they could have lost. For what they'd gained. Love, family, belonging.

"We're so sorry, Oncle Carris and Mademoiselle," Raine said between sniffles and sobs. "But after you put us to bed, Ronnie and I started talking, and decided the two of you should get married right away. We didn't want to wait until the morning to tell you, so we went on deck. We heard Papa had left, and Oncle, you sounded angry like you were before."

"So, we decided to run away." Ronnie picked up the tale. "Because you'd be happier without us."

"Never," Carris said, his voice betraying his emotion. When had these two come to mean so much to him? "I was wrong to be impatient and angry. I love you."

"We love you too." Raine said, and Ronnie nodded. "But you and Mademoiselle should marry and be our papa and maman. We will be very good."

"Don't make promises difficult to keep," Carris cautioned then grinned. "I'll understand if you engage in a bit of mischief occasionally. But don't frighten us as you did last night—ever." Both nodded solemnly.

"Mademoiselle," Raine said, "do you forgive us?"

"Of course. I'm so thankful you're safe."

"Have you told Oncle you'll be his beloved?" Ronnie asked.

Zorinda looked up at Carris. Her eyes were soft and her lips begged to be kissed. He would never let a day pass without telling Zorinda how much he loved her. If only ... "No, I haven't."

Carris's heart pounded painfully.

"Because I've been foolish. But I know where I belong." She kissed Raine and Ronnie on the tops of their tousled heads. "With you and with your uncle. I don't need to sail anywhere to find love."

Zorinda now looked directly at him, a beautiful smile lighting her face. "Yes, Carris, my beloved, I will marry you."

Raine and Ronnie looked at one another and nodded as though confirming their plan was working.

Only Carris knew this moment was the heavenly Father's plan. Then he kissed Zorinda, kneeling beside her on the floor of the San Francisco orphanage.

Zorinda refused Carris's plea to marry the next morning, demanding she be given adequate time to prepare, which included waiting for her new gown. When she and Carris shared their news with her father, tears of joy filled his eyes as he hugged them both, clapping Carris's back so forcefully, Carris nearly lost his balance.

Zorinda thanked God, his healing hands at work on her father.

The evening meal ended with music and dancing on deck, lasting late into the night. Carris granted Raine and Ronnie permission to stay up. At last, the excitement and adventure of the day caught up to the twins, and they both nodded off, propping each other up as they sat on a crate. Carris carried Raine, and Cavenley carried Ronnie to their cabin. Zorinda followed closely behind. Cavenley slipped out, leaving her and Carris alone.

"They look so angelic when they're asleep," Carris observed wryly. "One would never know they can wreak more havoc than a hurricane."

"Or how endearing they can be when apologizing. Lance is missing so much."

"He's afraid," Carris said. "Running is his way of coping."

"You don't seem as angry."

"I feel sorry for him. He's given a chance, which he throws away. I'm praying for him."

Zorinda smiled up at Carris. "So am I. You'll make a wonderful father."

"Only because I'll have you to keep me in line."

She trembled as he kissed her, clarifying why he was so eager to exchange vows. Tiny giggles erupted, and Zorinda looked over Carris's shoulder. She knew who was watching. So did Carris.

"Go to sleep," Carris growled with fake ferocity, "before I make both of you walk the plank." Giggles filled the cabin. Zorinda's next few nights would be sleepless. But the joy awaiting her was worth every missed minute of rest.

Clad in her gown of ivory satin, embroidered with the lovely Bird of Paradise flowers, Zorinda walked down the aisle of the orphanage chapel. Her hand rested on her father's arm. The space, devoid of all frills with hard wooden benches, was filled with Carris's officers and crew. The cross-patterned panes of the altar window emitted the bright rays of the late morning sun, bathing Carris in golden light. She moved slowly toward her captain, silently praying for God's blessing on their union. When she reached him, her father kissed her cheek and placed her hand in Carris's. Stepping back, he took a seat beside Mr. Cavenley on the nearest pew. Carris kissed her hand while Raine held out a breathtaking bouquet of gardenias, their scent gentle and joyous. How had Carris managed to find them?

Pressing the flowers to her chest, Zorinda smiled down at Raine, lovely in her new gown of coral silk. Ronnie, shifting from foot to foot, tugged at the collar of his new shirt. The smiling minister, and also headmaster of the orphanage, held his open Bible. Lifting her eyes to Carris, she no longer saw the mythical Poseidon, but a man of flesh and blood courageously facing life's challenges with a heart overflowing with love. Peace enfolded her as though God was bestowing his approval. When she and Carris turned to face the minister, Zorinda knew her real adventure was just beginning.

Epilogue

MID—FEBRUARY 1851

A feel of early spring was in the air the first morning after the *Bird of Paradise's* arrival in Norfolk. As Zorinda and Carris left the house on Bank Street, she spied jonquils blooming in the border of the garden.

"Are you sure you want to come?" Carris asked, gazing down at her with a melting smile as he tucked her gloved hand into the crook of his arm. How did he seem more handsome than the day before?

"I most certainly am. The Lord approves of me, which is enough. Besides, I have a few errands of my own. And we need to find the perfect present to give Mr. Cavenley now he's to captain the new clipper."

Carris had made the announcement two days earlier, Den Cavenley most deserving of the opportunity. The news had given cause for much celebration.

"I heartily agree. May I say you look most lovely this morning?"

"Of course you may." She playfully swatted at him with her free hand. "Any time and all the time."

"Absolutely, my love. I'll be stopping at the bank first."

Zorinda nodded. *Lord, I am your child, and I won't be afraid.*

"I hope the children won't be too much for your father."

"I wouldn't worry. If anything, he may prove too much for them. Especially if he starts spinning yarns."

Carris chuckled.

The bank was busy, but Banker Sharp immediately escorted them into his office. He seemed embarrassed. And uncharacteristically gracious, even though his cotton arrived in San Francisco after the agreed upon delivery date. His behavior suddenly made sense when he mentioned he'd already received a note from her father, his apology for his overly cautious handling of her financial affairs effusive. He rambled inanely as he shuffled papers, some of which he signed, some Carris signed—most of the documents they both signed. When Banker Sharp mentioned something about Mrs. Sharp's most recent social catastrophe, Zorinda took note. Apparently, Wil's Miss Southgate called off the nuptials two days before the wedding.

Carris gave her a lifted brow and a wink. She nearly laughed.

After payment was exchanged and the contract between Sharp and Carris stamped satisfied, they left. As they crossed the lobby, Taylor Darrow hailed them.

"Good morning, Mr. Darrow," Zorinda greeted and extended her hand, which Mr. Darrow shook enthusiastically. "How good to see you."

"And you, Miss, I mean, Mrs. Trewellyn. I wanted to tell you, Captain, the funds you returned have been put to good use. An addition is to be built on the Female Orphanage housing at least twenty additional young ladies."

Zorinda looked quickly at Carris, who appeared uncomfortable. He'd returned the money he'd accepted from the mission society? She'd had no idea.

"How wonderful," she managed before Carris spoke.

"Mr. Darrow, I do have one request—I'd like for the dormitory to be called Paradise Hall. My mother's favorite flower was the Bird of Paradise. And my lovely wife married me in a gown embroidered with the flower."

Mr. Darrow nodded. "Most certainly."

Zorinda smiled at Carris, his beloved face reminding her he loved her for the woman she was—not the one society preferred.

"Thank you," Carris said. "I pray much good will come from the expansion."

After making their goodbyes, they left the bank. Walking along the brick walkway, Carris cleared his throat.

"About the money—"

"Why didn't you tell me? You lost money. Perhaps if you return my painting to Mr. Arnell, he can refund—"

"Never, Zorinda," he uttered roughly in his most authoritative voice. He remained silent for several seconds. And when she tightened her hold on his arm, he covered her hand with his. "Are you going to take your new paintings to him?"

"I thought I might stop by his shop."

"No time like the present." Carris smiled.

When they reached Mr. Arnell's gallery, he was ushering out a gentleman carrying a vase. After seeing the customer climb into his buggy, the man opened his arms, enveloping Zorinda in a fierce hug.

"You did return. The missus and I have missed you. I hope you found things in order."

"Sarah has done nothing but sing your praises. I can never thank you enough."

"You'll be happy to know I managed to put Banker Sharp in his place a time or two. But look at you, Zorinda.

You look wonderful." He looked fully at Carris, his brows lifting in surprise. "If I'm not mistaken, we've met?"

"Briefly. Carris Trewellyn." Carris looked sheepish as he shook Mr. Arnell's hand. "You sold me a painting which changed my life. I discovered the meaning of charity. And I married the artist."

Mr. Arnell laughed. "Good for you. So, you're most satisfied with your purchase." Then winked conspiratorially at Carris.

"You grossly undercharged me. There's not enough money in the world to equal its value to me. A fortunate soul is the one who owns a *R.I.N.* painting."

"Zorinda," Mr. Arnell said. "Friends of the Sharps are visiting and saw your painting Mrs. Sharp purchased. The couple wants an original. Did you have a chance to paint on your voyage?"

"She completed eight and has nearly finished a ninth," Carris said proudly. "Each one more amazing than the one before."

"I fear my husband is blinded by newly wedded bliss. But yes, I do have a few I might consider selling. But three hold sentimental value, and I could never part with them."

She smiled up at Carris. He would know she was referring to the one of San Francisco Bay, the towering snowcapped peak of Cape Horn, and the waterfront of Papeete.

"Why don't I hold an exhibit? I'll clear out the back room for your paintings, improve the lighting, offer tea and a light repast." The man paced as he rubbed his chin.

"What a marvelous offer." Zorinda could barely contain her excitement. "Sarah and Li Ling can plan the menu. Once you make a guest list, I'll prepare the invitations."

"Mr. Arnell," Carris spoke, "what name will you give as the artist?"

Mr. Arnell looked at Zorinda.

Zorinda looked at Carris then replied.

"My name. I want to share the talent God gave me."

"About time." Mr. Arnell chuckled. "But Mrs. Sharp already knows. After she recovered from her swoon, she told me you showed promise. I wouldn't worry about her."

Carris slipped his arm around Zorinda's waist and drew her close. She could never have dreamed so dangerous a voyage would bring her such joy. God had taken her on a terrifying, yet miraculous journey and richly blessed her. The greatest gift of all was her discovery of something far grander than any paradise imaginable. Love.

Author's Notes

Much of *Far Grander Than Paradise* revolves around the opium trade and China's efforts in the 1800s to prohibit importation of the narcotic. Originally intended for medicinal use, it evolved into frightening and unrestricted recreational use with devastating consequences throughout the world.

The first Opium War, 1839-1842, between China and Great Britain, ended in a British victory and required China to accept unequal treaties, known by the Chinese as the "century of humiliation." Lance Trewellyn, Carris's brother, has involved himself in smuggling opium and has earned the notice of certain Chinese officials. Hence, in an effort to save his neck, he's thrown in his lot with an intermediary in Polynesia hoping to gain a reprieve from the Chinese. By now, you know his plan didn't turn out as he'd expected.

A second Opium War, this conflict involving the British and French versus the Chinese, occurred from 1856 to 1869, and again ended in China's defeat. This led to the nation's relinquishing of Hong Kong to Great Britain. You will discover in the sequel, Book II of the Charting the Course series, Carris has received a knighthood for his diplomatic and negotiating skills called upon in the second Opium War.

Clipper ships were the newest technology of the time, roughly mid-1840s to the late 1860s. Donald McKay, of Scottish descent and born in Nova Scotia, was probably the man most closely associated with the design and development of the clipper. He began his career building packet ships, went into business for himself in Boston, and introduced the world to the clipper. Most famous of his designs was the *Flying Cloud,* completed in 1851. Considered an "extreme" clipper, the ship went on to break numerous records, especially on those voyages around Cape Horn at the tip of South America traveling to gold crazed San Francisco.

In creating Carris, I came across the fascinating story of Captain Samuel Samuels and his ship, the *Dreadnaught,* both man and ship setting my imagination on fire. The *Dreadnaught* was one of the fastest sailing packets of the time. It was captained by a man who went to sea at the age of eleven, was shanghaied onto a ship bound for Liverpool, and went from cabin boy to captain by the age of twenty-one. When he married, his wife, and eventually their children, lived on the ship with him. He passed away at the age of eighty-five, leaving a record of his legacy in his autobiography, *From the Forecastle to the Cabin.*

I've been fascinated with French Polynesia as far back as I can remember. My father, a WWII vet, saw much of the area while serving as a Coast Guardsman aboard the *USS Aquarius.* He even kept a diary of his two years aboard the ship, a copy of which I sent to the National WWII Museum. During WWII, Bora Bora, where Lance's father-in-law was conducting his illegal activities, served as an American supply base. Until the late 1800s, Bora Bora was an independent nation governed by a monarch, protected under the Jarnac Convention, with official recognition as a kingdom by France and Great Britain. However, by 1895, the last ruler was removed and replaced with a French vice-resident. At the time of Zorinda's search for her father, Tahiti was already considered a French protectorate. Grand Chief Tapoa II ruled the kingdom of Bora Bora from 1831 until 1860. Though the island was the location of François Montagne's home, I used creative license as the location for his smuggling venture. There is nothing to indicate that Tapoa II would have permitted or condoned such activity.

Well aware of the limitations placed upon women in the mid-1800s. I added to Zorinda's difficulties by giving her mother Polynesian ancestry. Once Thad Wemblish is assumed dead, Zorinda takes the brunt of local prejudice as her father's status in Norfolk can no longer protect her. Considered something of a misfit, she's tolerated but not fully accepted. It's no wonder she not only wants to search for her father but wants to take control of her life and her choices. It's easy to see how Zorinda would resent the men in her life controlling and directing her activities. Once Carris accepts the fact Zorinda has a mind of her own, he sees her as his equal, anticipating smooth seas ahead. Lance's actions predictably derail his dream.

Zorinda's artistry was inspired by my mother's incredible talent. My mother could paint scenes so realistically a viewer often thought they were enlarged photos. One of the gifts presented to me when my husband and I moved into our first home was a painting of a ship at anchor at sunset on a tropical island. I never fail to think of her when I see it on my living room wall.

What's next for the twins? Is it the seafaring life or that of a starving artist? Now adults, Raine harbors a crush on the young boy (now man) who saved her and her brother from the horrors of Sydney-Town (which came to be known as the Barbary Coast) in San Francisco. Ron is a target for revenge. And what of Lance? Is he still living "looking over his shoulder?" Discover the truth in *Far Truer Than Promises.*

Visit my website at barbarablythebooks.com.

About the Author

Barbara's earliest writing efforts were geared to mainstream historical romance. Then the need to honor God and share her Christian faith redirected her writing. A lover of history, she's created faith-driven stories, entwining historical events with her characters who discover love in spite of complications and danger.

First bitten by the writing bug in sixth grade, Barbara was further encouraged in middle and high school. Upon graduation from Old Dominion University, she became a banker then an administrative assistant with a local school system. Barbara's husband passed away unexpectedly, and she had to refocus her priorities—unfinished manuscripts ended up in the file cabinet. In 2023, not long after retiring, she was contacted by a member of the local ACFW group. It was time to pull out the unfinished manuscripts and bring to life the historical stories she finds so fascinating.

Her published novels are: *Fire Dragon's Angel,* Virginia, 1676, *Ransom for Many,* North Carolina, 1718, and *Dance of Life,* mid-19th century Paris.

www.ingramcontent.com/pod-product-compliance
Lightning Source LLC
LaVergne TN
LVHW020524100826
845148LV00010B/1332
9798891344662